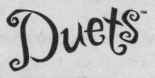

**Two brand-new stories in every volume...
twice a month!**

Duets Vol. #75

Isabel Sharpe kicks off the month with a very special
Double Duets on the theme of "manhunting."
Enjoy the chase as these heroines track down the
men of their dreams! This writer "pens a fresh tale
with solid characterization and snappy dialogue..."
says *Romantic Times Magazine*.

Duets Vol. #76

Two talented new writers join the Duets lineup
this month! Please welcome Sandra Kelly and
Wendy Etherington, who have crafted two funny
related tales about heroines fixing up "money pits"—
and the romantic chaos that ensues with
the heroes in their lives! Enjoy.

Be sure to pick up both Duets volumes today!

One Fine Prey

She was one very strange stranger!

"I look like a nut, I know, but there's a suit-wearing conservative in here somewhere." The woman laughed nervously and extended her hand. "I'm Allegra Langton, by the way. Allegra means fast. Lang means slow. A bundle of contradictions right there."

"I see." He hesitated for a second, wondering if he should make up a name, then decided not to when the only one that popped into his head was Chester Hoblinks. "I'm John. John Tyler Jones."

"John Ty-ler Jones, I'm awfully, awfully glad to meet you."

He stared past her crazy wig and clothes and fake glasses into her eyes and let his brain enjoy the singsong sound of his name on her tongue. *John Ty-ler Jones.*

Then he blinked. What the hell was this? "Look, I'm due at a meeting, so I really should—"

"I know we have a lot in common," said Ms. Fast Slow.

He couldn't help looking incredulous. A lot in common? He'd start with the fact that they were both human...and then he'd end there, too.

For more, turn to page 9

Two Catch a Fox

"So you think you give good relaxation?"

Cynthia said the word as if it had a different meaning altogether.

"I know I do." Adam took a swallow of his beer. "But I was actually talking about real relaxing."

"Oh." She clearly didn't believe him. "Like long walks in the rain? Discussing Chaucer in front of a roaring fire?"

"Wrong again. First…" He paused and lifted his glass again.

"First?"

He suppressed a grin at her impatience. "First I'd want your hair down."

"Oh, you would, would you." The scorn in her voice almost completely covered a breathless quality. "Next?"

"Next…I'd want the stuffy business jacket off."

"And then?" She smiled coolly, but a quick swallow gave her away.

"And then…I'd want to watch you."

"Watch…me…what?"

He let his mouth spread into a slow grin. "Dance the funky chicken."

For more, turn to page 197

HARLEQUIN DUETS

ISBN 0-373-44141-X

Copyright in the collection:
Copyright © 2002 by Harlequin Books S.A.

The publisher acknowledges the copyright holder
of the individual works as follows:

ONE FINE PREY
Copyright © 2002 by Muna Shehadi Sill

TWO CATCH A FOX
Copyright © 2002 by Muna Shehadi Sill

Visit us at www.eHarlequin.com

Printed in U.S.A.

One Fine Prey

Isabel
Sharpe

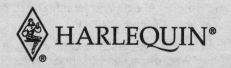

HARLEQUIN®

TORONTO • NEW YORK • LONDON
AMSTERDAM • PARIS • SYDNEY • HAMBURG
STOCKHOLM • ATHENS • TOKYO • MILAN • MADRID
PRAGUE • WARSAW • BUDAPEST • AUCKLAND

Dear Reader,

Welcome to a special double MANHUNTERS
Duets! This is Allegra's story, the tale of a woman
convinced she's not as she appears. (If you read my
April Temptation novel, *Hot on His Heels,* you've
already met her and the rest of the gang.)

I think most people struggle at one time or another
to reconcile the image they project and the reality
of who they are. When I lived in Boston, there was
an absolutely terrifying man I saw regularly in my
neighborhood. He always dressed in black leather
and chains. He had a long jet-black Mohawk,
multiple piercings, studded black belt, the works.

One day I bumped into him (thank goodness not
literally) at the supermarket. He was examining
packages of raw meat, and I half expected him
to tear into one on the spot. I sidled closer, totally
fascinated, and nearly dropped my basket when this
huge hulking man opened his mouth and out came
a high breathy squeak, "Ooh, pork chops are on sale
this week!"

I was so disappointed.

But it was proof positive that appearances are
deceiving. And as Allegra and John find out, it's
even possible to deceive yourself.

I love to hear from readers! You can write to me
through my Web site at www.IsabelSharpe.com.

Isabel Sharpe

To the Loopy Duetters who have provided me with more laughs, love and support than any bunch of crazed women I've ever known.

Prologue

Excerpted from Hot on His Heels, *Isabel Sharpe, Harlequin Temptation #873 April 2002*

Door County Wisconsin, Summer

"HAVE YOU EVER made eye contact with a total stranger and you just about die from the chemistry?" Tracy half-turned away from her three closest friends, Lake Michigan breeze blowing her short, dark curls onto her face. "It happened to me just now. It's like something inside you is wired to react to that person—it's something you can't help."

"So find him." Cynthia shrugged her linen-covered shoulders as if she'd worked out yet another of the world's pressing issues with a snap of her perfectly manicured fingers. "Get out there and find him."

Tracy rolled her eyes. "What, go running after him up the beach?"

"This is a small community. Ask around. Start right here at the party. A lot of people have been coming to Fish Creek for years. See what you can find out."

Allegra nodded eagerly, her long earrings swinging back and forth. "What could it hurt to ask around? We could all help. And even if we find out who he is, it doesn't mean you have to do anything."

"I don't know." Missy bit her lip. "It could be dangerous."

Tracy glanced around at her friends. The three women watched her expectantly—Cynthia challenging, Allegra encouraging, Missy apprehensive. Anticipation hung over the trio as if Tracy could be empowered to do something all three women wished they could share in.

All at once, a crazy, fabulous idea sprang into her head. Why couldn't they? She could take up the challenge herself then slap it right back at them.

"I'll do it on one condition." Tracy smiled and fingered the blue foil label on her beer. "That whenever this kind of instant attraction happens to any of us again, we'll pursue the guy."

"Ha!" Cynthia clapped her hands together and laughed, a flush rising attractively up her cheeks. "Great idea."

"Wow." Allegra's eyes shot open wide. "Double wow."

"But what if…I mean, I couldn't do this. I'd be horrible at it, I know." Missy bit her lip, looking as if she'd been asked to French kiss a tarantula.

"Think of it as science, Missy." Allegra peered over the tops of her fashion-accessory glasses with a fierce scholarly expression. "An experiment involving the chemical reaction of female to male."

"Is it merely an animal reaction?" Tracy donned an equally academic scowl. "Or a sign of deeper linkage?"

"In other words," Cynthia gave Missy a sultry smile, "do we fall in love or just get lucky?"

"Oh!" Missy gasped out.

"What should we call ourselves?" Allegra asked. "We should have some kind of name, just for fun."

"I've got it." Tracy put down her beer and held up her hands to sketch a giant marquee in the air. "The Manhunters."

Cynthia pretended to choke on her drink. "Manhunters! It's dreadful. I love it."

"Tacky in the extreme." Allegra grinned. "I love it, too."

They turned to look at Missy, who squirmed and made a face. "It's not very scientific. More…predatory."

"Exactly." Tracy lifted her drink for a toast; Cynthia's shot up alongside, then Allegra's; Missy's rose weakly. "To the newly formed Manhunters Club. Let all males between the ages of twenty-five and forty, who are straight, single, attractive, financially and mentally sound, non-reliant-on-their-mothers and dying-to-be-in-a-committed-relationship…beware."

1

"I'M SEEING...SOMETHING." Frau Hinkel's accented voice boomed through the tiny darkened room. She stared into the glowing probably-plastic crystal ball on the table, her heavily ringed hands making mysterious graceful gestures around the tacky pink orb. "Yes...yes...it's coming..."

"What? What?" Allegra leaned closer, gazing into the depths of the ball as if she expected mystic visions would actually appear, which of course they wouldn't in a gazillion years. If only Frau Hinkel would drop the mumbo jumbo and get to the point.

"I'm seeing..." Frau Hinkel's eyes flew open; she gasped and jumped as if a bee had stung her enormous rear. "Yes! It's clear! I'm seeing...the Internet!"

"Hmm." Allegra narrowed her eyes behind purple-framed plain-lens glasses and tapped a pencil against her notepad, sending six colored wooden bracelets cascading toward her hand. "You mean I should start conducting my seminars online?"

"It's brilliant." Frau Hinkel took her hands off the sphere and folded them into her lap. Immediately the rosy glow of the ball faded and the lights sprang up in the black material-draped room, which of course happened because she had a couple of switches under the table. "The spirits have always been good to me."

"You can say that again." The "spirits" had been good enough to get Frau Hinkel this chic lakeside condo in downtown Milwaukee. Underneath the faux-gypsy exterior lay a shrewd middle-aged business-woman who had already given Allegra good advice about expanding her self-help workshops from a small night-school class at the University of Wisconsin, Milwaukee, to a successful independent undertaking. In return, Allegra referred her psychic-seeking students to Frau Hinkel. "I'd been thinking of organizing a national lecture tour. But you—the spirits, that is—think there's enough of a market online?"

Frau Hinkel inclined her head and closed her eyes, displaying lids impressively decorated with bands of sparkling green shadow in progressively deeper shades. "The robins return. The planets are correctly aligned. Your personal aura is the right shade. And the fading boom of the last decade guarantees that hard-working people are becoming disillusioned."

Allegra laughed. "I see the spirits of the cosmic universe are remarkably in tune with the economy. But are these people logging on?"

"People all over the world need your workshops to relax and follow their dreams. You advertise the site properly, get the buzz going, and people will flock to you. Yes, even online."

Excitement churned Allegra's stomach into a mini-version of Lake Michigan after a part;ularly nasty storm. She sat back in the uncomfortable wooden chair and swished the long flowered folds of her yellow skirt into a more even and therefore harmonious distribution across her lap. "The thing is, I'm happy doing 'Am I the Me I Want To Be?' seminars locally. But people are so grateful when I help them see what they really want out of life. I almost feel I'd be selfish to keep the business local. Like I'm not fulfilling what I am put on earth to do." She threw up her hands; the bracelets clattered down to her elbow. "The rat race could be so much more bearable if everyone just got to like the cheese they're fed."

"You don't have the money right now for TV ads or infomercials. Travel expenses for a national tour would wipe you out. The Internet is the perfect solution for your need to expand. Which reminds me." Frau Hinkel winked and heaved herself up, nearly upsetting the black velvet-covered table on which the now-white orb was glued. "I have some extra flyers for my psychic services that the spirits instructed me to request you make available at your next seminar."

Allegra accepted the brochures and tucked them into her Mexican straw bag, thoughts tumbling over themselves in their quest to dominate her consciousness. "I guess you're right. But money's not the only reason a lecture tour would be difficult. It's a little hypocritical to complicate my existence to that extent when I preach the philosophy of keeping life simple."

"Exactly. The Internet is as simple as being complicated gets.'' Frau Hinkel gave a sharp nod that made her turban wobble. ''And thank you for the flyers.''

Allegra patted her bag. ''The spirits have been very helpful. It's the least I can do.''

''It is enough.'' Frau Hinkel bowed from her massive height and held out her hand. ''Or it will be once you've paid for today's session.''

Allegra fished out her battered wallet and deposited the cash in Frau Hinkel's wide palm. ''How's your daughter's wedding coming?''

''Oy. What a pain in the keister.'' Frau Hinkel dropped the booming psychic voice for her normal nasal tone. ''The sooner the happy day's over, the better. Flowers. Caterers. Bakers. Dressmakers. Plus, Flora needs somewhere to live, so I'm evicting a tenant and the *schweinhundt* is giving me trouble. These yuppies think God put the world here to make their lives convenient.''

''I'm sorry.'' Allegra stood, only half-listening.

She already had a Web site, one she'd done herself, but she'd need to put an ad in the *Journal Sentinel* and hire someone with more experience to advise her on how to get the classes started. Because the word had to get out, online and through national media— newspaper ads, radio, direct mail…

''Speaking of weddings, how's your love life?''

Allegra brought her brain back from its advertising campaign and ran her hands through her spiky brown hair, usually hidden under a wig to match her mood.

She sighed. "The usual. Namely nonexistent. I'm too…*unusual* or something. Every normal guy thinks I'm a kook. Every weirdo thinks I'm his soul mate. What I really need is a nice conservative gentleman. I need to get more in touch with my inner dullness."

"Hmm." Frau Hinkel stretched her arms out to the side, solemnly placed her splayed fingers to her temple and stared off into space. Her cat, Whisky, scratched at the door to come in. A horn honked from a nearby city street. "I'm seeing…that you will find this man soon…very soon…maybe even today."

Allegra raised a cynical eyebrow. *Uh-huh.* "The spirits told you that?"

"No." Frau Hinkel turned her eyes back to Allegra. "I sensed this myself. Some things I truly do."

Allegra gaped, startled by the intensity of the gaze directed at her. For a weird and entirely disorienting second she felt as if Frau Hinkel truly believed she possessed some psychic ability.

Right.

She fumbled her bag over her shoulder, the miniature wind chimes on the handles tinkling melodiously. "Okay, well, I gotta go. Thanks for the business advi—the *spirit* message."

"The spirits never lie, remember that." Frau Hinkel lumbered to the door alongside her. "Keep your eyes open for Mr. Right. He's out there."

Allegra waved and walked briskly down the hardwood hallway to the elevator. What made Frau Hinkel so sure Mr. Right lurked around the corner, when all the corners she'd encountered had been lurkerless for so long? Since the girls had made their Manhunters' pact last summer and Tracy found her true love Paul as a result, Allegra had been peering into masculine eyes all over town, hoping for that magic sizzle. But no. Nothing. Not even a spark. Not even a tingle.

She left the building and struck out on Prospect Avenue, enjoying the sun and the glorious still-cool May afternoon breezes off Lake Michigan. A woman and a man in conservative suits walked briskly toward her on the sidewalk, deep in discussion over a file. Allegra automatically began her Potential Mate checklist on the man. No ring. Well-dressed. Good-looking. Very attractive, in fact. Nice stride, nice build. Sandy hair, good complexion…what color eyes? She could almost tell. He was just about close enough to—

The man turned from his companion and met her stare. Allegra took in a sharp breath and held it. Adrenaline poured through her body. Adrenaline and some intense emotion so close to unbearable she would have broken the eye contact if she'd been remotely able to. Oh, gosh. This was amazing. This was really happening. To her.

A smile lifted the corners of his mouth; he nodded slightly and moved on. Allegra came to a stop, turned, and stared until he disappeared into Frau Hinkel's building without so much as another glance in her direction, which definitely ranked high on the disappointment meter.

But wow. Double wow. Total primal attraction. Her very own Manhunter moment, right on the heels of Frau Hinkel's prediction.

She lifted a shaky hand to adjust her glasses, her insides impersonating a dizzying trip on a merry-go-round. Okay. According to the Manhunters' pact, she had to go after him and ask him out. Right now. She took a few running steps back toward Frau Hinkel's building and stopped.

What on earth was she supposed to do about having her "big moment" over a guy in another woman's company? Even a woman who seemed to all appearances to be a colleague? The Manhunters' manual didn't touch on that.

But she couldn't leave without trying. And not because she was afraid of losing face in front of the girls. That heart-stopping, stomach-flipping, soul-invading kind of encounter happened so seldom. It had to signify something deep. They had to be in tune with each other's souls in a rare and special way.

Except she couldn't go charging after him and assault him with a request for a date. For one thing, men didn't exactly respond to her with openmouthed drooling like they did to Cynthia. Allegra had to approach them gently, subtly, get them used to the habitual colorful self-expression she hid behind, so they could see the normal, giving woman underneath. This man might be open to an overture, assuming he'd felt the chemistry. This man might even be interested, if she could get him alone to find out.

But that perfect stylish woman standing there, wondering what depths of desperation Allegra must have descended to, made that option too painful to consider. The assault would be doomed before it even started.

She walked back under the beige awning at the entrance to Frau Hinkel's building and stared miserably through the door into the empty lobby. Of course now that he'd disappeared, the decision had been made for her. Who was that unmasked man? Had he been tempted to look back and check her out again? Was he inside, upstairs, right now, wondering about her the same way she was wondering about him?

Did he live here? Did his colleague live here? Or were the two of them paying a professional call on one of the building's tenants?

Allegra scanned the apartment buzzers hopelessly. Who knew? She wasn't going to hang outside the building for the next three days to see if he came out. The girls were probably already waiting for her at Louise's, anyway.

Bummer.

She sighed and doubled back down the street to her car. Only two facts were certain. Whoever this amazing man was, he obviously wasn't planning to find out if the extraordinary moment of absolute connection between them had meant anything.

Allegra reached her lavender Ford Escort and dumped her bag disgustedly in the back seat.

And darn it, neither was she.

"AND YOU, MA'AM?" The waitress aimed her firmly fixed smile at Allegra, pad poised.

Allegra closed her menu. Every week she and her three best friends met at Louise's Italian Café for dinner, so routines were well-established. She always ordered last because it took her the longest, except maybe when Cynthia requested dishes not on the menu. This time the only difference was that the girls had spent time admiring Tracy's engagement ring, and more time hashing out Allegra's recent encounter.

"I'd like the corn soup without the crouton garnish, veal *piccata* made with olive oil instead of butter if that's possible, same for the roasted garlic mashed potatoes, easy on the garlic, please, then could you cook the broccolini extra crunchy, and hold the onions on the dinner salad, and I'd like the vinaigrette dressing for that on the side, and a glass of the non-sulfite Pinot Noir." She took a deep breath. "Please."

The waitress nodded, looking slightly dazed, and collected the menus.

"I don't know why you get so upset when people compare you to Meg Ryan." Fresh-faced Tracy plonked her elbows on the table. "You even order like her in that *When Harry Met Sally* movie. Remember? We saw it together in college."

"You're right, she does." Cynthia gazed at Allegra over her martini, then widened her eyes innocently. "Are you about to fake an orgasm at the table?"

"Shh!" Missy's cheeks turned a bright shade of pink; she looked around to see if anyone was coming to kick them out of the restaurant. "Someone might *hear* you."

"So what?" The tall elegant brunette shrugged. "Everyone saw the movie. Or if they didn't, they heard about that scene."

Allegra curled her lip. "Every review of Meg's movies mentions how 'kooky' she is. Blech. I'm sick of that label."

"Ahem." Cynthia looked pointedly at Allegra's outfit and gave a teasing smile. "Might I suggest a trip to Boston Store's Better Sportswear department?"

Allegra rolled her eyes and laughed. "It's not just the clothes, Cynthia. I could put on a navy suit and pumps every day and it still wouldn't change me. That kind of difference needs to come from inside."

"How do you plan on accomplishing that?"

"I need a man."

Tracy, Cynthia and Missy opened their mouths for immediate protests. Allegra held up her hands, expecting the outburst.

"I know, I know. It sounds stupid and sexist, but it's not. You know how some women want to bust out and be wild? Even though they're not wild all the way through or they would have been that way all along?"

Three pairs of eyebrows rose in a yeah-so-what's-your-point expression.

Allegra sighed. She was making sense. Really. "Then they find a guy who makes it safe for them to be wild, and with him they can be. Tracy, you know what I'm talking about.''

''Yes. I guess I do.'' Tracy nodded, beaming. ''When Paul and I first started dating I did all these bold sexual things I never dreamed I could do. He brought out a side of me I didn't even know I had.''

Cynthia toasted Tracy with her martini and grinned wickedly. ''The side of you that gets hot describing tomatoes.''

''Yeah.'' Tracy sighed dreamily. ''That side.''

''Bingo.'' Allegra smacked her hand on the table. ''Before she met Paul, Tracy couldn't get hot over tomatoes. Now she can. See?''

Missy's eyes widened in horror. ''Allegra, you...you want to get excited by vegetables?''

Allegra made an ''oh-pleez'' face. ''I need a guy who can make it safe for me to bring out my more normal side, Missy. And I think this guy would be perfect. But since he was with a woman who's probably his and every other man's idea of perfect, I panicked. I couldn't risk scaring him off until he sees how he can change me.''

Missy clucked her tongue sympathetically. ''I can understand that. I wouldn't have had the nerve, either.''

Cynthia shook her head. ''Well, I can't understand it. You let him go. Entirely against Manhunter regulations. Now how are you going to get him back?''

Allegra poked her faux glasses higher on her nose and looked mournfully at the steaming soup the waitress put in front of her, as if it could offer her comfort. "I don't really know. I guess I could start by ringing all the buzzers in Frau Hinkel's apartment building and see if he answers."

Cynthia dug into her salad and pointed a forkful at Allegra. "And this would help him not think you're kooky...how?"

"What about the psychic lady herself?" Tracy broke off a piece of her roll. "I know you use her for business advice, but maybe she could find him for you."

"Ha!" Cynthia rolled her eyes. "That mind-reading stuff is a bunch of hooey."

Allegra stopped with soup halfway to her mouth. Frau Hinkel's words floated into her consciousness like that echoing voice in the background of bad movies. *You will find this man soon...maybe even today.* Had she set Allegra up?

"If he lives in her building she might even know him," Tracy said. "Then you get your man and she can keep looking psychic."

Missy frowned. "I guess it couldn't hurt to ask...."

Allegra sat back. After all, he *had* gone into Frau Hinkel's building. Maybe he was even on his way to see her. Maybe Frau Hinkel figured Allegra would bump into him and find him attractive. Maybe that's what the prediction had been all about.

Allegra smiled, soup going cold in front of her, a certain man's eyes staying warm in the back of her mind. She could easily start her search with a visit to her not-really-psychic friend. Worst case, Allegra would be out some cash for the appointment. Best case, she could have finally found the perfect opposites-attract mate for life.

Her heavy mood shattered completely; the fragments turned into delicious dancing sparks.

"Okay." She nodded firmly and laughed. "I'll call Frau Hinkel tonight."

2

"YES, MR. TABACHNIK, customers will still be able to order all the products Brighton Pharmaceuticals makes. They'll just be ordering them from their computers instead." John twisted the phone away from his mouth and shoved in a Chicken McNugget, chewing as fast as he could before he had to speak again. Worst part of this job was convincing his clients' but-we've-always-done-it-this-way employees that their sacred companies would only benefit from going online. They hated the idea of anything new, all of them.

"I don't see how dis vill be any beddah dan usink a got-damn phone."

John swallowed hastily, imagining the partially chewed bite hitting his stomach like a bowling ball thrown into a pool. He twisted the phone back down to his mouth and started looking around his cluttered apartment for his calendar. "Look, why don't we set up a meeting where we can discuss this in person. Then we—"

"In person? You vant to talk to a person? You sure you don't need a computer dere to make you feel beddah?"

John rolled his eyes and pulled a jumble of clean

clothes off his favorite leather chair. "Let's see..."
He frantically pawed through a pile of catalogs and
bills. Where'd he put his damn calendar? "This week
looks pretty..." *Ha!* The kitchen table, where he'd
been penciling in appointments this morning. He ran
into the kitchen, skidded to a stop on the linoleum,
grabbed the calendar, and brought it back to his desk
and dinner. "Tuesday..." He flipped frantically
through the densely scribbled-on pages and pointed
triumphantly. "Wednesday. I have time at—"

Hell. His mother's birthday. Tomorrow. He'd remembered this morning, then it had gone clean out
of his overloaded mind. Too late for a card; he'd have
to find a florist. "Ten o'clock?"

"Dat's fine, yes. But I don't tink dis computer stuff
vill be any—"

The line beeped. "Mr. Tabachnik? I'm sorry, I
have another call."

"Vat? You can't even have a conversation vidout
some machine tellink you vat to do?"

"Sorry, Mr. Tabachnik. I—"

"All right, all right. See you Vednesday."

John grabbed another bite of chicken and pushed
the hangup button to connect the other call, making
a beeline for the oak bookcase his phonebooks were
supposed to be in. "Hello?"

"It's Katherine."

Katherine. He came to a total paralyzed halt in the
middle of his living room. She'd called him. He'd
worked with her all day every day for the past three
weeks at Brighton Pharmaceuticals while he'd turned

on all the subtle charm he could possibly turn on, and she'd finally called him. At home. Could she be coming around?

"I've been thinking about your little offer."

"Oh?" *Which one?* He'd asked her out several times, in various apparently platonic guises. She was everything he wanted in a woman—everything he wanted in a wife. Smart, slender, sophisticated, sexy… Everything.

"I haven't been to the opera in ages and I love *La Bohème.* I managed to clear that date. You said you had the tickets?"

"Right." *Hell.* He had to get tickets. He flipped through his calendar. *Double hell.* Wednesday the twentieth was the one evening he had free to look for a new apartment. "Yeah, my friend and I were going, but…well, I told you. His unexpected business trip…"

"Mmm. You told me."

The hair stood up on the back of John's neck. Her voice was like a rich dessert after a meal of overcooked vegetables. He pictured her to torment himself—slender ankles, endless legs, heart-shaped ass, perfect breasts, face like a—

The phone almost slipped from his fingers. Planted firmly on Katherine's magnificent body was the head of that flaky looking woman he'd passed yesterday, when he and a client were heading to his apartment to pick up some extra materials. The one who'd made no sexual impression whatsoever until he happened to catch her eye. Then *man,* he'd needed an airbag against the impact.

He shook his head to replace her face with Katherine's and found instead that her short, energetic, unspectacular body had replaced Katherine's worship-deserving one to complete the picture.

"John?"

"Yes!" He banished the image entirely. "I'm still here. I'll be glad to have company that night." Ecstatic more like it. He hadn't wanted a woman this much since he met his ex-wife. And that had been a brainless passionate mistake. Not this time.

"See you tomorrow, John." She breathed the words into the receiver and hung up.

John groaned in ecstasy and dropped to his knees. *Oh, mama.* His eyes shot open wide. *Mama. Birthday. Phonebook.*

He jumped to his feet and strode back to his desk, phonebook in hand, grabbed a French fry and dialed the first florist he came across. "Hello, this is John Tyler Jones. I'd like to send a dozen roses for arrival tomorrow." He gave the woman the necessary information, picturing his mother's careworn face brightening at the delivery.

His brows drew straight down until they almost covered his eyes. Not his mother's face. *Her again.* This time getting his mother's flowers. He wrestled them away from her and gave them back to his mom. Come on. The way that woman looked she'd probably try to replant the roses to rescue them from certain vase death. One of those save-the-world-with-crystals types.

His phone beeped. John groaned again, not at all in ecstasy this time, and connected the other call.

"This is Dolores."

John grabbed a fistful of hair that refused to stay in the neat side part he inflicted on it every morning. Dolores. Also known as Frau Hinkel to her unsuspecting marks. His landlady. Who'd insisted he move out so her soon-to-be-married daughter could move in.

"Dolores, so help me, if you're calling to move the date up again, I'll contact my lawyer. I keep telling you I will move out, but not this month. I have no time to find a new place to—"

"Settle down, settle down." She mumbled something about ants in his pants. "There's been a very interesting new development."

John frowned. He didn't trust Dolores Hinkel as far as he could throw her, which was definitely not far considering her size. "You're going to cut me a break?"

She gave a satisfied chuckle that set his teeth on edge. "Let's say I'm willing to compromise. For a small favor."

John narrowed his eyes. "Let me guess. You want me to paint the entire building with a brush held between my teeth."

"Smaller. I want you to be at the south west corner of Kilbourn and Prospect at 10:00 a.m. on Saturday."

"And?"

"And nothing."

"What's the catch?" What the hell was she talking about? "You'll tell the police I'm a pervert and let them know where and when to arrest me so I'm out of your hair?"

"No catch, no funny business. You do this for me you get another week."

"I need a month."

"Two weeks. Take it or I have you evicted."

"At least give me the reason I have to stand on this corner."

"No danger. No strings. No reason. Two weeks. Offer's good for the next thirty seconds only."

John closed his eyes. He had to oversee getting Brighton Pharmaceuticals' Web site up and running by the end of the month; already he was a week behind schedule. Moving at the same time was impossible. But with two extra weeks, he could avoid any hassle the very determined Dolores might give him at the worst possible time.

"Am I going to be framed for drug possession? Apparent drive-by shooting? Boiling oil out an upstairs window? Or will you have thugs throw all my stuff into the street while I'm gone?"

Dolores made a scornful noise. "Ten seconds…nine…eight…seven…"

John gritted his teeth and moved back to his food. The witch. She had him by the McNuggets and she knew it.

"Two…one. Well?"

He sighed and picked up his French fries, indigestion already stagnating his insides. Nothing could be as easy as this sounded; he'd be an idiot to agree. But what else could he do? Any other option would take time he didn't have.

"Okay, Dolores. In spite of my tremendously better judgment…I'll do it."

"WHICH LINKS aren't working?" John adjusted the cell phone more comfortably against his ear, and swung around on the sidewalk to face Lake Michigan, spinning out endlessly toward the horizon. It was 10:00 a.m. Saturday. Corner of Kilbourn and Prospect. Had Frau Hinkel wanted him here to admire the view? "Is there no reaction at all when you click on them or a 'document not found' message?"

He listened to the panicked female voice on the other end, trying to give the woman his full attention. Half his mind and both his eyes were constantly on the lookout. He peered at his watch. Five after ten. Twenty-five more minutes and he'd be free to go back to his apartment. If his apartment was still there.

"Okay. I'll be home in about a half hour. I'll log on and see what the trouble is. Until then, avoid any more coffee—you'll give yourself the shakes."

The panicked voice eased into grateful relief. John punched off the phone and smiled in satisfaction. Problem-solving always got his juices flowing. He rolled his neck around to ease the tension building from this ridiculous stand-on-the-corner charade.

So far not a mugger in sight. No one had accosted

him. With luck no one was back at 1508 Prospect effecting a forcible eviction.

His watch made another trip into view. Ten after ten. He groaned, thinking of the piles of unsorted paper on his desk, the mountain of phone calls he had to make, the glitches to work out, the staff to convince they needed training... This half hour would come directly out of his already-too-short sleep time tonight.

A flash of color caught the corner of his right eye. He glanced down the hill and froze, neck bent, hand gripping the muscles of his shoulders. *Her.* The world-peace, save-the-rain-forest, animal-rights, anti-global-warming, undoubtedly socialist, probably vegan New Age goddess who'd blindsided him a few days before.

Abruptly he turned his head away, praying his cell phone would ring again so he could be involved when she passed by. The last thing he wanted was to reestablish contact. The woman made him very uneasy—not in an unpleasant way, but uneasy still. And he was already uneasy enough waiting for whatever Psychics Unlimited intended to dish out. If he didn't look at her she'd be more likely to walk by.

A newly leafing maple became the object of his endless fascination...for about three seconds.

He turned back, unable to resist his curiosity, and watched her walk in his direction. No, walk *at* his direction. Staring purposefully. He exhaled a stream of air and clutched at the phone in his pocket. Why the hell was he standing here, padlocked into eye contact with a woman probably about to ask him to chain his body to an endangered alligator species?

She approached, not attempting to break the crazy eye-lock she had him in. Her bright patterned clothes flowed around her body like a belly dancer's veils. Her hair, which he remembered in light-brown spikes, had suddenly grown longer, curly and dark. She wore purple-framed glasses that didn't distort her large, hazel eyes in the slightest—probably just decoration. Her lips were full, mouth narrow, which made it look soft and childlike, and as if she were puckering suggestively.

He hadn't a clue what he'd say to her.

"Hi." Her voice was pleasant, if a bit loud. "I think we met the other day—well not *met* exactly, but saw each other. At least I did. And I think you did, too."

She pasted a smile over clenched teeth. He could practically hear her yelling at herself for starting out so clumsily.

He nodded, still off-balance, but unable to snub that kind of vulnerability. He'd certainly been there, most recently stuttering his way through an invitation to Katherine. "I remember."

"Oh! You do." She clapped her hand to her chest. "I thought it was just me."

He nodded again, wishing whatever Dolores had cooked up would happen now, so he could escape politely.

"So." She folded her arms across her chest and smiled, more naturally this time. Her movements were quick and decisive; she was graceful, more like an athlete than a ballerina. "I know it's weird of me to come up to you, you being a total stranger and everything, but I had this feeling we have a lot in common."

He couldn't help looking incredulous. A lot in common? He'd start with the fact that they were both human...and then he'd end there, too.

"I look like a nut, I know, but there's a suit-wearing conservative in here somewhere." She laughed nervously and extended her hand in greeting, causing a landslide of bracelets down to her wrist. Her hand was warm and dry; her shake firm, no-nonsense. "I'm Allegra Langton, by the way. Allegra means fast. Lang means slow. A bundle of contradictions right there."

"I see." He hesitated for a second, wondering if he should make up a name, then decided not to when the only one that popped into his head was Chester Hoblinks. "I'm John. John Tyler Jones."

She took a deep breath and let it out in a long sigh of contentment. "John Ty-ler Jones, I'm awfully, awfully glad to meet you."

He stared past her crazy wig and clothes and fake glasses into her eyes, and let his brain enjoy the singsong sound of his name on her tongue. *John Ty-ler Jones.*

Then he blinked. What the hell was this? "Look, I'm sorry, I'm due at a meeting in—" he looked at his watch "—oh, wow, ten minutes. So I really should—"

"I *know* we have a lot in common. Let me prove it." She tilted her head and raised her eyebrows, looking curious and coy all at once. "You buy your salsa hot, you never miss a Brewers game and your idea of a wonderful vacation is camping in the mountains."

"Sorry. Mild salsa. Basketball fan. Beachside condo." He turned away. This was too bizarre. Dolores could go to hell. He'd been here long enough.

"Let me try again." She danced around to face him, some weird jingling sound accompanying her movements. Her hand stretched toward his arm to keep him from turning away again, though she didn't touch him. "You're a night owl, you sleep with the windows open and you waltz like Gene Kelly."

Her stare was so hopeful he couldn't help smiling. She must be a bright light in whatever asylum she escaped from. "Wrong again, I'm afraid."

"Early bird, air-conditioning, two left feet, huh?" She twisted her face in disappointment.

"That's me." He moved to step past her, surprised that he did so a bit reluctantly.

Gentle fingers pushed his chest to stop him; her touch made him want to rear back, but not from distaste. For a second he felt the same wild rush as when he first laid eyes on her the other day, as if he'd been rammed from first gear straight into fifth.

Her hand fell away; she folded her arms and regarded him like a teacher disappointed in her pupil. "Microbrewed beer, cable movie channels, refuse to put on roller skates."

He raised his eyebrows. "Actually...yes."

"Figures." She shrugged wistfully. "None of those describe me."

He put on a polite smile. He really should get out of here. Intriguing as Ms. Fast Slow was, she might also be a stalking loony who could make the rest of his life hell. "I really have to—"

"Did you ever feel as if someone existed inside you who was dying to get out?" She gestured with her fists, expression painfully earnest. "Someone you didn't let have quite enough air to survive because this other part of you kept crushing the lid closed on the box you shoved her into?"

He gaped. If this was small talk with a stranger, he'd hate to be around for her in-depth discussions.

"Well, did you?" Her voice came up at him more softly this time; her eyes grew large and thoughtful, as if she was considering installing him in her living room next to the divan. Her question made him think back to how he felt when he'd fallen so madly in love with Cara, his ex-wife. Like part of him had come alive for the first time ever.

And died a slow shameful death soon thereafter.

"I don't think so. I'm pretty much as you see me."

"Ah." She gave a mysterious, rather satisfied smile. "Of course. That's what makes you so perfect."

"For...what?" The minute the words were out he wanted desperately to take them back. The last thing he should do was encourage any more of this surreal conversation. He opened his mouth to make an excuse to leave and no words came out, so he stood there like an idiot, watching the sun shine off the nylon strands of her wig and glint on the clear lenses of her glasses as she contemplated a sailboat out on Lake Michigan.

"I should tell you about me before I let you know what you'd be perfect for. I run a workshop—seminars, really, called, 'Am I the Me I Want to Be?'"

He tried not to cringe, but he couldn't dispel an immediate image of vapid-eyed disciples in an incense-clouded classroom, chanting and beating tambourines. "Look, I—"

"It's for people getting to that stage in their career where they ask themselves, 'What the hell am I doing here?'" She peered at him curiously through her purple glasses. "Have you ever asked yourself that?"

He clenched his jaw against the part of him that wanted to say, *not until five minutes ago.* "No, I generally know exactly—"

"I'm starting to think about expanding into online seminars, though I lack the technical know-how so far. What do you do?"

He bit off a twisted laugh. Right. He'd be totally honest and tell Ms. Organic Granola he was exactly what she needed. "I'm a used-car salesman. I love my work. In fact I love my work *so* much that I have to—"

"I know, you have to go." She slid him a shy sideways glance. "Would you like to go out some time? I could tell you then what I think you'd be perfect for, because I'd know you better. We could have a lot of fun.''

He swallowed, not even wanting to know what her idea of ''fun'' would be. ''Look. I'm very fl—''

''Stop!'' She put her hand out like a traffic cop. ''Never mind. You were going to say 'flattered.' Please, leave me what little dignity I have left. It's not like I ask strangers out all the time. You're my very first, in fact.''

Her honesty made him smile up at the dazzling sky in spite of himself, then he brought his eyes down to her face, steeling himself so he didn't jump at the by-now familiar impact of meeting her hazel gaze. ''Fair enough. Is just 'Goodbye, nice to meet you,' okay?''

She pressed those mesmerizing lips together and nodded. A sad nod that sent a little jolt of regret through his body. ''I take it that means 'no' on the date.''

''I...I...'' What the hell could he say? *Sorry, you're not my type and I'm too old for flings that go nowhere?*

''I know. I'm too much of a kook.'' She wrinkled her nose. ''Can I give you my phone number at least? So you can still change your mind?''

He didn't have the heart to say no. She scribbled on a torn-off piece of envelope and shoved it into his hand; the stiff glue side sliced a nasty paper cut into his forefinger. He suppressed the wince and curled his fingers into his palm so she wouldn't try to bulldoze him into being extensively cared for.

In any case, the pain would be something to remember her by.

She gave a wistful waggling-fingered wave and walked back down the block, jingling and flowing all the way. He glanced at his watch. Exactly ten-thirty. Assuming his apartment was still intact he'd survived this bizarre assignment with no ill effects.

And here he'd been worried someone would toss a grenade at him.

He turned to walk back to his building, Allegra's image firmly planted in his brain, nursing the paper cut on his finger and wondering why he felt someone actually had.

"You're back! How did it go?" Missy and Cynthia jumped up from Allegra's jet-black futon. The women had come over to her white, purple and pink Victorian house on Astor Street that morning to lend moral support in her hour of extreme nervous need.

Allegra slumped down onto a leather Turkish hassock, which emitted a deflating sigh at the same time she did. "Disaster."

"Oh, no!" Missy's eyes turned distressed. "I'm sorry."

"A real jerk, eh?" Cynthia shook her head sympathetically. "Isn't that always the way? The ones that look the sweetest leave behind the most bitter taste."

"No, no. It wasn't like that. He was wonderful. Nice suit, basic job, straightforward attitude…even his name is average. John Ty-ler Jones." She wiped off the dreamy smile which had imposed itself on her face. "Unfortunately, *I* behaved like an overqualified idiot the entire time."

"Oh, dear!" Missy folded the personals section of the *Milwaukee Journal Sentinel* and knelt next to Allegra to give her a hug. "What happened?"

"I was determined to show him who I really am. The high-school valedictorian, the woman who graduated college with honors, the woman who built a nice little business from the bottom up. A woman who has a lot of close friends, a lot to offer. The woman who lives here—" she gestured at her meticulously decorated living room, then screwed up her face, remembering the miserable sinking feeling when every word that escaped her mouth accomplished the opposite. "Instead I showed him a nutcase."

"It couldn't have been *that* bad." Missy patted Allegra's arm and put on a determinedly bright expression. "You must have at least…intrigued him."

Cynthia frowned, tapping red-nailed fingers on the mantel. "Maybe it's your clothes. Maybe you should try wearing something more…usual."

"It's not that. Everything I said shouted, 'kooksville.' First I tried showing what I thought we'd have in common, only I guessed wrong every time. Then I starting rambling on about alternate personalities lurking inside me, which probably made him think I escaped from an institution. Then, showing exquisite timing, I waited until things were at their absolute worst to ask him out."

"What did he say?"

"He said no." Allegra pulled off her wig in utter disgust. "Who could blame him?"

"Just like that? No?" Missy put her hands on her hips in outrage. "How rude!"

"Not exactly like that. He said he was flattered."

"Oof." Cynthia cringed. "That's worse."

"I know, I know. I told you it was a disaster. He even told me he was a used car salesman, which I know wasn't true."

"How did you know that?" Cynthia asked.

"Not him." Allegra shook her head emphatically. "Not John Tyler Jones. Something very corporate, but with a touch of creativity."

"How did you know *that?*" Cynthia held up her hand. "Never mind. You just knew."

"Did you feel that…that…thrill again?" Missy blushed, blue eyes round and curious.

Allegra closed her eyes, took in air and blew it out through pursed lips. *Oh, yes.* The minute she was close enough to see his very gray eyes, she'd felt the rush, the pull, the breathless body-warming connection. No wonder her brain had turned to cheese. "Yes. Yes, I did."

"Then he did, too." Cynthia folded her arms across her chest and glared down at Allegra from her considerable height. "So no disaster. You just got off on the wrong foot. We'll have to plan your next move more carefully."

"Oh, no." Allegra held up her hands to ward off the evil of good intentions, at the same time traitorously yearning for another chance. "I'm not going through that humiliation again."

"You know, he may have just been nervous about accepting an invitation from a stranger." Missy laid her hand on Allegra's arm. "Maybe if you could see him again…"

"Exactly." Cynthia strode over to Allegra's designer end table, grabbed the cordless phone and strode back, holding it out. "Call Frau Hinkel. Obviously she knows who the guy is. Get the scoop, and arrange to bump into him again. With that kind of chemistry between you, sooner or later things will heat up."

"Maybe he'd rather do the asking." Missy shrugged apologetically. "Some guys are like that."

Cynthia rolled her eyes. "Pathetic ego-driven idiots, all of them. If I had my druthers we'd chain men in the basement and only have them brought up for sex and heavy lifting."

Allegra snorted in an entirely unladylike way. "Now there's an idea."

"Cynthia Parkins, what will you think of next?" Missy giggled madly.

"Call." Cynthia pushed the phone insistently at Allegra. "The Manhunters' pact requires it. Where would the world be if everyone let one minor failure defeat them?"

"He'll think I'm a stalker." Allegra put on her best mournful look, excitement starting to shiver her insides in spite of her protest. See John again? She'd love to. She couldn't help it. Even though she'd behaved like a fool, she'd enjoyed being around him, trying to get a sense of who he was, how his mind worked. Not to mention having more of *those* kinds of hormones put into action than she'd needed in years. And glimpses of not-unkind amusement behind his exasperation showed he wasn't only being polite by talking to her as long as he did.

"Call."

"But...I'll be a worse idiot the second time because I'll be twice as terrified." Her mournful look barely hung on because a nervous giggle was fighting like mad for the right to break through to her features.

"Call." This time Missy took up the chant.

Allegra took the phone. Her friends stared expectantly. She grinned and shook her head, knowing she'd call, knowing she'd wanted very few things as much as she wanted the chance to get to know John Tyler Jones.

"Okay, I'll call."

3

"Ow." JOHN JERKED his hand back from the telephone and shook it, as if he could fling the pain away from his finger. Damn paper cut. Every object he touched had turned into a painful reminder of *her*. He'd even dreamed about her last night—as a masked evil sprite, slicing into his fingers with a machete made of envelopes, rubbing hot salsa in the wounds and forcing him to waltz with Gene Kelly.

He rolled the squeaky office chair toward the right wall of the minimalist cubicle Brighton Pharmaceuticals assigned him while he consulted here, and reached for the desk phone with his left hand, just as his cellular rang.

"Hello, this is John Ty—"

"I have another assignment for you."

His stomach dropped. Dolores. "What the hell is it this time?"

Heavy taps landed on his shoulder from someone standing next to his desk. "John, Mr. Tabachnik is throwing a fit at his terminal. He says it's possessed."

"She wants to go out with you." Dolores gave a disgusted snort. "Why, I don't know."

John held up a please-wait finger toward the shoulder-tapper. "Dolores, I've got one employee freaking out, another client on my back for a site supposed to be up yesterday, my boss here wants more reports than there is paper for on earth and I have no idea what you're talking about. Can I call you back?"

"Not if you want to stay in my building."

"What?"

"Jones!" Lester Prism's enormous bellow preceded his equally enormous bulk down the narrow corridor bisecting the rows of cubicles. The CEO of Brighton Pharmaceuticals loved to prowl the office and pounce on unsuspecting employees, having no apparent duties of his own. "Here at Brighton, we tolerate only the best. Excellence in all we do, m'boy. Excellence!"

"Dolores, I'll call you ba—" John frowned. *"Who* wants to go out with me?"

His shoulder got another heavy tap. "I think you better hurry before Mr. Tabachnik busts an artery. He keeps screaming, 'You vill not get the beddah of me, you big-screened tool of Satan.'"

"Allegra Langton wants to go out with you, who do you think?" Dolores mumbled something about lost marbles.

John's entire musculature bunched, then realigned. "Alleg—"

A hundred-page report slammed down on his desk with all the force of Lester's near-bovine arm behind it. "No charts in here. I like charts. No nice pictures. Too many diagrams. Too much technospeak. Clarity. Brevity. Excellence, m'boy. See what you can do."

Lester wiped the ever-present sweat off his blunt-featured puffy face.

"Okay...sure, Lester." John went to loosen his tie before he realized he had already loosened it. The strangled feeling continued anyway. The Granola Woman and Dolores in cahoots—he should have pieced it together. Except he had no reason to connect them. Bumping into someone twice in the same week wasn't all that unusual. In hindsight the overcoincidence was glaringly obvious. First sighting of *her* near Dolores's building. Then, "Go stand on the corner and wait." *She* shows up. Right.

"Mr. Tabachnik has a heart condition. I'm afraid he'll—"

"I'd like that report redone by the next team meeting Friday, m'boy. Cut down to about twenty pages. Lots of pictures. Don't waste words. Just the gist. I'm a busy man. See to it."

Mr. Prism lumbered back down the aisle. John covered the mouthpiece of the phone and turned to the heavy-tapping employee whose name he didn't know. "Ask Mr. Tabachnik if he remembered to use his new password."

"Right." The anonymous suited figure darted away toward the stairs.

John turned back to the phone. "Dolores, I'm sorry. This is a bad time to—"

"She says you don't want to go out with her."

John groaned. *Tattletale.* "That's right. I don't want to go out with her."

"Well, you do now."

"What?" The phone on his desk rang. He picked up the receiver and put it to his other ear, twisting the cellular away from his mouth. "Hello, this is John Tyler Jones."

A desperate voice launched into a litany of troubles at Randolph Cosmetics. Lipsticks were showing up the wrong color online; customers were confused by the placement of links on the screen; some products took too long to find...

John smiled. At least those weren't a programmer's problems. "Call Rick, he designed the site. It's not my—"

The voice continued. John's smile faded. Rick had gone into the hospital. John was the only person in the forty-eight contiguous states who knew the site intimately. Could he please—

"You want somewhere to put your head at night that isn't in a tent?" Dolores demanded. "You change your mind and go out with Allegra."

He brought the cellular back to his mouth and twisted the other phone away. "Standing in the street Saturday should have gotten me two more weeks. You can't do this to me."

"Two weeks? Who said that? Me? I remember nothing."

Damn. She *could* do this to him. And she would. And she was. Next agreement he got in writing. "Dolores..."

"I'm only saying it once, my little soft pretzel, so get a pen and write down her number."

"Why the hell does she want to go out with me?"

"God knows. She's a nice girl, and her business means a lot to me. You screw this up, you're going to have to *love* camping."

"Just a second." He clenched the receiver between his ear and shoulder and fumbled for a pen, wincing when he grabbed it too tightly and his kook-inflicted paper cut objected. He switched to the desk phone, placated the desperate voice with promises he couldn't keep in a million years, hung up, and went back to the cellular.

"What's her number?" He'd write it down, call her up, take her out, show her a decent time and be the hell done with it. "Fine. I'll call her. Goodbye."

John threw the pen down and punched Dolores off midsentence. He took a deep breath and stared at the memo-littered half wall in front of him, wondering why he hadn't fought Dolores harder. Legally she had a right to kick him out. But there had to be other ways of negotiating, other avenues open to him than going on a date with someone he wasn't interested in. Maybe because going out with Ms. Tofu was a lot easier and quicker than legal action.

He nodded, and picked up the office phone. Might as well get the deed done now. He dialed the number Dolores gave him, pushing away strange excitement. He'd offer to take her out to dinner. Informal bite someplace, then excuses—not too far from the truth—that he had to get back to work. Quick and dirty, get it over with.

Two rings and his cellular's shrill tone interrupted. He answered. "Hel—"

"Don't ever hang up on me and *don't* call her now, you spaetzle, I just got off the phone with her. She'll know I made you call."

The Granola Woman's line made a click of connection in his right ear; John slammed down the receiver. So much for getting it over with now. "Okay, okay, I'll call her tonight."

"Here's the deal, Tyler Jones."

"What deal, Dolores?" He rolled his eyes and picked up the report his boss had chucked at him. How the hell could he condense ninety-eight pages of vital information about Brighton's Web site into an illustrated sound bite?

"One more week at the apartment for every date."

John froze. "Excuse me?"

"You heard me. Those are the rules. You need 'til the end of the month? That's three weeks, three dates."

"Excuse me?"

"Get to know this girl. She's a gem. You'll have fun."

"Ex—" The office phone rang, saving him from repeating himself a third time. He had to go out on three dates? He barely got four hours of sleep a night. Where the hell could he squeeze in three dates?

"Hang on, Dolores." He switched to the desk phone. "Hello, th—"

"You called me. Who is this?"

His eyes shot open wide along with his mouth. He recognized that voice. *Her.* How the hell had she—

"I have caller ID. You hung up just when I answered. I hate missing calls. Who is this?" Her voice sounded curious, shy and a little hopeful.

"Uh...wrong number." He hung up, feeling rude and ridiculous and ashamed, the way he did in his teen years when his friends put him up to crank calls.

"What's going on?"

"Dolores, will you please—"

The desk phone rang again. He gave a silent groan of frustration. "Hel—"

"Are you *sure* this is a wrong number? Maybe I could help. Who are you trying to reach?"

He choked. His brain melted. He could think of no one. Who would he be? Who would he be calling? He couldn't be himself or Dolores would turn him into an unhappy camper.

"Who's on that other phone?" Dolores bellowed. "Tell me you didn't call Allegra."

He switched mouthpieces. "The line must have connected before I hung up. She has caller ID."

"Oy." Dolores mumbled something about decks missing cards. "Well don't tell her who you are or she'll find me out. Make up something. Tell her she reached Al's Pizza."

He twisted his face incredulously. *Al's Pizza?* "You've got to be—"

"Hello? Are you still there? *Who is this?*" The Vegan Queen's voice had become distinctly suspicious.

He closed his eyes, counted to ten, hung up on Dolores and switched phones back. "This...this is..."

Blank. Nothing. Wiped slate.

He sighed and adopted a thick Italian accent. "Al's Pizza. I call to check a order, gotta wrong number. *Mi scusi* and *arriveder—*"

"Al's Pizza, eh?" The suspicion turned sharper. "Well, *what* a coincidence. I'm *dying* for some pizza."

Oh, man. He shifted uncomfortably and tried again to loosen his already-loose tie. "Uh…okay, *bene,* what'll it be?"

"Large pepperoni, extra cheese. How much is that?"

"Oh…fifteen dolla'" He gritted his teeth. This was the stupidest, stupidest thing he had ever done in his life. Damn Dolores. Damn his brain for melting when he needed it most. Damn the nonsleep he'd been getting that slowed his usually high-speed reactions and logical thinking skills. This could not get any worse.

"Well, hel-*lo.*" The rich sultry voice came from two feet above his right ear and sent his male hormones into overdrive.

Katherine. He snapped his head around and up, grinning goofily. She'd never come by his desk before. Usually he made all the excuses to go by hers.

"*And* I'd like a Greek salad, romaine not iceberg, lots of hot peppers, easy on the feta, anchovies, real lemon in the dressing, plenty of olives, onions paper thin and the biggest diet cola you have." The Apparently-Not-Vegan Queen added a nice layer of sarcasm to her tone. "So. When should I come pick all this up?"

"Working hard?" Katherine smiled her dazzling smile, tipped her face up and shook her head so her blond hair bunched and swung luxuriously over the shoulders of her rose-colored jacket.

"Yuh." He laughed stupidly.

"When should I come pick up my pizza?"

"Uh…" He lowered his voice to a husky mumble in hopes Katherine wouldn't hear his horrible Godfather cast-member audition. "Justa minute."

"In just one minute?"

"No! We deliver for you. Twenty minutes." He hung up the phone, and faced Katherine with a somewhat strained smile.

"Is…something wrong with your voice?" She stopped the hair thing and perched on the edge of his desk. Her perfume wafted toward him—a bit sweet for his taste, but a nice scent anyway, and one he associated with her. He tried to keep his eyes from straying to her long perfect legs, idly swinging off the edge of his desk, further interfering with his ability to function.

"My voice?" He cleared his throat. "No, no, I'm fine."

"I'm looking forward to the opera."

"Yeah." He nodded rapidly, feeling totally off-balance around her as usual. "Me too."

She leaned forward and wrapped long pink-nailed fingers around his tie; he swallowed so convulsively he was afraid his Adam's apple would bruise her skin. "Your tie's crooked, John."

He let out a horrible guffawing sound that made

him wish he could do something noble and dramatic, like have a heart attack. "Yeah. Well. You know. Tough morn—"

The desk phone rang. Katherine released his tie. He swore under his breath and picked up the receiver. "Hello, this—"

"I just changed my mind. I want sausage instead of pepperoni. And you forgot to take down my address."

Something he swore were smothered giggles sounded on the line. Okay, so he made a lousy Italian. At least she didn't know who he really was. That could get very awkward when he had to call and ask her out tonight.

"Is it too late to change my mind, Al? This *is* Al, isn't it?"

He tightened his lips, fighting absurd laughter. Whatever else, the woman had a decent sense of humor. But what the hell could he say about a pizza order with Katherine right there? "*Si.* That item can be…upgraded. No problem."

Katherine peered at him curiously.

He covered the receiver, wondering when he could take his next vacation. "Mr. Scallopini from Warburg's—another client. He understands me better if I use an accent."

"Oh." She nodded politely and smiled. "Well, I see you're busy. I better get back to work myself. See you later."

"Yes." He gave her his warmest smile back and watched her lean body undulate down the aisle. *Man,* she was hot. Someday he hoped to be able to act remotely normal around her. Maybe after they'd been married ten or twelve years.

"I *still* haven't given you my address." The irritated voice on the phone had turned unmistakably mischievous.

"Okay, okay, I'm ready." He leaned out past the flimsy cubicle wall to watch the rest of Katherine's long-legged journey around the corner.

"Two, four, three, nine…you with me?"

"Si." He caught himself just as his chair was about to tip over and scooted back into the cubicle. "I'm with you. Two, four, three, nine . . ."

"Upper Torch. That's *U-P-P—*"

"I can spell that." *Torch?* He frowned. Where the hell was—

"Sta-tue of Li-ber-ty, New York Har-bor…"

He choked down a burst of laughter, and the weird urge to let her know who she was really talking to, so they could share the joke. "You gotta nice view up there?"

"The best. You should come visit me." Her voice dropped into a husky, shy invitation. "I'll show you around."

John blinked. He blinked again, trying not to think about those wide hazel eyes. Forget that. Forget ever having been flattered by her attention. The woman was totally desperate. First she'd asked him out after catching only one glimpse. Now she was trying to pick up an obviously phony pizza man she'd never even seen. "Okay, *bene*…one large sausage, Greek

salad, diet Cola delivered to New York Harbor—
twenty minutes.'' He hung up the phone and shuddered. Ms. Sausage-Instead-of-Pepperoni was a piece
of work. He'd have to wear armor on their dates.

He turned to his computer, trying to refocus his
scattered brain on his actual duties for the morning.
Three weeks and Brighton's Web site would be completed, employees trained. Three weeks he could use
to find a new apartment, and move safely out of
Dolores's reach. Three weeks and three dates with a
man-eating resident of the Statue of Liberty. He could
survive. Miserably perhaps.

But at least without pain.

He pounded in his password and winced when the
paper cut from the woman he couldn't seem to get
out of his mind stabbed into his finger.

ALLEGRA SAT RIGIDLY on the black futon in her living
room and took a gulp of ginger-apple tea, briefly reg-
istering the spicy sweet taste. Apple for pure inno-
cence, ginger for a pungent kick—a nice schizo combination that fit her mood perfectly.

She set the cup in the exact center of a circular
coaster on her coffee table, next to her barely touched
plate of cheesecake and scowled at Tracy, who'd
come over for dinner and consolation and had now
disappeared into an issue of *Vogue.*

''I mean the setup was so obvious. I call Frau Hinkel saying I want to see John again, she says leave
everything to her, then he calls me five minutes later
and hangs up.'' She scrubbed her spiky hair into a

short frizz of frustration. "He doesn't want me. Frau Hinkel *made* him call. It's like when Mrs. Zdanowski forced her jock son to take me to the cotillion Junior year because she was so sure no one else would ask me."

Tracy looked up from her magazine and sighed. "Are we going through this again?"

"Not the cotillion, no."

"Okay. Let's try it this way." Tracy held up her forefinger. "One, even if Frau Hinkel had something to do with John's calling you, how on earth would she be able to pressure a grown man into asking you out if he didn't already want to, at least on some level? It's not like she'd hold a gun to his head."

"Well, no..." Allegra contemplated a perfect white orchid she'd taken endless pains to grow, and considered crushing it. "But then why didn't he ask me out?"

"Two." Tracy held up another finger. "John obviously *intended* to ask you out, or else why would he call? Maybe his boss came by while he was on the phone and he didn't want to get caught."

"So he pretended he worked at Al's Pizza? Wouldn't that make a slightly worse impression than a normal personal call?"

Tracy shrugged. "I thought that was kind of cute. Most men's first reaction would be to pretend they were second in command at Microsoft. However, that's beside the point." She patiently held up a third finger, the one weighted down by the diamond engagement ring she'd gotten out of her own Manhunter adventure. "Three, maybe he lost his nerve. Maybe Frau Hinkel is encouraging him, not forcing him. Maybe he's shy."

"Ha!" Allegra dismissed the idea with a floppy-wristed wave. "No one's *that* shy. I did everything to make it easy for him. I called him back those two times, I made him laugh, I even flirted with him. Nothing."

"You flirted?" Tracy's eyes opened wide; she rubbed her hands together like a miser sitting down to count his gold. "Oooh. You didn't tell me that. What did you say?"

Allegra adopted a Mae West stance, one hand to her hip, one to her hair, and brought on the attitude. "I invited him and his large sausage to come up and see me sometime…." She dropped the pose for a black scowl. "Only he practically broke the sound barrier getting the phone back into its cradle."

"Hmmm." Tracy narrowed her eyes thoughtfully at the cleavage-y supermodel on the cover of *Vogue,* then snapped her fingers. "Of course! Think about it. John calls, having no idea he's very much on your mind because you just spoke to Frau Hinkel about him. Then, even though he discovers you have caller ID, he's sure you don't recognize his work number. Third, he thinks he's disguising his real voice, even though he knows you don't buy the pizza act. So he's under the understandable impression you think he's some harmless crank caller."

Allegra frowned. "You don't think—"

"So from his perspective, the female stranger who

asked John Tyler Jones for a date after only a brief encounter on the street is now flirting madly with Mr. Pepperoni Pizza.'' Tracy held out her hands. ''What's he going to think?''

Allegra swallowed. ''That I'm a man-eating kook?''

''No wonder he wanted off the phone.''

''But...but how could he not know I knew who he was?''

''How *would* he know you knew who he was? *I* know you knew. *You* knew you knew. But *he* had no way to know you knew.''

''Oh, no. Who knew?'' Allegra put her hands to her ears as if to ward off any further complications. This couldn't be happening. She'd been so aware the voice belonged to John, so aware of the pull between them, it never occurred to her that he'd think she hadn't guessed. ''But I didn't give Mr. Pizza my *real* address.''

''You could have been leading up to it.''

''Oof.'' Allegra slumped back against the futon's ebony frame, feeling the one bite of cheesecake she did manage to eat knocking to get back out. All the time she thought she was dazzling John with her wit over their shared joke, he'd been thinking she was Mata Hari. ''I see your point.''

''So what you need to do now, is make sure John—''

''Finds out I knew he was Pepperoni Man.'' Allegra stood and punched her fist into her palm. ''Convince him he's the only person I've ever approached like this—the only person I've ever had the *nerve* to approach like this."

"Yes." Tracy smacked her hand on the super-model's pouty face. "That even now you can't quite believe you're pursuing him, because it's so out of character—"

"And I never would have if we hadn't had that killer eye contact in the first place."

"All of which is pretty much—"

"True." Allegra gave a firm nod. "All right."

"Then to prove it, keep your hands to yourself on your first date." Tracy grinned and picked up the dessert plates to take them to the kitchen.

"No good-night kiss?" Allegra wrinkled her nose, remembering John's very nicely shaped mouth and aware she'd leaped way ahead of herself in the day-dream department. "That's going a little too far."

Tracy laughed. "Play it by ear. Maybe he'll make that decision for—"

The phone rang. The women froze. Allegra stared over at the Instrument of Eternal Promise, her heart jumping into overdrive. "It's him."

"Now, Allegra." Tracy drifted cautiously back into the living room and put the plates down. "It could be anyone."

"I know it. I can feel it." Allegra walked over to the phone, glanced at the unfamiliar number on the caller ID display, and straightened her skirt, feeling like an idiot for worrying about her appearance. But for some reason it mattered. This call mattered. She picked up the receiver.

"Hello?" The deep voice resonated into her ear, around her brain, and through her entire body, causing sympathetic vibrations all the way down.

She closed her eyes, whirled around to face Tracy and nodded.

"Hi, John." Her voice came out an ecstatic whisper.

He cleared his throat. "How…did you know it was me?"

"Actually, I'd recognize your voice anywhere." She winked at Tracy who put her hands over her mouth to stifle a giggle.

"You mean…I mean…does that mean…"

"Did you enjoy your trip to New York, Mr. Ty-ler Jones?" She adopted a gently teasing tone, intended to bewitch him.

"My trip to—"

"Did the pizza get cold?" She smiled wickedly at Tracy who dove onto the futon and buried her face in the cushion.

Silence.

Allegra's smile grew less wicked, flattened, and eventually drooped into sheer panic. *Oh, no.* She'd done it again. Bothered and bewildered instead of bewitched. Around John she was doomed to behave like a complete—

"I was wondering…"

She inhaled at the sound of the words and dared to hope again. *I was wondering.* In that deep sexy male voice. "Yes?"

"Would you…like to go out for dinner some night?"

Ohhh, yes. Yes. Yes. Yes. She gave Tracy a thumbs-up; Tracy answered with a silent cheer. "I'd love to."

"Is tomorrow okay? Around seven?"

"Tomorrow." She turned to Tracy, and mouthed *to-mor-row* in a silent scream. "Tomorrow sounds—wait, what am I saying? I have a class tomorrow."

"Saturday? No, I can't Saturday. Sunday?"

"I'm in class. Monday?"

"I'm in a meeting. Tuesday?"

"In class. Wednesday?"

"In Cleveland. Thursday?"

"Thursday…done." She grinned and pumped her fist into the air, then stilled. She shouldn't make any move that might damage the fragile fact of their next meeting, but she had to know. "What made you change your mind about me, John?"

Silence.

Allegra rolled her eyes and pummeled herself mentally. Who cared? He asked her out. She had a chance now to correct all her first impressions. Why didn't she just shut up and—

"Let's say the reason *not* to call became less compelling than the reason *to* call. Give me your address. I'll pick you up Thursday at seven. You like Thai food?"

"Yes!" *Yes. Yes. Yes. Yes. Yes.* The tidal wave of excitement rolled in again. She gave him her address, all the while doing the samba around her apartment, forcing Tracy prostrate on the sofa again. "I'll see you at seven on Thursday."

She hung up the phone and rushed to hug Tracy, then whooped and made a dismal attempt at clicking her heels.

"Ha! Whatever Frau Hinkel did or didn't have to do with it, Thursday at seven o'clock John Tyler Jones begins the night of his life." She let her adrenaline out in a gale of laughter and struck a hands-out command-the-masses pose.

"From this moment forward, the Manhunters are back on track."

4

ALLEGRA FASTENED a small brooch that had belonged to her mother onto her demure ivory cotton sweater and smoothed her burgundy skirt, both barely worn hand-me-downs from her fashion horse third-oldest sister, Maureen. Tonight, she'd look the part. Tonight, she would not be displaying her kook side, she would be displaying Ms. Good Taste Conservative. She would show John Tyler Jones how much they had in common. She would explain about the Great Pizza Caper and make sure he understood she didn't pick up guys randomly, that he was tremendously special and sexually arousing. Then if that went well, she wanted to tell him how he could help her change.

As long as she could act normal enough to get the mood right. Those kinds of confessions didn't work well when your date was horrified by you.

She stood back from the mirror, patted her wig of auburn curls and frowned. The right look, the right idea.

Except…the outfit needed perking up. She glanced at her watch and fought down a surge of excitement. Ten minutes to seven. It needed a *fast* perking up.

Aha! She had just the solution. She opened the top

drawer of her antique black bureau, snatched a brightly patterned silk scarf out of the jumble inside and draped the material casually across her shoulders. Much better.

Except…she scowled at her bare arms and opened the top to the pink pop-up ballerina jewelry box her oldest brother gave her for her tenth birthday. Just a couple of bracelets. Two at the most. There. Red and blue.

Except…if she wore them *all,* they'd pick up the colors in the scarf and make for a real ensemble.

She pushed the bracelets on, nodded in satisfaction and stared some more. Very nice.

Except…the skirt looked kind of drab against the brightness of all those colors. She had one that would be perfect—not *quite* as conservative, but hardly kooky. Red was very fashionable these days, and even high-society women were wearing short, short skirts.

She rummaged in her closet among the packed hanging clothes. Which meant the skin-colored panty hose would have to go. No point emphasizing a lot of bare leg, not that hers were exactly endless. Maybe those blue tights with the black flower pattern. She dug them out from her underwear drawer, pulled them on carefully and smiled. Perfect.

Except…she didn't look conservative anymore. And it was seven o'clock. She put her hands to the waistband of her skirt and began to take it off. She should have let well enough alone. Burgundy would be—

Her doorbell sounded, scattering nervous sparks through her body. John. No time. She pulled the red skirt back up, gave the hem a quick tug down, as if covering a half-inch more of her thighs would somehow help, and rushed downstairs to the front door.

"Hi." She said the word in a silly breathless rush. He looked gorgeous. Gorgeous. He had on a silk jacket that matched his fabulous eyes in endless shades of gray, a plain white shirt and a burgundy patterned tie that would not only have looked *fabulous* with the skirt she discarded, but would also have made them into a perfect complementary couple.

Lesson one: next date, if by some miracle he wanted one, the first outfit would stay as is.

He smiled a greeting, eyes flicking over her ensemble. No reaction. None. Of course. She'd started out dressing for him, then changed into an outfit more fitting for a date with Boy George. Why did she do this? Why didn't she have the nerve to be herself?

His gaze went past her and around her hallway and living room. *That* got a reaction. "Nice place." He looked at her again, then around her home, clearly comparing.

"Hard to believe Ms. Kook has decent decorating sense?" Except for her bedroom, which she preserved as a wild, cluttered oasis.

He shook his head. "Only that the inside doesn't match you the way the outside does. All that pink and purple trim..."

"My inside doesn't match my outside, either. It's what I was telling you before, about being trapped."

"Right." He put his hands in his pockets and rocked on his heels. "Trapped. I remember."

Uh-oh. His kook overload button was flashing red already. New topic. She gestured gracefully around her. "I decorated according to the principles of feng shui. To maximize the flow of energy and promote spiritual peace."

"Oh. Well." He nodded thoughtfully. "Feng shui looks nice. Elegant, and sophisticated and sort of…minimalist."

Allegra folded her arms across her chest and started her platform sandals tapping on her scratch-free pickled oak floors. "So if I don't match my decor that makes me inelegant, unsophisticated and maximalist?"

He grinned into her eyes, which made her scowl sag into disbelief. *How* did this man make her feel so many emotions with mere eye contact? Their first kiss would probably ignite. She absolutely had to make sure that tonight she found out whether it would or not.

"While *you* are carefree, and…joyous, and complicated."

He said the words as if he were reciting the contents of his sock drawer, but they still managed to produce a flush on her face. *Carefree? Joyous? Complicated?* If nothing else, he'd managed to find a better way to describe her than kook. The date was a success already, if the extra-fuzziness of her already fuzzy feelings was anything to go by.

She glanced at the creaseless perfection of his suit. "I can imagine your apartment. Antique wooden furniture, humidor for the Cuban cigar collection, portable wine cellar, hand-painted duck decoy, not a speck of dust anywhere..."

"Hmm." He cleared his throat and pushed impatiently at the thick tousled mass of hair that fell across his forehead. "Now that you mention it, my apartment doesn't match me, either. I'm a total slob."

"Aha!" Allegra's eyes widened, first in surprise, then in triumph. "There's something we have in common. Our homes don't match our appearance."

"I guess." He smiled and gestured to the door. "Shall we go? There are a couple of Thai restaurants downtown. Which one's your favorite?"

Allegra raised her eyebrows. He hadn't planned the evening? Hadn't gotten them a nice quiet corner table? "Would you like me to call for a reservation? We could have a drink here, and then go when our table's ready."

"A reservation?" He blinked. "Oh, well, I thought we could leave it to chance. Thursday evening shouldn't be too bad."

Allegra shrugged and followed him out her front door. Maybe it was just as well. Get out in the crowds while they got to know each other. One-on-one drinks in a house with a bedroom might seem like forced intimacy. Maybe Tracy was right, and he was shy.

Maybe Allegra would have to nudge a little to get their relationship going in the right direction. That was fine. She wasn't above a nice little nudge or two when the outcome would so clearly be worth it.

They drove down Kilbourn Avenue in John's navy Honda Civic, heading for The King and I restaurant. Miraculously, John got a parking place right outside the building, making Allegra glad she hadn't pointed out a space several blocks before as she'd been tempted to do. Whoever got a space right in front of their destination? In a silly schoolgirl way, it made John even more attractive. As if he had power to get whatever parking he wanted when he wanted it, and maybe other things, too. She liked that kind of power.

They entered the restaurant, crowded as usual, gave John's name to the hostess and stood waiting for a table.

And stood.

Allegra put on a bright smile. Now for some nice ordinary small talk, perfect for a getting-to-know-you date. Then she could ease into all the heavy stuff. Explain the clumsy way she'd handled telling him she knew about pizza man, and make sure he understood that as far as men were concerned, she wasn't the type to go for the sampler platter. Then ask him for help in bringing out her inner dullness. "Chilly this morning, wasn't it? And so warm yesterday."

"The usual mix for this time of year."

"Indeed." She beamed at him. "You know, sometimes I think spring in Wisconsin is some kind of spiritual test of man's soul. To see whether we have what it takes to withstand the rigors of life and whether we have the strength to resist moving to Florida.''

"Ah." His phone rang and he smiled apologetically, though, she thought also with a touch of relief. Darn. She should have just said, *Yes, spring in Wisconsin can be the pits.*

"John Tyler Jones... Hi, Jennifer." His voice turned slightly weary. "Uh-huh. Yes, I see. Okay. I'll call them later tonight and see what's up. Right. No problem."

He punched off the phone. "Sorry about that. I know it's rude, but I can't be out of touch or people panic. You were talking about having the strength to resist Florida."

"Oh. So I was." She tried not to let her concern for him show. He was not happy at all about having to be at people's beck and call. "Well, I love this time of year, even if the weather suffers from multiple personality disorder."

He glanced outside. "After all the snow, it's a relief to see some green."

"Absolutely." Allegra tapped her finger against her chin. "Green is a really restful color, don't you think? I mean there you are outdoors in all this green, and you just want to immerse yourself in it, you know? Spring is such a blissful green season. I can't pass a nice lawn or meadow without wanting to go roll myself around and around in all that green. Smell it, touch it, practically become it. Do you feel like that?''

He turned from his perusal of the bar and looked into her eyes. ''I never thought about it in quite that way.''

Allegra gave him a sick smile. ''No. I guess not many people do.''

Damn, damn, damn, damn.

He held the eye contact though, which made her skin get shivery and warm at the same time. ''Maybe I'll start.''

''Start?''

''Thinking about it that way.''

''Oh.'' She gave him a shy smile. Maybe he still thought she was okay. Or maybe he was just being very very polite in case she went berserk and started foaming at the mouth when contradicted.

''So...John. What do you do when you're not at work?''

''I work more.'' He was still staring at her thoughtfully. As if he were trying to figure out how anyone like her could have survived into adulthood.

Allegra laughed, though she had a feeling he wasn't joking. ''Seriously, what do you do?''

''I *was* being serious.''

She frowned. Workaholism was not a healthy lifestyle. He could probably use one of her seminars. ''Okay. What *would* you do if you could stop selling used cars long enough?''

She crossed her fingers. If he kept up the pretense

of being a used car salesman, she'd have lost the battle before she could really begin fighting. If he confessed, if he seemed to want honesty between them from now on, she still had an outside chance. Even if it was a way outside chance. Like in a cow pasture miles and miles away.

He tightened his sexy mouth, tipped his head and half-rubbed, half-scratched the back of his neck. "Allegra."

"Yes?"

"I'm not a used car salesman."

She smiled demurely, though her internal works immediately began a vigorous celebration. "I know that, John."

"You do?"

"Of course. You have some office job, something technical which allows you some creativity."

He opened his mouth and closed it. "How did you know that?"

"Because…I can tell that's who you are. Nothing dramatic." She put her fingers to her temples in a comic imitation of Frau Hinkel's psychic pose, anxious to reassure him. "I can't read your mind or anything."

"Well, *that's* good." He nodded, looking at her as if she might have gone over several edges all at once. "I'm not wild about that quality in a date."

Especially in a date like her. Because if she could read his mind she might find she scored about zero on the enticing scale and he'd be too kind to want her to know that. "I have a pretty good intuition, that's all."

"Is this the same intuition that knew we had a lot in common?" He grinned to show he was teasing her.

She grinned right back. He was irresistible when he smiled. All these sexy grooves appeared on either side of his mouth, like ripples around an object thrown into water. And he lost that weight-of-the-world look that had her positively itching to help him, which she undoubtedly could if he'd let her. But first she had to remember to keep her unusual side under control so as not to terrify him before he could fall for her.

"Your table is ready." A woman in traditional Thai dress appeared and escorted them to the nice quiet corner table he was supposed to get a reservation for.

She sat opposite him and opened her menu, scanning the choices as quickly as possible. Nothing worse than the awkward silence when you felt you had to keep talking to prove how much fun you were having, but at the same time you did have to choose food or risk looking like an indecisive idiot when the waitress showed up.

"So, what *do* you do, John?"

His phone rang. He answered it, instructed someone to write down an error message and report it to another number and punched the phone off. "I have a consulting business. I help train client employees on computer software."

He answered her question as if the phone call hadn't interrupted them. She had a feeling he probably lived his whole life in little disconnected fragments. Very detrimental to optimal energy flow.

"I see." She looked up from the noodle section and nodded rapidly, searching through her brain files for some intelligent and thoroughly normal observation. "That sounds nice."

"Boring you mean?" He closed his menu with a smile. "At times it is. But for the most part I like what I do."

Allegra slapped her menu on the table. Now *here* was a topic she could comment intelligently on. "How do you *feel* about your job? An instinctive answer, not the party line."

He got a strange hunted look in his eyes which he was probably unaware of. "Fine, thank you."

"Does your work complement who you are?" She gestured into the air. "Do your daily accomplishments make you feel like you are a truly fulfilled version of yourself?"

"Well, I can't...really..."

She leaned forward eagerly. "Because so many people live their lives on autopilot. They don't really pay attention to how they *feel*. How they feel about what they're doing for a living, how they feel about the people they're with. In my seminars, I challenge people to tune in. Pay attention. Ask themselves, 'How do I feel?' Do I ever wake up and say, 'What the hell am I doing here?' Do I ever ask myself, 'Am I the me I want to be?'"

His very handsome features took on an expression of bewilderment. "Actually, I'm happy in my work."

"Sometimes people fool themselves into thinking they're happy. Because fooling themselves saves them from really having to examine their lives and make changes."

"I'm sure that's true. But in this case—"

"Sometimes people can live that way for years and years and after it's too late, they realize their whole lives went by and they were never really happy. But they keep saying they're happy because they've conditioned their minds to believe it."

"Allegra." He held up a hand to stop her torrent of words. "Sometimes people say they're happy because they *are* happy."

She reined herself in and sat staring stiffly across the table. Oops. There she went again.

"Of course. You're right." Except she didn't think he *was* right, in his own case at least. But she should probably wait until he trusted her a little before she brought this up again.

The waitress came to the table and asked for Allegra's order.

"I'd like the pad Thai, please." She took a deep breath. "And could you keep the oil to a minimum and could I have extra peanuts sprinkled on top and could you also please give me double the usual carrot garnish and three lime wedges? And could you make the seasoning extra, extra hot. Please." She handed the waitress her menu, her lips pressed together to keep back any further requests. Meg Ryan had not been invited along on this date.

"Extra, extra hot?" John shuddered and ordered green curry mild. "Doesn't that erode your insides?"

Allegra tipped her head to one side. "Actually, capsicum is very beneficial for digestion. It also has loads of vitamin C, promotes healthy circulation, can ease cold symptoms and if you sprinkle some into your socks in the winter it can help keep your feet warm."

"You're kidding." He took a long swallow of beer.

Allegra beamed at him. "Just don't forget to tell your lover *before* she sucks your toes."

John jerked forward over the table, clapped his hand to his chest and swallowed convulsively. Then looked up, eyes moist from his little brush with choking to death. "Don't ever say things like that while I'm drinking."

She'd just opened her mouth to apologize, when his mouth widened into a groove-cheeked smile. Allegra immediately decided that sitting across from John Tyler Jones and smiling into his eyes was pretty much the best thing that had ever happened to her, or that could ever happen to anyone.

"I'm sorry I pounced all over you before. I'm sure you're happy in your work. I get kind of carried away with enthusiasm."

He waved off her apology. "I like that you're passionate about what you do. I think your field is probably very...interesting."

She stared at him, trying to ignore how her heart had just about laid down to die when he said he liked that she was passionate. She had to concentrate; tap into his mood and expressions as minutely as possible to see if he was being sarcastic about respecting what she did. But his gray eyes were only clear and friendly across the table.

A slow blush found its way up her face. "It's been a terrific career. Now I want to expand into online seminars. You work with computers, do you know anyone who could get me started? I have an ad in the *Journal Sentinel,* but I haven't found anyone suitable yet."

"Uh." He pulled at his tie and lined up his knife and spoon more evenly on the white cloth. "I—"

His phone rang; he answered, gave out the necessary information and punched the call off. "Not off the top of my head. I'll give it some thought, though."

"Thanks." She smiled again and relaxed as far as she could while becoming a trifle irritated at his phone for ringing so much. He did want to help her. That was good. That was terrific. This date could still turn out to be everything she'd hoped, which was admittedly plenty.

The rest of the meal she managed to keep the conversation light and fairly normal. Okay, maybe she didn't quite manage normal, but she didn't have much experience at it yet. She couldn't be expected to master the transformation overnight. And he only had two more calls during the meal, both of which annoyed him, though he was probably in denial about that too, and hadn't noticed how he clenched his teeth at each ring. So at least he wasn't dying to escape her. But he certainly needed her help to free himself from phone imprisonment.

And she still had to find the right time to talk about the important topics they needed to talk about, to clear the way for their future, short- or long-term, though she hoped very very long. But so far she hadn't really been able to manage a clear patch of normal conversation that would put him at ease. Maybe their fabulous good-night kiss would set the proper mood. Maybe she should wait until then.

They split the check at Allegra's insistence and left the restaurant, stepping out into the now-cool evening air. Regardless, she needed to keep this date going. He needed to loosen up so they could connect better, so she could relax, so he'd turn his phone off and she could kiss him and then they could really talk.

What should she suggest now? The outdoor roller rink opposite Uihlein Hall had been her first choice in planning the evening. Roller-skating was so freeing and so rejuvenating. John simply wouldn't be able to help having fun. And if he kept having fun in her company maybe sooner or later he'd give meant-to-be a chance.

Even though she had to be nothing like the wife he envisioned for himself.

Unfortunately, he stepped directly across the sidewalk to his car. And stopped, darn it.

"Allegra, thanks for coming out with me. I hate to make an early night of it." He smiled down at her, avoiding her eyes after one quick glance, his voice politely regretful. "But I really need to go home and do some work."

She stepped closer and made him look right at her by making sure her own gaze was clear and direct. People couldn't avoid gazes like that, no matter how much they wanted to. Honesty was one of the great and awesome powers in the universe. "You do?"

"Yeah." His voice came out husky and lower this time; he looked surprised, as if he'd found out that maybe he'd been telling the truth after all, and he *did* hate to make an early night of it.

Allegra put her hand to his arm and felt the nice hard muscles under his silk jacket and white shirt tense at her touch. "I thought we could go do something fun."

"Fun?" Instead of surprised, he looked vaguely terrified.

"You like to roller-skate?"

"...Roller-skate."

Okay, so that answered her question. But if he was going to be loosened, as he desperately needed to be, tonight and forever, and if he wouldn't admit he didn't like his job and if he wouldn't admit he liked to lie in the grass and if he wouldn't risk a little hot pepper in his food, then the very *least* he could do was roller-skate.

"There's an outdoor rink right opposite Uihlein. They ice-skate there in the winter. You can rent skates and everything."

"Allegra, I would love to, but I really have to—"

She took another step toward him, keeping her earnest gaze fixed on his sexy eyes and moving her hand up from his forearm to his shoulder. "I think you could use a little fun."

She said the words very very plainly so he wouldn't misunderstand, but at that moment, with the cool night air swirling around them, special delivery from Lake Michigan a few blocks away, and with his Adam's apple dipping in a practically audible swallow, she didn't really care if he did misunderstand and think she was referring to…that other thing.

"Yes." His Adam's apple did another bobbing trip up and down and the intensity of his stare intensified so she felt that he'd really been caught, spiritually, and maybe even sexually, in the power of what lay between them. "Okay."

"Good." She stepped away, beaming at him and danced a few steps down the sidewalk and back. "You'll love it."

He nodded and they walked the rest of the way to the rink in silence. She knew for sure he was wondering what the hell just happened to him. So much the better. He'd think again before underestimating their rare and wonderful link.

Half an hour later, she had to admit that while roller-skating could be freeing and rejuvenating, it helped very much if you knew how. And apparently John didn't. He didn't look so much freed and rejuvenated as clumsy and horrified. But he was getting better. He'd managed seven or eight strokes last time before he had to clutch the railing or fall down.

So maybe this hadn't been the very best idea she'd had. Maybe she should have pity on the poor man and let him go home. Chances were, when he entered the paper-laden confines of his apartment and settled down to work, he'd be carrying a picture of her that involved fresh air and laughter, and maybe he'd start to realize the depth of his yet unrealized discontent.

But they did have one matter to settle before she let him go. That, she absolutely wouldn't give up. Because kissing him meant hurdling over to a new level, one where she'd feel safe talking to him about what needed to be said. The pizza, and the fact that she wasn't a stalker, and the de-kooking she needed his help with.

She skated smoothly up to where he stood embracing the railing and stopped about a foot from his really very magnificent body.

"Had enough?"

He nodded, not even trying to disguise his discomfort, which she liked about him. "I'm afraid this isn't what I'm meant to do in life."

She smiled and pushed herself a little closer. "Just one more thing."

"You're not going to make me try pole-vaulting now, are you?"

"No." She nudged forward so that only about an inch separated them, and tipped her face up. "But I would really love you to kiss me. I could kiss you, but I think being kissed is so much more romantic, especially because you're so much taller than I am and frankly I couldn't reach."

"I…I…" He clenched the railing more tightly. His phone rang. Allegra watched politely while he took the call, all the while imagining herself disguised as a phone repair technician armed with a jackhammer. But if he thought an obstacle as easily surmountable as a phone call could deprive her of this all-important good-night kiss, he was entirely, completely, rigor mortis wrong.

The very second he ended the call, she continued.

"Don't you believe in kissing on the first date? Because I thought it might be a good idea to have our first kiss now. I like getting it over with so then I can stop worrying about it, you know?"

She moved forward and back, just a little, so their bodies touched and came apart again. The frantic frozen look on his face started to thaw.

"I mean," her voice dropped to a whisper because being this close to him made the crowded rink blur to a dark whirl of movement, and made producing tone somehow impossible. "I hate that moment at the door after a first date when you keep talking except neither of you are thinking about anything but that kiss and whether it will happen or not. You know?"

"Yes."

He seemed to be having as much trouble with vocal volume as she was. She scootched her skates closer until she practically pressed against him. His hands came up to grip her upper arms, slowly, as if he wasn't the one in control of moving them.

"I mean in that situation at the front door, you want the kiss to happen, but sometimes it's so damn awkward that it's not worth the stress and then you skip it, and that would be a shame in this case, don't you think?"

She ended in a big hurry on a breathless rush of air because he was leaning slowly toward her tipped-up face as if he was in some kind of trance, and she knew what that meant.

He kissed her, and the kiss was perfect. Warm, lingering, with a promise of passion to be explored at another time.

Wow.

He drew back and she kept her eyes closed for a second or two to savor the warmth and the residual fireworks before she launched into all the important things she had to say, then opened them and smiled shyly. "Thanks."

"Don't mention it."

His eyes were so beautiful, gray and clear, and at

the moment slightly confused and questioning, as if he couldn't quite believe what had just happened.

Then suddenly the emotions were all too much, all too intense, and she was horribly afraid that in the throes of a tremendous rush of euphoric energy, if she stayed in reach for even another millisecond, instead of calmly talking things over, she'd jump into his arms, wrap her own around his neck and tell him she never ever intended to let go.

And that was a lot more awkward than getting past the first kiss.

So she turned her shy smile into a cheerful one and pushed firmly away on his wonderful broad chest for a calming turn around the rink, forgetting in all her fabulous unsettled romantic excitement, that John Tyler Jones was not tremendously steady on skates.

5

JOHN WALKED INTO the conference room at Brighton Pharmaceuticals with five copies of the newly pared-down report Big Boss Lester had wanted for the transition team. He'd stayed up all night working on it. All damn night long. His brain was a pea-souper, his eyes felt like clay balls that had been baking for days in the sun and his muscles didn't seem at all interested in obeying his commands in a timely fashion.

''Hi, there.'' The musical voice lifted his barely functioning pulse into a nice jazz rhythm. Katherine. Fresh, stunning, unimaginably lovely. In one of those miniskirted suits that showed her legs from here to eternity.

Hubba-freaking-hubba.

''Hi.'' He gave her an intimate smile, tossed his briefcase on the conference table with a flourish, and keeping friendly-but-meaningful eye contact, lowered himself into the seat opposite.

And shot out of it with a furious shout of pain.

Jeez. His hand started toward his painfully bruised tailbone, and halted when he saw Katherine's narrowed eyes looking at him as if he were one of the Marx Brothers in a posthumous movie.

He was never ever roller-skating again. Never.

And he was never again letting a tiny kook of a person entice him into kissing her while he wore any kind of footwear that could possibly slide.

"What's the matter, John?" Katherine tipped her head to one side so her blond hair fell over her shoulder in a luxurious cascade. For some reason, the gesture made him think of Allegra, of how quizzical and odd and endearing she looked when she did the same thing.

"Oh. I, uh, fell and bruised my…" He laughed awkwardly. "My…"

She leaned forward so her shirt gaped open and exposed a bit of heaven. "Your *coc*cyx?"

He swallowed. *Oh my God.* "Yes."

"I bruised my coccyx once, too, ice-skating. It sucks, doesn't it?"

His hands gave an involuntary start; he clutched the reports tighter. No one who looked like Katherine should be allowed to say the words, "sucks" and "coccyx" in such close proximity.

"It's pretty painful." He smiled and prepared himself for one helluva fantasy. Strangely, though, he started thinking instead about Allegra. How she'd sped back to him when she saw him sitting on the rink floor, clenching his teeth against the pain. She'd knelt next to him and put her hand on his arm, squeezing tightly, head bowed, not speaking, instinctively knowing he needed time to work through the agony and embarrassment, sending a silent signal that she was there.

When he'd been able to focus again, she'd lifted her head. Their eyes had met, and that crazy impossible chemistry took over. Her full bottom lip had tucked anxiously behind her front teeth. Her forehead wrinkled into furrows of concern. And under the hideous auburn wig, her always-unexpectedly beautiful hazel eyes filled with vulnerability, as if she was waiting for him to lash out at her.

He'd had the craziest urge to take her in his arms and kiss her again, feel that soft mouth against his—

"Good morning!" Lester Prism entered the room, bringing with him three other members of the team and the smell of stale cigarettes and perspiration. "Morning. Morning. A new day. A new beginning. Room for excellence. John, what do you have for me? What can you show me?" He lowered his bulk into the chair at the head of the table and rubbed his hands together.

John pushed Allegra out of his pea-soup brain and gingerly tried sitting again. He managed to make contact with the chair without yelling and leaned forward to keep his...coccyx out of trouble. "I shortened the report as you asked. From one hundred pages to twenty." *And damn near died in the process.*

He pushed a streamlined copy toward Lester, one each for the other members of the transition team, and a specially delivered copy to Katherine, who beamed and swiveled back and forth in her chair, the corner of a gold Cross pen stuck between her lips.

Oh, yes. Sexy lips. Though not quite as full and beautifully shaped as Allegra's, now that he noticed.

"So, then." Lester settled into his chair, picked up the report, and began leafing through the pages. "Let's have a look-see, Jones."

John nodded, glancing at Katherine, who winked. He winked back, hardly daring to believe what was happening. She was flirting with him. *Oh, mama.* He leaned back, drumming his fingers on the table.

And stifled another yell.

Jeez! Paper cut still hurt his finger, bruise hurt his tailbone. Would this Allegra person never leave him alone?

Worse, he couldn't shake the sudden image of her face, tipped up toward his when she asked him to kiss her. How her mouth had been so sweet and inviting. How her nuttiness receded so completely behind her femininity, how her short sturdy body suddenly seemed waiflike and wildly tempting. But most of all those eyes had drawn him in, had made kissing her seem inevitable and natural and right.

He hadn't resisted. It hadn't even occurred to him. And the moment their lips touched, the crazy inappropriate out-of-place attraction gelled into a restless nagging need that hadn't left him alone all night.

If only Brighton Pharmaceuticals made a pill that could numb that feeling as easily as the ones that could numb the pain in his—

"Jones!"

John's head snapped over to Lester, who sat glowering at him at the end of the table. "What is this?"

John's teeth clenched into a death grip. His head added to the pain throbbing in his finger and his tailbone. "This is the abbreviated report you asked for."

"What can I learn from this? Only twenty pages? Stuffed with pictures? It's filler. Excellence, m'boy. I need to know what you are talking about. See what you can do to beef it up. Something this important should be several times this length. I'll assign someone to help you. Tabachnik. He can talk you through what we're all about here."

John's jaw clenched harder; he imagined all his teeth gradually cracking into dust.

"Lester?" Katherine leaned forward. Lester noticed. His eyes began doing a strobe dance up to her face and down to her gaping blouse. "I think I should be the one assigned to work with John."

"You do." Lester wiped at his moist forehead and took a deep breath. "Why?"

"Because I care so *deeply* about excellence, Lester. So deeply."

"Ha!" Lester pounded his fist on the table. "You see that, Jones? That's the kind of dedication we need. Good. You help him. Next business item."

John stared over at Katherine, who winked and sent him a sexy smile. His teeth unclenched.

The woman of his dreams, the exact type he'd been

praying for nightly since recovering from his divorce, wanted him. He was as good as married again.

He dismissed the strange lack of euphoria as merely a stunned reaction.

This time he'd get it right.

"So?" FRAU HINKEL folded her huge arms across her brightly patterned caftan. "What do you see in this boiled cabbage of a man you are so hot for?"

"Oh." Allegra let out a huge sigh, stretched her arms up and folded them dreamily across the top of her blond Marilyn wig. "Only that he's everything I want."

"Everything?"

"Everything short of having 'Am I the Me I Want To Be?' become a huge nationwide success."

"Ah." Frau Hinkel's bushy eyebrow rose skeptically. "Well you see more in him than I do. Have you found anyone to help you take the seminars online?"

"None of the résumés I've gotten so far have hit me the right way. John thinks he might be able to find someone. I hope so."

"I see." Frau Hinkel said the words as if she didn't think John could do basic arithmetic and mumbled something about brain-damaged idiots. "Well, I think the ideas you and I discussed today are *wunderbar.* Can the spirits be of any more help to you before you go?"

"There is one thing." Allegra wrinkled her nose,

considering. Frau Hinkel might be annoyed when she found out Allegra suspected some earthly and easily explainable connection to John. But she had to know. Their last date had gone really well, but she couldn't help being anxious. Couldn't help worrying that John had been out with her for some other reason than that they were meant for each other. "How did you get John to go out with me?"

"Me? Me?" Frau Hinkel clutched her enormous bosom. "I did nothing. The spirits intervened. They made your inevitable Fate possible. You would have met him anyway, believe me. You were destined for that…that…Jones person."

"Frau Hinkel…" Allegra wagged her finger reproachfully. "Men like John don't generally want women like me."

Frau Hinkel narrowed her eyes. "Did the *dumkopf* give some indication he didn't want to be out with you?"

"Oh, no, not really. The date was fabulous. Except that he had to spend so much time on the phone, poor thing. I'll try to help him with that. But I wanted to explain to him about…me, and it never seemed the right time."

"No intimacy on this date?"

"Well, I wouldn't say *no* intimacy…" Allegra tried to keep a gooey smile off her face, then said what the hell and let it rip.

"Hmm." Frau Hinkel's right eyebrow shot skyward. "He a good kisser, this John?"

"The very best."

"Aha." Frau Hinkel nodded as if John's kissing ability impressed her mightily. "There's some hope for him yet. As for the other problem, I don't have time to contact the spirits right now, but if I *did* have time, no doubt they would tell you to chill the heck out, my little cupcake. Intimacy will come when intimacy is ready. You'll know when the moment is right. The spirits will guide you. Don't push or they'll screw everything up for you, understand?"

Allegra nodded. "Yes. I'll try to be more patient. Assuming John ever wants to see me again."

"Oh, he will." Frau Hinkel uttered the words as if she was swearing a solemn oath. Or issuing a dire threat. Which made Allegra all the more suspicious that the pseudo-gypsy was involved with John's turnabout interest in her.

She pinned the larger woman with her clearest most direct give-it-to-me-straight gaze. "Frau Hinkel, why did John agree to go out with me?"

"You really want to know?"

"Yes."

"In that case—" Frau Hinkel stretched her arms out wide, then brought her splayed fingers up to her temples "—ask him yourself. He will be outside this building sometime in the next half hour. Just go out there and wait."

Allegra shot out of her seat with a gasp and gestured at her second-most comfortable cheer-herself-up outfit. "Oh no! He can't see me dressed like this.

I swore up and down that next time he saw me I'd be totally conservative.''

"Get over it, babushka. Men never notice clothes. It's what's inside that counts. That and being a wild Amazon slut in bed.''

"I have to go.'' Allegra pulled her wallet out of her bag and threw some bills into Frau Hinkel's outstretched palm. Assuming Frau Hinkel knew something about John's movements, Allegra should get the heck out of here before he showed up.

She ran down the hall and yanked open the door to the stairs, skidded onto the landing and half-ran, half-slid down the railing to the first floor. Then she peeked through the door. All clear? The tiny window didn't give her much of a view.

Whatever. She had to get out of here one way or the other. On their next date, assuming the spirits sent her the proper mood, she absolutely had to clarify the pizza incident, and let John in on how she wanted him to help bring out her more conservative side. But if she looked like a refugee from a seventies yard sale, he might think she was beyond help.

She pushed her way out of the door and scanned the street one way... No sign of him. So far so good. Other way...John. Striding up the block, one hand on his briefcase, the other holding the *Milwaukee Journal Sentinel,* which, thank goodness, he seemed to be engrossed in.

She moved cautiously back toward the building and edged quietly along its side, hands scrabbling over the warm cream-colored bricks behind her, staring at the sidewalk in case her eyes held any message of longing that managed to communicate itself to his subconscious awareness. If he could just keep his eyes on whatever fascinating article currently held his interest, and if his peripheral vision wasn't particularly tuned into hot pink and purple, then she might have some prayer of—

"Allegra." His pant legs came into view and stopped in the middle of the sidewalk. No doubt he was staring at her, thinking she was a fashion nightmare who had an unnatural fondness for the sides of buildings.

"John." She braced herself to meet his eyes. And then suddenly she didn't care that she looked like Bohemia warmed over because happy chemicals were madly buzzing and fluttering up and down her body. More amazing, unless she was totally mistaken, the chemicals were doing a number on him too, because he shot off enough positive energy to light the Empire State Building.

"What are you doing here?" He asked the question at the exact same time she did, which made them both laugh and then stand there gawking some more.

"I met with Frau Hinkel. My spiritu— My business adviser." She clutched her large straw bag to her chest, trying to hide the hot-pink shirt, swarming with tropical butterflies, which didn't even begin to approach the number swarming in her stomach. "What about you?"

"I'm…I live here."

She gaped at him in dismay. Frau Hinkel was his landlord. Maybe she did have some way to put the screws to him. "How…was work today?"

"Great." A dynamite smile broke out on his amazing face, making him so irresistibly handsome she almost couldn't hold all the feeling in.

"Something happened?" She smiled back. She couldn't help it. His moods reached out to her, swallowed her up and carried her along for the ride.

"Yes. I was assigned to work on a certain project with a…colleague I…respect."

"Oh." She nodded, feeling an inexplicable sense of foreboding. "He's lucky."

"…She."

She. The happy chemicals evaporated along with her smile and her hopes and her self-esteem. Allegra wasn't making him glow like that. Allegra wasn't making him radiate happiness like that. Some *she* person was. Undoubtedly a long-limbed blonde who shopped at Ann Taylor and had matching everything. Who radiated calm sensual confidence instead of scattered jittery wackiness.

"That's great." She swallowed and nodded and stared down at her scuffy purple plastic sandals, wishing they would sprout magic wings and carry her into another dimension.

"Allegra." Her scuffy purple plastic sandals suddenly had company. Men's brown dress shoes. "Do you…want to take a walk?"

Her head shot up to encounter an expression not, as she expected, full of pity, but a kind of contrition, touched with what might even be tenderness. Maybe. If she wasn't imagining it. Which was entirely possible. "A walk? With you?"

He smiled. "That was the general idea, yes."

Wow. "I'd...love to. Thanks."

"Okay." This time Allegra had most definitely put the smile on his lips because she felt that smile all the way down to her neon-pink-and-purple alternating-color toenails.

"Wait out here for me. I'll go change."

She waited. Yes, oh yes, she waited, brimming with impatience. He wanted to take a walk with her. Frau Hinkel hadn't forced him to do that. Nope. His earlier mood might have been because of some other woman, but he...he...

Her giddiness took a nosedive. Unless he wanted to take a walk so he could break up with her. Not that he really would be breaking up with her since they weren't technically going out, except in her passionate imagination, but maybe he was about to give her the dreaded this-is-going-nowhere speech she'd heard so many times.

Oh, no. Her shoulders slumped. He couldn't. Could he? After that wonderful kiss they had? After which she'd shoved him onto his ass and practically splintered his tailbone. After which he hadn't called and she'd bumped into him today in the middle of ecstatic happiness over getting to work closely with some to-tally-perfect-for-him woman.

Oh gosh. He could.

She sat on the low stone wall at the edge of the sidewalk and leaned against the wrought-iron railing, plucking aimlessly at the hem of her purple skirt. She'd been really excited about this guy. Really excited. Beyond all the show, all the chemistry, all the furor about finding her perfect opposite, deep inside her a wise little head seemed to pop up at the sight of John and whisper that this was for real.

Now in about one minute, that wise little head was going to get its brains crushed into vanilla pudding.

"Hi." A warm male body looking absolutely fan-amazing-tastic in jeans and a polo shirt sat down next to her. Carefully.

Allegra winced and looked over at his strong legs stretched out next to her. "How's your butt?"

"Unhappy." He reached and touched her pink tights-covered knee, a cautious warm touch. "Is something the matter?"

She dared a glance up at his face. Oh no. *That* face. That thoughtful, pitying, tender, I'm-about-to-lose-your-sorry-ass-from-my-life face. "I'm expecting some rough weather any minute."

He quirked an eyebrow up at the perfect blue May sky and quirked it back down at her. "Oh?"

Allegra shrugged. "Just a feeling."

"Okay." He shoved a hand through the thick hair over his forehead. "How about that walk?"

"Sure." She rose to her feet, feeling hollow and hopeless in spite of the beautiful weather and the even more beautiful man beside her.

They headed south on Prospect Avenue and crossed into Veteran's Park. The lake stretched endlessly ahead, like a tiny peaceful ocean. The breeze blew fresh scents of water and spring; the unfurling leaves whispered quietly overhead; seagulls soared; pedestrians strolled.

She'd hate this place for the rest of her life.

"Are you about to stop, drop and roll?"

She lifted her heavy head and gazed at him mournfully. "Why, am I on fire?"

He gestured to the grassy lawn. "I thought green made you want to roll."

"Oh." She glanced around. "I guess it does."

She hated grass. She hated the color green. But she hated most having to wait until he worked up the nerve to broach the subject they both knew was due any minute.

"Look, John. I know what you're doing here."

He looked at her in alarm. "You do?"

His phone rang; he answered without breaking stride, gave detailed technical instructions to the caller, and hung up.

"Yes." She threw her hands out and let them drop, knowing by now that he would have remembered his question in spite of the phone call and her answer would make sense. "So why don't you just say what you have to say and get it over with."

"Uh...okay. Fine." He rubbed the back of his neck. "Except I don't know what you think I have to say."

Allegra came to a full stop in the middle of the lawn. "You don't?"

He hunched his shoulders, put his hands out and shook his head in a show of genuine cluelessness. "Nope."

Her breath caught in her throat, then escaped in a sweet rush out her wide-open mouth. "You're not about to tell me you don't want to see me anymore?"

His brows drew down, his lips parted. His startled gray eyes stared into hers and relit the sparklers that were tuned to his special power of ignition. "Why would I want to do that?"

"I..." She shrugged and burst out laughing, feeling like she'd been given a presidential pardon two seconds before her execution. "I don't know."

He grinned. "Let's walk."

"Let's." They continued walking on the raised grassy park with the stunning lake view. "What a gorgeous day. I love this place. The lake and all this beautiful green. Maybe I will drop and roll after all. What do you think?"

"Whatever floats your boat."

She tipped her head and stared at him shyly. "Will you join me?"

"I...don't know. I'm out of practice."

Something an awful lot like hope started singing a

quiet little song in her head. "You mean you used to?"

"When I was a kid."

She took his strong warm hand and held it. He tightened his grip in an almost an affectionate squeeze, and the little song became a nice full-volume operatic aria. "Tell me about it."

"When I was a kid…"

His tone became quiet, slightly awkward, not the assertive businessman's voice at all. It was a boyish, almost vulnerable voice. Allegra held her breath, afraid that if she even moved air out of her mouth the wrong way she'd upset the balance of the universe and he'd stop talking.

"…I used to lie in the grass and pretend I was part of the bug world. I even used to talk to them."

"You did?" Allegra stopped and turned to face him. *Double wow.* They might be kindred spirits after all. "I thought that was just me."

He grinned and seemed to come suddenly alive. "I was Captain Ant. Ruler of Bugania. Faster than a speeding centipede. More powerful than a pill bug. Able to leap blades of grass in a single—"

"Come on." She laughed and tugged his hand, flopped down into the sweet warm grass and folded her hands under her chin, wondering if it was possible to die of unexpected happiness coming so soon on the heels of expected rejection and misery.

He knelt awkwardly beside her. "Uh. I haven't done this in a long time."

"So." She patted the grass opposite her. "It's like riding a bicycle. You never forget."

He glanced around for spectators, then lay stiffly across from her and doubled his hands under his chin as she had.

"Now." Allegra peered down into the grass. "We watch."

Except she found it much harder than usual to concentrate on whatever might be happening in and on the earth below them. Because in the excitement department ants and bugs and worms and growing grass didn't remotely compare to John Tyler Jones's long lean body and his handsome gray-eyed face inches away. Lots of inches. Too many inches.

She moved her body forward, imperceptibly, she hoped. Like an inchworm. Ease the front up, then follow with the back, all the while pretending to search for insect life and thinking of casual conversation to distract him from her subversive mission.

"So...why did you stop?"

"Stop what?"

"Speaking in bug."

"I don't know." He met her eyes and the breeze blew across and over them and the sun poured down warm on their backs. "I must have had a sensible reason, but I seem to have forgotten it."

Ms. Inchworm managed another discreet wriggle forward. "Oh?"

"Oh." He must have figured out what she was up to because he looked suddenly wary.

Immediately she lay still and pretended fascination with something as totally dull as bug-watching. Not only because she didn't want him to freak, but also because she suddenly knew, as if Frau Hinkel's spirits were sitting on her shoulder whispering in her ear, that now was the time. "John?"

"Yes."

"Could you turn off your phone?"

He stiffened. "But…then it wouldn't be…on."

"Right." She made her voice very gentle. "That's the point."

"I don't think I'd better do that. I'm sorry. People need to be able—"

"To reach you. I know." She wrinkled her nose, conceding the battle but hardly the war. "John?"

"Yes."

"I tried to tell you once before, but I don't think it worked. I did know it was you trying to sell me pizza."

He groaned and shook his head. "Sorry about that. I called you and then I was suddenly afraid I shouldn't be calling you and work was crazy and I…panicked."

"Why shouldn't you have been calling me?"

"Because…Allegra…because…I don't know. Because I barely knew you."

"But you knew I wanted you to call me."

"Yes. I knew that."

Allegra inched forward again so that she was almost close enough to smell his clean thick hair, and if he lifted his face they'd be very close indeed. Which was exactly what she was after. "I wanted you to know I knew you were Pizza Man because I was afraid you'd think I tried to pick up strangers all day long."

He lifted his head and they were, in fact, very close indeed. Which seemed to startle him, but unless she was way way off in her perception, which she generally wasn't, their closeness didn't make him feel particularly unhappy. That made her feel extremely happy. And safe. And bold. And crazy about him.

"Did you think that about me?" she whispered.

His gaze dropped to her mouth, which she tried to make look as enticing as possible. "I did wonder."

"I'm not like that."

"No?"

"No. It's only you, John Ty-ler Jones."

He took in a sharp breath and his eyes came back up to hers. He seemed to be totally out of his element, totally lost, exactly the way she suddenly felt. As if the scene around them had shifted and gone underwater-indistinct and the only really real reality that existed in the universe was this crazy chemistry between them and the crazy burning need to kiss him and be kissed by him.

Thank goodness that's exactly what happened.

He moved his body up toward her, but not in an inchworm wriggle, in a smooth powerful movement, so his lips could reach hers and his hand could cup the back of her head to bring her as close as possible and to make the kiss deep and fabulous.

Which they did. And it did. And it was.

Oh my goodness, kissing John Tyler Jones was glorious. If you could talk about something as noble as glory with every atom crying out for sexual satisfaction.

But then the kissing was over. And the look on his face did not reflect at all the joyous hallelujah-the-crops-are-saved look on her face. His face looked more like, what-the-heck-do-crops-have-to-do-with-it?

He pushed himself up on what must be very strong arms considering how easily he did it, and sat looking very confused and wary again, with the breeze ruffling the fabulous tumbling wheat-blond locks of hair across his forehead.

Okay, so John Tyler Jones might not be quite as swept away as she was. Yet. But he hadn't dumped her, and he had kissed her, and he did look a little like the passion between them was a surprise, and maybe even a nice one, so she wasn't at all going to give up. Full steam ahead, in fact.

"John?"

"Yes." He looked as if he were trying very hard to rouse himself out of a dream he wasn't sure he wanted to be having, but was enjoying in spite of himself.

"Remember when I said you'd be perfect for

something, but I didn't want to tell you then what you'd be perfect for?''

"Uh. Yes. I think.''

"I'd like to tell you now.''

"Okay.'' Wary and wary and more wary.

She pushed herself up and waddled toward him on her knees, then sat and clutched her knees to her chest. "I want to lose my kook image.''

His eyes flicked over her hot pink butterflies and purple skirt and alternating purple and neon-pink colored toenails under her purple plastic sandals. "Oh?''

"I think you can help me.''

"I can?'' He put his hand out and brushed aside strands of her blond Marilyn wig, then drew his hand back distastefully so that she swore she'd go home and burn her entire wig collection that afternoon, except that the fumes would probably be toxic.

"Yes. Because you are so normal and…normal. I think you can bring out that side of me. It's something I'd really like to try.''

He shook his head. "I'm not sure what I can do.''

"Inspire me.'' She got to her feet and stretched her arms out wide, then smiled down at him, still kneeling on the sweet green grass with the sun lighting his face and a bee buzzing around his head. "Be yourself and inspire me.''

He grinned and brushed away the bee. "I guess I could do that.''

"Good.'' She laughed and gave in to a tremendous burst of energy by doing a cartwheel before she remembered that cartwheels probably weren't going to set her off down the road to normalcy.

She turned to grin ruefully at the very-probable love of her life who might not know that he had actually just agreed to fall deeply in love with her, as well. Unfortunately, she didn't turn in time to warn him about the bee, which had just landed next to his eye.

6

JOHN PUNCHED OFF his cell phone and gave a long frustrated groan. If Mr. Tabachnik referred to the Internet as "Satan-dot-com" one more time…

He sighed and glanced at his watch. Six-fifteen. He had about five minutes to shower and change before picking up Allegra for their date. Date number two, which, according to Dolores's Rules for Dating Allegra, meant another week of assured residency in this apartment.

Terrific. The rules might buy him time, but they also endangered his sanity. Twice, in spite of himself, the desire to kiss Allegra had been so strong as to impair his usually sound judgment. *Danger. Danger. Code Red.* She was nothing like the woman he wanted. Katherine was everything like the woman he wanted. The woman who would be so good for him, who would complement his life like a fine wine complemented a good roast.

Being with Allegra would be like pouring ketchup over chocolate cake. Nothing wrong with ketchup. Nothing wrong with chocolate cake. They just didn't belong together. Ketchup needed French fries. Chocolate cake needed frosting. Allegra needed to find a nice French fry to settle down with. He needed Katherine to frost him.

Mmm—

His stomach growled. Damn, he was hungry. Whatever Allegra had planned for them tonight he hoped the evening included French fries and chocolate.

He jumped into the shower, lathered, rinsed and toweled himself off, wondering why he had been so anxious to clean up for a duty date. Truth was, he was sort of looking forward to seeing her. She had so much energy, so much passion for everything she did. Her work, her bug-watching…

Her kissing.

He closed his eyes, inhaled a long breath and blew it out quickly. Yes. She could do some serious kissing. He had to stay away from that dead end, in his thoughts as well as his actions. Dwelling on those kinds of feelings could turn them into something more than what they were. No doubt as soon as he kissed Katherine, his world would be turned back to right side up.

But there was no denying that Allegra charged him up in a way he hadn't been charged in a long time. Not like the hot sexual flashes he got when he saw Katherine. But charged up. Kind of like…charged up.

He shook his head. He wasn't going there. Bad enough she counted on him to perform some sort of kook-ectomy on her. As if she could possibly contain that exuberant personality in something approaching normalcy. Women who watched bugs and turned cartwheels were simply doomed to be irrepressible. Joyous. And eternally kooky. He could no more imagine her happily strapped into an average lifestyle than imagine a lioness thrilled to be in a cage.

The strangest part was that she called to something in him, something long-forgotten and kid-like. As if the fun, happy childhood he hadn't had still lurked inside him, patiently waiting its turn.

Wait a second. Didn't he say he wasn't going to analyze this anymore? Didn't he say that dwelling on feelings like this was nothing but dangerous? Next week he'd have his first date with Katherine. Then he'd be on the straight and narrow to heaven. Allegra would recede in comparison, a lively curiosity.

He buttoned up his patterned cotton shirt, tucked it into his khakis and grabbed his keys and wallet off his dresser. Six-twenty-five. He'd be politely late, not bad.

At six-thirty-six he turned onto Astor Street and pulled up in front of her house, a tall narrow Victorian painted stark white, with elaborately decorative trim accented in rather bilious shades of deep pink and purple.

In bizarre contrast, low, beautifully landscaped shrubs grew around the house in varying colors and textures. An old stone staircase led up to the front door; at the top sat two very dignified stone lions, streaked green with mossy age, each lifting a regal paw in greeting. He imagined they were probably tremendously uncomfortable with the paint job that had been foisted on them behind their backs.

The overall effect was that of a house from some faraway Oz-type country, dumped here on this quiet residential Midwestern street, instead of the other way around. A house that stood out on the quiet street like…Allegra in a crowd of businessmen.

The front door opened and the woman herself burst out onto her front walkway, wearing some crazy pink-and-orange outfit. She crossed the street, waving, and jumped into his car.

"Hello, John Ty-ler Jones."

"Hi." A huge smile helped itself to his mouth, and his heart gave a racing jaunty salute. Okay, so he liked her. No harm in that. And he loved the way she sang his name as if it was her favorite tune. She looked nice today, in spite of the pink giraffes parading all over her. She wasn't wearing one of those god-awful wigs, though she had gelled her hair into forbidding spiky clumps. But without the fake hair, the high-cheekboned lines of her face stood out undisturbed and he liked that, even behind the outrageous pink fake glasses. She was really pretty attractive when you took the time to notice.

"So what's on the agenda for tonight?" he asked.

She settled back against the seat and tilted her head so her chin came up and she looked sassy and sweet. "We're going to the zoo."

"The zoo?" He tried to suppress a smile. What did

he expect, dinner and a movie? "I thought the zoo closed at five."

"There's a special event tonight." She looked away, then met his eyes again with a touch of defiance. "Gorilla Night."

"Gorilla Night." He gave in and let the grin spread over his face, watched a defiant vulnerable blush spread over hers, and had the crazy dumb idea of leaning over to kiss her again. "Sounds great. I haven't been to the zoo in years."

She broke their eye contact and buckled her seat belt. "I originally thought we could go to Fun World and play, pretending we were there with our kids, but then I thought that might be not quite the starting place for my new adventure in sedateness."

"Probably not." He turned right on Brady Street, right again on Farwell, and headed south to pick up I-94, feeling strangely energized. He should be working. He should be *wanting* to be working. Getting Brighton's Web site ready for its launch at the end of the month. "Gorilla Night sounds positively tame compared to Fun World."

"Would you rather have gone to dinner? That's what I planned originally, but it seemed to lack something. And I think the wander-and-chat method of getting to know someone is so much more effortless than being pinned across the table from them and having to provide scintillation for two hours, don't you?"

He chuckled and pushed away a sudden image of

him and Katherine after the opera on their date next week. "Now that you mention it, I guess I do."

"Not that I didn't enjoy dinner the other night, I did." She made a sound of exasperation. "I'm sorry. My foot's in it again."

"I suggested dinner last time because I don't have your…imagination."

"Ha! No one without imagination would strive to become ruler of a bug empire. You might have distanced yourself from it for a while, but I don't think you can lose imagination permanently."

"Maybe not." He glanced over at her again. She looked troubled and thoughtful and his insides contracted with the need to cheer her up. "So is there food at this Gorilla Night? I'm starving."

"Oh, yes. Everyone will be wearing gorilla costumes and we all have to eat what gorillas eat. Bananas and lettuce and orange peels and wanga fruit."

His knuckles went white on the steering wheel. "Wanga fruit?"

A tiny undignified snort sounded from the seat on his right. He pulled off the highway, stopped at a red light and turned his body toward her, putting his arm behind her seat. "I take it I've been *had,* Ms. Langton?"

The snort turned into red-faced giggling. "I'm sorry. But the fact that you believed me is an indication of how far gone you think I am."

"How far gone?"

"Into kookdom." Her giggles faded; she turned a

flushed pleading gaze on him. "You will help me, won't you?"

He wasn't going to kiss her. He wasn't. He wasn't even leaning toward her soft open mouth. Nope. He was—

A car honked politely behind them; John spun back to the wheel and the car lurched forward toward Blue Mound Road, turned right, then turned right again into the zoo entrance. He extracted the entrance fees from his wallet, waving away Allegra's attempt to share the expense, found a parking place and walked beside her to the entrance amid thronging families, trying not to think about how fun it was to be caught up in her near-running enthusiasm, wondering when he'd ever met someone who seemed so thrilled to be awake and alive every day. She definitely reminded him of Cara, his ex. And a little of that sexy wacky actress Meg Ryan, especially when she ordered food.

Don't go there, John.

"What do you want to see first?"

He shrugged and smiled down at her. "You decide."

"Okay. Food first, since you're starving."

They ate burgers and fries outdoors and watched parents herding their excited or cranky or sleepy kids through the crowds. John handled a couple of phone calls during the meal, but without his customary zeal. For some reason he was getting irritated at being interrupted so much. As if somehow the zoo should be out of bounds for business. Which of course was ridiculous since he couldn't ever afford to be out of bounds. His clients depended on him to be available. But it would be nice to feel unreachable. Private. For a while.

When they had finished their dinner, Allegra stood, brushed crumbs off her lap and announced the arrival of animal time. They saw penguins first, then the big cats, the rhinos and elephants, the giraffes, sea lions, camels, bears, fish, reptiles and finally, the gorillas.

They got matching gorilla temporary tattoos and decorated gorilla masks. They pitched coins into a gorilla statue's open jaws, bought gorilla mugs and went bowling for gorilla dollars to trade in for gorilla ice-cream bars, which they took outside to eat.

"That was fabulous." Allegra tore the paper from her ice cream and bit off a chocolate gorilla ear. "And your phone only rang three times."

"Amazing, wasn't it."

"Can I see the offending creature?"

"What, the phone?" He fished it out of his pocket and handed it to her.

"Ah! The vile instrument of torture." She looked at it thoughtfully for a minute, then suddenly pointed off into the trees. "Look! Another peacock with its tail up."

John peered into the trees and grinned. They'd seen at least five, and she got just as excited every time. He accepted his phone back and watched her dance along the path ahead of him and plop down on a vacant bench.

Man, she got him going. When they were playing pin the banana on the gorilla, right before she placed the banana perfectly onto the gorilla's privates and laughed herself into tears, she'd asked him again if he knew anyone to help her with her quest to take her classes online. For one crazy second, he'd entertained the idea of offering his own services. Sheer lunacy of course.

"I'm beat. How do these kids have so much energy? Are we that old?" John sank down beside her on the bench and crossed his legs, aware he still had enough energy left for a 6K run at least. She did that to him. He unwrapped his ice-cream bar, aware of Allegra watching him somewhat apprehensively, and took a cold smooth bite.

"Ha!"

He started and turned to her. "What?"

"You're a biter, too."

He looked at his ice cream, then back at her. "A biter."

"Instead of a sucker or a licker. People who bite their frozen treats dive into life headfirst. No caution. No savoring. Grab life by the stick and make short work of it. We're probably more the same than I realized." She smiled at him, her face glowing, a tiny smear of chocolate on her lower lip.

He wanted to lean over and lick her mouth clean, feel her lips under his tongue, taste the sticky sweetness mixed with her own—

"You can if you want." Her smile turned wicked, her voice come-hither sexy.

He stared at her in total bewilderment. "I thought you couldn't read my mind."

"No offense, but it wasn't your mind I was reading."

He glanced down at his pants. Was he—

Allegra burst out laughing. "I meant your face. You had 'I want to kiss you' written all over your face." She leaned forward. "And…"

"And?" He swallowed.

"You can."

He froze. What the hell was happening to him? This was all wrong. He had to explain, had to let her know. He couldn't let her keep thinking they had any future to look forward to.

"I…was married before." He winced. Why the hell had he said *that*?

Strangely, she didn't look at all confused, if anything the opposite, but her smile faded. "To a biter?"

He pushed away a sudden image of Cara's teeth trapping his earlobe and cleared his throat. "Ice cream, you mean?"

She blushed and bobbed her head up and down. "Yes, of course."

"I can't say I remember. But she was extraordinary. A lot like you in some ways."

The embarrassed blush turned to a blush of pleasure when she smiled. "Oh?"

"Allegra…" He pressed his lips together. How the

hell could he tell her he'd only started going out with her to keep his apartment? He couldn't. And he liked her enough that his apartment wasn't the entire reason anymore anyway. But one look into that hopeful shyness when he compared her to his ex was enough to send up a three-alarm warning. "It didn't work out. We were too different."

"Oh." Her hopeful pleasure diminished. "I see."

"You do?"

"Yes." She gestured with her ice cream. "I'm like her. Things didn't work out with her. Therefore you don't think they will with me."

"She cut my hair. That's how I met her. She was...passionate and intense the way you are, and a little far out. I was young, just out of college. She intrigued me. My parents said she wouldn't challenge me in the long run, that I'd get bored of her, that passion wasn't enough, that shared interests and lifestyles and plans for the future were more important."

"And they were right?"

"Yes." He made his voice as gentle as he could, feeling like a puppy killer. "They were right."

"No." Allegra shook her head firmly. "*She* was wrong."

"Since the divorce, I've thought a lot about what makes a marriage last. I know what I need now, what will make me happy."

"And it's not a kook like me." She sat thoughtfully, clutching her ice-cream bar. A drip ran from the gorilla's fudgy back down the stick and plopped onto her orange skirt.

He couldn't tell if she was angry or hurt or relieved. He couldn't tell if he was, either. Right now he felt a combination of all three, and had this very strange desire to be talked out of his opinion.

"So." She turned cheerfully, licked up the melted ice cream, then bit off the gorilla's head. "That's why you need to help me change. So I can be what I know I can be and so you can get what you want, too."

He paused with a mouthful of ice cream. How did she manage to turn that around so quickly? When he thought he'd done a brilliant job of letting her down easy? Of course he did need to go on seeing her to keep his apartment. And it wasn't as if being around her was a strain. In fact she was a lot of fun. And cute. And sort of sexy in a wildly unlikely way.

"Why do you want to change so badly?"

"Because I want to be taken more seriously. Because I believe that my seminars can really help people all over the country. But to help people you have to get them to trust you. And it's easier to trust someone in the mainstream of looks and behavior."

He gestured to her outfit. "Seems like the looks wouldn't be hard to change."

"That's just it." She lifted her hand and let it slap down on her thigh. "They shouldn't be. I started out ready for this date wearing black pants and a white top. Then I thought that looked sort of like a waitress, so I changed the black pants for this skirt. Then I thought the white top seemed a little bland in comparison, and since we were coming to the zoo, after all, I figured the giraffes would be perfect and they matched the orange skirt somewhat, in spite of the pink. Then by the time I realized what I'd done, it was time to go.''

He grinned. He couldn't help it. She looked so mournful and frustrated over not being able to wear boring clothes. "You did leave the wig off."

"Yes." She patted the top of her head, eyes shining. "You noticed that."

"So there's progress."

"Thanks to you."

"Me?" He took a bite of gorilla belly. "What did I do?"

"You inspired me. I knew you would."

He narrowed his eyes dubiously over the smile that didn't seem to want to leave his lips when he was around her. "So when did all this kookiness start?"

"When I was a kid. I grew up in a huge family, and I guess I wanted attention. But this isn't me, not really. I'm actually sort of shy and insecure underneath. I just haven't been able to figure out how to stop. I haven't felt…brave enough to let the real me out."

He nodded, still not quite understanding how she thought he could change her, but taken with the image of Allegra standing out among drab faceless brothers and sisters like a flamingo among crows. "I see."

"What were *you* like as a kid?"

"The opposite. I did whatever it took to be invisible."

Allegra frowned. "From whom?"

He suppressed the images of drunken conflict, glanced around suspiciously, then leaned toward her. "The shaved pod people. They're everywhere."

She burst out laughing so hard that a few people turned, first in alarm, then to smile and chuckle themselves. No doubt about it. Allegra Langton was contagious.

"I'm sorry." She wiped away a tear with her non-ice-cream-holding hand, then surprised the hell out of him by leaning over and squeezing his arm. "I'm really sorry."

"For what, laughing?" He tried to keep his voice light, but he felt uneasy, as if she'd hacked into his subconscious again and figured out what he hadn't said.

"No." She met his eyes, hers clear, strong and supportive. "For the tough times growing up."

Emotion walled off the back of his throat until he cleared it. "It's okay. Thanks."

A mom walked by pushing her sleeping baby in a stroller. He and Allegra watched her pass, absorption in the sight allowing the awkward intimacy to fade naturally.

"So. Enough about you, John Ty-ler Jones." She said the words teasingly, but he sensed the compassion and sensitivity behind them. "Back to me and my fascinating problem, which only you can help me with.''

''Why me?''

Her eyes widened and she stopped in the middle of licking the last melting bump of ice cream off the stick. ''Well, obviously.''

''Obviously?'' His stomach tightened with a mixture of anticipation and dread; he tossed the rest of his bar in the trash.

''You and I…I mean, we…'' She waved the stick as if it were a baton. ''Don't you *feel* it?''

Yes, he damn well did. And he was a fool to have walked into that one. *Now* what the hell could he tell her? He put his hand up to his temple and winced when he jabbed his bee sting. ''Allegra…''

She put up her hand. ''Stop right there. Forget it. You're going to say, 'Oh, Allegra, I like you, you're a very nice woman and maybe I'm the eensiest bit attracted to you, but seriously, you are wearing a shirt with giraffes on it and that pretty much says everything I need to know.'''

''No.'' The word came out of him more forcefully than he intended. Because that *was* pretty much what he was going to say. Except he didn't really care that her shirt had giraffes on it. And he would never ever use the word ''eensiest.''

''No?'' Her sexy mouth twisted in confusion. ''Then what?''

About a million words and phrases rose up and jammed tight against his larynx. He couldn't think of a damn thing to say because he hadn't a clue which one to pick, or how he felt about her. Except that the feeling was there, and more compelling than he ever would have expected.

"It's okay, John." She patted his hand. "I didn't mean to push. It's our second date, for heaven's sake. I had a wonderful evening. Let's just go home."

He nodded and rose with her, feeling like he'd let her down, and even more curiously, like he'd let himself down.

They walked back though the primate house and out through the front, past the shops and restaurants and into the parking lot, over to his car. He wasn't even worried about getting back to work, or worried about how much he could get done tonight, or how little sleep he could manage on.

He hadn't thought about work since his last call. He frowned. Strange. His phone hadn't rung in—

"John?"

He turned from unlocking her door, unnecessary since he could have used the keyless entry to unlock all the doors at once, but he liked the gesture, and felt it was important this evening especially.

She stood quite close to him, the fading light dulling the gel shine in her hair. "Would you like to go out again next Wednesday? There's a concert I thought you might enjoy. The Hot Armadillos are playing."

The Hot Armadillos? This couldn't go on. He couldn't let her keep thinking this relationship could continue, not when she had hinted at some kind of future together.

"I can't Wednesday." He made his voice as gentle as possible, hating to hurt her. "I…have another date."

"You mean with a…woman?"

"Yes. A woman I work with. I'm taking her to *La Bohème* at the Florentine Opera." He purposely left out the fact that he'd arranged the date before he started seeing Allegra. Better to let her think he was a jerk who kept his hand in multiple cookie jars.

"Oh. So I guess that's your answer on the Hot Armadillos."

If her voice hadn't cracked, he might have stayed strong. He might even have gently told her he was halfway in love with Katherine without even spending much time with her, and that as soon as he fell the rest of the way, he planned to ask her to marry him.

But her voice did crack. And for one horrifying second he thought he saw her lower lip go soft, then pull in tight, as if it was trying very hard not to tremble.

He put his hands to the sides of her face and took off her pink glasses, reached and put them on top of his car, stared down into her pretty eyes, shining reflections of the streetlights in the dusk.

He heard her breath go in and not come out, as if she thought he was going to kiss her and couldn't manage to breathe while she waited. But he wasn't going to kiss her. He was going to tell her. Now.

Before either of them got in deeper and before either of them got hurt.

"Allegra." He put his hands to her shoulders. "I—"

"Mommy?"

John frowned and turned to see a little boy standing behind him, cheeks grimy with tear-smudged dirt. What the heck was this?

"Hey little guy." He knelt beside the child. "Are you lost?"

"No." The boy shook his head emphatically. "I'm not lost. I'm here. Mommy is lost."

"Okay." John glanced up at Allegra, who had put her glasses back on and was scanning the parking lot. "We'll find her for you."

"I swallowed my gum and I feel sick and my shoe-lace is untied." The boy sniffed and rubbed his eyes, leaving new smudges.

"Oh." John looked down at the little sneakers with bulb-nosed cartoon characters on them. "Well, the gum is probably a lost cause and you'll feel better when we find your mom, but I can help you with the shoes. Okay?"

"I got more gum." He dug another piece out of his pocket, unwrapped it with chubby fingers and put it into his mouth.

"I don't see anyone." Allegra's voice came up behind him; she knelt next to the boy and patted his shoulder. "After John ties your shoes we can go find Mommy, okay?"

"Okay."

John fumbled with the little laces, feeling tender and clumsy and out of his element. He glanced over at Allegra who was watching him help the boy with a gooey smile of longing on her pretty face.

Oh no. Bad news.

He didn't know which was worse. That gooey smile of longing she was sending him, or the one he was pretty sure he was sending back to her.

He bent his head over the little sneakers, more confused than he'd ever felt in his life. What had possessed him to smile at her over a child? Didn't he know what that meant? What kind of hearth-and-home wanting that signified? He had no business toying with her, no business sharing that kind of intimate connection with someone he had no intention of seeing after—

Something hit him on the top of his head. Something warm, about the size of a small marble. Something that stuck.

"Uh-oh." The child's singsong voice struck dread into his heart. "I dropped my gum."

7

"YOU'RE KIDDING."

Allegra shook her head, enjoying Cynthia and Missy's outrage even through her dulling misery.

"Nope." She built up a huge satisfying forkful of one of Louise's chopped salads and dumped it back onto the plate. "He's dating someone else. He's seeing her tomorrow."

"Oh, *no*." Missy's blond eyebrows formed a perfect upside down vee of distress. "How could he *do* such a thing?"

Cynthia's empty martini glass hit the table with a thud. "The bastard."

"They're going to the opera." Allegra stared gloomily at her friends. "The *opera*. And I suggested we go see the Hot Armadillos for crying out loud."

Missy winced. "Are you sure the two of you are suited?"

"*Yes*." Allegra's voice rose to a near-shout and she had to tamp it back down. "I'm just afraid he won't figure himself out in time. I'm just afraid I won't be able to change fast enough. That he'll fall in love with this woman and we won't get the chance to be deliriously happy for the rest of eternity."

"Oh, gosh." Missy shook her head helplessly. "That would stink."

"So what are you going to do about it?" Cynthia pinned Allegra with her no-nonsense stare. "Make an action plan. Fight for what you want, for what you believe."

"I don't know how to handle this." Allegra rounded up a piece of rogue lettuce on the rim of her plate and pushed it back into the middle. She couldn't ever remember feeling this low, this powerless. Here she'd been cheerfully telling John all about how his life should and would go, and how that life would certainly include her once he realized it, and he had other female plans the whole time.

"Do you know this woman?" Missy asked.

"No, but I can imagine her." Allegra sighed. "One, she doesn't own a wig, or wear fake glasses, or shirts with giraffes on them. She probably has a nice respectable job she's brilliant at. She'll probably make him the wife he's always dreamed of, that every normal nice guy has always dreamed of. And I'll end up bitter and alone, or married to Pee Wee Herman."

"Look, Allegra." Cynthia leaned across the table and shook her finger. "I understand the shock, but you can't let this babe beat you. You are a fabulous, dynamic, passionate, caring woman. Most guys are scared to death of strong women, at first anyway. Believe me, I know."

"They don't exactly flock around meek ones, either," Missy said.

Cynthia put her arm around Missy and hugged her close. "We'll work on you, honey. You need your life to involve more than the building at work, the building that's your home, the supermarket and the personal ads. And for the record, *you* are a fabulous, passionate woman, too. You just…suppress it a lot."

Missy blushed and examined her soup. "But Allegra doesn't, and she's in trouble, not me."

"Yes, indeed." Cynthia punched a fist into her palm. "First, isn't it true, Allegra, that on your dates with John up until this little bombshell about the other woman, you were starting to be pretty sure he was into you?"

Allegra sighed, remembering their kisses, the way John lowered himself onto the grass to watch bugs, the way he'd thawed enough at the zoo so that he allowed himself to be a little silly, and even started to open up to her. Not to mention that when he helped the little boy, he'd glanced over at her with definite tenderness, right before he ducked his head and got gum in his hair, which the boy tried to extricate and ended up cementing to a good solid square inch of John's scalp. "Yes. I thought so."

"So what makes you so sure now you were wrong? What makes you so sure he'll prefer this other bimbo to you? Maybe they'll go out and have a horrible time."

"Maybe." Allegra pushed her untouched salad to the side and gazed mournfully at the steaming bowl of *pasta arrabiata* the waiter set in front of her. "But she's obviously more of what he's looking for than I am. If he was into me even half as much as I'm into him, why would he ask someone else out?''

Cynthia frowned for a moment, then her face cleared. "How do you know he asked her *after* you two started seeing each other? Going to the opera isn't generally a spontaneous event, you know. And you guys have only known each other two weeks.''

Allegra stared at Cynthia while her entire body went through a slowly accelerating process of restoring hope and energy. "Do you think that's possible?''

"Of course it's possible. I don't know if it's true, but you don't know for sure it isn't.''

"She must be right." Missy nodded happily. "Once John saw you he was completely smitten, but he's noble enough to honor this date with the other woman since he made it so long ago.''

"Hmm." Allegra took her glasses off and pressed her hands to her eyes. As much as she wanted to believe this new version of events, something didn't quite work. "But then that might mean he's some kind of serial cheater. That it's only a matter of time before he sees someone better than me and takes off after her.''

"Possible." Cynthia shrugged and patted back her hair. "But Manhunter chemistry doesn't happen that often. I'm betting Missy's right.''

"Wow." Allegra put her glasses back on. Maybe John *had* asked Ms. Perfect out before they met. That could explain why John seemed so conflicted at first, why he initially resisted her. But maybe he had been as drawn to Allegra as she was to him, and eventually felt he had to explore the attraction. Maybe their chemistry and compatibility had surprised him.

At the same time, he would still feel bound to go on a date that had been planned a while back. She could buy that. It might be a ridiculous stretch, but things *could* have happened that way, and she sure as hell wanted them to have. If only she could see John and this woman together, she'd know right away what he felt. But of course that idea was silly. She couldn't exactly tag along on their date.

Could she.

A mischievous shot of adrenaline slid through her body and lit up her brain. She couldn't exactly find out if there were any last-minute tickets available and wear something really nice and attend the performance and keep an eye out for John and Ms. Who-ever-she-was in order to find out what depth of emotion lay between them and therefore where she stood in John's affections.

Nope. Uh-uh. No way.

''So, I'll wait and see how he acts toward me after their date, on our next one.'' Allegra picked up her fork and shoveled in a mouthful of pasta.

''I have a better idea.'' Cynthia narrowed her eyes and tapped her temple.

''Better?'' Allegra raised her eyebrows hopefully. She'd love to hear. Any idea would be better than the crazy one she had. Her friends would think she'd

cracked. They'd be horrified. Call her a stalker. Tell
her to keep her passion under control and not resort
to such ridiculous childishness. And they'd be absolutely right.

Missy clapped her hands and laughed. "What,
what?"

Cynthia adopted a mysterious about-to-give-away-
the-secret stare. "Allegra? How would you like to go
to the opera?"

"I'D LIKE another glass of champagne, please." Katherine beamed at the waitress at Eagan's Restaurant,
eyes brilliant blue against the soft flush of her face.

John shifted uneasily in his seat. How many drinks
did that make? At least twice what he'd had, and he'd
only half-finished his third beer.

"So anyway." She plunked her chin on her hands
and blinked at him. Several strands had come out of
the fancy bun thing she'd arranged on top of her head,
and hung forlornly around her face. "What were we
talking about?"

"I…" He searched wildly for an answer. Truth
was, they had been talking about the same thing
they'd been talking about since they met at Uihlein
Hall, took their seats, sat through the fabulous and
moving production, stood through intermission, sat
again for the second half and walked over here for a
post-opera dinner.

Pretty much nothing. "I'm sorry, I don't remember."

"That's okay." She sent him a dazzling smile. "So."

"So." He grinned back, but it was admittedly an effort. "How are things at Brighton for you? Lester is a character, huh?"

"Oh." She started giggling. "He is something. I think he has not a *clue* what goes on in that company."

"I think you're right. Which is a shame considering he runs it." He chuckled as much as the concept warranted, which wasn't a whole heck of a lot.

"You're so right!" Katherine, however, appeared to find the idea hilarious. "Running a company he knows nothing about, can you imagine? It's like…it's like…a person in charge of something who is totally clueless, you know?"

She went off on another gale of giggles at her analogy, then snorted, apologized and giggled some more.

"So." He looked around at their fellow diners, starting to feel desperate. "I guess the consensus is that Lester is incompetent."

"You said that right." She giggled a few more times, then even her capacity for enjoyment of Lester's idiocy faded and they were met with silence again.

John took a sip of his beer. Why the hell wasn't this working? Could he just not relax enough around her? Or did he and Katherine really communicate on such different wavelengths that they couldn't intersect? There had to be some question he could ask that would help them connect on more than a superficial level. There had to be.

He pushed his fingers through his hair and winced when they met the empty space resulting from Allegra's gum-extraction process, even as he remembered her gentle hands and her gentle teasing. He and Allegra found plenty to talk about, and look how different they were. From their first date when she started in with all that talk about—

Ha! He resisted the urge to rub his hands together with glee. "Katherine."

"Yes, John?"

"Have you ever woken up, figuratively or literally, and asked yourself, 'What the hell am I doing here?'" He strained to remember the rest of Allegra's question, though he could picture her passionate concerned expression without any trouble. "Have you ever wondered if you are the *you* that you want to be?"

Katherine's eyes warmed; her breath came out in a little gasp. "Oh, John, that is so *deep*. I know what you mean, too. The problem for me is work at Brighton. I hate the place. I feel so—" she hunched her shoulders and made tense claws of her hands "—boxed in. You know? Like part of me is *suffocating* there. I mean—"

The waitress brought her glass of champagne and she took a long luxuriant sip.

"Can I tell you something, John?"

"Sure." He sat back, a little surprised by the response, and guilty for borrowing from Allegra's repertoire to make progress with Katherine.

"Sometimes…sometimes I get so closed-in feeling, so trampled down, that I want to tear off my clothes and run to the lake and…and…and *dive* in and swim and swim forever, sleek and wet and graceful like a dolphin." She took a long breath and ran her hands down her body. "Do you ever feel like that, John?"

"Uh." He tried very hard to look as if he were attempting to remember feeling like that, wondering why the image of Katherine naked and wet, gallivanting among the waves and the sight of her hands on her own body wasn't making him wildly hard. "A dolphin. No. I can't say that I do."

"Well, I do." She sighed. "I suppose that must sound sort of strange to you."

"Not much sounds strange to me anymore." He thought again of Allegra, as he had been thinking of her at the oddest and most frequent moments during what was supposed to be his most fabulous erotic date ever. Katherine was everything he wanted. He kept telling himself that. And kept telling himself that. "I know someone else who would probably get into the dolphin thing, however."

Oh, man. There it was. An image of Allegra's slim strong body skimming the waves, gleaming wet in the sunlight, diving and arching, bursting up for air, laughing and joyous.

Boi-i-ng.

Katherine arched an eyebrow. "You might as well tell me who she is."

John's head jerked up. "Who?"

"The woman you've referred to about every ten minutes all evening."

John instructed his face to resume motion, because right now it was frozen in shock. Had he been talking about Allegra that much? He couldn't remember talking about her more than once. Or twice. Maybe three times. And then that time when he— Four. Four times tops. Or was there another...

Damn. But she was just so interesting. She dominated his thoughts simply because she was unusual. Because she was charming and fresh and curious and unlike anyone he'd ever met. That was it.

"She's a friend." He shrugged, all the while instructing his pants to lie down and play dead. "Someone I took out a few times because my landlord made me...told me...asked me..."

He clenched his teeth. For some reason he couldn't reduce Allegra to a duty. Couldn't make her seem like a burden he had to carry in order to get what he wanted.

"Your landlord *made* you to take her out? How on earth did she manage that, threaten to evict you?" Katherine succumbed to another wave of giggles.

"...yes." The word barely made it out of his tightened lips. Katherine's giggles died a swift and terrible death.

"Oh, poor John. And poor her, not being able to

get dates otherwise. You were sweet to be nice to her.'' Katherine tsk-tsked, then abandoned all pretense at sipping her champagne and drained her glass. ''You are, you know.''

''I am…what?''

Katherine leaned forward and probably tried to narrow her eyes to sultry slits, but the alcohol had beaten her to the punch. ''Sweet. And gorgeous. And sexy as hell. Even with that funny bald spot on top of your head.''

She reached out and touched his face; he had to steel himself not to pull away. It wasn't that Katherine repulsed him, hell no. She was a total babe. It's just that…he wanted her sober. He wanted her hot for him without alcohol fueling the reaction. He wanted her…different. More like…more like—

''Well, hel-*lo,* John Ty-ler Jones.''

—Allegra. Oh my God, Allegra. Wrapped in some colorful flowery drape thing that made her look like a punk gypsy. His heart launched into a musical production number and the smile he couldn't seem to contain around her erupted onto his mouth. There she was. Right here in the restaurant. *Jeez.*

Out of the corner of his eye he saw Katherine tilt her lovely head to look up at Allegra. Then turn back to look at him, so he had to work to tear his eyes away from the invigorating sight of the beaming punk gypsy woman in front of him.

''Allegra.'' He managed to wrench his head over to Katherine, who was looking at him with entirely too much of the "aha" look that women were so damn good at. "Katherine, this is Allegra, my...friend. Allegra, this is Katherine, my...other friend."

"Happy to meet you." Katherine shook Allegra's hand and sent John another speculative look. "Does she happen to know your landlord?"

"Yes." Allegra glanced at John. "I do."

Katherine put her hand to the side of her mouth in an aside to John. "So she's the one," she whispered loudly.

"What one?"

Katherine turned to the beaming gypsy with a smile. John clenched his fists, knowing that in her alcohol befuddled state, Katherine was going to spill the beans and ruin everything. And worse, hurt Allegra. "Katherine, I don't think—"

"You're the woman he can't stop talking about."

A flush of pleasure crept over Allegra's face; she turned bright, hopeful eyes to John. He found himself gazing back at her with something like yearning. At least it felt like yearning. God knew what it looked like on his face because he was still terrified that Katherine would say something about Dolores and her dating contract. Allegra would totally misunderstand. He'd been an idiot to admit to the arrangement.

Katherine cleared her throat. "Aren't you going to ask Allegra to join us?"

"I—" He searched Katherine's face for signs of jealousy and found none. Terrific. They had nothing to say to each other and the arrival of the woman constantly on his mind and on his lips didn't bother her in the slightest.

"Would you *like* to join us?" He tried not to sound too hopeful. At very least Allegra would liven up the evening. At most... He didn't much care to analyze "at most." Because "at most" had something to do with reluctance to let her out of his sight.

"The more the merrier." Katherine gestured clumsily to their tiny table for two, then frowned. "Well, we're done eating. Let's you and me move to the bar, Allegra. John can pay and catch up. Here, John."

She fumbled in her beige purse, tossed him money for her meal, rose with her customary grace and nearly fell over. Allegra moved in to support her and sent John a look. A look that said, "What the hell kind of man are you to be out with a gorgeous boring drunk when you could have me any time you wanted?"

John sent her a go-figure grin, bursting with a strange euphoria. In that tiny moment, without saying a single word, he and Allegra had connected more deeply and openly than he and Katherine had during their entire friendship.

He signaled the waitress and pantomimed signing a bill; she smiled and nodded. His phone rang. He dug it out of his pocket and looked at the display. Oh, for Chrissake, Mr. Tabachnik. He glanced up and met Allegra's eyes across the room for a split second before she paid Katherine her full attention again. He shook his head, knowing what she wanted him to do. She'd turned his phone off at the zoo, while she'd distracted him with the peacock. And he'd enjoyed the respite. Enjoyed having the rest of the date uninterrupted by business.

To hell with Tabachnik. He put the phone back into his pocket. Voice mail would take the message. He'd deal with it later.

The waitress brought the bill; he paid the check and walked over to join the women deep in conversation at the bar, struck by the contrast between Katherine's sultry elegance and Allegra's energetic color. Katherine leaned toward Allegra, still talking earnestly. Allegra nodded and patted her arm.

"I understand. The dolphin response is quite common actually."

John chuckled and shook his head. Why did he *know* she'd take the naked wet dolphin woman in stride?

"It's like sometimes…" Katherine flung out her arm; Allegra neatly caught her champagne just before it tipped over. "Sometimes I wake up and say, hey, what the hell am I doing here? What? And then I ask myself something else. I ask myself, am I the…the *me* I want to be? Am I? Am I? Who the heck knows?"

Allegra's eyebrows shot to the top of her forehead. She turned and fixed John with a pointed stare. He gave her a who-me? shrug and winked.

Katherine kept talking. People in the bar kept talking. And drinking. And smoking. And eating. He was pretty sure. But after he winked, Allegra's face softened to a parted-lips look of longing that would have knocked him to his knees if there was room in the bar to kneel, so he didn't care who the hell else was around or what they were doing.

Jeez. He'd been attracted to her before, but nothing like this. He had to look away before he embarrassed himself by clearing the bar with a sweep of his arm and making love to her in front of the Milwaukee night crowd.

He pulled himself together and tried to concentrate on what Katherine was saying, aware by the look on Allegra's face that she was having as much trouble taking the words in as he was, and not because Katherine was mumbling. The undercurrent buzzed between them, powerful and magnetic, a nearly tangible other presence in the bar.

"Uh…here's my card." Allegra rummaged in a tiny bright red night bag and came up with a business card for Katherine. "Come to one of my seminars this week. I think I can help you."

"You can?" Katherine's face crumpled into tenderness. "You are so *sweet.* I love you. Isn't she sweet, John? Isn't she?"

Allegra and John exchanged glances, moved toward Katherine and took an arm each. "Time to go home."

"Home? No, no. Oh, no-no-no-no-no. I don't want to go home. I want to *party.*"

"Party's over. Bedtime." John put an arm around Katherine's waist and half carried her out of the restaurant.

She flung her arms around his neck. "Oh, John. You are so *sweet*. I love you. Isn't he sweet, Allegra? Isn't he?"

"Yes, he's very sweet." Allegra's voice nearly bubbled over with amusement.

John grinned at her over Katherine's flowery-smelling hair and shook his head, because he finally had Katherine's fabulous body pressed against his and it did absolutely nothing for him. While one parted-lips smoldering glance from a tiny gypsy woman was enough to send him into orbit.

"Will you undress me and put me to bed, John?" Katherine stumbled and he had to lurch to one side to avoid running her into a street sign.

"I think maybe I better not." He sent Allegra a panicked look.

"I'll come help."

"Would you?" Katherine untangled herself from John and embraced Allegra. "Oh, I'd be *so* grateful. I don't feel quite up to it."

They bundled Katherine into John's car and John drove her home, keeping his eyes on the rearview mirror for Allegra's headlights. He had it bad. No question. When you even had a tender spot for headlights there was no other conclusion to be drawn.

So what the hell was he going to do? Why couldn't he feel this way about Katherine? Why was he drawn once again to a free spirit that wouldn't fit into his life? He'd tried that with Cara. The passion they had was amazing. When they were alone together or in bed, they operated as a single person. But you couldn't spend your life alone or in a bedroom. Marriage was about more than passion. Marriage was about sharing lives. And he and Cara had had little in common, very few things they enjoyed or liked to do together. He thought her friends were irresponsible and immature and she thought his were stuffy and materialistic. Eventually they'd stagnated, suffocated, separated.

He wasn't going through that again.

They arrived at Katherine's house in Whitefish Bay and managed to get her inside. John waited in the opulent living room while, judging by the full-throated rendition of "Love to Love You, Baby," Allegra had a hell of a time getting Katherine into bed.

Finally his crazy gypsy appeared at the top of the stairs and descended, disheveled and beautiful. His heart got a dangerous ache just from looking at her. *Steady, John.* He couldn't let the disappointment over Katherine push him into something he didn't want long-term. Because that's all this was. All it had to be. Starting something with Allegra on the rebound wasn't fair to either of them.

"She's out." Allegra glanced at him, then studied her clasped hands. "John."

His body went on red alert. "Yes?"

"Did you really start going out with me to stay in your apartment?"

He opened his mouth to protest, to explain, to tell her everything he had felt and, more importantly, everything he was feeling. Except that he hadn't a clue how.

"Allegra, it wasn't like that. I never meant—"

"I know." She walked up to him and put her tiny hands on his chest, making him feel protective, pumped up and incredibly humble at the same time. "That's okay. I'm not upset anymore."

"You're not?" He looked down at her tipped-up lovely face and knew there was no way that more than about ten seconds would go by before he kissed her.

"Well, I mean things changed. Didn't they?"

She stared up at him, wide-open vulnerable and anxious. Three…two…one, and he kissed her. Not the kiss of a clumsy idiot on roller skates about to wet himself from terror; not the kiss of a boy-wannabe inspecting the ground for bug life. But the kiss of a man who had gone crazy over a crazy woman.

His phone rang. And rang. And rang.

"John…your phone."

"To hell with my phone."

"Oh, John."

He kissed the corners of her mouth, her chin, her cheeks, her temples, gentle savoring kisses. She responded with a very sexy "Mmm" and pressed herself rhythmically against him. He held out for three more seconds before he turned the kisses hot, tasted her tongue, ran his hands over her firm lines and felt himself go rigid.

This was crazy. This was nuts. What had he told himself in the car? About him and Cara? That he absolutely positively *wasn't* going through that again.

He kissed down to her throat, painted tiny wet circles with his tongue in the boundary of his lips, savoring the softness of her skin. Absolutely…positively…wasn't…

She moaned, a soft helpless sound. He lifted his head and saw the dark glaze of passion in her eyes, felt her body's strong hunger.

Okay. Maybe he was.

8

"THE EMERGENCY MEETING of The Manhunters' Club will now come to order." Cynthia banged her fist down on Allegra's Naguchi coffee table. "The purpose of this meeting is to get Allegra ready for The Date."

Tracy nodded, eyes gleaming. "The date that will live in infamy."

"The date that will show John what a warm, caring, totally normal person you are." Missy gave Allegra a hug. "The date that will give him—"

"The finest orgasm man has ever known." Cynthia waggled her eyebrows á la Groucho Marx. "He won't be able to walk for three weeks."

"*Cynthia!*" Missy burst into giggles.

Allegra sat stiffly on the futon in her living room and forced herself to smile. All of this was a lot of fun. All this planning, all this support, to make sure her date turned out to be perfect. She'd made reservations at Chez Mathilde, one of Milwaukee's finest restaurants. The girls had assembled to do her hair, makeup and nails and make sure she didn't stray into unnecessary accessories. Her plain black dress and usual plain white cotton underwear were already laid out in her bedroom. All perfect.

Except she was terrified.

Because after the other night when she'd ''bumped into'' John and Katherine at Eagan's; after they'd gone back to Katherine's house and Allegra had endured a drunken rendition of every Donna Summer hit known to man getting Katherine into bed; after she'd processed the information about the dating-apartment arrangement and decided it wouldn't matter, she'd gone downstairs and John had kissed her.

Triple and quadruple wow.

Because this time he'd kissed her like he meant it. Each time he'd kissed her before, it had felt like he meant it, too, but this was an entirely new and extremely powerful level of meaning it that she hadn't thought was possible except in fantasy.

In response, she'd come up with a torrent of emotion that made her realize exactly how deeply she felt for this man. The feeling had blindsided and unsettled her so much she'd broken away from him, in spite of the fact that her body was ready to beat her to death for not allowing it a chance at satisfaction. Of course the fact that Katherine started snoring like a congested rhinoceros upstairs had watered down the mood somewhat, too.

Maybe she thought she loved him before, in a nice happy unthreatening way that would still leave her plenty of time for her business and quirks. But now she realized she loved him with a capital *L* and that this meant things were extremely serious and that tonight mattered more than anything had ever mattered to her since she first emerged into daylight as an infant and got a taste of what mom-arms felt like.

The problem was, a nanosecond before she'd broken away, she sensed John starting to pull back. And once she extracted herself from his arms, there had been no protest from him, no passionate declaration of the feeling he'd been broadcasting through his kisses. Only a confused look on his face, as if he'd started kissing the wrong person in the dark and the lights had just come on.

She knew exactly what that was about.

Tonight she had to show him she could be Katherine. Or at least a Katherine type. One he could let himself fall in love with, since he obviously hadn't made much progress on that front with the real one. Tonight she had to show him she could be the woman he had such strong feelings for that he could practically make her explode with the way he kissed her, but also that she could be the normal-woman fantasy he obviously still clung to.

And she had to prove to herself that she could be that woman, too. That she *was* that woman inside somewhere. That the kookiness she had clung to her whole life was a front. That she could grow out of it and dare to be herself, Allegra. That she had enough of her own personality to make him fall in love without resorting to gimmickry. That—

"Uh…hello?" Fingers snapped in front of her face. "Anybody home?"

"Sorry." Allegra blinked and brought her eyes back into focus. "I'm just—"

"In love?" Tracy beamed and chuckled. "Welcome to the club. It's a great place to be."

Allegra let her head drop back to stare at her ceiling. "I wish I didn't feel down to my bones that tonight was a make or break deal. I know he doesn't love Katherine, but he does still love the *idea* of her. What if I can't be that way for him? What if I don't turn out to be interesting enough? What if I can't—"

"Allegra, Allegra, Allegra. This is not going to cut the mustard, honey." Cynthia wagged her finger and her head at the same time. "You are a fabulous, fabulous woman. I'm still not sure what this inner dullness is all about, but I will tell you straight out, that whatever form it takes, and that form might surprise you, I'm betting you have exactly what he wants."

"Amen to that." Tracy slumped onto Allegra's Turkish hassock. "Or at least what he *thinks* he wants."

Allegra lifted her head. "What do you mean?"

"Obviously the guy has this idea that he wants someone like Katherine. At the same time, he's drawn to you. You can't dispute that."

"No…"

"So," Tracy threw up her hands and let them slap down on her thighs. "He's conflicted. If you give him what he *thinks* he wants, if you show up looking and acting like every brain-dead-male fantasy of woman, I'll bet my farm he'll find himself missing the way you really are.''

"But it's *not* the way I really am. The way I really am is the way I'll look tonight. I'm done with being kooky. Kookiness was the coward's way to cover my shyness, a crutch to make sure I stood out in a crowd. I've got to have more self-esteem than that.''

"Oh, honey.'' Missy knelt at Allegra's feet and patted her knee. "Your self-esteem is not in your clothes. It's in your heart.''

"Oh, Missy.'' Cynthia gave a long sigh. "You should have married Mr. Rogers.''

"Missy's right. John will be blown away by the way you look tonight,'' Tracy said. "Just don't forget he was blown away before, too.''

"Hear, hear.'' Cynthia brushed off her spotless black linen pants and picked up a makeup case that could double as a pet carrier. "So let's get cooking. I can't wait to get my hands on that gorgeous skin of yours.''

Tracy brandished a comb and advanced menacingly. "And I can't wait to tame those spikes in your hair.''

Missy rubbed her hands. "I'll do your nails and run interference on any kooky clothes items you get the urge to put on. You'll look so normal and pretty you won't recognize yourself.''

For the next hour, Allegra submitted to their care. Tracy washed and fussed over her hair until little wispy bangs hung over her forehead and the rest layered into a sleek flattering style. Cynthia dug into her makeup and gave Allegra bigger eyes than she ever knew possible, accented their color and shape with subtle smoky touches of shadow, oohing and aahing over Allegra's cheekbones and mouth while she applied blush and lipstick. Missy made her nails into glossy better-than-nature works of art, firmly turning down Allegra's suggestion of painting them black to match the dress.

"And finally, my own special surprise gift." Cynthia leaned down next to her purse and came up with a Victoria's Secret package. "The ultrasexy, eye-and-fly-popping underwear."

Allegra giggled and bit her lip, torn by a sudden rush of emotion. She peered into the bag, praying she wouldn't cry and smudge all the goop on her face. Black lacy panties. Black lacy bra. John and her, together tonight.

"Wow," she whispered. "Double wow."

"I wish there was some way to sneak in a mini-camera so we can all see the expression on his face when he gets a load of *those!*"

Allegra escaped the burst of girl-giggles and went upstairs into the haven of her haphazard eclectic riotous bedroom, which she supposed the New Her would have to clean up and organize and weed out to make as feng shui as the rest of the house. But right now she had sexy underwear to try on.

It fit. It was fabulous. Even on her short, sturdy

unremarkable body. She straightened her spine and struck a seductive pose. He'd go crazy when he saw her. This was what he wanted, after all. And equally as important, she loved how she looked and how she felt. Loved the New Her.

She pulled on the simple black sleeveless shift the girls had helped her pick out three days before. The simple silver earrings, necklace and bracelets they'd bought to complement the style. There. She smiled at herself in the mirror.

For three seconds.

She looked fine. Really. Lovely, even. But so... plain. The outfit really needed a little—

"No." She said the word so loudly all three women came charging up the stairs.

"You okay?"

"Allegra?"

"Anything wrong?"

She nodded smartly to her tremendously normal reflection and stalked out onto the landing to the appreciative cheers of her best friends.

Tonight she would prove what she'd known for so long. She didn't need the frills and trappings. She didn't need the New Age lingo. She could be who she really was and still be worthy.

Tonight was the beginning. Of the new Allegra, and of her lifetime of love and happiness with John.

JOHN WALKED up the front steps to Allegra's door, returning the raised-paw greetings of the little stone lions. He pushed the hair the kid's gum had left him back from over his forehead and adjusted his tie. For some reason he was reluctant to knock yet. For some reason he wanted to stand here a little longer and enjoy the anticipation. To imagine what nutso outfit Allegra would be in tonight. How she'd stand out in the elegant restaurant like a ruby-throated humming-bird in a black-and-white movie. How her joy and lively energy would make his own jump up to match her.

He had it bad. Whether that was or wasn't good, he still hadn't been able to decide. On the one hand there was Cara. But of course Allegra wasn't Cara, and he wasn't the same man he was then. On the other hand, there were still women like Katherine. After he'd gotten used to Allegra, after her special brand of surprise didn't surprise him anymore, would he turn back to his fantasy of elegant lovely sophistication? The kind of woman who would match him so well, who wouldn't keep him quite so on edge, wondering what sort of debacle would arise next?

The kind of woman who wouldn't leave him scarred, bruised, stung and bald after four encounters.

He frowned, contemplating the restful greenery contained in the low stone wall around her pink and purple trimmed house. Of course the last time he saw her he hadn't sustained any physical damage. Unless you counted the possibly indelible mark she'd left on his soul. Which was useless if they weren't a good match in the long run. Because the long run mattered.

The long run was either fulfilled passionate happiness that lasted, or that faded into dismal imprisoning emptiness.

Allegra's musical voice came through her door. "You can do this. You can do this."

He cocked his head, grinning. Do what? She sounded like the little engine that really really wanted to.

He rang her bell, unable to stop smiling, unable to contain the warm anticipation spreading through his heart. Call him nuts, but he couldn't wait for the door to burst open. Couldn't wait for the first glimpse of his hummingbird, to see what outlandish—

The door swung open slowly. "Hello, John."

"Allegra."

His eyes made a lingering sexist journey, top to bottom. Her hair, instead of being wigged or spiked up into shiny points, lay in short soft waves around her face. Her eyes looked enormous and vulnerable, shaded subtly with midnight blue that enhanced their color and shape. Her mouth and cheeks had been touched with a deep rosy pink, and her dress...

Oh my God, her dress. A nearly off-the-shoulder, above-the-knee little black number that managed to look innocent and way-the-hell sexy at the same time. Black stockings. He loved black stockings. They made a woman's legs look like touchable sin. And heels, so that she stood a few inches taller than normal, and the top of her head could touch his chin instead of his shoulder.

The better to kiss you, my dear.

No question, he felt like the Big Bad Wolf. She looked stunning. Sophisticated. Elegant. Lovely. The whole package.

Oh, Mama.

"Allegra."

She tilted her head, not in the usual quirky puppy-dog fashion, but as if she had Katherine's long hair and was letting the ends sweep over her shoulder. "Yes?"

"You look…" He shook his head. Where were the words? "Amazing."

"Thank you." She reached out and touched his tie, a slow, graceful gesture. "So do you."

He swallowed convulsively. *Oh, man.* She was… she was…

"Amazing."

One Allegra eyebrow quirked up. "You said that already, John."

He took a deep breath. The sound of his name spilling sensually from those rose-colored lips just about undid him, though not to the same degree as when she warbled the entire thing. *John Ty-ler Jones.* "Shall we go?"

"Yes." She went back into her house after an over-the-shoulder glance that made him practically overheat. He imagined steam hissing out of his pants at some point during the evening, restaurant patrons coming to his aid with glasses of ice water.

"I'm ready." She'd added a cream-colored shawl

and a tiny black purse. He stood too close behind her while she locked her door, wanting to feel the warmth generated between their bodies, wanting her to feel the promise of future intimacy, watching her pretty-nailed hands as she put in the key, to see if they trembled.

They did.

Good. At least he wasn't the only one rattled.

On the way to the restaurant, his fascination increased. He practically rear-ended several vehicles because he couldn't keep from glancing over at her. She was so damn sexy. He'd never dreamed she had that kind of beauty. Not as cover-girl obvious as Katherine, but an intriguing, second-look kind of beauty that got to you gradually and hooked you much harder. Her relative silence added a layer of mystery that made him hope the service at Chez Mathilde was really really fast.

Because if he didn't get to make love to her tonight he would probably suffer injury of a very intimate nature.

They parked half a block from the restaurant. He caught her appreciative glance and smiled. "Here we are."

"Yes." She pushed open her door, and exited his Honda without visible effort in a motion that pushed her skirt well up her thighs and made a Sharon Stone moment possible had he been sitting in the right spot.

Jeez!

He fell into step beside her, touching her shoulder

to guide her around a tree, touching her elbow to guide her into the restaurant. Not that he thought her incapable of guiding herself. Just that he was incapable of keeping his hands off her.

The maitre d' showed them to a quiet corner table. Allegra sat and allowed her chair to be pushed in as if she was the queen herself. As if she came to this kind of restaurant all the time, which, now that he thought about it, was entirely possible. Just because she generally dressed rather...unusually, didn't mean she hung out at fast-food joints every day.

They settled themselves in at the table. Allegra leaned forward, making his eyes flicker down to the neckline of her dress in spite of himself.

Down, boy.

"So, John, I never asked you how you liked the opera the other night. *La Bohème* is one of my favorites."

"It was wonderful." He put his napkin in his lap to hide his...delight. Sitting here opposite a beautiful woman talking about opera, how much better could it get? "A new production for the Florentine by a local director. Very effective."

"I saw the Zefirelli production at the Met when I was a child. I remember mostly how crowded and colorful the stage was. Fabulous, really."

"I love Puccini." He grinned at her. She was perfect. The change absolutely stunned him.

"His music goes straight to my tear ducts. I can't

sit through a single one of his operas without sobbing my eyes out.''

He nodded. *This* was the discussion he'd been trying to have with Katherine. ''Like at the end of *Bohème,* where he realizes she's dead and calls out her name?''

''Yes! Oh, gosh.'' She fanned herself delicately with her hand, moisture apparent in her eyes. ''It about kills me.''

John passed over a handkerchief, which she declined, obviously fighting to get herself back under control. This woman couldn't even *talk* about the opera without crying. Katherine had sat politely through the whole performance, but John had the feeling she could have been watching herself in the mirror with the same amount of interest, maybe more.

''So, John.''

''Yes, Allegra?'' He found himself grinning again, looking forward to whatever outrageous question she was going to ask. Did he ever want to get up in the middle of an opera and sing along? Did he think people really died of love? Did he think a sky-diving trip would make a good wedding present for a friend of hers?

''What did you study in college?''

His grin faded. ''I was your basic English major.''

''English. I see. What did you do your thesis on?''

''Henry James.''

''How interesting.'' She perched her chin on delicately clasped hands. ''I'd love to hear about it.''

"Are you a James fan?"

"Not particularly." She sent him a polite flattering smile. "But I'm sure whatever you wrote about was fascinating."

John accepted a menu from the waitress and bent over the choices, starting to feel a little disoriented. What the heck was this? Maybe she was nervous. Maybe the level of emotion they'd reached together last time made her uncomfortable. Maybe—

"Oh! Prawns."

He looked up from his menu at her cry of delight and waited hopefully for an insightful prawn news item to follow. Their breeding habits; her adventures fishing for them in Australia; any bizarre medicinal properties—possibly aphrodisiac?

"I love them." She met his eyes briefly and bent back over the menu. "They're delicious."

John frowned at the top of her head. Did her idea of becoming "normal" mean she had to annihilate her personality along with her outfits? Or did her crazy clothes somehow give her permission to act in ways she didn't dare now? Was it the black dress? The restaurant? Him?

She raised her head and met his eyes. He held her gaze and indulged himself in the familiar jolt of attraction at the same time noting that her usual full-tilt sparkle had dimmed. Funny he hadn't noticed before. Maybe he'd been too busy drooling.

"So. How is Katherine?" She spoke in a formal cadence totally unlike her usual singsong speech.

He cleared his throat. This was decidedly bizarre. "I imagine she didn't feel too great for a day or two after the other evening."

"You haven't spoken to her?"

"No."

"Oh." She tried to suppress a smile, but judging by the fact that the corners of her mouth widened and turned up, the effort was a failure. "I see."

He put aside his menu impatiently. Where had their easy connection gone? "You look incredibly beautiful tonight, Allegra."

"Thank you." She blushed a beautiful natural blush. "You see, I *can* do it."

"Yes. You can." He nodded. "Congratulations."

The waitress appeared at their table. "Are you ready to order?"

John gestured to Allegra and nearly rubbed his hands together with anticipation. Bring on Meg Ryan. She wouldn't be able to resist this one.

"I'd like the prawns, please. Then the veal." She closed her menu and handed it to the waitress with a gracious smile.

John's stomach sank. This was unbelievable. How could he possibly miss a habit of hers that made him writhe in embarrassment every time they were out together? He ordered his own meal and a bottle of wine. Maybe that would help loosen her up.

They chatted aimlessly until their first course arrived. He started to fidget, to pull at his tie like a restless kid in church. Was she going to be like this all the time, now? And why did he find himself so disappointed? Wasn't this what he wanted? Didn't this transformation waive away any objections he had about not being able to fit her into his life?

Allegra stared at her prawns, crunchy tails still intact, lined up in a neat, orange-pink succulent row. At her elbow the waitress had placed a finger bowl with a floating lemon slice, to rinse her fingers after touching the shells.

He couldn't help it. He wanted her to take a shrimp, shout, *Be free!* and have it go swimming in the little bowl. He wanted her to take the leafy garnish on her plate and explain how the antioxidants would attack his free radicals and make him live twenty years longer. He wanted…he wanted…

Her.

In all her kooky wonderful glory. Not this trampled on, suffocated version. Did they have a long future to look forward to? He didn't know. But he sure as hell wasn't interested in this Katherine impersonation.

The waitress cleared their first course and brought the second. He barely glanced at what he ate. Barely tasted a single flavor. All he wanted was to get Allegra home—to his or hers, and take off the costume, mess up her hair, wipe off the makeup, and make love to her until they both took a nice figurative trip out of earth's atmosphere.

"Your phone hasn't rung all evening." She daintily patted her lips with the napkin.

He sent her a mischievous glance. "It didn't ring at the zoo, either, after you got hold of it."

"I'm sorry." She blushed and tilted her head, pressing her lips together. "That was wrong of me. I shouldn't have—"

"No." He repeated the word more softly when the first one came out nearly a shout and several people turned. "It was rude of me to keep interrupting our dates. I enjoyed having the phone turned off. Nothing came up that couldn't have waited an hour or two. You taught me a good lesson."

She got a pleased and puzzled look in her eyes. "So, is your phone off now?"

He shook his head and leaned forward over the table, gazing intently into her damn gorgeous eyes, letting his hunger for her show in his. "No."

Her lips parted; her hand crept to her throat. "Then why…hasn't it rung?"

"Because, Allegra." He leaned closer, took her hand and drew a circle on her palm with his thumb. "I didn't bring it with me."

Her face lit up for one joyous second before she brought the emotion back under control. He held her gaze, desire and frustration going nuts through his system. He couldn't wait another second. Couldn't wait to take a jackhammer to the concrete she'd encased herself in. Free the woman he loved. Ravish her all evening and to hell with tomorrow.

"Let's go home." The words came out forceful and hoarse and left no doubt as to his meaning.

Her eyes widened, delight at first, but then touched with what he could have sworn was sadness that made him feel helpless and passionate and confused.

She glanced down, then back up at him, biting her lower lip.

"Yes, John." She nodded. "Let's."

9

SHE'D DONE IT.

The phrase looped over and over in Allegra's head like one of her nephew Bobby's kid-song tapes. She'd done it.

An entire evening dressed like anyone else on a date, engaging in thoroughly normal conversation. Ordering dishes exactly as offered on the menu. Resisting the impulse to make her shrimp go swimming in that little bowl they gave her.

She shifted in the front seat of John's car and returned the smile he sent over. And John had eaten it up. From the second she opened her door until the moment when he made his intentions plain in the restaurant. *Let's go home.* He'd been captivated.

She'd done it.

So why wasn't she bouncing off the walls? Besides the fact that she no longer practiced any form of bouncing. This was exactly what she wanted, right? She'd succeeded beyond her wildest dreams. He was hot for her, passionate, tender, everything she'd dreamed of.

And she'd been normal beyond normal. Her inner

dullness had sprung, grown and blossomed, all in one evening.

So why couldn't she get rid of the feeling she'd been stuffed into a straitjacket? Sedated instead of sedate. Composted instead of composed. Poisoned instead of poised.

John parked in her driveway; she got out and he took her arm to lead her to the front. She stood stiffly unlocking the door while John's warm lips drew heavenly designs on her neck. Why wasn't she responding? Was the New Her frigid to boot?

She pushed open the door. This was ridiculous. She couldn't expect a total transformation overnight. Changing personalities was bound to take time, to be a little confusing, a little conflicting at first. She needed time to adjust, time to relax. John would understand. He'd give her the time she needed, to make their lovemaking slow and long and—

"Allegra." He kicked the front door shut, drew her to him in the dimness of her hallway and kissed her wildly, put his hands to the back of her dress and started unzipping.

So maybe she needed to warn him about the lovemaking being slow and long and—what she'd been about to say before he interrupted, which was languorous.

"I want this off you," he whispered.

Except the zipper stuck in the material of the dress's seam and he had to work like mad to get it down and pinched her skin in the process, quite painfully if the expletives that wanted to get past her lips were anything to go by. Another sign from the Fates that their relationship shouldn't progress quite this quickly?

On the other hand, his mouth felt very nice…and he, um, certainly knew how to…um…use it.

She made a silly whimpering noise of protest or pleasure, she wasn't quite sure which, since his strength and heat in the dark were pretty effectively impairing her judgment.

"You okay?" He'd finished unzipping the dress, but he held the sides together at her nape and fumbled for the light switch next to her front door.

"I'm…yes." She smiled tightly, squinting at the sudden bright surge of light.

"You don't look okay."

"It's…a little…soon."

He grimaced. "I'm sorry. It's just that you look so—" He held up both hands and backed away, which of course made her dress slide right off down to the floor and left her standing there in the black lacy New Her underwear Cynthia had bought for her.

He tried very very hard not to stare. She could tell, by the way he held his head straight up and sort of set his shoulders, but his eyes couldn't quite manage to stay glued to hers, and he let drop several words not allowed in church.

Allegra stooped down, pulled the dress back up and clutched the material in front of her body, tempted to let it slide back down. Because in that one moment when she stood in her underwear, watching his eyes extend out of their sockets by several millimeters, something powerful and female and fabulous had risen up in her.

"Allegra, you have no idea what you do to me."

His voice came out hoarse and humble and the powerful female fabulous feeling swelled so tremendously that she was afraid she'd start looking puffy. He wanted her. She was enticing. She was lovely. She was sexy. She was...*woman.*

She dropped the dress.

He practically lunged for her, swept her into his arms, his mouth a tight tense line. "Bedroom."

"Upstairs." She bit her lip, calculating. Better use the guest room. The sheets were clean there, and the bathroom had fresh soap. "Third door on the right."

And truth be told, she didn't want him in her own bedroom yet. Something didn't quite feel right, letting him into that room, where feng shui wasn't invited— or rather where feng shui had taken one look and run away screaming. Her bedroom was just so...*kooky.* Better the guest room, perfect and in order, the way she was tonight. He'd like that. Making love in that perfect space would be a perfect ending to a perfect—

John kicked open the door and barged in, obviously forgetting that she lay crosswise in his arms and therefore wouldn't fit through the door, because her ankle bone experienced a jarring sharp pain accompanied by an alarming thud, which made John stumble and practically hurl her onto the bed in the semidarkness.

She rubbed her ankle, trying not to wince too obviously, waved off his apologies and at the same time gestured to a large rose-colored candle on the dresser opposite.

John lit the candle and sat next to her on the bed, his eyes dark and glittery in the romantic yellow glow.

"Did I hurt you?"

"It's nothing." She smiled bravely, wondering if by morning her ankle would look as if a purple plum had been glued to the side of it. "I'm fine."

"You're sure? You're okay with this?" He touched her chin and gazed at her so tenderly that she started feeling hot and melty again.

"Oh, yes." She lay back on the bed and smiled invitingly.

He took in a deep slow breath, then pulled off his shoes and socks, undid his pants and shirt and stepped and shrugged out of them, all the while watching her, pausing now and then to stroke his warm hand along her waist or thigh as if he couldn't stop touching her.

She tried to relax, pushing away the nagging worry. Something about lying here about to be ravished by the man of her dreams wasn't quite as fabulous as it should be, and she hadn't a clue why. The evening had worked out perfectly. She should be thrilled. She should be—

John stretched out over her and she chopped her thought right off. Because the feel of his warm male body lying so intimately over hers made her think she could probably at some point remove her underwear by singeing it off with the heat from her own skin.

"Allegra." He kissed her and her doubts and worries ran for cover under the onslaught of emotion, a lot of it admittedly rather carnal. But you couldn't lie there under the love of your life's magnificent body and be even remotely disinterested.

He unfastened her bra, pulled off her panties, touched her everywhere, taking his time, forcing her to be greedy by refusing to be touched back, making her feel like a queen, like a goddess, making her feel and feel until the feeling grew so great she was afraid she'd rise up off the bed.

And then he put on protection and slid inside her, whispered sweet everythings, moved slowly and beautifully until she actually thought she *would* rise up off the bed, thank you very much, except, somehow it didn't quite happen that way. In fact, after a while she realized that nothing was going to happen at all.

Oh, no.

So much for being Woman Herself. Katherine probably would have climaxed by now. In fact Katherine was probably one of those women who orgasmed by mistake. Out of the blue. *Oops! Sorry! What was that? Oh, gosh, don't mind me. Just another pesky orgasm. Probably my fourth or fifth, but I always lose count.*

"Allegra? You okay?"

"I don't think I'm going to…I mean, I'm too tense or something."

"It's okay." He stroked her hair, her cheeks, her eyelids. "I was too quick. I should have spent more time—"

"No, it's not you. It's definitely not you." That, she could be very, very definite about. Which is why she just was.

"I was too crazy for you, Allegra."

His words made liquidy warmth spread all over her once again. "You go ahead."

"No." He started to lift off her. "Let me—"

She stopped him. "Please."

"Are you sure?"

"Yes." She looked him straight in the eye with her direct, most honest gaze so he'd know that taking his own pleasure was absolutely what she wanted and she didn't hold him at all responsible for the fact that she was only half a woman, and the wrong half at that.

He went ahead. And even though she knew she wouldn't join him at the final destination, the ride was really really nice, and she clasped his body to her and ached to be a bigger part of him.

She could tell the moment he lost control, when his thrusting became irregular along with his breathing, when he stiffened and held her tight and whispered her name and something that sounded very much like, "I love you."

Allegra sucked back in the sigh of satisfaction

she'd just let out and froze under him. "What did you say?"

He disentangled his face from her left shoulder and looked down into her eyes, traced her mouth with the tip of his finger. "I love you."

She tried very very hard not to panic, since panicking wasn't a polite thing to do when someone declared love for you, but with his words came a sudden realization of what had been bothering her, what hadn't felt right all evening. She loved him. She'd loved him all along. And he only loved the woman she'd become tonight.

That woman wasn't really her.

"You don't have to say anything if you don't feel it," he whispered.

She closed her eyes against the tears. "I do love you."

He gathered her up against him, rolled to his back and kept her close, held her tighter than she'd ever been held.

She buried her face in his strong comforting shoulder. "But you don't really love me, John."

"I don't?"

She didn't blame him for sounding a bit wary. She popped her head up so she could speak honestly and openly to him once again. "You love the woman I became tonight."

He quirked one eyebrow up as if she had suddenly become fluent in Sanskrit and couldn't help but show it off. "I don't think you have that quite right."

"Yes." She pushed up on her elbows. "Yes, I do. Because tonight you couldn't keep your hands off me. That never happened before, not like this."

He rolled his eyes. "Allegra, you were standing there in black lace underwear and a smile. Forgive me. I'm human."

"No, before the underwear modeling. Before that."

He put his hand under her chin and brought her face closer, even though she resisted slightly so her cheeks squooshed forward and probably made her look like a goldfish impersonator. "Allegra, did it ever occur to you that I was just glad to see you? And that you looked beautiful tonight? Do you think I'm so shallow that I would suddenly fall in love with gel-free hair and makeup whereas before I had absolutely no feelings for you whatsoever?"

She bit her lip, which was hard to do with her face squooshed up. Okay, so maybe he had her there. "But you said Katherine was what you wanted."

He sighed and let her cheeks return to their natural habitat. "You're right. I thought she was what I wanted."

"You said I was too much like your ex-wife."

"Yes. I said that, too."

"John?"

"Yes, Allegra."

"Are you absolutely sure I'm what you want?"

There it was. A sort of haunted shadow that came and went across his eyes. Ghosts of Cara and Katherine and Indecision and Uncertainty. "I know I love you. But I can't tell the future. I don't know what we're going to face or how we'll do together. But I know how you make me feel."

"How?"

He struggled to sit up, with this look on his face that said, *Why do women always insist on the full-color illustrated guide?* "You make me feel good."

"Good?"

He sighed. "*Really* good. I don't know, Allegra. I'm not big with words."

She nodded. "I'm sorry. I guess I was a little paranoid. I'm not used to having changed into the New Me yet."

"Yeah. About that…"

"What?"

"I liked you the old way."

Her jaw dropped and she had to bring it back up to its regular position in order to say, "You did?"

He nodded. A glorious glow of happiness started down at the tips of her polished fingers and spread up to the carefully styled ends of her hair and back down. "You mean, I don't have to wear boring clothes all the time? And talk about nothing?"

He laughed. "I really wish you wouldn't. I missed you tonight."

She blinked at the tender halting tone in his voice and then started to laugh and cry at the same time. "Oh, John Ty-ler Jones, I love you."

She threw herself into his arms and nestled there,

hardly daring to believe her Manhunter moment could work out so well. "We can move out to the country and have busloads of dogs and babies."

His arms stiffened slightly. "I wasn't really thinking of moving out of the city."

"Oh."

He nuzzled her neck. "But we could buy a condo together."

"You want me to give up my house?"

"No. Of course not. Not if you want to keep it."

"I do." She kissed his strong smooth shoulder. "You can move in here."

"Uh, right." He nodded and squeezed her close. "That *could* work. Possibly."

"Good." She laughed out loud to give her overflowing happiness somewhere to go. "Let's celebrate tomorrow by going dancing."

"...Dancing."

"Okay, sorry. Not dancing. And I know roller-skating is out. How about..." Her excitement became tinged with perplexity. "How about..."

"What am I thinking? I have tickets to a Brewers game tomorrow. Would you like to come? My friends Stu and Joe will be with me. You'll really...uh...like them." He rubbed the back of his neck. "Maybe."

"...Baseball."

"No?"

She shook her head. "We could go out to dinner. Again."

"Sure, sure. That would be nice."

"Yes." She smiled at him. "Nice. Then maybe after we could go lie in the sand by the lake and count the stars."

"...Okay. By the way, I meant to tell you, Brighton Pharmaceuticals is having a launch party for the Web site I designed for them next week. Would you like to—"

"Web site?" She extracted herself from his embrace and turned to face him. "You designed their Web site?"

His face immediately broke all previously set wary-looking records. "I'm sorry, Allegra. I should have told you sooner. But I wasn't sure I wanted to—"

"That means *you* can help me! We can be lovers *and* business partners!" She flung herself back on top of him, positive that no relationship which had started so much by chance had ever turned out quite so meant-to-be. "Now you can quit your horrible job that's making you so unhappy. We can make 'Am I the Me I Want To Be?' a national phenomenon together!"

He rubbed the back of his neck harder. "Allegra, my job isn't making me unhappy. I swear to you I have never asked myself 'What the hell am I doing here?' Not once."

She looked at him very very seriously. She didn't mind when he didn't tell her about dating her to keep his apartment; she understood why he didn't. And she didn't mind when he held back what he did until he knew he loved her; she understood why he did that, too. But it really bothered her that he wouldn't be honest about how his job was slowly suffocating him.

"Oh."

The candle flickered and flared up with a sparking spitting sound, then dwindled down again.

"So." He touched the tip of her nose. "I love you."

"Oh, me too." She made a supreme effort and managed a smile. "Me too."

John moved on the bed and his skin made a nice swishy sound on the soft organic cotton sheets. "Well, why don't we get some sleep."

"Yes. Okay. Good idea."

"Good night, Allegra."

She nestled up against him, feeling strangely cold and empty when she should most have felt warm and filled to the brim. "Good night, John."

JOHN DRIFTED into consciousness. Something was very wrong. His alarm hadn't—

His eyes shot open; he sat up and peered blearily around the room. Clock. Clock. Where the hell was a clock? He was late. He felt it in his bones.

Beside him Allegra opened her eyes. "H'llo."

"Hi." He reached over and retrieved his watch from the table next to the bed. *"Damn!"*

Allegra sat up. "Late?"

"Yes." He swore again and hurled himself out of bed. "Today is the launch day for Brighton's Web site. I can't believe I overslept."

"Maybe your body is telling you something."

"That I need more sleep?"

"That you want to lose this job."

He jammed his legs into his pants. This had to stop. "Can we put that subject to rest, please?"

She watched while he yanked on his socks and shoes. He probably owed her an apology for snapping at her, but honestly, the woman didn't let the subject alone. Nothing was more annoying than someone who thought she knew you better than you knew yourself. Last night was terrific. But even last night things had gone wrong. She hadn't been relaxed with him. They couldn't agree on a future. She didn't want a condo; he didn't want to live in feng shui land. They couldn't even decide what to do tonight. He knew he loved her, but unless they could actually agree on something, they couldn't last long. He should do some serious thinking about whether they were meant to be.

But right now, he had to get the hell to work. He pulled on his shirt, fastened his pants, and reflexively patted his pocket to make sure his phone was—

Damn. He'd have to swing by his place and get his phone. He should have brought it with him last night.

"I'll call you later." He kissed Allegra hurriedly and hightailed it out of her crazy pink-and-purple trimmed house, drove like a wild man to his apartment, grabbed his phone, noting the number of voice mail messages with dread, and hit the highway.

And hit the brakes.

Traffic. Backed up as far as the eye could see. Inching. No. Millimetering.

Damn. He started to sweat in spite of the cool morning air coming through his rolled-down windows.

Then even the millimetering slowed, and the lines of cars stopped. Completely. Twelve miles to get to a job he was already late for on a crucial day and he was sitting in a parking lot.

He put the Honda into park, switched off his engine, pulled out his phone and retrieved his voice mail.

"This is Jennifer at Randolph. Our Web site is down. Please call me ASAP."

"Dis is Mr. Tabachnik. Vee gotta problem. Big problem. Ladies go to our site, dey type in 130 pounds, your compudah says dey're morbidly obese and go see a doctor. People vat are 350 pounds, it tells to stock cheesecake. Vat de hell is dis? Lester is ballistic."

"It's Jennifer again. The Web site is still down. Where the hell are you?"

"This is Dolores. Time's up, my pancake. My daughter moves in one week from tomorrow, like it or not."

"Jennifer again. The Web site. *Help.*"

John loosened his tie and pushed back his seat. *Jeez.* One evening off and the entire world collapsed. The Randolph site down, Dolores evicting him and the Brighton site suffering from a major screw-up. He must have programmed the weight questionnaire after one of his dates with Allegra. He couldn't even be around her without his brain turning into a mass of confused wiring. Was that the way he wanted to spend his life?

A woman of Katherine's type might not engender the kind of passion he had with Allegra, but could he share her tastes; he wouldn't be heading for that sickening sense of letdown, of being betrayed by his overly romantic dreams, the way he'd felt when his marriage to Cara dissolved. A woman like Katherine was steady, predictable. No ugly surprises.

His phone rang. "John Tyler Jo—"

"John, it's Katherine! I'm so glad I reached you before I left."

"Left?"

"I'm at the airport now, we're just boarding. I took one of your friend's seminars, and guess what?"

"Wha—"

"I've discovered the me I want to be! I quit Brighton and I'm joining a lesbian potato-farming commune in Idaho."

His mouth dropped open. "You—"

"Oh, gosh, we're boarding. I gotta go. Thanks so much! I love you. I'll miss you. Bye."

She clicked off the line. John stayed frozen with the receiver next to his ear, trying like hell to process the fact that his perfect fantasy female was going to become a lesbian potato farmer.

Where the hell did that leave him in terms of predictability? Of sharing? Of no ugly surprises? Couldn't you count on anyone being the "them" they actually seemed? Or would Allegra work her way through the entire population and change everyone?

He grinned, feeling love for her swirling pleasure through his heart. He wouldn't put it past her.

His phone rang. "John Ty—"

"It's Jennifer. Where the hell have you been? My boss is on my ass, our customers are furious, we've probably lost a ton of sales. This is our one-day, two-for-one sale, in case you forgot. This is totally unacceptable."

"Yes. Okay. I'll call the Web-hosting company, see what's up. I'm sorry, I—"

"I don't want to hear it. Just fix the damn thing. Now."

He punched off the call and took a deep breath. Okay. He could handle this.

His phone rang. "Jo—"

"Jones!" Lester's bellow nearly burst his eardrum. "Where the heck have you been?"

He pictured Allegra, warm and sleepy and soft in bed beside him. "I've been—"

"I don't care where the heck you've been. We have a notable lack of excellence here. If you're not at work in twenty minutes, you're fired."

"Lester, I'm sitting on I-94, not moving. There is no way I can—"

"Read my lips."

"I can't *see* your damn lips, Lester."

"Get. Here. Now."

The line clicked off. John punched off the phone and laid it on the seat beside him. Immediately it rang again. Cars all around him started honking their frustration, as if the noise would somehow magically clear the jam. *Rrring. Honk.*

He turned the key toward him in the ignition and pushed the button to rolled his windows up tight and block out the noise. Nothing. Nothing happened. *Rrring. Honk.* He turned the key the other way to start the engine.

Click.

The battery. The phone. The damn honking. His whole damn life.

He took a deep breath and finally allowed the voice screaming inside his head to be heard.

What the hell am I doing here?

10

ALLEGRA WAVED away a pestering fly buzzing around her front steps, carefully dipped the tiny brush into bright red nail polish, carefully wiped it on the mouth of the bottle and carefully approached her target. Careful, careful and more careful. She didn't want smudges.

There. Perfect. One nail done, nineteen to go.

Ten minutes later, she stepped back and examined her handiwork critically. Nice. Of course the polish wouldn't last forever, but stone lions looked very very cute in navy bows, white baseball hats and red nail polish.

Next, the flags. She picked up a bag of them and arranged them in groups, sticking out of the low bushes around her house. Very nice. So they weren't all American flags, but she'd wanted lots for the desired effect, and the party store had run out of the U.S.A. variety, it being Memorial Day weekend and all. They still looked festive and fun. Spruced up those plain green bushes a lot.

She eyed a dwarf Japanese maple next to one of the lions. Maybe she should decorate the tree with crystals and origami birds. It would only take her an hour or two to make the birds. And that would be one less hour or two she had to spend staring at the wall feeling her heart cracking.

John hadn't called. He'd bolted from her house yesterday morning and she hadn't heard a word since. Of course she hadn't called him either. But for some reason every time she reached for the phone something stopped her. Probably the reality that she had no idea what to say.

Hi, John, I know we have virtually nothing in common, but would you like to spend the rest of your life feeling frustrated and doing nothing together?

Except there were moments of true connection, many of them. Just not last night. Not when it mattered. Not during sex and not when they'd verbalized their feelings. She was ready to explode from frustration. Because a man who enjoyed watching bugs and eating gorilla ice-cream bars simply *had* to have lots in common with her. But damned if he'd let it out.

Allegra sank onto her front steps and rested her chin on her fists. She'd tried being more like him and that hadn't worked. The next move had to be his.

"Allegra!"

She raised her head to see Cynthia and Missy bundling out of Cynthia's Jaguar convertible.

Cynthia held up a white paper bag. "Donut therapy."

Allegra gave a wistful grin which only half her mouth agreed to participate in. "How did you know I needed it?"

"Because we figured if the date had gone really well you'd have called by now." Missy crossed the sidewalk and stopped in front of Allegra, her brow furrowed with worry.

"And if the date had gone really *really* well, then we figured you wouldn't answer the door when we showed up this morning." Cynthia leaned forward and put the bag into Allegra's lap. "Come on, honey, take us inside and spill. We'll stuff you with fat and sugar and listen."

Allegra led the way to the house and on into the kitchen, then stopped when the girls didn't follow her past the hallway. She backtracked and found them staring into her living room, which, now that she saw it with their eyes, did look a tad as if her last visitor had been a cyclone.

"Um." She gestured at the clutter. "I haven't picked up."

"This is *one* day's worth?" Cynthia exchanged glances with Missy.

"I get a little hyper when I'm...hyper." Allegra wrinkled her nose. "I was moving furniture around, and then I thought maybe I'd add a few items from my bedroom and from the basement. To liven the place up. It got feeling too...neat. It didn't at all match my mood."

Cynthia picked up a wobbly clay pot, glazed in rather sloppy stripes of green and pink. "What's this?"

"I made that in grade school." Allegra shrugged. "I thought it added some fun to the room."

"Yes. Fun." Cynthia replaced the bowl carefully on the knickknack-strewn coffee table. "Let's go eat."

"Let's." Allegra led the way into the kitchen and set out mugs, plates and coffee-making paraphernalia which she put into action.

"So, what's up with John?" Cynthia settled herself at Allegra's blue-green kitchen table and folded her hands.

"He hasn't called."

"Since..." Missy prompted.

"Since he left here yesterday morning."

"Oh." Missy clamped her lips together and sent Cynthia an anguished glance.

"Bad sex?"

"Sex was okay. Bad conversation."

"The sex was merely *okay?*" It was Cynthia's turn to look worried.

"I couldn't relax. I couldn't...you know."

"Oh."

The coffeemaker sputtered and made liquidy indigestion noises.

"That happens to me all the time." Missy smiled bravely. "Don't worry."

"Missy, you only had sex *once*."

"Ha!" Missy shook her hair back. "A lot you know."

Allegra and Cynthia turned to stare; Missy shrank back, blushing. "But this isn't about me."

"We'll get to you soon. Tell us everything, Allegra," Cynthia said. "You might as well."

Allegra nodded, passed out the plates and donuts and coffee and told them. About how last night she felt as if she'd put herself in a mental straitjacket, and how the black lace underwear had made John's eyes and other things bulge out, and how she'd been so sure he loved her only for her Katherine impersonation, which wasn't really *her* after all, so she couldn't enjoy the sex, and then after when it started looking as though he really loved her for herself, the *real* her turned out to be someone he couldn't relate to.

"And that's the last I heard from him."

Cynthia frowned as if she was concentrating hard on sipping her coffee without making noise. "Okay, wait. Something's not right about your conclusion."

"No?" Allegra clutched her mug anxiously, clinging to whatever hope she could dig up.

"Why do you assume that if you're not completely normal, you have to be completely kooky? Why can't you be a normal person who happens to express herself rather...rather..."

"Expressively." Missy smiled through a dusting of powdered sugar on her upper lip.

"So he doesn't like dancing and you don't like baseball, and he hates your house and you hate his condo, this is enough to drive you apart?" Cynthia handed Missy a napkin. "If you want to go dancing, go with us! He can watch baseball with his friends. You can buy a new house together. Sometimes you can dress up like the other night and the rest of the time you can indulge the kook side of you.''

Allegra blinked and slanted a look sideways to think that one over. Somehow when Cynthia got hold of complicated issues they always became sensible and manageable within seconds. They should send her to Congress. ''I guess that could work. I suppose I kind of saw this as an either/or proposition. Which I guess it doesn't have to be.''

''So what's the big deal?''

''His ex-wife for one thing.'' Allegra finally managed a bite of donut, which rewarded her by falling like a lead ball into her stomach. ''She was a little like me and the marriage didn't last.''

''So he needs to do some work on himself.'' Cynthia smacked her hand on the table. ''Call him.''

''And say what? 'John, in order for this relationship to succeed you need to change?' What guy would hear that and say, 'Yes, dear, you're right, I do need to change, and I will right now.'''

''She has a point.'' Missy sipped her coffee, grimaced, and added more sugar. ''My mom always said never marry a man thinking you can change him.''

Cynthia rolled her eyes. ''All moms say that. But that's because their generation didn't have the know-how and the female balls to do it.''

Allegra scooched up a skeptical eyebrow. ''And you do?''

"Maybe, maybe not. But it seems to me if John loves you, which he does, he won't let the relationship drop like this. He's probably out there figuring out how to change for you right now."

Allegra snorted. "More likely he's out buying me an exact replica of Katherine's wardrobe."

The phone rang. Missy and Cynthia immediately stiffened and stared at Allegra. Allegra stared back. The phone rang again.

"Well *answer* it for heaven's sake."

Allegra bolted to the phone and picked up the receiver.

"Hello *mein* cupcake, this is Frau Hinkel."

"Oh." Disappointment shot out her standing power; she sank onto a nearby stool in prime position for disappointed slumping.

"I found the perfect person to help you get your seminars online."

"Oh?" She tried to summon enthusiasm, but found enthusiasm difficult when her entire universe had essentially been crushed.

"He's had lots of experience, he's handsome, and…" Frau Hinkel let out a devious little cackle. "He's a lot like you."

"Like me?"

"You know, unusual."

"Oh." She tried to smile until she realized Frau Hinkel couldn't see her so she might as well save herself the effort. "Great."

"He'll be at your place any second."

"*What?*"

"For the interview. He couldn't wait. Very impatient. I told him to go right over."

"You—"

"Goodbye my little jelly roll. Enjoy."

The line clicked off. Allegra slung the phone back into its cradle and swiveled on her stool to face her anxiously waiting friends. "Great. Frau Hinkel arranged an interview with some megageek and I can barely—"

The doorbell rang. Allegra slumped back against the wall. "Oh, for crying out loud. I don't feel like talking to anyone."

"Want me to get rid of him?" Cynthia stood menacingly.

The bell rang again.

"No." Allegra sighed and slid off the stool. "I'll do the interview. If he's exactly what I need, it might cheer me up."

She dragged herself to the front door and opened it.

John.

Only not John.

Not at *all* John.

This man wore narrow punky dark glasses. And a tiny gold stud earring in one ear. And the most godawful riotous Hawaiian shirt she'd ever seen. And yellow pants with little black ants printed all over them.

And the most amazing thing was that somehow he still managed to look unbelievably sexy.

"John."

He took off his glasses and revealed those intense gray eyes that sucked the breath out of her body in an audible whoosh.

"*This* is John?" Cynthia's incredulous voice floated over from behind Allegra, followed by a gasp from Missy. "*This* is Mr. Conservative?"

"Cynthia." Allegra spoke very very calmly, not taking her eyes from John's. "Missy. Don't you have somewhere extremely important to be right now?"

"Yes. Absolutely. We do." Cynthia and Missy immediately came into view in front of and then next to and finally behind John before they disappeared out the door.

"Can I come in?"

"Oh, gosh." Allegra backed up a few steps. "I would have been happy staring at you in the doorway for the rest of my life, but you can come in if you want, sure."

He advanced into her hallway, shut the door behind him, and gave her yellow and green leaf-patterned outfit an appreciative once-over. "You look great."

"So do you." She gestured up and down. "More than great. Edible."

"Oh yeah?" His face broke into a grin. "So eat me."

She burst out laughing, then thought maybe that

wasn't quite the sex goddess thing to do, so she sobered up and nodded. "Maybe later I will."

His eyes which could absolutely not have gotten any more intense, got more intense. "Allegra, I want to design your Web site for you. I want to be part of your business and your dreams, and your life."

"You…you do? Really?" She swallowed. "This isn't some surreal German movie?"

"Nein, fraülein." He shook his head. "You know how you felt that night you dressed up to go to Chez Mathilde's with me?"

"Which part, suffocated? Sat on? Squelched?"

"All of the above." He took a step forward and pushed the bangs off her forehead with a gentle hand. "I've felt like that all my life."

"Oh, John."

"Until I met you." He trailed his fingers down around her face and held her chin, tipped her face up. "You make me feel like the kid I never got to be. You make me feel like I'm alive. You make me feel like…dancing."

She stepped forward even though there was very little space left between them to step into. "Isn't that the title of a BeeGees song?"

"I guess it is. I'm not much good with words."

"Oh, John." She said his name in the most disgusting gooey-in-love fashion and didn't even care. "You're perfect."

He kissed her then, the way he had the night when Katherine was upstairs snoring like a rhinoceros, only this time they hadn't left any big problems unsettled between them. This time they'd gotten everything right.

"Can I tell you something?"

"Mmm." He lifted his mouth from her throat. "Tell me."

"Those are the ugliest pants I've ever seen."

"I was making a point."

"I think you should take them off." She reached down and tugged on the button at his fly. "Now."

He ran his hands down her back, over her rear, and pulled her hard against him. "Now that you mention it, I'm not particularly fond of your outfit either."

She rocked against him. "Off it goes."

Then everything got very very lustful and serious very very fast. She swore she'd been standing there only a few seconds, but suddenly she was naked and he was naked and touching her everywhere. And she couldn't help but touch him back because he was so hard and smooth and inviting everywhere she put her hands.

"Should we go upstairs?" she whispered.

"Not yet."

He lifted her and set her down on the black futon, his hands continuing to wander in a rather delightful way that made her heart feel full and her body feel very very empty and greedy. Then his touching became more insistent and she decided that upstairs could go to hell because she wanted him *now* and if they were here or upstairs or in the middle of Uihlein hall during the third act of *La Bohème,* she couldn't care less.

She opened her legs for him, eagerly, without restraint, and with only the faintest fear of what happened last time when she couldn't…manage. Which would be a terrible shame to happen again, when things promised at last to be so good between them.

He held her gently, pushed inside her and began to move in a slow, steady rhythm, murmuring tender words, and the faint fear became a little more distinct. Oh, gosh. That kind of failure twice would be *horrible.* This time she simply had to…had to…

Oh my.

She gripped his shoulders and cried out from the sheer intensity of the wave that flared through her, cried out again when the wave broke into pulsing contractions.

John thrust harder, grabbed her close and said her name, not whispering this time, but rather loudly, before he followed her over the edge, before she'd even quite made it back down from her own heaven.

"Oh my goodness." She lay under him, and said the words again because she simply hadn't adequate poetic ability to describe everything she felt. "Oh my goodness."

He lifted off her and smiled, stroked her cheek and her breast. "I think we got it right that time."

"Oh, yes. I think we did."

He got up from the couch and swept her up into his arms. "*Now* we can go upstairs."

She giggled, not quite down from the physical high and finally allowing herself to believe the emotional high was here to stay. "Second door on the right, this time."

He quirked an eyebrow, but went into the colorful jumbled chaos of her bedroom, this time not smacking her ankle on anything.

"Wow," he murmured. "This looks like my place."

"See?" She smiled and kissed him, knowing they had what it took to be the John and Allegra they wanted to be. "I told you we had a lot in common."

We'd like to send you **2 FREE** books and a surprise gift to introduce you to Harlequin Duets™. Accept our special offer today and

Indulge in a Harlequin Moment!

HOW TO QUALIFY:

1. With a coin, carefully scratch off the silver area on the card at right to see what we have for you—**2 FREE BOOKS** and a **FREE GIFT**—**ALL YOURS! ALL FREE!**

2. Send back the card and you'll receive two brand-new Harlequin Duets™ books. These books have a cover price of $5.99 each in the U.S. and $6.99 each in Canada, but they are yours to keep absolutely free!

3. There's no catch. You're under no obligation to buy anything. We charge nothing—ZERO—for your first shipment and you don't have to make any minimum number of purchases—not even one!

4. The fact is, thousands of readers enjoy receiving books by mail from the Harlequin Reader Service®. They enjoy the convenience of home delivery… they like getting the best new novels at discount prices, BEFORE they're available in stores…and they love their *Heart to Heart* subscriber newsletter featuring author news, horoscopes, recipes, book reviews and much more!

5. We hope that after receiving your free books you'll want to remain a subscriber. But the choice is yours—to continue or cancel, any time at all. So why not take us up on our invitation with no risk of any kind. You'll be glad you did!

SPECIAL FREE GIFT!

We can't tell you what it is…but we're sure you'll like it! A FREE gift just for giving the Harlequin Reader Service® a try!

Visit us online at www.eHarlequin.com

The **2 FREE BOOKS** we send you will be selected from **HARLEQUIN DUETS**™, the series that brings you two brand-new, full-length romantic comedy novels for one low price.

Books received may vary.

THE HARLEQUIN READER SERVICE®—Here's how it works:

Accepting your 2 free books and gift places you under no obligation to buy anything. You may keep the books and gift and return the shipping statement marked "cancel." If you do not cancel, about a month later we'll send you 2 additional books and bill you just $5.14 each in the U.S., or $6.14 each in Canada, plus 50¢ shipping & handling per book and applicable taxes if any.* That's the complete price and — compared to cover prices of $5.99 each in the U.S. and $6.99 each in Canada — it quite a bargain! You may cancel at any time, but if you choose to continue, every month we'll send you 2 more books, which you may either purchase at the discount price or return to us and cancel your subscription.

*Terms and prices subject to change without notice. Sales tax applicable in N.Y. Canadian residents will be charged applicable provincial taxes and GST.

If offer card is missing write to: Harlequin Reader Service, 3010 Walden Ave., P.O. Box 1867, Buffalo NY 14240-1867

DETACH AND MAIL CARD TODAY!

BUSINESS REPLY MAIL
FIRST-CLASS MAIL   PERMIT NO. 717-003   BUFFALO, NY

POSTAGE WILL BE PAID BY ADDRESSEE

HARLEQUIN READER SERVICE
3010 WALDEN AVE
PO BOX 1867
BUFFALO NY 14240-9952

NO POSTAGE
NECESSARY
IF MAILED
IN THE
UNITED STATES

Two Catch a Fox

Isabel
Sharpe

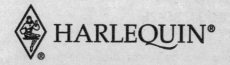

HARLEQUIN®

TORONTO • NEW YORK • LONDON
AMSTERDAM • PARIS • SYDNEY • HAMBURG
STOCKHOLM • ATHENS • TOKYO • MILAN • MADRID
PRAGUE • WARSAW • BUDAPEST • AUCKLAND

Dear Reader,

This book is the last in the MANHUNTERS miniseries,
which started with Temptation #873, *Hot on His Heels*.
I admit, I will miss these characters!

Tracy, Allegra, Cynthia and Missy have been my
constant companions over the past nine months and I
have enjoyed their friendship, struggles and, of course,
their happy endings.

Here's wishing all of you the Manhunt of your dreams!

Cheers,

Isabel

P.S. You can e-mail me through my Web site at
www.IsabelSharpe.com.

Books by Isabel Sharpe

HARLEQUIN DUETS
17—THE WAY WE WEREN'T
26—BEAUTY AND THE BET
32—TRYST OF FATE
44—FOLLOW THAT BABY!

HARLEQUIN TEMPTATION
873—HOT ON HIS HEELS
    (*Manhunters* #1)

HARLEQUIN BLAZE
11—THE WILD SIDE

This book is dedicated to all those
who could use a little laughter in their lives.

1

"'Everlasting and eternal, my heart to yours, our souls entwined. If you are my lady, I will be your knight. Once our passion kindles, it will blaze until death parts us.'"

Cynthia closed the newspaper and restrained her cynical left eyebrow which was too obviously expressing its opinion of such garbage.

"Oh!" Missy practically expired onto Cynthia's kitchen counter in an orgasmic slump. "Read it again."

"Forget it. I'm getting heartburn." Cynthia slapped the paper down on the breakfast bar and picked up her coffee mug. The girls had come over to her condo on this beautiful Fourth of July morning for a healthy round of donut therapy, though Cynthia stuck to whole-grain toast, and had spent the entire time reading and speculating on the ad in the newspaper personals section that Missy had discovered and freaked over. "You read it. Or maybe Allegra wants another turn."

"Um…no thanks." Allegra grinned and rolled her eyes over Missy's prostrate head. "I read it four times already. Your turn, Missy."

"I don't know if I can handle it." Missy's voice came out muffled by the counter and her arms wrapped around her head.

Cynthia sipped her coffee and tangled her legs in the rungs of her counter stool to keep from kicking Missy, much as she adored her friend and co-worker. "Missy, you are being ridiculous. If the ad affects you that much, *answer* the damn thing. I'm telling you right now, in my book this kind of reaction counts as a Manhunter moment just as much as if you'd seen him in person and gotten all hot and bothered. According to our Manhunters' pact when you encounter that kind of chemistry with a guy, you have to pursue him."

"I can't." Missy sat up and propped her head on her hands so her bobbed blond hair spilled over her fingers. "What if he turns out to be a fake? Some evil-doer with a book of poetry putting ads in to lure nice girls like me to their ruin."

"Their *ruin?*" Cynthia gestured impatiently with her coffee and nearly scalded her fingers. "What century do we live in, Missy?"

Allegra sent Cynthia a gentle warning glance through her purple-framed glasses and brushed donut crumbs off the merry-go-round on her pink sweater. "Missy, I agree with Cynthia. You've been reading the personal ads for years, and were never even tempted to answer one. This means the guy knew subconsciously that an ad was the best way to reach out to you. You two have a serious spiritual link."

"Yeah, whatever." Cynthia waved away Allegra's wacky theory with her newly manicured fingers. "In any case, you have to answer it, Missy. You've been mooning over this ad for three days. Do you want to spend the rest of your life wondering who this guy was? Because you will, you know. You'll be signing on for the worst thing life can throw out, a huge, tantalizing, eternal 'could-have-been.'"

Missy's eyebrows were visible enough through the curtain of hair over her face to be seen rising in distress. "I know, I know. You're right. I just... I just... It's just that..."

She slumped down again and buried her face in her hands.

"Missy." Allegra patted Missy's hand. "Let's try something. It might be a good catharsis. Just for kicks, why don't you write down what you *would* write back if you had the nerve?"

Allegra sent a sly look to Cynthia who gave her a thumbs-up and winked. Sometimes Allegra was way too kooky for Cynthia's taste, but there were moments, like now, when she could be very attractively devious and manipulative. Cynthia could respect that in a woman. As long as the end was good.

"Ha!" Missy lifted her head. "You think I'd fall for *that?* The minute my back is turned you'll call up the response line and answer."

Allegra put her hand to her heart and stared unwaveringly into her long-time friend's blue eyes. "I swear to you, Missy. I will not."

"Really?" Missy gazed back hopefully. "Because I was kind of working on what I would say…you know…if I was *going* to respond, which of course I'm not. Probably."

"Of course." Allegra patted Missy's hand again and managed a totally guileless glance at Cynthia.

Cynthia buried a snort of laughter in another sip of coffee. *Like a lamb to slaughter.*

"Well…" Missy blushed. "I was *going* to say something like—"

"Hang on." Cynthia put down her mug and opened a neatly organized drawer under her counter for a fresh pad and sharp pencil. "Okay. For posterity. Or, you know, for if you were *going* to respond, which of course you're not. Probably."

Missy's eyes grew dreamy; she absently trailed her hand down her throat. "Okay, here it is. 'I have waited for you, I have longed for you, my love; I will be your lady, I will ride with you down the path of life; we shall be inseparable as…as…'"

"Siamese twins?" Cynthia suggested not-at-all-helpfully.

Allegra shot Cynthia a dirty look. "Go on, Missy."

"As inseparable as are love and loving…and life and living." Missy gave a huge sigh, still enjoying her vacation in La-la-land.

"Um…wow." Allegra nodded carefully. "That's really…wow."

"Life…and…living." Cynthia scribbled the last

word and tore off the sheet. "Perfect. Though I would have added 'hump and humping.'"

Missy's eyes snapped into focus. "Sex, sex, sex. Isn't there anything else in your head?"

"You find something better, I'll replace it." Cynthia grinned and waggled her eyebrows. "Okay, I'm sorry, I was being inappropriately crude. Your answer is fabulous. A guy like him will love it."

"Wait a minute." Missy clutched fists to her way-impressive chest, which she'd tried to camouflage as usual, with a loose pink-and-blue plaid cotton blouse. Entirely unfair that a woman with Missy's prudish outlook be given the body of a centerfold, while Cynthia, who fairly burst with lust for loving, got the tall bony twig look. "You said you weren't going to phone it in."

"No, *Allegra* said she wasn't going to. I made no such promise."

"*Cynthia!*" Missy slid off her stool and stood with her hands on her hips. "You dirty double-crosser."

"Well?" Cynthia waved the paper with Missy's note. "Think love, think happiness, think Siamese twins until death or surgery do you part, and ask yourself, did Cynthia promise she wouldn't phone in the ad?"

"No, but…but…" Missy gestured at Allegra, eyes starting to sparkle. Her nervous stuttering dissolved into a giggle. "You *can't*."

The protest was entirely lame, giving Cynthia the permission she needed. She snatched up the *Journal*

Sentinel and found the ad, circled with a yellow high-lighter. "Number 0524. I'm calling now."

"*No!* No, you can't. I mean I can't just give a stranger my phone number." Missy tried to grab for the paper. "He might be a serial killer."

Cynthia shrugged, easily holding the paper out of reach. "So, I'll give him *my* number. If he calls and he's nice, I'll set up a date for you. If he's a serial killer, I'll tell him you're not interested. Okay?"

"I...I..." Missy covered her mouth with her hands, eyes alternately dismayed and excited. "Well, okay. If you're sure it's okay."

"I'm sure." Cynthia dialed the number, feeling suspiciously envious. The four best friends had made the Manhunter pact last summer. Here they were, a mere year later, Tracy on her honeymoon, Allegra as good as engaged, and Missy about to embark on her own adventure...while Cynthia was still unattached.

Ironic. Because of the four of them, Cynthia was by far the most open to carnal attraction. In fact, though she'd never admit it to the other women, during the past year, she *had* had some Manhunter moments. She always had them. Men were drawn to her and she was drawn to them. But she hadn't told the girls, for a really lame reason. Because she couldn't help feeling there might be something bigger out there. That what Tracy and Allegra and now Missy had experienced wasn't the usual sexual charge Cynthia got when she locked eyes with a man who desired her. But something truly special and deep and lasting.

Which put her in her current conflict. Because she wasn't even sure she *believed* in the idea of love as anything more than good sex plus good friendship. Except she sure as hell had been holding out for something.

The line connected; she listened to the recorded instructions, then punched in the ad code.

"Wait, Cynthia, I can't…I don't—"

"Shh." She winked at Missy. "It'll be okay."

Missy wrung her hands helplessly and turned to Allegra who grinned. "You don't have to go out with him if you don't want to."

"What if *he* doesn't want to?"

The beep to begin the message sounded in Cynthia's ear. She read Missy's message and left her own phone number, making the words as emotional and sincere as possible, all the while trying not to gag.

"Whew!" She hung up the receiver and beamed at Missy. "After all that goo I need to go rent a porn flick or something."

"Oh, Cynthia." Missy jumped up and down and clapped her hands. "Do you think he'll call?"

"Of course he will." Cynthia smoothed back her hair, pushing away a second jab of envy. Missy deserved to find someone wonderful. That girl had wasted herself on TV and mooning for too long.

"But what if someone else leaves a message he likes better?"

"Missy." Cynthia folded her arms sternly. "Repeat after me. I am a fabulous woman…"

Missy rolled her eyes and blushed. "I am a fabulous woman…"

"I have intelligence, humor, honesty…"

"I have…those things."

"And breasts women would kill for and men fight to the death to—"

"*Cynthia!*"

Cynthia shrugged. "And from now on, I will go after what I want."

Missy took a deep breath. "I'll try."

"Good for you." Cynthia stepped forward and gave Missy a hug, completely unable to understand Missy's reluctance to get out there and live her life. You only got one shot, why waste it? Cynthia sure as hell hadn't. She'd ditched a childhood of North Carolina poverty, traded in her Southern accent and softness for the more powerful and effective Yankee grit, graduated from Yale with honors and followed job offers around the country, building her career until she landed in Milwaukee with a dream job at Atkeson, Inc. No one could accuse her of hiding her light under a barrel while waiting for a man.

Cinderella she wasn't. But let's face it, when it came to long-term relationships, most men hated strong women. The ones that didn't were generally looking for a mommy to take care of them or a rebellious daughter to keep in line. Sorry, but Cynthia wasn't into dating family members.

Besides, she had plenty of other successes in her life to celebrate. This year she planned another even bigger one: to win Milwaukee's coveted Foster Award, for the businessman or woman who had contributed most to the community. She'd entered the day the applications were circulated among area businesses. This was her year. She was certain.

In the meantime, unlike her friends, she wasn't above enjoying temporary liaisons with guys who clearly weren't her "happily ever after." That could see her through many more years quite contentedly.

Cynthia turned away from the sight of Missy's pink cheeks and shining eyes. As always, she had her own agenda. One that would bring a lot more richness and dependable happiness to her life than finding a man ever could.

"OH, MAN, she was so beautiful, you know?"

"Yes, Ken, I know." Adam leaned back in his favorite leather chair and blew a disgusted breath up at his ceiling. He knew. He knew everything about Ken's ex-girlfriend. Everything. What her toes looked like, how she liked her tofu, what kind of organic cleaner she preferred for the toilet...

"I mean, she was my first, my last, my *everything*." Ken clutched his heart and tossed back the rest of his drink like a cowboy downing his eighteenth shot of the evening.

Orange juice, straight up. Adam rubbed his stubbled chin and contemplated emptying about half a bottle of vodka into the juice. Maybe a good buzz would cheer Ken up. Or put him to sleep.

Two weeks ago, in a moment of regrettable warm fuzziness, Adam had invited his emotionally flattened co-worker to move into his neat, uncluttered two-bedroom condo until Ken could find another apartment after his ex evicted him, physically and emotionally, from theirs. A favor to a friend. Out of the goodness of his heart. Charity, to a man kicked in the groin by a Birkenstock-wearing female foot.

The longest two weeks of his life. His neat uncluttered condo felt messier and more crowded every day. And he hadn't heard this much whining since his last visit with his cousin's kids.

``Ken, at some point you're going to have to realize that this woman treated you like dirt for three years, then ditched you.''

Ken pushed his glasses up his nose with his middle finger, a rude gesture Adam still hadn't decided if Ken knew he was making.

``She was a princess, a goddess, a—''

``Manipulatrix.'' Adam grabbed the *Journal Sentinel* and slapped it down in front of Ken on his grandmother's antique coffee table. ``There.''

``You want me to read the paper?''

``Your ad. Remember? The one you wrote and didn't have the guts to send in?''

Ken's blue eyes slowly widened; he stared at the paper, then up at Adam. ``You didn't.''

Adam solemnly crossed his arms over his chest, as if he were going to admit to being the ghostwriter of the Declaration of Independence. ``I did.''

"Oh, wow." Ken gave a shout of laughter and slapped his thighs, which stuck out of his bright red shorts like pale hairy saplings. "I can't believe it. Lemme see."

He opened the Weekend Cue section and skimmed the ads. "Men seeking women. Where is—oh, *wow.* There it is! I can't believe it! My words! Me! I wrote this!"

"So..."

"So?" Ken stabbed his finger on the ad to hold the place and turned questioning eyes up to Adam, smiling for the first time in two weeks.

"So, call and see if anyone has answered."

Ken's smile faded. "You mean call? And see if anyone has answered?"

"Believe it or not, that's exactly what I mean."

"But...I'm not sure I want to know. I mean, what if no one did answer? Then what?"

"*Then* you hang up and try again later." He spoke patiently and kindly as if he was talking to a small boy, wondering if Ken should have his testosterone levels checked.

Ken clutched his stomach and slumped back on Adam's couch. "I don't know if I can take any more rejection."

"Fine." Adam grabbed the paper. "I'll call."

"Hey! My ad!"

"I promise I'll give it back when I'm finished." Adam strode to the cordless phone in his kitchen and dialed the number on his way back into the living room, praying someone in Milwaukee was sappy enough to respond to Ken's ad. If the guy didn't cheer up soon, Adam was going to send him to a hotel.

It was totally beyond him how any adult male—he'd leave out the word ``mature'' in Ken's case—could wallow so deeply in his own tragedy. So, life stank sometimes. You couldn't control what happened to you. Shrug it off. Take some time to work through it, sure, but then concentrate on what was good about life instead of what you couldn't change. Get out there and do what felt right, seek out what made you happy. Live in the moment, not in the past and not in some imagined future. Granted, Adam's brush with mortality three years ago had given him new appreciation for being alive, but it frustrated the hell out of him when people resisted all that was new and potentially wonderful about each day.

He listened to the instructions on the phone and punched in the message code. The tape started playing. He held up a finger. ``Okay, here's the first message....''

Ken sat up ramrod straight and clutched the edge of the table.

A tiny whispering female voice came onto the line. Adam leaned forward, phone pressed to his ear, as if bending over would somehow improve his hearing.

``Um, hi.'' The whisperer took a long quavery breath. ``I'm Betsy. I thought your ad was sweet. Call me.''

She hung up without leaving a number. Adam

rolled his eyes. It figured. Weird ad, weird responders. ``That was Betsy. I think she had to get back to the Home For the Very Very Timid. Message two.'' He repeated the mechanical words.

``Hi. My name is Dora, and I thought your ad was really cute, you know? I'm like *way* romantic myself, I mean that knight and lady thing was like poetry! I'm a poet, too, you know. In fact, I thought to best tell you about myself I'd read you some poetry I wrote.''

Paper rustled over the line. Adam passed his hand over his eyes. ``She's going to read some of her poetry.''

``Yeah?'' Ken shrugged his slender shoulders under his bright green shirt. ``Repeat what she says so I can hear.''

``This is ridiculous. Why don't you—''

``Love.'' Dora's voice broke in. Adam rolled his eyes and repeated the title to Ken, who nodded hopefully.

``Love. Love. *Love!* Lovelovelovelove…*LOVE!* I love. Therefore…I…love. My head loves. My nose loves. My bed loves. My toes loves. My nipples—''

Adam held the phone out to Ken. ``I am *not* repeating this aloud.''

``That bad?'' Ken's face crumpled mournfully.

``That bad.''

``Okay. See if there are any more.''

Adam sank back down in his chair, rested his temple on his hand and put the phone back to his ear, hoping Ms. Nipples-in-love was finished. "Next message."

"Hi. This is Missy."

The low, rich voice sent a bolt of chemical lightning through Adam's chest and into his stomach. The sexiest female voice he'd ever heard.

"I have waited for you, I have longed for you, my love' I will be your lady, I will ride with you down the path of life, we shall be inseparable as are love and loving, and life and living."

"Well?"

His friend's normally gentle voice was so irritated Adam had a feeling Ken had been trying to get his attention for a while.

"I—" He cleared his throat. "This one…you might want to hear."

"No kidding!" Ken leapt to his feet. "No kidding. What does she say?"

"Why don't *you* dial and—"

"No. No." Ken backed away, arms rigid, waving his hands as if he was warding off a swarm of killer bees, until the couch hit the back of his knees and he sat down suddenly. "You call. Please."

Adam let out an exasperated sigh and dialed again, chiding himself for the nerves churning his stomach. This was nuts. He'd had an immediate desire to know the woman on the other end. In every sense of the word. How could he possibly be so attracted to a voice? She'd responded to Ken's ad. Ken's words. All that syrupy stuff obviously turned her on. Not his kind of woman, even if her voice made his thoughts need an R-rating at least. He liked his women tough, sassy and sexual. The kind who would double over laughing if he mentioned knights and their ladies.

He waded through Betsy and Doris and got the message again, bracing himself this time so the sound of her voice wouldn't affect him as deeply.

Hi. This is Missy.

No good. If anything the reaction was worse this time. He forced himself to concentrate on the ridiculous words she was saying and managed to repeat them out loud to Ken, then got up to write down the woman's phone number on a discarded envelope, conveniently ignoring the fact that his hands were unsteady.

``Oh!'' Ken clutched his chest. ``My lady! My soul! My heart! My—''

``Ass. You don't even know her.'' Adam punched off the phone and faced Ken with his hands on his hips. He was being cruel, but the grumpy feeling souring his stomach had spread to his mood.

``I know her. How could I not know her? She is my destiny, my soul mate, my true love.''

``Yeah, well here's her number. I'm not getting into some Cyrano de Bergerac thing. You want her, you woo her.'' He tossed the envelope with her number down in front of Ken, wondering what evil force in the universe had made him use the word *woo*.

Ken fidgeted and scratched his chin again, then gave Adam the glasses-back-up finger. ``Adam?''

Adam's shoulders slumped. He knew that voice, that look. "Yes, Ken?"

"I know I've been a burden to you for the past two weeks, but I promise this will be the last thing I ask you for. Can you call and set up the date?"

"Ken." Adam kept his voice gentle with a tremendous effort. If he didn't know by her syrupy words that the woman on the phone with the incredible voice was meant for Ken, he'd be after her in a flash. She'd affected him that deeply. Just as her words affected Ken. You didn't ignore signs like that. Life threw them at you for a reason.

Up until three years ago, he hadn't been able to read the signs so clearly. Up to his ass in work, work, work, and then for a change…work. Always after something he didn't have yet, always pushing for the next big deal. Wasting his precious time on planet Earth.

Now his mission was not only to pile as much of life's amazing here-and-now smorgasbord onto his plate as he could, but to make sure people he loved— he glanced at Ken—or tolerated—weren't making the same mistakes he had. "You've got to learn to make the life you've got into the one you want, Ken."

"I will, I will. In fact I'll go out this afternoon and actually look for an apartment."

Adam turned on him incredulously. "You haven't been looking?"

Ken's mouth worked for a few seconds before words actually came out. "Well, I've needed time to…recover from my loss. But now I have hope of a new wonderful life with my lady. I promise I'll be out of here by the end of next week…or the next.''

''I'll tell you what.'' Adam drew his hands over his face. He couldn't believe he was going to do this. ''I'll call Missy for you and set up the date—''

''Oh, thank you!'' Ken dropped to his knees, hands clasped.

''The minute you find yourself a new place.''

Ken's eyes widened, then he lunged for his baseball cap, grabbed the *Journal Sentinel* real-estate section and ran for the door. ''I'm as good as gone.''

As good as gone. Adam stared down at the number in his hands, the woman's rich, sultry voice playing over and over in his mind.

For some reason, he knew what Ken meant.

CYNTHIA SLUNG two bags of groceries onto one arm and dug the keys to her condo out of her purse. Tired. Very tired. And she still had reams of notes to transcribe and organize into a report from the day's interviews. Plus Internet research to dig out a site for the year-after-next's Playground Project banquet.

She stuck the key into the lock and swung the door open, breathing a sigh of relief at the cool air and peaceful order of her home.

Two steps into her hallway, she stepped out of her shoes, lined them up perpendicular to the wall with her toes, and glanced at her message machine. Nothing.

Her kitchen beckoned. Man, she was hungry. She dumped the groceries on the counter and ran upstairs. First things first. Relieve the discomforts in the order of their severity. Number one: panty hose. Number two: tight skirt. She slipped on a pair of plaid linen shorts and a black cotton sleeveless top, brushing dryer lint from the shoulder. Ahh, better. Next: hunger and thirst. Then off her feet.

Half an hour later she let her fork drop contentedly onto an empty Skinny Dinner tray and felt some semblance of humanity returning. Except that her beloved little condo in downtown Milwaukee felt lonely tonight. She could use someone to talk to. Someone to say, *Tough day at the office, dear?* So she could answer, *You bet. Let's get naked.*

Richard Croshallis, or as she sweetly referred to him, Dick Crotchless, a working woman's worst nightmare, today had become…worse. She'd gone out to his company, IT Consulting, to interview senior management. A local venture capital firm had become interested in his astounding entrepreneurial success and was considering investing a wad of money in his business. First, though, the investors wanted to make sure he was running a healthy company. Enter Cynthia Parkins, Senior Engagement Manager at Atkeson, Inc., and her trusty partner, Russ Hawkins. Able to ferret out the truth behind the success.

She got up and went to the freezer for strawberry fat-free frozen yogurt. Unfortunately, Dicky turned out to be arrogant, cocky and lecherous, with several questionable business decisions under his belt despite the phenomenal growth of his company. Worse, he wanted the investment capital badly. Which didn't sit at all well with his I-run-the-place-and-no-one-can-do-it-better mentality.

But that wasn't the worst part. Ohhhh, no. The worst part was that his father, Frank Croshallis, sat on the panel that decided who got the Foster Award. Russ, bless his idiot heart, had blurted out that Cynthia was in the running. If you could call it running. More like sprinting, scrambling, clawing tooth and nail...

When he found that tidbit out, Dicky's little eyes had lit up like a rat smelling a garbage dump. Aha! Leverage. Immediately he'd started in on her.

Cynthia wanted that award. She wanted that award badly enough that she hadn't immediately told him where he could stuff his company. Anyone who got the Foster Award could write his or her own ticket. With the financial award and more importantly, the prestige, she could finally overcome any objection people might have to her starting out life as a poor Southern girl. Join the Centurion Club and network with the cream of Cream City's businesspeople.

She'd be playing with the big boys on a level field. Golfing without a handicap. Seated at a feast for one. Dumped on an island with sterilized, undiseased, big-bicepped men.

She could start her own firm. Granted, she could and would do that someday with or without the Foster

Award, but a little help would be wonderful. Now she had to keep little Richard happy or he'd go screaming to daddy about how she blew his chance to get one-hundred million dollars sunk into his screebly little company.

Terrific.

The phone rang. She considered not answering, but frankly, she could use a human voice right about now. She could even stand chatting with a telemarketer.

"Hello?" She crossed her fingers, hoping the person on the other end was in the mood for good conversation.

"Is this Missy?" The voice was deep and rich, full of life. The kind of male voice that could make, "Is this Missy?" sound like a sexual invitation.

Cynthia closed her eyes and enjoyed her reaction, a shivery mixture of curiosity and a strange instinctive anticipation, as if she'd met someone she knew she'd be in bed with very soon. God, she loved voices like that. Especially when she couldn't see the guy on the other side, because then she didn't have to deal with the fact that he was probably four feet tall and round with no hair and bad skin.

Which, unfortunately, he invariably was if he'd responded to Missy's gooey note. Men with voices like that shouldn't be allowed to look like anyone but Pierce Brosnan. "Yes, this is Missy."

She braced herself to hear the voice again. Of course Missy would want her to check him out. As long as all she had to do was listen to him, that would be fine. Enjoyable even. Though the second he pulled any of that knight-and-his-lady garbage, she'd have to plug her ears.

"This is…uh, Ken."

"Nice to hear from you, Ken." *Keep talking, keep talking. Say anything.*

"I liked your answer to my ad. Very much." A certain suggestive tone crept into the words *very much* that had Cynthia ready to propose phone sex.

"I'm glad." She put enough warmth into her own voice to melt Antarctica. What the hell. Even if she was reeling him in for Missy, might as well make the job fun.

For a second Cynthia heard something that sounded like whispering, then paper crinkling. Odd.

Ken of the to-die-for voice cleared his throat, somewhat uncomfortably, as if he was about to do something he didn't care to do. "Soul to soul we have connected. Life to life, voice to voice, breath to breath."

Cynthia held the receiver away from her ear and waved at the air in front of her face as if it suddenly reeked. *What* a fantasy blaster. A voice like that coming up with such total garbage. Ken was perfect for Missy. No question. But his voice was perfect for Cynthia.

"Um. Yeah." She glanced helplessly around her apartment. What the hell would Missy say to that? Soul to soul? Breath to breath? "And…body to body. Let's not forget that one."

A deep chuckle came over the line. "Indeed."

The hand in front of Cynthia's face was suddenly needed to fan her rapidly warming cheeks. *Aye yi yi.* Steam heat.

"So, Missy."

Cynthia closed her eyes, ready to sail away to anywhere on the smooth undulations of that voice. "Yes, Ken?"

"I'd like to meet you."

"Oh, I'd like to meet you, too." Except that finding out what Mr. Breath-to-Breath really looked like would probably be totally devastating. Good thing she was landing the guy for Missy.

"The thing is..."

"Yes?"

"Well, I'm kind of shy."

Huh? His voice radiated confidence. Shy? "Oh, yeah. Me, too."

"So, I'd like to bring a friend the first time we meet."

Cynthia's *huh?* expression ascended to new and more profound levels of *Huh?*-ness. The guy wanted to bring a *friend?* She shook her head and stifled a giggle. This was absolutely incredible. What a major geekoid waste of a sexy voice. What would Missy think? Chances were she'd welcome the chance to avoid the pressure of a one-on-one date.

"Sure. That would be fine. What's your friend's name?"

"...Adam?"

That strange feeling of electric anticipation came over her again and amputated her giggles. *Adam.*

"Well, great! Great!" Why the hell was she suddenly so curious about a geek's doubtless also-geeky friend?

Cynthia paced back and forth in her kitchen, trying to make some sense of this whirling mass of emotions. Her emotions never whirled. They sat in nice little compartments and came out one by one at the appropriate time. Right now she felt as if they'd all hurled themselves out for a barroom brawl.

She had to go along on this date. She was dying to see for herself what all these feelings were about. Meet the guy. Meet his friend. Put the emotions back in their boxes. Reassure herself she wasn't losing her mind.

"Meet us at Chicken Curly's at seven."

Chicken Curly's? She raised her eyes to the ceiling. Ugh. It figured. "I'll…be bringing a friend, too. Her name is Cynthia."

"Cynthia."

She stopped pacing. Her emotions instantly ended their brawl, like those movie scenes where one person shouts for quiet amid total chaos and everyone freezes.

Sex. No way could she hear her name spoken in that masculine take-me-baby voice and think of anything else. This was crazy. The guy was talking about souls and knights and breathing on people and he thought Chicken Curly's was a good place for a date.

Obviously they hadn't a thing in common. And here she was, absolutely drooling for a glimpse of the complete nerdoid perfectly destined for her good friend Missy. What kind of freakish sleazeball did that make her?

They agreed on a date for Saturday night. Cynthia hung up and dialed Missy's number before she gave herself any time to think about what had just happened. Because what had just happened was too weird to bear thinking about.

Missy answered on the second ring. "Hello?"

"Missy, great news. I made you a date with Mr. Knight-and-his-lady. I pretended I was you."

Missy squealed so loudly Cynthia had to hold the phone away from her ear. "You did? You did? You really did? You really, real—"

"His name is Ken. He's got a totally dynamite voice." She clenched her teeth together and released them. *Down, girl.* "He said, 'soul to soul'…uh…life to life, breath to breath'…whatever the hell that means."

"Oh!"

Cynthia didn't have to be in the same room with Missy to know that her lower lip was doing that trembly thing. *Man,* some people were corny. She walked over to her sink and started rinsing dishes, squelching yet another entirely inappropriate pang of envy. "So we're set. Saturday night, seven o'clock at Chicken Curly's."

"I *love* Chicken Curly's."

Somehow that didn't surprise her. "And he's shy so he's bringing a friend."

"A *friend?* Oh, gosh, I can't do this. Two men? Two? Cynthia, help. You've got to come with me. I can't—"

"Relax." Cynthia let out a breath of relief. Not that she'd hesitate to drop out if Missy didn't want her there. "I've already invited myself along. I thought you might need reinforcement."

"Oh, *thank* you, Cynthia. You're the *best.*"

"Yeah, don't mention it." Cynthia winced. Not very comfortable to have praise gushed all over her when she'd just spent the last ten minutes lusting over her friend's geek date, sight unseen.

"Um…Cynthia?"

Cynthia sighed. She knew that voice. "Ye-e-es?"

"Can you do me another favor? Can you keep pretending to be me, at least on the first date?"

"What?" A mug slipped out of her fingers and clunked into the sink. "Missy, that's a really bad—"

"It's just that for one thing he already knows your voice. And this way I can watch him and get to know him without feeling like I'm on display. I get so *nervous* when I am desperate to make an impression. I freeze up and I can't say anything. So you can be me and just not talk to him a whole lot and I'll pretend I'm your pushy friend, and when it gradually becomes obvious that he and I are much better suited, then we can confess the joke and everything will be fine."

"Missy…" She groped for the words to express

how completely idiotic this idea was at the same time trying to suppress her persistent fantasy of what The Voice would look like. If she pretended to be Missy, then he'd think *she* was his ad-answerer. ``Starting any kind of relationship based on dishonesty is a horrible idea.''

``But the only dishonesty would be the names we use. I mean you don't have to pretend to act like me. It will be obvious which of us is destined for whom right away. I mean jeez, when Ken says his knight and lady stuff you'll just throw up, and that should be a dead giveaway, right? In the meantime I can be so much more relaxed. Because if I have to feel any worse pressure than I already do I'll break out in hives. Will you do it? Please?''

Cynthia shut off the water and pressed a hand to her forehead. That pleading panicky voice Missy used brought out all her big-sister protective impulses. She knew what being shy and scared felt like. But she'd fought to overcome those feelings years ago, while Missy had given in to them all her life.

She sighed, knowing she couldn't turn her friend down. ``All right, all right.''

She ended the call with Missy practically sobbing in relief and sighed. Okay. She could handle this. Heck. Maybe the friend Adam would be cute. And she might as well see this Ken guy and explode the myth of the perfect voice so she could get it the hell out of her mind.

She ran a sponge around the sink and wiped the chrome faucet clean of water spots.

Because she had this weird instinctive feeling that nothing less than an explosion would do it.

2

``HOWDY FOLKS! And welcome to Chicken Curly's, home of the rootin-tootin, good-time, happy-chicken, fun—''

``Yeah, thanks, whatever.'' Cynthia eyed the short-skirted, cowboy-booted bimbette hostess with total distaste. Way to put human dignity on hold. ``We're meeting two gentlemen here, have they arrived? Adam and Ken.''

The faux-cowgirl pored over a white clipboard with a plastic grinning chicken stuck on the clip. Missy tugged excitedly on the back of Cynthia's sleeveless linen top. ``Do you think they're here yet? Isn't this place *great?* Doesn't the hostess look pretty?''

``I don't know if they're here. This place is something else. And she looks like an escapee from Rogers and Hammerstein's worst nightmare.''

``Oh, jeepers.'' Missy gave Cynthia's arm a playful smack. ``Relax, would you? This place is really fun.''

Cynthia rolled her eyes. The last thing she expected was for Missy to have to tell *her* to relax. But she couldn't help being tense. Theme restaurants irritated her. Theme restaurants in the Midwest pretending to be in the Wild West irritated her more. Throw grinning chickens into the mix and things got much, much worse.

Then there was a certain amount of tension involved in going to meet the owner of that voice. That tension irritated her the most. She could go on a date with a Mel Gibson clone and barely get nervous. In fact, she did fairly regularly, thank you very much. She'd worked hard to acquire that level of confidence. Frustrating as hell to have her cool shaken now for no earthly reason.

``Yessiree! Adam and Ken! They're in coop number forty-two! Follow me, gals!'' The hostess flashed perfect teeth in a perfect smile and whirled enthusiastically so her skirt flared up over her perfect twenty-something legs.

Cynthia sneered at the smiley chicken briefly visible on the hostess's perfect rear. Okay, so Cynthia Parkins was on edge. Not that she could ever relax in a place that made its employees wear happy-chicken heads on their butts. But until she saw The Voice and could put her bizarre, out-of-place feelings out to pasture, she'd just have to deal with being unsettled.

They followed the hostess, negotiating bales of hay topped with various plastic nesting fowl and went down an aisle of booths separated by chicken wire on which hung utensils and plastic eggs and pictures of happy people shaking hands with giant chicken-costumed idiots.

"Here we are, gals!" The hostess stopped at a booth. "Coop forty-two."

Two men rose. One relatively short, blond thinning hair, glasses, bright plaid cotton shirt and yellow shorts. The other...

"Oh, gosh, the tall one is *gorgeous!*" Missy whispered. "Do you think that's Ken? Ooh, I hope so."

Cynthia swallowed without needing to swallow, which was damn uncomfortable. If ever there was a perfect Pierce Brosnan kind of guy... Which meant the voice probably belonged to the geeky one. Because it wouldn't be fair if one guy got it all.

The tall vision of perfection extended his hand to Cynthia as if Missy and the Geek didn't exist, which they didn't the minute she met his eyes. The chemistry between them flared so intensely, Cynthia had to look away. And she *always* won stare-downs.

"Hello. I'm...Ken."

Missy gasped behind her.

Prickles ran down Cynthia's skin. *The Voice.* Him. All of it. The perfect package, ruined by gooey poetry and the fact that he had chosen Chicken Curly's. This man. This perfect man was perfect...for Missy.

She wanted to throw up.

"I'm...Missy." She nearly choked on the fake name, shook his hand and dropped it before she gave in to the urge to run his fingers all over her body.

For one strange second she could have sworn she saw disappointment in his eyes at the mention of her name, before he turned his warm attention to Missy.

Had he hoped she wasn't the woman who answered his ad? Did that mean *Missy* attracted him more?

Wait. She reprocessed the information while the strange second dragged out into a truly disorienting minute. One thing Cynthia knew was chemistry. She'd minored in it in college—outside of the classroom. She and the Stud had chemistry in spades. So why would he be disappointed to learn she was the one who answered his ad?

She brushed the thoughts aside and introduced herself to the Geek, Adam, who stared with outright lust.

Ewwwww.

Missy and The Geekster exchanged shy smiles and handshakes. Why couldn't *they* be the ad couple instead of Missy and Stud? Then Cynthia would be free to drag Stud home to her cave and ravish him.

The four of them sat down in the booth and opened large egg-shaped menus, filled with cartoon drawings, pictures of greasy food and painful why-did-the-chicken-cross-the-road jokes.

Cynthia hid a grimace. Practically every entrée was deep-fried, served with fries or smothered in a cream sauce. Every salad was loaded with saturated fat: chicken strips, tortillas, bacon, sour cream or gunky cheese dressings. She rarely ate food like that, and in her current totally unfamiliar state of unrest, she would still be digesting this meal by the end of the month.

``So.'' The Stud hurled the syllable into the awkward silence. Missy, Geek and Cynthia looked at him expectantly. "What looks good here?"

Cynthia's eyes narrowed speculatively. A hopeful sign. "You haven't been to Chicken Curly's before?"

He smiled, which made his dark brown eyes slant down at the corners. Very, very sexy. "A friend's suggestion. What do you recommend?"

"Chicken Came First turnovers, extra gravy and fries." Missy and the Geek said the words at the exact same time, stared at each other in surprise, then burst into laughter.

"*What* are Chicken Came First turnovers?" Cynthia glanced at Stud, wondering if she could get away with a chicken orgasm joke. He grinned and shook his head, almost as if he'd been reading her mind.

"Chicken stuffed with cream cheese in cream sauce wrapped in butter pastry with pan gravy." Missy patted her stomach which, predictably, drew the attention of both men to her chest and made Cynthia put Wonderbras on a mental shopping list.

"I call them Chicken Curly fat bombs." Geek made the announcement proudly and Missy laughed so hard she had to cover her mouth with her hands.

"Fat bombs." Cynthia's blood thickened at the thought. She searched her menu desperately for something she could stomach.

"So, Missy." The deep voice resonated over the table.

No answer. Cynthia looked expectantly at Missy, who kicked her.

She took a deep breath. Okay. Time to pull herself together. Coming face-to-face with The Stud of Life and the concept of chicken fat bombs in one evening had flustered her, the Great Unflusterable One. Not for nothing was she called Ice Empress at Atkeson, Inc. She was Missy for the day. Her date was a geek in a stud's body. She'd be eating ninety-seven percent of the evening's calories from fat.

No problem.

"Yes?" She smiled coolly.

"I enjoyed your response to my ad." Stud put his elbows on the table and leaned forward, which made her want to do the same. "Do you answer personals all the time?"

She gave a snort of laughter. "No way."

Missy cleared her throat and turned her lovely blue gaze on Stud. "She's never answered an ad before, Ken. But this one called to her, as if someone wrote it just for her, across all boundaries, across time itself."

Geek and Stud both snapped their heads over to Missy, then snapped them back to Cynthia like spectators at a Ping-Pong match.

Cynthia silently cheered Missy on. The sooner Stud fell for her, the sooner they could confess the lie and get the hell out of this ridiculous situation.

"Oh." Stud narrowed his gaze on Cynthia. "Is that so?"

"Yeah." Cynthia nodded. "What she said."

Stud looked at her quizzically, as if he couldn't

quite believe she was the person she said she was.
Which was most likely because she *wasn't* the person
she said she was. He'd figure out soon that unlike the
real Missy, she lived in a goo-free zone. Then she
could go home, eat her own food and have some hope
of a normal life expectancy.

"Your answer to his ad touched me, too." Geek
stared at Cynthia adoringly. "As if your words could
reach through my body and wrap themselves around
my heart."

"Oh my." Missy's head snapped over to Geek,
then back to Stud.

Cynthia sighed. Figured Stud would have brought
a friend who also hailed from Goo Planet.
"Well...good. Words that can get into your body
are...good. Maybe you've opened some frontiers in
surgery for—"

"Howdy ho, Curly customers!" The waitress arrived at the table, beaming as if she'd never seen such
wonderful friends in all her life.

"Howdy ho, Curly server!" Geek and Missy
shouted out the words in tandem.

Cynthia snuck a glance at Stud to see how he handled such excesses of perkiness. By the frozen horror
on his face, which he quickly hid behind a smile,
she'd say not terribly well. Interesting. He must be
one of those intellectual brooding romantics. Missy
would love that. Missy would adore that. Missy could
focus all her efforts on bringing joy and chicken fat
into his life.

He turned his eyes on Cynthia while her glance was still mid-sneak. She managed to muster a friendly grin into those deep magnetic eyes, but again had to drop her gaze first. *Why* was this attraction so damn powerful? Was this heart-pounding brain-scrambling reaction what the other girls felt during their Manhunter moments? Why the *hell* was Cynthia the only one to feel it over someone already taken—by one of her best friends, no less?

Of course her confusion could just stem from attraction complicated by guilt. After all, Missy flipped over Stud's ad and he flipped over her response, and here was Cynthia wanting to take him home to enter the Multiple Orgasm Olympics. That could confuse anyone.

"Now what would you all like from the henhouse today?"

Cynthia gestured at Missy, who ordered a small Cock-a-Doodle soup and Chicken Came First turnovers.

"Chicken…came…*first!*" The waitress scribbled on her pad, still beaming. "And *you,* ma'am! What would *you* like from the henhouse today?"

"Hmmm." Cynthia tapped her finger to her lips and decided the woman could use a little friendly deperking. "I'll have the Henny Penny chicken salad, dressing on the side, and to start I'd like the Cock-a-doodle soup, too. And can you write down that I'd like a really *big* order of Cock-a-doodle soup and that I like my Cock-a-doodle soup really *hot?*"

"Oh, *sure!* At Chicken Curly's the customer *always* flaps away happy! I'll write it right down!" She beamed again and wrote Cynthia's order on her pad. "One big, hot coc—"

Stud coughed suddenly into his fist. Missy kicked Cynthia under the table. Geek looked confused. The poor waitress turned bright red and wrote down the rest of the order in silence.

Cynthia kept her expression scrupulously innocent. That was *too* easy. She might even be able to enjoy herself.

Forty-five minutes later, after they'd made dents in their meals, it became apparent that she wasn't going to enjoy herself. Geek was practically breathing fat bomb fumes down Cynthia's neck, even sitting cater-corner across the table; Missy was obviously way-smitten with Stud, not hard to tell why; and in spite of Cynthia's continuing efforts to throw Stud Missy's way, her own attraction was only growing. He was funny, charming and obviously intelligent. If only he'd spout some more of that knight-and-his-lady garbage, Cynthia could become comfortably nauseated and remind herself what kind of a guy he was.

To top it off, when she thought at least she'd gotten used to the horror that was Chicken Curly's, Chicken Curly's got more horrible. A huge gong rang out, practically making her spit Henny Penny chicken salad back into its egg-shaped bowl. Missy and Geek immediately started bouncing up and down, shouting,

"Hoedown! Hoedown!" along with the waitstaff and other assorted idiot patrons.

She lifted an eyebrow at Stud who lifted one back, enough to make her want to throw him to the floor and do naughty things to his big, hot Cock-a-doodle soup.

Then just when she'd started to realize, in the middle of her lustfest, that she'd be expected to dance some goofy corny dance with a man she wanted to be ravishingly graceful and sensual for, Missy scooted over, nudged Cynthia out of the booth, and crossed to Stud with totally uncharacteristic boldness, as if she'd already picked out their wedding colors. "It's a hoedown. Everyone gets to dance!"

Cynthia pressed her hand to her forehead and groaned. "Let me guess. The Funky Chicken."

Geek sidled up to her and took her arm. "Oh, so you've been here before!"

One wistful glance over at Stud escaped from her control before she allowed herself to be led onto the dance floor, but not before she mouthed, *help* and got a fabulous grin in response. He definitely didn't belong here any more than she did. The two of them belonged in her apartment. On the bed. Doing the funky chicken in their own special way.

The dancing started. She moved to the beat, refusing to do *that* dance, and smiled at Geek, suddenly enjoying herself because *nothing* in the world was funnier than watching Geek dance. Nothing. And with all the other families and couples crowding the dance floor, flapping their elbows, she could quite happily pretend she'd landed in her worst nightmare and would soon wake up and have a bracing breakfast. At least the dance wasn't intimate. At least she didn't have to see Stud take Missy into his arms.

She peeked over at him again, apparently unable to keep her eyes off him, and wasn't particularly surprised that he could make a rooster imitation sexy. Not that he was so fabulously graceful, but he was grinning and unselfconscious and…into it.

She sighed. Maybe he was perfect for Missy after all. How many more signs did she need? Except for the wild yearning he produced that made her—

"Hey, folks." An announcer voice boomed over the restaurant PA system. "Are you having a rootin-tootin' good time?"

"Yes!" the crowd shouted.

"Okay. All you families skedaddle back to your tables. We're going to change the pace now, have an adults-only slow-struttin' rooster waltz."

Her enjoyment died a swift painful death. Slow dance. Ick.

Geek advanced, arms outstretched, his long skinny nose morphing in her imagination to look like a yellow rooster beak. She sighed, closed her eyes and allowed him to lead, reminding herself she was doing this for Missy. Except then she thought about Missy in Stud's arms and wanted to cackle at the injustice.

"You are lovely like the night sky, Missy." He gathered her closer into his surprisingly strong arms;

she moved back as politely as possible. "I confess I am totally smitten."

"Adam—"

"I know it seems too much too soon, but can I ask you a favor?"

Oh, help. "You can ask, sure."

"Could I have a token of our first meeting, milady? That I might carry with me into the jousting tournament of life? A ribbon, a kerchief, a lock of your hair?"

She scrunched up her face in bewilderment. Where did these medieval people time warp from? "I have a used tissue in my pocket, would that be okay?"

He drew back and looked at her curiously. He did have really nice blue eyes once you could look into them through his glasses. Under the major geek exterior he was probably a sincere and forthright and sensitive...major geek.

He shook his head, obviously confused and pulled her close again. She resisted. He trailed his fingers across the back of her neck and she considered forcefully introducing her knee to his fly. *Here's a token, baby.*

"May I cut in?"

The deep voice behind her entered her body and took a slow, sexy sightseeing tour. She closed her eyes for a second to process the thrill. Man, she loved that feeling.

"You want to dance with her?" Geek gave his friend a not-at-all-friendly look.

"She did respond to *my* ad."

"Yeah, right. I forgot. *Your* ad." Geek glanced over at Missy who was standing next to Stud looking sort of bewildered, as if nothing was quite the way it should be. Apparently Stud hadn't left her quite as glowing leaving the dance floor as leading her on to it.

Cynthia squashed down any evil pleasure the thought brought her. She was *not* going to stand in the way of Missy's happiness because of a few wayward hormones. Though why Stud would want to dance with Cynthia when he had the goo-love of his life right there....

Stop! No hope allowed. Not until she got the word straight from Missy's mouth that *she* wasn't interested. Cynthia wouldn't even begin to allow herself to go there.

Stud handed Missy gracefully off to Geek and stepped in front of Cynthia. He took her into his arms as if he not only had title to her, but also an ownership manual which he'd studied carefully. Nothing she liked better than a man who had that kind of confidence. Who simply took what he wanted of her as long as it was relinquished gladly.

And she was feeling extremely gladly relinquishing, though she'd draw the line at outright propositioning.

"So, Missy." He drew her into the dance, not a real high-school slow dance, but a down-tempo number. "What do you think of Chicken Curly?"

"Appalling." She grinned up at him. "What do you think?"

"Harmless fun." He held up his arm and guided her in a slow turn. "What really bothers me is you."

"Me?"

"I can't figure you out."

She suppressed a shiver of excitement that he'd been trying, even knowing he meant she didn't measure up to his romantic expectations. "How's that?"

"You don't seem like the type to respond to my ad."

"Well, I guess I'm just chock-full of surprises."

He grinned, a lazy do-me-now grin that made her practically fall off her heels. "Surprise me, then. Tell me something about you I couldn't guess."

She sighed. Might as well drive the last nail into the coffin of his hopes. Time to let him know she wasn't a dreamy-eyed maiden waiting around in her ivory tower for His Knightship. "I'm the best damn businesswoman in the city."

"Really." He spun her again and pulled her closer to avoid a couple behind them.

"I work for Atkeson, Inc. We investigate businesses for venture capital firms, see if they'd be investing their money wisely." She tensed her arm to avoid pressing closer and running her fingers over his shoulder to test its strength. "Does that surprise you?"

"No. Try again."

``Hmmm.'' She wrinkled her brow at him. ``How about…I'm going to win the Foster Award this year.''

He grimaced. ``A waste of energy.''

``Excuse me?'' She stiffened in his arms. ``Do you have any idea what winning that award can do for a career?''

``Ah!'' He quirked a devilish eyebrow. ``But what can it do for your soul?''

Cynthia rolled her eyes. There. Finally. The goo, damn him. Why couldn't he be perfect for *her?* ``My soul doesn't need shelter and three meals a day.''

``I bet you'd be surprised what your soul needs.''

``Oh, really?'' She gave him a challenging half grin, swaying to the music. ``Surprise me, then.''

He narrowed his eyes as if he were considering her at an auction. ``Let me get to know you better, first.''

``Deal.'' She kept her expression bland while a sensual shiver made the rounds of her body. It wasn't what he said so much as the way he said it. As if he conjugated the verb ``to know'' in ways not allowed in public. ``Now your turn. Surprise me with something I couldn't guess.''

He chuckled. ``Okay. Let's see. My family has enough money to buy small countries in South America.''

``Impressive, but not surprising.''

``No?''

``You have that air of privilege.''

``I *did* shower.''

She laughed. ``Try again.''

"Okay. I *was* the best damn businessman in Milwaukee."

"Before I replaced you?" She smiled teasingly. "What did you do?"

"Same thing I do now. I manage my family's money. Oversee our investments and the Bradson Foundation."

Cynthia rolled her eyes. "Sitting on a mountain of cash, throwing out bills to the starving rest of us?"

"Something like that."

"So…" She tipped her head to look up at his face. "What changed?"

"I had a heart attack three years ago at age thirty-two."

Her jaw dropped.

"Surprise." He grinned and widened the gap between them since the couple behind them had moved on.

Cynthia swallowed the weird lump in her throat and held herself tight so she wouldn't move closer again. *Get a grip, woman.* "Are you okay now?"

"Fine. There was minimal damage. But it brought home all those clichés about brushes with death showing you what's important."

Cynthia narrowed her eyes. "Are you about to tell me that what I want in life isn't important? Because I don't sit still for that lecture."

"I won't say a word. It's your turn again. Surprise me."

She let a minute go by, pretending to consider, but

savoring the feel of his hands on her and the graceful way they moved together. ``I grew up without anything. My family couldn't even buy a bus ticket to one of those South American countries you own.''

``Ah, that explains it.''

She frowned. ``What?''

``Your hunger.''

She shot him a seductive look before she realized what she was doing and turned it into a polite querying one. ``What do you know about my hunger?''

``That it's deep. Strong. Ravenous. And that the food you are going after won't ever fill you up.''

``This sounds like a lecture.'' She curled her lip. ``Are you one of those guys who thinks claiming he knows more about a woman than she does is sexy? Because frankly that attitude pisses me right off.''

He chuckled. ``And you know why that attitude pisses you right off?''

``Yes. But not the reason you think it does. Not because you're right. Because it's arrogant and meddling.''

He nodded. ``You're right. I apologize. Shall we go back to the table and join the others?''

Cynthia's insides contracted. *Ouch!* And she was just beginning to enjoy the fight. Maybe he wasn't as tough as he looked. She adored a good verbal battle with a worthy adversary. ``Not up for the full fifteen rounds?''

He grinned and swept his arm around the dance

floor. ``The hoedown is over and we're the only people standing out here.''

Cynthia blinked and glanced at the empty space around her. She'd been totally oblivious to anything but the man. Since when was she not aware of every detail of her surroundings? Her dad had called her Commando when she was a girl.

Confused and unsettled, she walked with him back to the table where Missy and Geek were laughing over some doubtless goofy joke. Cynthia *never* felt confused and unsettled. Not since she'd figured out who she was and what she wanted from a very early age. Since then she'd simply identified the steps required to achieve her goals and gone for them methodically, one by one.

They reached the table. Geek turned lovelorn hopeful eyes to Cynthia, and Missy did the same to the man standing beside Cynthia. A man whose body radiated warmth and strength she could feel without touching him. Whose mind intrigued her the way few mens' minds did. Bodies, sure, she could get intrigued by bodies in a heartbeat. But there was something different about this guy. A combination of the typical hard-driving career man she recognized, and a softer person who worried about his soul and hers, who'd been able and willing to pour his heart out to a newspaper ad in the most revolting romantic drivel imaginable.

She sat and again lost the battle to keep herself from glancing into his eyes, a glance that stuck there and held while the chemistry between them scorched her insides clean of everything but wanting.

He broke the gaze instantly when Missy spoke to him and leaned over to hear her better, answered, smiled and chuckled warmly.

Cynthia sank back against the booth and stared mournfully at the remains of her Henny Penny salad.

Missy and the Stud. That damn ad.

For the first time in many, many years, Ms. Cynthia Parkins desperately wanted something she had a feeling she couldn't have.

3

MISSY SIGHED and tapped a sheaf of papers on her desk to straighten the edges. What was the matter with her? She usually worked with the high level of concentration and energy befitting a statistician employed at Atkeson, Inc. But today for some reason she just couldn't summon any enthusiasm. Friday afternoons were always the pits. And to be honest, she was kind of distracted. She'd been distracted all week.

After last Saturday night, meeting that totally hunky Ken and everything…well what were the odds he'd turn out to be someone so *gorgeous?* Usually guys who were on her wavelength, romantically speaking, looked more like the other guy, Adam. Of course he was cute, too, in his own way. And pretty funny a few times. But he wasn't her soul mate. Only the man who'd written that ad could fill that role.

She giggled and stretched back in her chair. Who would *ever* think that she, Missy Beckworth, would have her very own Manhunt to go on! And with someone who looked like a movie star! Tracy, Allegra and Cynthia probably never thought she'd even manage to trap a nerd. Heck, *she* never thought she'd manage. But here she was, hell-bent on getting under

Hunky Ken's gorgeous tall, dark and handsome exterior to find the perfect match within. Funny how he hadn't really let his romantic side out the other night. When she tried to connect with him while they were dancing, he'd seemed sort of embarrassed.

And even though he did think Cynthia was the one who answered his ad, it hadn't felt really terrific when he'd wanted to dance with her, because she obviously thought he was cute, too. Imagine! Some guy meant for *her* that Cynthia wanted. She still couldn't believe it. Not that she'd want Cynthia to feel bad ever. Cynthia was a really good friend. And even though she was so sexy and so aggressive with guys, Missy totally trusted her to keep her hands off Missy's man.

Missy's man. She giggled. What a great phrase. Of course, come to think of it, she did have a good time dancing with his less-gorgeous friend. He was really easy to talk to, and a great dancer. That was good that she liked him. She wanted to like all her future husband's friends.

At any rate, she knew Hunky Ken was shy, and that's probably why he didn't let his romantic side out. Even shyer than *she* was if anyone could imagine such a thing. Except on Saturday she'd felt so *bold,* so comfortable, so excited to be facing the man who inscribed those beautiful words straight onto her heart. Her soul mate probably just needed a little more encouragement. Good thing they'd made another date for the four of them for next Monday night!

She glanced at her watch and rolled her eyes. Oh,

gosh, this day was going to take for-*ever*. Maybe she could take half a vacation day, or a quarter of one, even, and get out of here. She had about a million days saved up, waiting for that perfect romantic vacation that never quite seemed to materialize. And as hard as she worked and with her near-perfect attendance record, except for that time she got the flu last winter, she probably wouldn't even get in trouble.

Go for it, Missy.

She giggled at her unaccustomed daring and headed off to personnel, where that really nice Mr. Henley worked. If only he'd talk to her face instead of her chest.

Nice Mr. Henley gave her breasts the rest of the day off and she gathered her things and left the building, feeling as if she were emerging from an egg or a cocoon or something.

This was so great!

She wasn't really even sure where she was going except that she really could use a giant frozen custard cone to get the afternoon rolling.

She stopped into Andy's on Old World 3rd Street and bought a double turtle cone, then took it outside to eat on one of the benches set down low by the river. *So nice!* Even if melting ice cream eventually dripped onto her chest the way it always did. That's all she needed. A big blotch on her nicest flowery sundress.

She took a big wonderful lick and closed her eyes

to let out an equally big wonderful sigh of contentment, when a shadow fell over her.

"Cynthia?"

Oh, gosh. Only two people in the world thought
her name was Cynthia, and though unfortunately the
voice hadn't been deep and sexy enough to belong to
her soul mate, it must belong to his nice friend, Adam.

She squinted up at him, and smiled when she saw
him holding the exact same kind of cone she had. A
double and everything. "Hi, Adam."

"Can I join you?"

"Sure." She patted the seat beside her. *Too perfect!* She could get to know the man of her dreams
through Adam. She could find out more about Hunky
Ken, so she could get through his shyness to the perfect man she knew waited for her underneath.

Adam lowered himself to the bench and turned to
smile at her and her ice cream. "Great minds think
alike."

She couldn't help smiling back. He had a really
nice smile. And really nice blue eyes to go with it.
He wore green shorts and cool scuffed hiking boots
and a nice neat bright yellow cotton shirt with a collar. He looked really gentle and friendly and sweet.
"It was too beautiful to stay inside."

"That's exactly how *I* felt!"

"Really?" She laughed and found herself staring
into those really nice blue eyes *way* too long. What
was she doing? "I had a great time the other night."

"Me too."

She took a cool bite of her ice cream, aware of his eyes on her. For some strange reason, she wanted to stick out her tongue and lick really sexily like she'd seen people do in the movies. Crazy idea. "Your friend seems very nice."

He took his eyes off her and leaned back against the bench with his strong-looking legs splayed out so one thigh nearly touched her dress. "Your friend does, too."

Missy blinked. She could have sworn she heard him sigh wistfully at the exact same time she did. They were like *twins* or something. "So what is he like? I mean, my *friend* really wants to know, since she absolutely *loved* his ad."

"She did?" He took a long lick of his ice-cream cone. Missy found herself watching his tongue on the ice cream and she started feeling very…warm. "What did she say about it? The ad, I mean."

"She said…" Missy wrinkled her nose. Did she dare share her response to the ad with this guy? He might laugh. Except that she felt awfully safe with him. Not the way she usually did around guys. Even if he thought she was corny like the girls did, Missy knew instinctively he'd be polite. And he *had* said a few really sweet romantic things the other night at the restaurant. It figured that Hunky Ken would have a friend as sensitive and sweet as he was inside. "She said that his words touched her heart. That reading the ad was like coming home. Like hearing from someone she'd carried in her heart all her life, just knowing that someday she and he would be together...forever.''

''Oh, *wow.*''

She turned, almost weepy with gratitude at his appreciation for her words, expecting to find him gazing dreamily off into space, thinking romantic thoughts. Instead, he was gazing at *her,* and that warm and melty feeling got a whole lot more warm and...meltier. ''So what did *your* friend say when he heard the response to his ad?''

''He said...he said the signal he'd sent out into the world had been read by the one person it was destined for.'' His voice thickened with emotion. Ice cream began to drip over the edge of his cone and onto his long, nicely shaped fingers. ''He said hearing back from your friend made his world suddenly whole, brought pieces together he didn't even know were missing, to make a complete picture of his soul.''

''Oh, *wow.*'' Missy tried to stare dreamily off into space, imagining the dark handsome picture of male perfection she'd met so recently saying those wonderful things about her words, but instead found herself staring dreamily at the man next to her. When he talked that way it was as if *he* was saying the words, instead of quoting Hunky Ken. Jeepers, she'd have to be careful to keep it straight. ''He's so poetic! Missy has flipped over him.''

''Yeah. He's such a good guy. He works so hard.'' He licked the sides of his cone clean and extracted a wet wipe from his fanny pack to take care of his sticky fingers. "Can I tell you a secret?"

Missy jerked her gaze up from his really quite beautiful hands. "Of course."

"My friend. I did him a favor. On the sly."

"Ooh, *what?*" She leaned closer to catch his low voice and noticed his gaze flicking down to her chest. For some reason she didn't mind so much when he looked. In fact she leaned forward more, practically hyperventilating with excitement. She'd never done this in her *life*. At least not with someone she barely knew. Meeting Hunky Ken the other night and hearing how he felt about her response to his ad must have given her all kinds of female confidence she'd only dreamed about having.

Adam waggled his bushy blond eyebrows up and down. "I entered him into an award competition without telling him. He's too modest. He never brags enough about what he does for this community. And he's done a lot for me, too."

"Oh." Missy laid her hand on his arm. Then she stared at it, lying white and nervous on his tanned, slightly hairy skin. She couldn't believe she was touching him. But it felt so normal. "You are such a good person to do that for him."

"You think so?"

"Yes. I do." She found herself staring into his eyes again. What was her deal today? They must have put something in her ice cream. "My friend wants an award, too. Really badly."

He scrunched up his face in what looked kind of like horror. "She *does?*"

"Yes." Missy looked at him curiously. "What's wrong with that?"

"Nothing, nothing." He frowned and shook his head. "It's not what I expected from her."

"What do you mean?"

"Oh, nothing. Nothing." He crunched down on his cone and she couldn't help noticing his teeth. Even his teeth were really nice. She couldn't stand bad teeth.

They finished their ice-cream cones in silence. But not hostile silence. Nice comfortable silence, which baffled Missy. Usually she hated silence. Silence meant she was failing, that she wasn't interesting enough, that she couldn't think of anything to say. But this felt fine. It felt okay. They weren't "not talking," they were just eating instead.

She was supposed to be spending the time finding out about his friend, her life destiny. But for some reason she didn't want to. Silence with this man felt so good.

"That hit the spot." He cleaned his fingers again with the used wipe, offered her a fresh one with a smile, and the warm melty feeling inside her got an added dose of fluttery.

She accepted the cloth and rubbed her fingers and mouth. What were the odds after a lifetime of unrequited crushes and unfulfilling relationships that she could be attracted to two guys at once. Two guys who seemed to be interested back? One tall and movie-star gorgeous, whose ad showed clearly that he was her destiny—though she had some breaking through to do in person—and one simple honest-seeming guy whose smile made her insides wobbly.

If only she could combine the two, she had a feeling she'd never want for love again.

"RICHARD, I'D LIKE—"

"Please. Call me Dick."

Believe me, I already do. Cynthia adjusted the phone to her ear and gritted her teeth. "I won't pretend we don't have some concerns about IT Consulting. I'm of course trying to represent you in the best possible light to the—"

"My left side is my best. And I do well in candlelight. Across a dinner table. For two."

Cynthia made a face that would best belong on a superheroine named Countess Castrator. The man was *impossible* to talk to. "I wonder if you could be a little more specific about the competitive advantage your company has in the marketplace."

"We're the best."

She could practically hear the shrug of his shoulders that accompanied the remark. "I'm afraid that's not quite good enough for—"

"It's good enough for me."

"Rich—"

"Dick."

"*Dick.* Unless we can show in more detail how

your company compares favorably to its chief competitors, we can't—''

''Look, honey. In three years, I've taken this company from nothing to forty-three million in revenues. Your investor friends don't need to know anything more than that. Other companies can't touch me.''

''I understand that—''

''But *you* can.''

Cynthia took the phone away from her ear and stared as if it had spouted green alien ooze. ''Mr. Crosh—Richa—Dick. This is totally inappropriate. I want to work with you, but I would appreciate it if you would keep our relationship professional.''

''I want to work with you, too, Cindy. And we'll see where our relationship goes, okay?''

Cynthia ended the call with icy politeness and hung up in disgust. Snivelling, parasitic, mutated, gender-bending, gnat-faced dog-person.

Richard Croshallis, Boy Wonder. As in—wonder if he's a boy? Or a rat. The man was making their investigation nearly impossible. Little hints were emerging that indicated his company might be on shaky ground, that his judgment might not be the best. Which might leave her having to recommend that VF Capital not invest in his firm. Which might lead Dick Crotchless to recommend to his father that she not get the Foster Award.

She swiveled in her chair and gazed out the window at the Milwaukee River. For one strange moment she had a tremendous urge to be out of this office, heading for the lake in shorts and a bikini top, to hang out on someone's yacht with a giant frosty mug of beer in her hand and a keg on standby. Not to mention someone who looked a lot like Stud beckoning to her from the cabin, wearing nothing but a smile.

Oh no, not again. She'd had a tough time since their date last weekend. Missy had done nothing but glow over Stud and his ad. Which spelled hands- and thoughts-off for Cynthia. The truth was, she'd always been so good at tamping down attraction when she needed to. The few times she'd been superficially attracted to married men, she'd chopped the feelings off at their first showing, without mercy and without much trouble. But all the usual suppression techniques weren't working in Stud's case, and she hadn't a clue why. He was gorgeous, but not so much more gorgeous than other men she knew. He had an attractive personality as well, but so had dozens of men she dated. Then on the negative side, he had that gooey streak a mile wide. That alone proved he was totally wrong for her, even without Missy in the picture.

Enough. She needed to refocus on her job and forget Stud and forget her escape fantasy. She loved her work, relished the challenges. Richard Croshallis was merely another pesky speed bump on the road to success. She didn't need a vacation, she needed to buckle down and come up with a strategy for how she'd string Dicky along in case VF Capital decided against investing while the Foster committee was still debating. She couldn't recommend his company for investment with the current problems. Questionable hiring practices, a management team shut out of big decisions, too much money and time planned for acquisitions. Not a pretty picture.

She needed solutions. She needed strategies. She needed… She needed…

Below her, the gates on the drawbridge across the Milwaukee River descended to stop street traffic; the drawbridge rose slowly to allow a stunning white yacht to pass. A tall man with dark hair stood at the wheel, carefully steering the ship. Not *him.* But a vague resemblance. Enough to set her heart pounding like an adolescent with puppy love.

She needed…

Cynthia stood, put her blue-green suit jacket on over her ivory silk shell, patted her hair into place and grabbed her purse.

She needed that beer.

``WELL, I'M NOT SURE.'' The quavery old-woman voice on the phone held a hint of impatience. ``Next week looks pretty busy.''

``I understand, Mrs. Lemmingster.'' Adam pitched his voice to a purr of persuasive sympathy while on his desk pad he doodled an admittedly childish big-nosed, buck-toothed caricature of the elderly benefactress. ``You give so much of your time and talent to the city, no wonder your schedule is full.''

``I believe what goes around comes around. The

Lemmingsters have always been pillars of this community.''

"Indeed they have." He made his voice at once hearty and slightly awestruck and added devil's horns to his caricature and flames shooting out of her eyes. "But I'd love to take you to Lake Park Bistro and talk about the community center. Or does a lovely lady like you already have a full week of dinner dates lined up?"

Mrs. Lemmingster emitted a ghastly creaking sound, probably supposed to be a girlish giggle. "Oh, you flatterer."

Adam chuckled along with her and added a stealth bomber to his artwork. "So do we have a date? Wednesday, August fifth?"

"Well…"

"The city needs you! I need you!"

She cackled again. "All right, young man. Wednesday, the fifth. Pick me up at seven."

"It's a date." Adam chopped his smile off with a grimace and hung up the phone. Negotiations. Ego-stroking. Manipulation. Sometimes he wanted to say, "Look, building a community center in the inner city is a good idea that will benefit everyone so fork over the damn cash and shut up."

But no. Mr. Pennypincher needed his ego stroked. Mrs. Too-rich needed her flattery. Mr. and Mrs. Big Corporation needed endless assaults for Adam's cause to be noticed among all the others with their hands out. All of his targets needed wining and dining and assurances of their importance to the community, of their ongoing involvement in the project, of their visibility. His own family's foundation could only pour so much money into the city. The rest had to come from other sources.

He got up from his desk and walked to the window. Gorgeous day. Not hot. Not humid. Perfect day to blow off work and grab a beer at the Rock Bottom Café. Watch the river slide by. Watch people. Man wasn't meant to stay in an office building on a beautiful Friday afternoon. Life was simply too short to deny oneself simple and easily available pleasures. He could make the rest of his calls on Monday.

He swiped his suit jacket off the back of his chair, grabbed his Palm Pilot and headed for the door. Out on Old World 3rd Street, he sniffed the sausage-making smells from Usinger's factory and descended the steps down to Riverwalk, the low walkway that rambled beside the river through Milwaukee's downtown. The Rock Bottom Café had outdoor tables beside the water, perfect for a late July afternoon drink.

Most of the tables were full when he arrived, doubtless the weather had planted the same idea of escape into other people's minds. He scanned the crowd briefly, then zeroed in on the back of a shapely brunette head.

Missy?

He almost laughed. What were the odds? He hadn't been able to get her out of his mind all week. Something about her totally intrigued him, beyond the obvious fact that she had a dynamite body, beautiful face and radiated intelligence. Never in Adam's wildest dreams did he expect the woman who answered Ken's nauseating ad to resemble his every fantasy of woman.

Of course Ken was nuts over her, which spelled do-not-enter for Adam. The poor sop had barely taken his eyes off her all evening and had even emerged from his usual passive state to shoot daggers at Adam when Adam couldn't resist the temptation to dance with her.

Unfortunately, the time he'd spent with her in his arms only increased his confusion. Because to look at her and talk to her, you'd think she was a hardboiled warrior woman, jolted by a past of poverty into achieving success at any price. She had to have been badly hurt at some point to be so good at hiding the overly romantic soul capable of pouring such syrupy sentiment into the response to an anonymous newspaper ad. He hadn't been able to tap into the soft middle under her armor, hadn't even begun to be able to figure out her enticing puzzle.

He grinned and walked over to her table, signaling his arrival to the waitress. But even keeping in mind she was Ken's territory, he'd be damned if he wasn't absolutely crazy to try.

4

"HOW ABOUT ANOTHER?" Adam watched Missy as she set down her second empty glass. She could attack a pint of beer with determination he rarely saw. Not weakness that would suggest a problem with alcohol. Strength. As if the excellent microbrewery beer was a foe to be conquered, drunk up before it had the chance to be anything but a part of her. He wasn't sure she'd even bothered to stop and taste it.

She reminded him of someone.

"Sure. I'll take another." She smiled coolly and settled back into her seat, raising her face to the late afternoon sunlight. He wished it was cloudy so she'd take off her sunglasses and he could see her dark eyes. He wished it was warmer so she'd take off her jacket and he could see more of her skin. Hell, he wished they were in his bed making it like ravenous love beetles. How could a woman like this be right for Ken?

So far they'd chatted impersonally about the business community in Milwaukee. Who they both knew. Where those people were going. How far they'd get. Right now he was itching to get personal. Extremely personal. He couldn't remember having this primal a reaction in a long time. Either he was getting desperate or he and this lovely woman were a sexual explosion waiting to happen.

Except that while he couldn't stop shifting in his seat, adjusting his cocktail napkin, tapping his foot, she sat there, still and graceful, unshaken and unstirred by alcohol or emotion, even under the impression he was her newspaper-ad soul mate. But inside that slim sexy unmovable rock he bet there was volcanic activity. Or at least a soft core. The woman who wrote the response to Ken's ad was in there somewhere. He wanted at her.

Their beers arrived; she raised hers to him, took a long swallow, and thumped the glass back down on the table exactly in the middle of her napkin. That feeling he'd seen her before, or someone like her, increased.

"Do you attack everything with that kind of determination?"

Her eyebrows shot up from behind her sunglasses. "I guess I do, yes."

"You never sit back and let things wash over you? Never allow words like 'linger' and 'savor' into your life's vocabulary?"

She folded her arms across her chest. "Are we starting with this lecture again?"

"Yes."

A smile worked its way onto her full mouth. "Maybe you should let me live my life the way I want and I'll let you live yours the way you want. Deal?''

He put his arms on the table and leaned toward her. ''What if I think you should live your life the way I live mine?''

Only one eyebrow made it over the top of her sunglasses this time. ''Then I'll probably say something to you along the lines of 'butt out, buddy.'''

He grinned. '' 'Butt out?' This from the woman who wrote, 'I will be your lady, I will ride with you down the path of—''

''Yeah, well, that was a moment of weakness.''

He tapped a finger on her linen-covered forearm, wishing he could stroke and explore instead. ''I'd like to see more of that weakness.''

''Don't hold your breath.'' She lifted her beer and drained half of it. ''I only play the knight-and-lady gig for men who don't try to change me ten seconds after they meet me.''

Adam narrowed his eyes. He couldn't imagine anyone holding herself so tightly without cracking. And yet, he could imagine it. Because he'd seen it somewhere. Felt it...

She was exactly the way he used to be.

Out of nowhere with the realization came an overwhelming, strangely tender desire to help her. Show her how good life could be when you relaxed and let it happen instead of always trying to force it.

''Okay. How about if I stop trying to change you. Will you let that weakness out for me to see?''

She stopped with her glass up to her mouth and put it down slowly and deliberately this time, her movements graceful and feminine. One slender perfectly manicured hand rose to her temple and removed her sunglasses. Her eyes were the deep soul-piercing brown he remembered and unless his male radar had malfunctioned, they were flashing sex signs a mile high.

"Honey," her voice came out a soft seductive drawl, as if she'd morphed into a Southern belle. "If you stop trying to change me, I'd let just about anything out for you to see."

He swallowed. *Ken's woman. Ken's woman. Ken's...*

Oh, hell. Ken didn't deserve a woman like this. He wouldn't know the first thing about how to handle her.

He leaned back, as if he was calmly considering her offer, trying to pretend her words hadn't shot him to the moon and back. "I don't know about that. Because I think you need some serious...relaxing."

She laughed and finished the last of her beer as if it were sexual ambrosia. "So you think you give good *relaxation?*" She said the word as if it had a different meaning altogether.

"I know I do."

"Hmm. What most guys don't know about me and...*relaxing,* is that the more relaxing they give me...the more relaxing I want. Which doesn't end up being very relaxing." She put her glasses back on, then tipped them down her nose and peered at him over the top. "Does it."

"I guess not." He grabbed for his beer, feeling himself start to get hard under the table. She damn well better be doing the female equivalent under her side. He hated teases. "But I was actually talking about real relaxing."

"Oh?" Either she had X-ray vision and could see under the table, or his eyes and body language were giving him away because she clearly didn't believe him.

"Not that I don't think relaxing you in *that* particular manner could have its benefits. But I was thinking of trying other methods."

"Oh." She wrinkled her nose and put the sunglasses back down on the table. "Like long contemplative walks in the rain and evenings discussing Chaucer over a glass of Port in front of a roaring fire?"

He chuckled. "Wrong again."

She tipped her head to one side, obviously curious, and he congratulated himself at the same time condemning himself for being so smug. He hadn't felt this alive in a long time. Hadn't been engaged in a sexual power struggle that excited him this much since...ever.

"Would you like another beer?"

She shrugged, but he detected a hint of disappointment at the change of subject. "Sure."

He made her wait until the beer had been served,

feeling the alcohol warming his own veins, and wondering how a woman nearly half his weight could manage with so few signs of intoxication. Except that she was softening a little. The lines around her mouth had eased. A hair or two dared escape from that tight twisty thing she had going on at the back of her head. And her accent slipped from time to time, allowing glimpses of North Carolina, aside from her deliberate use of the Southern drawl when she was teasing him.

"First…" He lifted his glass and took a cold bubbly sip, then licked the foam off his lips, aware of her watching him intently.

"First?"

He suppressed a grin at her impatience and made sure his words came out slowly. "First, I'd want your hair down."

"Oh, you would, would you." The scorn in her voice almost completely covered a breathless quality. She made a dent in her own beer, then put her hand to her hair, pulled out a pin or two and shook her head so rich brown hair tumbled around her face. "Next?"

He tightened his lips, daring himself not to react visibly when his entire body was reacting to beat the band. Impossible to say who was the seducer and who was the seduced. He'd never met a woman who could match him like this. She was making him completely crazy.

"Next…" He let his eyes wander over her body. "I'd want the stuffy business jacket off."

She affected a bored look and pulled off the jacket to reveal a thin silk shell through which he could see her lacy bra. The combination of that incredible length of thick hair and the visible underwear made him go semi-hard again. If he hadn't seen her fingers shaking just a little when she unbuttoned her jacket, he'd surrender and go home before his pride slithered onto its jelly knees and had him begging for her favors.

"And then?" She smiled coolly, but a quick swallow gave her away.

"And then…" He leaned toward her. To his surprise, she leaned toward him until she was only inches away. He could smell the light touch of perfume she wore, could imagine her breath on his face. "Then…I'd want to watch you."

"Watch…me…what?" She enunciated carefully, her full lips puckering and pouting as they formed the words.

He let his mouth spread into a slow grin. "Dance the funky chicken."

She reared back so hard she almost tipped her chair over. *"What?"*

He affected an innocent stare. "What did you think I was going to say?"

She glared at him and fumbled for her purse. "If you have to ask, then I'm not interested."

"Oh, come on." He rolled his eyes, pretending total exasperation. "Women. Damned if you come onto them, damned if you don't. I told you I was going to try alternate relaxation methods.''

''Hmph.'' She stood and slapped enough money to cover half the bill on the table. ''I'm fine tense.''

''I see.'' He slapped down enough money to cover the other half and followed her on the walkway by the river.

''So you'd rather I offered to have meaningless sex with you?''

She stopped walking and turned to him, her back to the railing by the river, eyes shooting sparks, mouth curving enough to show she was enjoying this game as much as he was. ''At least meaningless sex is human, and healthy. Not like that chicken fixation you have.''

''What is inhuman or unhealthy about having a good time?''

''Nothing. But given a choice between screaming and squawking, I'll take the screaming.''

He raised his eyebrows. Man she was good. The image of her screaming in ecstasy was making the blood slowly drain out of his brain to other places it was needed more. ''You don't mince words.''

''I know what I want.''

''I'm not entirely sure you do.'' He sent her a deliberately superior challenging gaze, feeling practically effervescent with the high of this kind of sparring.

''Right.'' She crossed her arms over her chest and

lifted her chin. "So you're going to teach me all about the real meaning of life, is that it?"

"I'd like to try."

"And pretending to be a chicken is my first lesson, because you'd rather see me in a beak and feathers than butt-naked."

He gritted his teeth. For all her attitude—or maybe because of it—he wanted to kiss her very, very badly. In fact, he was going to. "Don't knock imitating a chicken 'til you've tried it."

She put her hand to her temple and shook her head. "This has got to be a very weird dream."

He took a step toward her. "I can make it weirder."

"No." She put her hand out and touched his chest, her lips barely curving into an unwilling smile. "Nice of you to offer, but it's weird enough, believe me."

"I believe you." He took another step toward her, liking the feel of her hand on his chest. But then he had a feeling he'd like the feel of her hand just about anywhere.

"*What* are you doing?" She pushed against him and for some reason that hardened his resolve and something else for the third time in the past hour or so.

"I'm trying to back you up against the railing so I can kiss the life out of you."

"I see." She took a quick breath and tried on a well-how-about-that expression that didn't quite convince him. "And this is a good idea why?"

As if she didn't know. "Because, Missy, I have this feeling we could be very, very good together."

At the sound of her name she stiffened and swallowed. "Well, Ken. That might be your impression, but I'm not so sure."

Ken. Holy freaking hell. She still thought he was Ken. *Nice one, Adam.* What the hell was he doing? Betraying Ken with the woman he was completely crazy about? Whose response to Ken's stupid ad had shown they were made for each other?

He nodded and backed off a step. Her hand lingered on his chest, then slid slowly down and off his body, but not before he'd had to clench his teeth again and think multiplication tables.

"So." She smiled tightly, put her jacket back on and started replacing the twist in her hair.

"So." He put his hands in his pockets, feeling like a kid with his favorite toy pronounced unsuitable and taken away. "I sense that we are stopping there."

"You sense correctly." She patted her hair efficiently into place, but her voice was heavy with disappointment. "I guess."

He stopped thinking, reached for her and drew her tight against him, held her there, hands gripping her arms, feeling the thin firm length of her body, smelling the flowery shampoo scent of her hair, pressing his jaw against her temple. She stood still in his arms, then took a long, shuddery breath he'd bet a million dollars she thought would go in smoothly. Behind them a luxury yacht cruised slowly by, crowded with shirtless thirty-something men. A mom and her kids rambled noisily by behind them.

Then she moved. Not a lot. A slight motion of her face toward his. A slight tilt of her head that brought her forehead up and available to his lips.

He moved them gently, a kiss so light it practically didn't exist, except that he could almost taste her skin and feel her body shiver. They stood like that while a breeze swept over them and past, then she tipped her head toward him so her nose nestled into the skin under his ear and her mouth just touched his throat.

Yowzah.

He bent his head down, moved his mouth over her eyelids, her cheeks, then gently brushed his lips across hers, feeling electricity jolt through him at the contact. Her body changed. He could swear it did. Instead of feeling strong and slender and capable she became voluptuous and pliable and defenseless in his arms. As if she'd let go of all her tight female armor and let her true sensual self out.

God she was sexy. This was as close to heaven as he'd been with a woman in a long time. He could stand here all day and hold her like this. As long as she didn't say—

"Ken."

Damn. He lifted his head, looked down at her wide unexpectedly vulnerable eyes. "Yes, Missy?"

Her eyes snapped back to invulnerable. She pushed herself gently away. "Uh. I was just going to say that we really can't do this. I mean, we really can't get involved this way."

No kidding. "Why? Didn't you answer my ad intending to start a relationship?"

"Oh. Well, yes. I did. Of course. Except that…" She gestured helplessly in a way that indicated she hadn't a clue what to say. "Except that…"

He frowned. He had a feeling she was at a loss for words maybe once every five years. He also had a feeling she wasn't exactly shy about getting her desires met by men of her choosing. What was going on? He'd bet his trust fund she was crazily attracted to him. Why the hesitation?

He practically smacked himself. What difference did it make? He couldn't get involved with her, either. Not without giving Ken the first shot or at least talking it over with him. He'd just overlook the fact that the idea of Ken even ogling her made him want to scream with jealous rage. Very unlike him.

"Except that what?"

"Except that…" Her eyes cleared; her gestures settled down to their usual purposeful economy. "My friend Cynthia is crazy about you."

"Cynthia?" He frowned. That cute little mousy blonde? She *had* launched herself at him when the dancing started at Chicken Curly's. Which amused him because he hadn't pegged her for the launching type. And which annoyed him because he'd been dying to dance with the gorgeous sexy brunette in front of him.

"If I do anything with you it would break her heart."

His frown deepened. Convenient and unconvincing. "Aren't you being a bit overloyal?"

"Oh…no. See the last time she fell for a man, years ago, he left her for me, even though I didn't want him. As attractive as you are…" She took a deep breath and gave him the look of a starving dog turning down a pork chop. "I mean *seriously* attractive, I just can't risk—"

He grabbed her and kissed her, hard, the way he'd wanted to since he first laid eyes on her. No woman could look at him with that kind of hunger, and not get the sense kissed out of her. He'd looked at enough women with that pork-chop kind of look to know what she wanted from him.

Unfortunately he discovered rapidly that once he started kissing this woman, he didn't seem to want to stop. Because her mouth was soft, her tongue talented, and her passion unrestrained. He was pretty sure that unless someone pried them apart, he'd be happy spending the rest of his life kissing her right here on this spot, in spite of all the other things his body was yelling at him to do to her.

Think of Ken. He broke off the kiss and pulled back. "I'm sorry. I shouldn't have done that."

"No?" She appeared to have forgotten entirely about her fierce loyalty to her friend Cynthia. "Why not?"

"Because. Because...because my friend Adam is crazy about you."

"Adam?" She said his name with her eyes wide and troubled and he had to clench his fists and root his feet into the concrete beneath them to keep from grabbing her again.

"Yes. He told me after our date at Chicken Curly's."

"So. That clinches it." She looked crestfallen.

"Yes." He *felt* crestfallen so he probably looked that way, too, all miserable-eyed and hangdog heavy in the features.

"Okay..." She nodded a few times. "Okay. I can deal with that."

He stared at her, so cool and gorgeous and elegant in her blue-green linen suit, but with a flush on her cheeks and love-me-now in her eyes and he felt that same pork-chop look come over him, like in the cartoons where one character is so hungry, the other starts to look like food.

She blew out a sigh on a soft, "oh hell" and moved forward into his arms, raising her face to find his mouth as if she had sonar like a bat. She kissed him with such passionate heat, that he felt light-headed and disoriented, and something in his soul moved a little, in a place nothing had ever moved before. That wasn't true of the moving in his pants, which had happened quite a bit over the past few decades.

This time she broke away and they stared helplessly at each other while the breeze blew her mess of a hairstyle all around her face.

"So I guess we're not getting involved." He leaned forward and kissed her again.

"No." She wrapped her arms back around his neck and traced his mouth with her tongue. "Absolutely not."

"It would be—" He kissed her.

"—disloyal to—" She kissed him.

"—our friends, and—" More kisses.

"—not worth the—" More.

"—pain...and...and..." *Oh, man, more.*

She was killing him.

They broke apart, both panting and, if she was anything close to what he was, wildly aroused. This was nuts. They had something totally hot and special between them. Nothing like what Ken could ever have with her.

"Look, we have to face the fact that—"

"—nothing is going to happen, I know."

He ran his hands over his face and jammed them into his tight pockets. Okay. Nothing was going to happen today.

But he'd make reservations for a vacation in hell before he'd go much longer without this woman in his bed.

5

"OH, THAT WAS SO MUCH *FUN*!" Missy dumped an armload of shopping bags on Cynthia's kitchen table and flopped into a chair.

Cynthia smiled tightly and went to the refrigerator for a can of diet iced tea. *Yeah. Fun. Fabulous.* Missy had called her early that morning. She didn't have anything suitable to wear for their date tonight, to attract that totally hunky Ken. Could Cynthia *pleeease* take her shopping at lunchtime for something really sexy? Cynthia knew all about fashion. Couldn't she? *Pleeease?*

Cynthia offered a can of diet tea to Missy and popped the top off hers with a satisfying swish. What could she do? How could she refuse? She and Missy and Tracy and Allegra were practically blood sisters, and Missy had always brought out Cynthia's protective side. Missy was so much like herself...at about age ten. So they'd spent a very long lunch hour scouring stores for something Missy could wear that would knock the socks off the man Cynthia wanted more than she'd ever wanted any male in her life.

She slugged down a huge gulp of tea. What was with her? Maybe she was into the forbidden aspect.

Maybe she was avoiding intimacy by falling nutso crazy for a guy she couldn't have.

Except it wasn't her habit to be attracted to unavailable men. In fact, she was quite happy taking up the spare time of available ones. That theory demolished, she was left with her confusion intact.

"I am just *so* excited! I can't wait until he sees me in that dress. Do you think he'll respond? I mean, do you think he'll find me attractive?"

"Honey, a dead man would find you attractive in that dress. Don't give it a second thought." Cynthia's can of tea gave slightly under the crushing pressure of her grip; she put it down and folded her hands in her lap. Missy had never looked so happy. The entire time they were shopping she had babbled on about "Hunky Ken" and that dorky friend of his as if both men were her own personal property. Her eyes were snapping blue, her cheeks flushed. And by the time Missy's makeover was finished, there wasn't a prayer either man would take a second look at Cynthia.

Was there? She grabbed for her tea again. Since when had she been unsure of her power to attract men she wanted?

Since she met Missy's Hunky Ken.

He was hands-down the best kisser she'd ever encountered. Hands-down the best. Something incredibly powerful sparked between them when they were together. If only she could be sure he experienced that degree of power as well. That she wasn't just another attractive woman to him, that his attention couldn't just as easily turn to Missy when she showed up as decked out as she was going to be tonight. Lush and curvaceous and sexy in that blond farm girl way that men wet themselves over. That made them rush up to offer protection and worship, hoping to fulfill their ultimate fantasy of the good girl who liked bad-girl sex.

Men took one look at women like *Cynthia* and either tripped over themselves running away to find someone they could be tougher than, or they clung, tight and unwelcome, wanting to feed off her strength. Or, like Dick Crotchless, they saw her as a challenge to be overcome, and employed leering condescension to try knocking her down several pegs—probably to compensate for single-serving-size penises.

That's what she'd enjoyed so much about Ken the Stud when they were down by the river. He took her boldness in stride, matched it. She got the feeling they were both enjoying the power struggle, playing a game where the ultimate goal was not to win or lose, but to find a way to fit together.

"...will be anyway, so can we get started? I'm about to *burst* with impatience."

Cynthia put away her polite-listening face, which had been smiling and nodding at poor chattering Missy for the past five minutes, and tuned in for real. "Of course we can start. It's five-thirty, we meet them at seven. Should be plenty of time."

She shoved down her own desire and put on a burst of faux enthusiasm. Missy got first try at Stud. The exchange of ads showed they bonded at least on some level. They deserved a chance to have a good syrupy medieval wallow. Then if that didn't work out, Hunky Ken could shower off the goo and hop into the sack with Cynthia for a sheet-melting night of fun. Or two. Or many, many, many.

She showed Missy how to turn her head upside down and spritz with hairspray to give her hair volume. Missy peeked at herself in the mirror when she was right side up again. Her eyes widened. "Oh, gosh. I was always such a flat head. Look at me!"

Feeling slightly queasy, Cynthia led her to a chair. *Ugh.* She hated feeling this way. Skinny and bitter and bitchy. A mood she detested all the more in this particular instance because it made her seem like someone who depended on men for her self-esteem.

As if.

"Here. Let's do your makeup."

She outlined Missy's eyes with brown liner, added a touch of shading to the corners, mascara, blush and a sexy deep burgundy lipstick. Her skin was already perfect.

"And now. The male-mind-blowing push-up bra and the dress-that-will-slay-him."

"Oh, gosh." Missy crossed her arms over her chest. "I don't know if I can put that thing on."

"Of course you can." Cynthia gave her a gentle shove toward her bedroom. "Go do it."

While Missy was changing, Cynthia gathered up the empty cans of tea, rinsed them and put them in the container she reserved for metal recyclables. Of course she hadn't given a thought to what *she* was going to wear. Not that it would make any difference. Even the Geek would be smitten with Missy when he got an eyeful tonight.

"Um, Cynthia?" Missy's horrified voice floated out of Cynthia's bedroom. "Is this dress supposed to make me look like breasts and nothing else?"

"You bet." In fact, though the Geek had quickly turned his tongue-hanging-out attention to Cynthia, she could have sworn he was taken with Missy. Maybe he just went for anything in a skirt. Some of the most unlikely ones were blessed with extra testosterone. In any case, when Cynthia and Hunky Ken had come back to the table after dancing, Geek and Missy had been chatting as if they'd known each other all their lives. As if *they* were the ones who—

Cynthia froze in the act of wiping tea drips off her kitchen counter. *Hello? Hel-lo?* Was it even remotely possible?

"Oh, gosh, Cynthia, I'm not sure if I can do this." Missy came in from the other room, knees clenched tightly together under the short hemline, hands covering her abundant cleavage, displayed to advantage in the little black nothing they'd settled on today. "It was scary enough in the dressing room. I can't go out there looking like this. Men will think I'm some kind of *tramp*. The guys will... Uh, Cynthia?"

Cynthia stared at her, brows furrowed. *Was* it possible?

"Why are you looking at me like that?" Missy wrapped her arms around her chest. "It's the dress, isn't it? Even *you* think I'm a tramp. Oh, gosh, I—"

"Missy." Cynthia walked up to her and stared earnestly into her eyes. "Did Hunky Ken ever say anything that sounded like that ad you answered? Did he ever use any of those flowery type phrases?"

"No." Missy's lower lip pushed out and she scrunched up her face, which should have made her look extremely stupid, but somehow she managed to look vulnerable and sexy and adorable. "I think he must be really shy."

"Missy." Cynthia grabbed her shoulders. "Does he strike you as a shy person?"

Missy sighed. "Not at all. I sorta don't get it, to be honest."

"Missy."

"*What?*" Missy took a step back, out of Cynthia's grip. "Why do you keep saying, 'Missy?' You're acting all weird."

Cynthia put her hands to her cheeks. She *felt* all weird. Not entirely in a bad way, either. "Does his little *friend* strike you as a shy person?"

"Ye-e-s." A blush started on Missy's neck and spread everywhere.

"The kind who maybe would ask someone *else* to pretend they put his ad in?"

"Well…he *could* have done that. I mean *I* did it after all, and—"

Her eyes shot open wide at the same time as her

mouth. She gasped repeatedly and clamped both hands to her chest, which made it look as if she were trying to keep her breasts from flying out into orbit. "You mean...you think Hunky Ken isn't the one...that his *friend* and I are—"

Cynthia held up her hands. "I don't know for sure. It's a hunch I had a few minutes ago." A hunch that would crush the barrier between Cynthia and the sexiest guy she'd ever met and make an all-night hormone party next to inevitable.

"Oh, gosh!" Missy sank into a chair and stared helplessly at Cynthia. "It makes sense. I'm such an idiot, thinking someone like Hunky Ken would be into me. I'm such an idiot."

Cynthia's heart contracted with painful guilty tenderness. "Missy, you are *not* an—"

"Forget it." Missy stood up, put her hands to the back of her neck, and unzipped the dress. "I'm not wearing this dress."

"Yes, you are."

"No. It's ridiculous to try and pretend I'm like you. I'm just *not.* I knew it was too good to be true."

"Missy. Missy." Cynthia grabbed her friend's dress and held it back together at her neckline, turned her around, and shoved her over in front of the mirror. "Look at you. You're gorgeous. You're sexy. And if little Adam is the guy who put the ad in, and he's not quite as...obviously attractive, so what? You fell for his *words,* remember? The knight and his lady stuff."

A tear rolled down Missy's cheek. "Yes. I remember."

"So all you have to do is come on the date, and allow yourself to realize that Adam is the one for you."

"He *is* pretty cute and everything..." Missy sniffed, then met Cynthia's eyes in the mirror. "You're happy about this, aren't you? You wanted Hunky Ken for yourself."

Cynthia scrunched her face up the way Missy just had. Except it looked awful on her. "I am attracted to him. I'm sorry. But as long as I thought you wanted him, I wasn't going to—"

"I know. I know you wouldn't do that to me." Missy turned and held out her arms for a hug, which made her dress fall down to her ankles.

Cynthia burst out laughing. "I love you, Missy, but I'm not sure I'm up for that kind of closeness."

Missy turned beet-red and, giggling, yanked the dress back up. "Oh, gosh. That was hysterical."

"Listen." Cynthia smoothed back Missy's hair and squeezed her shoulder. "Let's go to your house and get you dressed in something totally comfortable that looks equally fabulous. We'll sort this out. Okay?"

Missy nodded and stepped out of her dress. "Okay. This is good for enticing a hunk, but not a sweet guy like Adam. He'd want me to wear something closer to who I really am."

"That's good. That's what it's all about." Cynthia picked up the dress, shook it out and held it up.

Strangely, the skirt was shaking, as if it was dying to boogy all on its own. Cynthia clenched her fists over the soft material.

Not since her junior year of high school when she had to work up the nerve to ask Charlie-Bob Curtis to the prom had she been this nervous at the prospect of a date. When Charlie-Bob had turned her down with a why-the-hell-would-I-want-to-go-with-*you* sneer, she'd decided immediately that no man would ever be worth getting nervous over again.

"Well, even if he's not cover-model material, that Adam really is kind of sweet." Missy pulled on the mauve skirt she'd worn during the day.

"And once he finds out I'm not the one who answered his ad, I bet you guys will be a great couple." Cynthia folded the dress and put it back into the shopping bag.

"You think so?" Missy bit her lip doubtfully. "I bet you and Hunky Ken will make a good couple, too."

"It's possible." Cynthia nodded, butterflies doing a disco dance in her stomach. It was very possible.

And damned if she was going to let some stupid case of the jitters keep her from finding out for sure.

"SO WHAT YOU'RE SAYING is that the green pants don't look good with the yellow shirt?" Ken frowned at his reflection. He liked these green pants. They were cool. And green and yellow belonged to the same color family. You had to add yellow to blue to get green. So that should work. Besides, the yellow shirt had a little green stripe running through it.

He was nervous, going on a date with a major brunette babe like *her*. Last time he'd been nervous, too, but he hadn't known what to expect then. He certainly hadn't expected dark and sensual—what he'd always dreamed about. He expected the woman who answered his ad to look more…well, more like her friend, the nice blonde. Not so amazing, but then not so bad either. But *this* woman. He hadn't been able to keep his eyes off her.

"I don't think it's such a good look, no." Adam twisted his face and then straightened it again, which he did when he thought Ken was being clueless, which was probably most of the time. Adam epitomized cool. And on top of that, he was one of the nicest guys Ken knew. A rare combination. Usually guys who epitomized cool wouldn't come near someone like Ken. But Adam had opened his home to Ken when he really needed comfort, after Tina kicked him out.

He'd been pretty sure his life was over, until Adam put his ad in the paper and then called and read that answer out loud. Those words had been like a door opening and letting a dust-swirled beam of sunlight into the dark basement of his existence.

Ken grinned. He loved it when he got poetic.

"I think the green pants would look better on the hanger, Ken."

Ken sighed. Of course he better listen. Adam knew

about these things. Adam knew what dark, sexy beautiful women wanted. Because most of them wanted him. "Yeah, okay."

"Do you have any black pants?"

"Black." Ken examined his closet dubiously. He was pretty sure he didn't— "Wait. I think my weird Aunt Charlie gave me some. I never wore them, though."

He pawed through the racks of clothes and found them, still with the tags on. "They're not really my style."

Adam took the pants off the hanger and looked them over, nodding. "Yeah. These."

Ken shrugged and put them on over his too-skinny legs. He bet way-hot women were turned off by guys with skinny legs. The pressure was pretty intense on this date. Sometimes he almost thought it was too bad Missy's friend, the blonde, hadn't answered the ad. She wasn't so scary. She responded to him in a way that made him feel good. And she had the nicest pair of hooters he'd had the pleasure to gape at surreptitiously in quite a while. Now *that* was something he could handle.

He snorted at his own joke. *Get it? Handle?*

"Those are nice pants, Ken."

He looked at himself in the mirror he had nailed up behind his closet door. They were okay. Kind of drab. "You think?"

"Do you have any black shirts?"

Ken screwed up his face incredulously. "Black shirt with black pants?"

"Or a shirt with black in it...or gray? Any other crazed relatives give you something like that?"

Adam peered into Ken's closet and rolled his eyes at the colorful assortment. Ken liked colors. They helped him stand out where he would usually be invisible.

"Wait. I think Aunt Tommy gave me something a few Christmases ago."

"Charlie? Tommy?"

"Yeah, their parents wanted boys." He crossed to his dresser and lifted just the corners of the piles of shirts so they wouldn't get mussed. "Here we go."

The shirt wasn't all cotton, it had a black and gray pattern of tiny diamond shapes. Kind of goofy. Like something a lounge lizard would wear. Ken liked honest, clean, nice-guy clothes. This shirt looked like something a lounge-lizard womanizer would wear.

"That's a *great* shirt." Adam held it up approvingly. "Wear that."

"Yeah, okay." Ken put the shirt on, over his too-skinny torso. Missy wouldn't go for that. She'd rather have Adam's nice pumped build, he was sure. He did spend a lot of time at the gym, but his muscles just got stronger, they didn't seem to get much bigger.

He'd noticed the cute blonde checking him out when they were eating ice cream together. Maybe she didn't mind so much that he was skinny. He'd had a really nice time with her. But he didn't react to her the way he'd reacted when he saw her friend's dark beauty the other night at Curly's, knowing she'd answered his ad. His heart had jumped clean out of his chest like a cuckoo coming out of its clock.

Lord, she was hot. The thought of touching her made him...it made him...he scrunched up his face. It made him kind of terrified, actually.

He tucked in his shirttails and zipped and buttoned the pants. "There."

"Very nice." Adam tightened his lips. "She'll think you look very nice."

"Yeah?" He turned toward the mirror and his eyes widened. He *did* look very nice. Not really like himself. Sort of...cool.

"Wow." He started laughing. "Wow. I *do* look nice." He laughed again. He couldn't seem to stop laughing. He laughed so hard he snorted. That was not cool. He couldn't do that tonight.

Of course Missy's friend had snorted when he told her his favorite joke about the guy in the bar and the piece of string, when they were sitting on the bench together. She'd laughed really hard behind her hand as if she was embarrassed to do it out loud, then she'd done it and blushed like crazy, which made her look kind of cute.

He liked her. He felt comfortable with her. And she made him kind of antsy in a way he couldn't really explain.

Almost too bad *she* hadn't answered his ad. Except that, for a guy like him, who grew up ignored by women, to have a chance with a hot megababe…well it was almost too much to take in.

"So you think she'll go for me this way?" He adopted a pose he'd seen cool guys adopting. Sort of tilted to one side with their hip thrust out, arms folded. Except he just looked like he had a bad back. This macho stuff was really wasted on him.

"You look good." Adam dropped into one of Ken's old camouflage director chairs from college. There was something sort of hard and almost angry in his voice.

Ken turned to check him out. He looked kind of upset. Ken wanted to ask, but last time he did that, Adam had looked at him as if he were some kind of homosexual for wanting him to share his feelings. Ken turned away. Okay, so Adam could suffer in silence if he liked it better that way. Ken was no homosexual. He just liked to know what people were thinking. He liked to be able to help his friends.

"Well I hope she goes for me." He glanced hopefully at Adam. "I hope I can break through this time."

Adam stared at him as if he'd just said something very interesting, which was an unusual way for Adam to stare at him. "What do you mean?"

He frowned. "Last time I thought…well it was hard to believe she'd been the one to answer my ad."

"What do you mean?" Adam narrowed his eyes. "I mean *exactly* what do you mean?"

Ken smiled to himself. Even Adam could sound

clueless. That made him feel better. "I mean when I was dancing with her I tried to talk to her about my heart's desire, and it was like she didn't have any idea what I was saying." He laughed bitterly. "I had better luck with her friend."

Adam's eyes got wide again. Extremely wide. Then he got the same look on his face that he got when he was coming up with an idea he really liked. "Better luck?"

"Talking to her. Getting through to her." He waved his hand and let it slap down on his thigh. "I was probably just so nervous with such a totally hot woman that I couldn't relax."

"Ken." Adam got up off the chair like some wild animal about to pounce. "Did you try any of that knight and his lady sh—*stuff* on her?"

"Yes." He grimaced, reliving his near-despair. "She didn't seem to get it."

Adam took a step closer and stared down into Ken's face as if Ken's brain held a magic spell that might set Adam free forever. Which Ken was pretty sure it didn't.

"Did you try any of it on her friend? The cute blonde?"

"Not...really." He struggled to remember. He'd been so focused on the wild brunette fantasy he hadn't really— "Wait, yes. She was talking about how my—your ad had affected her. I remember thinking it was amazing that both women were able to speak with such—"

"Ken." Adam held his hands out to shut him up. "Do you think it's possible they're doing the same thing we are?"

Ken stared at him. "Uh, getting ready for the date? Yeah, probably. Who cares?"

"No. I mean do you think the blonde wrote the ad and is too shy to admit it?"

Ken's brain started whirring. Little pictures came into it. The cute blonde's interest in Adam on their first date, thinking *he* wrote the ad; her way-romantic words when they were sitting on the bench, which she attributed to her friend, but which came to her lips so easily; the way she made something dance way down inside him which he hadn't really paid attention to; her tongue on the ice cream. Those breasts...

Oh, those breasts. *Those* he had paid attention to. A man could get lost in them for weeks and never come up for air. They were sort of out of place on such a sweet, innocent person.

He laughed, a dorky nervous laugh, wishing he could rumble richly like Adam did, and punched his fist into his palm, hoping it looked manly. "Wouldn't that be something."

"Yeah, it would be something all right." Adam stood and headed for the door, apparently dying to get going on their date. "Something very fabulous."

Suddenly the obvious dawned on Ken, as the obvious always did eventually, with a twinge of unpleasant jealousy he wished he wasn't feeling. "*You* want her, don't you? This clears the way for you."

Something angry and dejected settled into Ken's chest and stomach. Guys like Adam always got the babe. Guys like Ken got the homespun sweetheart. Granted, she was a pretty-built homespun sweetheart. And if she'd answered his ad, he could probably fall in love with her ordinary sweet ways and live happily ever after, just like he was supposed to. Just like his dad and all his older brothers had done, and what the heck was taking Ken so long they'd like to know, and was he holding out for Cindy Crawford, ha ha ha.

But just once. Just once, before he fell and got married and had lots of little Kens, he wanted to land a megababe.

6

CYNTHIA WALKED up to the entrance of Chez Mathilde restaurant and turned to beckon Missy up next to her. Missy sidled to the front steps, her body back to being camouflaged in another of her sweet loose flowered sundresses that looked great on her and quite honestly fit her much better than the bombshell outfit. Though Cynthia would love to see the male tongues of Milwaukee dragging on the pavement if Missy ever got the nerve to wear it.

"I'm so *nervous*."

"Relax. You'll be fine. One glimpse of him and you'll know it was right all along." Cynthia adjusted her body-hugging red dress, trying to reconnect with her usual feeling of being the huntress who knew she'd get her buck tonight. That of course depended on her insight into the Great Personal Ad Mixup being correct, that of course, it might not be. But the more she thought about it, the more sense her instinct made. Missy got Cynthia to read her answer into the machine—didn't it make sense that the Geek would have Hunky Ken do the same? Which would explain why Hunky Ken never spouted any goo Cynthia's way. And maybe why he'd held back when he was kissing her by the river, for the same misguided reason she had—out of unnecessary loyalty to her friend.

She opened the door and gestured Missy inside, heart pounding in anticipation. Were they here yet?

They were.

Two men, the taller one looking so heart-stoppingly handsome, that Cynthia fixed her eyes on his shorter companion. She needed just a touch more time to settle herself down. And his friend was looking remarkably sharp in dark fashionable clothes. Unfortunately, after a quick smile at Missy, he immediately glued wistful, longing eyes on Cynthia.

"Look at him," Missy whispered. "He still wants *you*."

"He thinks I answered his ad." Cynthia nudged Missy forward. "Go tell him you did."

"I can't. What if he doesn't want me?"

Cynthia pasted on a smile and gave Missy a nice shove. "Go."

Missy stumbled forward and said hello to the Geekster rather sadly, giving a wistful glance of her own at the tall man to his right. Cynthia sighed. This would take more than she imagined to straighten out.

"Don't I get a hello?"

She turned, keeping her face oh-so-nonchalant, while her heart was singing Handel's *Messiah*. "I don't know, do you deserve one?"

He was dressed with his usual sophistication in clothes he wore so easily that they became less a statement of fashion than a part of him. "Yes. I do."

"Then hello." She used a sultry tone that usually made men prostrate themselves and promise diamonds.

His eyes flicked over her dress. "You look beautiful."

"Thank you." She smiled coolly. No prostration. No diamonds. This guy made her nervous.

"And sexy."

"Oh?" She arched her eyebrows, feeling her lips wanting to give one of Missy's dopey tremulous smiles. He wasn't playing fair. She'd been told plenty of times she was beautiful and sexy, but usually by men slavering so hard she'd want to offer them tissues. This man gave the compliments out as if they were statements of fact any idiot could have figured out. Yet she felt them down to her...everything. "Well, thank you."

"You're welcome." He smiled and his eyes did that totally irresistible slanty thing at the corners. "I think in a short time I'm going to want to kiss you very badly."

"Hmm." She fought to keep the shivers at bay and swallowed a lump of some strange emotion in her throat. "I'd rather be kissed very well."

He chuckled. "I can do that, too."

"I look forward to it." The words were supposed to come out in a bold-yet-enticing murmur. Instead they exited her mouth in a shameful hoarse whisper that sounded as if she were begging for it on her knees. For crying out loud. The guy had her so rattled she'd probably dribble soup in her lap during dinner.

At least she'd picked someplace a little more fun than Chicken Curly's. At least they could have a decent dinner and some good conversation.

Except it didn't turn out that way. Missy and her dweeblet enjoyed Chef Mathilde's excellent cooking, which sort of surprised Cynthia, because she half expected them to try and order chicken fat bombs, but they seemed totally subdued. In fact the entire occasion was totally subdued. Not that Cynthia missed it when their waiter didn't shout, "Hi-ho, Chez Mathilde diners." But the level of excitement was low and conversation jumped and bumped and strained instead of flowing the way it had the other night. As if the lovely ambiance was strangling the life out of the party.

On top of that, Dweeblet kept looking from Cynthia to Missy and back, opening and closing his mouth like a fish in an aquarium. Hunky Ken enjoyed his meal, but didn't seem to have much to say either. He kept glancing at Cynthia, then throwing speculative looks at Missy.

Had he figured out their ruse? He *did* promise to kiss Cynthia later. Or did the fascination with Missy stem from some other source? Cynthia gritted her teeth and dug into her fresh fruit dessert. The sooner they were out of here and she could talk to him about the ad mixup the better. And if it turned out he *had* written the ad Missy answered, then there was a perfectly simple and reasonable solution, which was to wish the happy couple well, go home and empty her liquor cabinet down her throat.

If Hunky Ken *wasn't* the ad-writer, she could get him into the sack for an evening of Mr. Happy Dancing and prove to herself he was a man like any other and she had not turned into a drooling doormat. Cynthia grinned and congratulated herself. *Very neatly worked out. Thank you very much.*

The second the waiter came with the check, she snatched it up, handed him her credit card and plonked her arms on the table. "Let's drive downtown to McKinley Marina and go for a walk on the pier there. It's such a nice night."

The chorus of "yeas" gave her hope the evening could be salvaged. They settled the bill, bundled into their cars and drove the mile to the lakefront, found a parking place and emerged out into the cool night air.

Cynthia fell into step beside Hunky Ken, dying to link her arm through his. What was it about being outside in the dark that brought out the romantic in her?

"It's a beautiful night." She gazed up at the clear night sky, pretending to study the stars, aware only of the warm body next to her.

"Are you thinking what I'm thinking?"

"I think so." She said the words like a sexual invitation and glanced over to find him searching the sky with intense concentration. Okay, maybe not.

"Lotta room out there."

"And we are *so* insignificant here on this spinning rock, and it just makes you *wonder* what it all means. Right?"

"Nope." He put on a smug smile. "I know what it all means."

"Really." She put on a teasing well-aren't-you-special face to counteract his smugness. "My goodness, congratulations. And what is that?"

"Nothing."

Her well-aren't-you-special face fell off. "Nothing? You think life has no meaning?"

"That's right." He spoke without bitterness or sadness.

"But...but...that's *terrible*. I mean, what do you work toward?"

He shrugged. "Death."

Cynthia stopped walking and stared at his dimly lit gorgeous face in horror. "You have got to be kidding me."

"Why?"

"Because...because then what is the *point?*"

"The point of what?"

"Going on." She gestured out into the darkness around them. "The point of getting out of bed."

"Being alive gives me pleasure. Knowing people gives me pleasure. Making love to them gives me special pleasure."

She was so flabbergasted she couldn't even respond to his sexy tone. "Isn't that meaning?"

''No. It's pleasure.'' He moved a step closer. ''Sometimes very intense pleasure.''

Cynthia swallowed and stared up at him. ''That's the saddest thing I've ever heard.''

''It's not sad to me.'' He shrugged, very close now, the breeze lifting dark locks of hair off his forehead. ''What do *you* think life's purpose is? Winning the Foster Award?''

She glared at him. ''Making something of myself. Leaving a mark on humanity. Using every day to its absolute fullest.''

''Is that what you think you do?''

''Yes.''

He leaned forward so his lips were close to her ear and those gimme-sex shivers started through her body. ''I think you're wrong.''

She reared back, wanting only to make immediate and violent contact between her fist and his hard gut, the romantic night spoiled. How could she still be so attracted to such a smug, arrogant butthead? And why, when he resembled so many domineering male annoyances she'd run into, was she still hanging around wanting to figure him out? Why did it matter at all what he thought of her? What did she care whether they fit? ''Prove it.''

His eyebrows shot up. ''Huh?''

''Prove me wrong. Show me that I don't take every second of every day and make it count.'' She put her hands to her hips. ''I dare you.''

His grin started slowly and spread into aggravating wickedness over his face. "I've won already."

Her glare turned into a frown. "How the hell do you figure that?"

"Because you're standing there arguing instead of kissing me."

"You...I..." She came very close to stamping her foot like her four-year-old niece back in North Carolina. "Fine."

She moved forward, grabbed his necktie and yanked his head down for a long full-mouth kiss. Ha! Take that, big macho jerk. And as soon as this kiss was over, she'd turn on her heel and walk away. Just walk right away and leave him standing there with his tongue hanging out and his pants looking triangular. Ha!

As soon as this kiss was over.

...Yup. She'd just turn right away from him. And walk...and...she'd...

Oh, crap. He was a good kisser. A really, really good kisser. No reasonable woman could turn her back on a good kisser.

Her brain suddenly clicked back into action and gave her an answer she'd forgotten she wanted. Lust. Pure and simple. Granted, lust more powerful than any she had encountered, and she'd encountered her share, but still just lust. It made perfect sense. Because who cared if someone was a bit of a jerk if you only planned to spend temporary time with him, and most of it horizontal at that. Right? She wasn't losing her mind. She was on totally familiar ground.

Case closed.

She broke the kiss and stood tight against him, her heart beating wildly. Well, *of course* it was beating wildly. The man could get a rock hot for him.

"So." She managed to steer her voice toward the casual bantering tone that was her trademark. "Do you accept my challenge to prove I don't live life to its fullest?"

"I can't wait to get started."

"Ha! I feel an easy victory coming on." She grinned, totally back in balance and finally remembering the entire point of getting him out here, before he hijacked her by spouting his meaning-of-life theories.

Before she moved one inch more into this territory, and before she gave into any more urges where this man was concerned, for Missy's sake as well as her own, she had to make sure once and for all, that he hadn't spouted the goo in the newspaper.

She glanced behind her to make sure Missy and The Geek were well out of earshot on the long stone pier that thrust out into the lake. "I want to ask you something."

"Well, that is a coincidence." His voice was low and sexy next to her. "I want to ask you something, too. You first."

"Okay." She picked a random spot and leaned her elbows on the railing. "If you're all into that knight-

and-his-lady stuff, why haven't you ever tried any of those lines on me?''

"Hmm. Good question." He angled his body toward her so the wind ruffled his dark hair. "How about I try some out now?''

Cynthia tried to swallow the sick feeling invading her throat and stomach. She *couldn't* be wrong, could she? Did this man really belong in Missy's gooleague, romantically speaking? "Uh...sure. Go ahead.''

He cleared his throat and stood away from the railing, one hand on his heart, the other gesturing rather comically toward her.

Cynthia braced herself. The end of her fantasy. On its way. Maybe she should just hurl herself into the lake to avoid it.

"Oh, fairest damsel-type-person. Would you like to come back to my place so I might show you my most fabulous tapestries?''

Laughter burst out of Cynthia's mouth at the same time the world became suddenly a much more fabulous place. "Oh, uh, yeah, sure, good sir knight. Tapestries are pretty much my favorites. And from what I have seen so far, I'm betting thine are most totally awesome.''

"Ah!" He stepped toward her, took both her hands, brought them up and around his neck, then slid his down to circle her waist. "This makest me megaglad. For that red dress on thy most fabulous bod has me crazy-nutso to know thee, if thou knowest what I mean, Missy.''

"I'm Cynthia." She blinked sweetly into his surprised face. "And I am way-desirous to know you as well, Ken."

He grinned wickedly. "I'm Adam."

She laughed again, feeling free and joyous and a little wild. No, a lot wild. Just the way she liked herself best. "So the ad was Ken's. The real Ken's."

"And the response you read on the phone was Missy's. And that means I don't have to stay away from you for Ken's sake."

She shook her head and pitched her voice down into an enticing purr. "You don't have to stay away from me for anyone's sake."

"I don't think I will." He kissed her, once lightly, then again, a slow lingering kiss that made her insides heat up instantaneously. See? This was easy. Cynthia Parkins's adult specialty.

Lust, pure and simple.

MISSY TURNED away from the sight of Cynthia kissing Hunky Ken. Oh, gosh, it hurt. Just a little. Even though they obviously belonged together. Even if Cynthia turned out to be right and Ken wasn't the one who placed the ad, and even if nice Adam here next to her had, she still hadn't quite thrown off the fantasy of a man like Ken wanting her. But really all night, though he'd glanced at her occasionally in a sort of measuring way, he'd only had eyes for Cynthia, so it wasn't like seeing them together was a shock.

"Hey." Adam pointed to Ken and Cynthia. "They're kissing."

He looked sort of miserable, which made her want to comfort him. He did look pretty nice today, though she didn't mind him dressed in casual clothes, either. "I think they belong together, Adam."

He turned and looked at her, his face really quite handsome in the soft lights of the city. Quite, quite handsome. "Does that mean that you and I..."

He gestured back and forth between them. Missy held her breath. She hadn't been sure she was ready to transfer her happy-ever-after to him quite so quickly. But somehow, in the night air, with Cynthia getting all hot and bothered barely ten yards away, it *would* be romantic for them to have their own moment, since she did feel something for him. Something that could grow once she realized the kind of man he was, once she made the leap to thinking of him as the man who placed that wonderful, dreamy ad, instead of his friend.

Adam's slender shoulders slumped in despair. "But she was what I wanted."

Missy bit her lip and snatched back her hand, which had been extending to caress his arm in a comforting and possibly seductive way, if she could manage something like that. Oh, gosh, that hurt. That hurt more than the sight of the kissing. Her eyes filled up a little and she kept them open extra wide so the tears would drain instead of spilling over and giving her away. So, she wasn't really a prize. Cynthia they wanted to take home. Men just wanted to stare at Missy's body and probably while they were staring they were thinking what a waste it was on her. Obviously they assumed she didn't know what to do with it. And she never ever got to prove them wrong.

Adam took off his glasses and wiped them, then put them back on, frowning. For all Missy's wide eyes, a tear did slip down her cheek. She reached and pretended to be brushing away some bug that had flown onto her face.

He glanced at her, then did a double take and his features crumpled into contrition. Obviously she hadn't disguised the tear well at all. "Oh, Cynthia, I'm sorry. That must have sounded horrible."

"I'm Missy. And it's okay."

He stared at her in confusion. "*You're* Missy?"

"Yes. I answered your ad."

His bushy brows drew down. "How did you know it was *my* ad?"

"Because." She shrugged. "It fit you better, Adam."

"I'm Ken."

"Oh." She giggled and immediately hated the little-girl sound. "Hi, Ken."

He laughed, a wheezy noise that made her feel a whole lot better about her little-girl sound. Except even a wheezy laugh seemed appealing on him.

"Hi, Missy." He pushed his glasses back up his

nose with entirely the wrong finger, which was even more appealing since he was so unaware he was doing it. "This is very confusing."

"Yes." She swayed toward him. "So I guess this means that we're...I mean, your ad was really amazing."

"You thought so?" He nodded, still obviously trying to sort everything out. "I liked your answer."

"I'm glad." She moved a little closer. The wind was sort of chilly and he looked very warm and inviting. In fact he was suddenly turning her way on. She'd never felt it quite this strongly before. Hot and sort of...desperate. "You know what this means, right?"

He scrunched up his face in concentration. "That you and I...that we're meant for each other?"

"Yes." She said the word in a low, breathy, drawn-out voice, the kind of voice she'd never dared use before. The kind of voice that made no difference what you were actually saying because the voice itself was the message.

"Cool. That's cool." He nodded very rapidly and folded his arms tightly across his chest. "So. What do we do now?"

"Oh, Ken." She laughed, and this time managed to make it a low, sultry sound. She was on such a roll! "I think you can probably guess."

He looked off to the right, then to the left. "No, I can't. I've never met anyone I was destined for before."

"You could kiss me." She could have squealed with excitement. She, Missy Beckworth, had just used the perfect, perfect line at the perfect, perfect time.

"Oh. Okay." He leaned forward and put his rather cold lips against hers for a minisecond, then leaned back and grinned nervously. "Hey, that was nice."

She narrowed her eyes. No one. *No* one was going to take her romantic lakeside mega French kiss away from her tonight. Especially not the guy who was going to turn out to be the man of her dreams.

Darn it. She should have worn that dress.

Well, tough. She didn't. She could manage without it. She reached and grabbed his face in her two hands, pulled it toward her and kissed him like a starving woman.

7

CYNTHIA OPENED her eyes to a strange room in a strange bed. Mmm. Nice. She stretched lazily, then turned to glance at Adam's clock, feeling that wonderful familiar soreness between her—

"Oh, *no*." She tossed off the sheet and rocketed out of bed.

"Whah?" Adam threw out an arm to intercept her and missed. "Where you going?"

"Work! Where do you think? It's seven-thirty." She scanned the room, retrieved her bra from a table lamp and dragged it on. "I have to get home, get changed, go over my notes for the meeting with—"

"No you don't."

"What do you mean no I don't?" She grabbed her earrings off the floor by his bed and jammed them into her ears. "Of course I do."

"If you say so." Adam yawned, got out of bed and made his way to the bathroom.

"Where are my panties?" Cynthia dashed around the room. Panty hose, she found in a ball on his bedside table. Dress, she found on top of his bureau. Panties…

Another loud yawn sounded from the bathroom,

followed by the sound of flushing water, and then a crinkling, unwrapping-type sound that was vaguely familiar...

"Try under the bed."

"Under the bed. Under the bed." Cynthia dropped to her hands and knees and scanned anxiously under the—

"Adam!"

Strong warm hands had helped themselves to her naked rear sticking up in the air. She was suddenly aware of him getting to his knees behind her....

"Stop that! Stop that right now." She tried to stand, but he clasped her around the waist and lifted her upright until their bodies were touching, his front to her back. "Adam, I don't have time for this, remember?" He found her nipples with his very, *very* skillful fingers and commenced delicious torture proceedings. "I mean we already did this...several times, and in order for me to live life to its fullest I have to vary my...*oh, man*...my activities, remember?"

"I remember." He kissed her temple, painted a thin line on her neck with his equally skillful tongue and rocked against her, with his most impressive and overridingly skillful condom-clad male thingy very much in evidence. "What better way to fulfill your destiny as a human than to interact intimately with another human?"

She pulled forward, dropped to her elbows, found her panties and lofted them triumphantly. "Enough.

I have to get to the office. I have to...*what* do you think you're doing?''

His fingers had found a rather vulnerable place and appeared to be preparing her to receive his most determined male bounty.

"I'm going to help you live life to its fullest. See, I'm at *my* fullest right at the moment, and I'd sure like to help you."

Cynthia giggled, then clapped her hand over her mouth. "I can't believe I just giggled."

She twisted her rear to one side, away from his heat-seeking missile. She really couldn't take the time to do this, much as she wanted to. He was so strong and funny and fun and they'd had one hell of a night together.

"Why can't you believe you just giggled?" He put both hands firmly on her hips and realigned her for the attack.

"Because I'm not the giggling type." She tried to twist away again, but probably not as hard as she should have. "This is your fault. You've done something to me."

"You're falling in love."

"In your dreams." She sent him a scornful look which he undoubtedly didn't see since he was busy kissing her shoulders and neck and making her wild for him. Again. "I got laid, is all."

"You're sure about that?"

She opened her mouth to say *Of course. Sex isn't remotely the same thing as love, not even fabulous sex.* But just as soon as she opened her mouth, his missile found its target and he began to move inside her. He'd wrapped his arms tightly around her, so she felt joined to him and protected at the same time. Something very, very strange shifted inside her so that she felt suddenly helpless and a little disoriented and a lot crazy about him.

Uh-oh.

One of his hands slid down her stomach to where it could do her the most good. He started to do things with his fingers that were enough to make her a panting, pleading, grateful mess instead of a Sex Goddess Of Life.

She wasn't used to this.

"You didn't answer." He murmured the words against her ear and she turned to his mouth and kissed him. And suddenly, even worse...*far* worse, she wasn't just enjoying the sensation of the smooth pressure of a male mouth, she was kissing *him.* Adam. All of him. His entire soul joining hers through the contact between their bodies and their mouths.

She broke away and mumbled something that sounded like, "Oh, hell."

"You're *sure* this is just sex, Cynthia?"

No. She'd never been blindsided like this before. She'd always been firmly in control of the situation and the physical activity and the man. This wasn't just sex.

"I'm not going to answer."

"On the grounds that it may incriminate you?"

"On the grounds that I'm trying to have an orgasm here, so if you wouldn't mind shutting up, I'd appreciate it."

He chuckled, drew her back against him and very quickly made sure she had a giant, amazing, earth-shaking orgasm, which he followed with one of his own.

She slumped back against him, panting and sated and *completely* freaking out because now she might possibly be late for her morning appointment with The Crotchless One and she was absolutely never late.

"I have to go."

"So you said." He caressed her up and down and she had no luck whatsoever getting her body to obey her signals to pull away.

"I have to *go*."

"So go." He kissed her temple, her cheek, then turned her to him and kissed her mouth again. But this time without the sex to make things...sexual, the kissing was ten times more emotional and personal and...

Terrifying.

Cynthia pulled away and stood unsteadily. "Okay. Panties."

She pulled them on and balanced on one foot to get on her panty hose, gaping at Adam who slipped back into bed. "What are you doing? Don't you have to get to work?"

"Sure. But I don't feel like going right now."

She stared at him as if he had just announced that he ate children for breakfast. "What does not feeling like it have to do with anything? You have work to do, you go."

"I'll go later." He grinned. "When I feel like it."

Cynthia shook her head. "That's irresponsible."

"No. It's smart. If I go when I don't feel like it I won't be productive. I won't get anything done. I'll resent the job and the time I have to spend there. If I relax here for half an hour and think about how you look when you're falling in love with me, then I'll be happy, and I'll go to work and get a whole hell of a lot done."

Cynthia scowled and staggered trying to balance while she shoved her other leg into her panty hose. "I'm not falling in love with you."

"No?" He smiled. "Well, I'm falling in love with you."

Cynthia froze, a bad idea when she wasn't balanced in the first place, and fell sideways onto the floor where she rolled to her back and lay staring up at the ceiling in shock. "What are you talking about?"

His head appeared over the edge of the bed. "I'm talking about falling in love with you."

She struggled up onto her elbows and glared at him. "You can't be falling in love with me after this short a time."

"No? Then explain to me why I am."

"Because...because..." She got to her feet and

grabbed for her dress. "We'll have to discuss this another time. When my brain is functioning."

He lunged for her and brought her down on top of him on the bed. "Your brain isn't functioning because you're in love."

"Will you stop with the love stuff? It's—"

"Irritating."

"Yes. And—"

"Presumptuous."

"Yes. And—"

"Hits too close to the truth."

"Ye— *No.*"

He put his hands to her cheeks and kissed her sweetly, which made her feel about as gooey as that awful ad his friend wrote. Give her ten more seconds of this and she'd ask him to be her knight.

"Go to work, Cynthia. And think about me, okay?"

She swallowed and two tiny tears made guest appearances in the corners of her eyes. "Yes. Okay."

Like she could remotely do anything else. She was a mess. An absolute mess. And Cynthia was never, ever, *ever* a mess over men. Men were fun. Men were just one whole hell of a lot of fun. But this man was beyond fun. This man had made her giggle. Blush. Orgasm with her heart as well as her body.

What the hell was she supposed to do now?

Work.

She pushed off him, stepped into her shoes,

grabbed her purse, headed for his door, then stopped
and turned around, strangely hesitant.

"Thanks. I had fun."

Oh no! Now she sounded *shy,* for God's sake.

He grinned. "We'll do it again."

"Yes." She managed an awkward wave, then...oh
for crying out loud...she giggled again.

CYNTHIA SHUFFLED her notes from that morning's
meeting with Richard Croshallis, which, to the total
openmouthed shock of her co-workers she *had* come
rushing in late for, probably disheveled and shiny-
eyed and soundly kissed-looking. She needed to get
a grip.

The meeting had been a near disaster. Cynthia being disoriented and way off her usual cool, Dicky had
taken full advantage, doubling every ounce of
smarmy insinuation he'd ever used. Didn't she know
what influence his father had on the choice for the
Foster? Think of what it could mean to her career.
Oh, and had she ever been to Eagan's downtown?
Great food, open late. Would she by any chance like
to have dinner with him tonight?

She'd said yes.

Cynthia fought back a combination surge of tears
and nausea. She still couldn't believe she'd accepted.
Of course on the outside, having dinner with him
meant only that she was having dinner with him. But
of course also on some level it meant she was whor-
ing around for the Foster.

The worst was when she started imagining Adam's reaction. Imagining him laughing at her, or condemning her, told-you-so-ing her. *Is this living life to its fullest, Cynthia? Having dinner with someone you detest and don't respect so you can move up the corporate ladder?*

No. The *worst* was when she imagined Dicky getting fresh and Adam bursting in to punch Dicky's lights out. Since *when* did Cynthia have rescue fantasies? Since freaking *when?*

Since apparently last night.

Oh, man. If this was falling in love, she hated it. First you were a nice strong stable person, with your life in order and your goals worked out. Then you fell in love and you became weak, dependent, stressed out with uncertainty—when he says this does he *mean* this or does he mean something else? Why hasn't he called? Why is he calling so much? Why doesn't he kiss me? Why didn't he touch me right then when he could have? What does it mean? Is it love? Is it lust? Is it forever? Is it for now? Is it love? Is it lust?

Ack! She looked down in disbelief at the crumpled ball of notes that recently had been on its way to becoming a neat pile. This was bad. Way bad.

Her phone rang. She patted back her hair in a ludicrous attempt to restore order to her brain, took a deep breath and answered it.

"Joe Collins here."

She rolled her eyes. Collins, the bigwig from VF Capital. She had a feeling she knew what this call was about, and it spelled disaster in bold VF-Capital letters.

"We received your latest report on IT Consulting and Croshallis. I can't see VF Capital investing in a company with these kinds of problems as is, but with the information you just gave us, I am afraid we aren't inclined to go through with the investment."

Cynthia winced, and moved the phone to her other ear. She'd known this was coming, ever since she'd sent in her latest report which showed, among other things, that Richard Croshallis was a regular at a local porn video shop. Renting *Horny Amazons at The Prom* six times in a month would not get you one hundred million dollars from a conservative firm like VF Capital.

"I understand. Is the decision final?" She crossed her fingers. If the decision wasn't yet final, she could kill time until the awards banquet. Four weeks. All she needed. Then she could break the news gently.

"Yes. We voted last night."

Damn. That left Cynthia with a delicate balancing act. If she told Richard now, he'd hold her responsible, knowing she'd provided information to VF Capital that strongly influenced its decision. One Dickytantrum to daddy and there, totally unfairly, went her chance at the Foster.

"Very good. I'll relay your decision."

She ended the call. Yes, she'd relay the decision. At some point.

What harm in putting it off a little? Things moved

slowly in the corporate world, right? Decisions took time. Especially important decisions that involved a lot of money. Dicky knew that. A couple more weeks, give or take, then she'd tell him. Honest.

A timid knock sounded at her door. "Yes?"

Missy poked her head into the office. "I know you're busy, I'll only take a second."

Cynthia's heart contracted. Her friend looked miserable. "Come on in, honey."

She got up from her massive desk, pulled out one of her newly upholstered teak visitors' chairs for Missy, then sat in the other herself. "What is it? You look like your life is over."

"Oh, it's not that bad." Missy sat and clenched her hands together. "It's just…well, it's…"

"Ken."

"Yes."

"Missy, what happened? What did he do?" Cynthia braced herself. If that weenie-dick treated Missy one *iota* badly, he'd have to face the wrath of Cynthia.

Missy's face crumpled. "Nothing."

"Nothing." Cynthia eyed her carefully. "And that's…bad?"

"Yes." Missy gulped a swallow and sniffed. "Oh, Cynthia, we were out there in the beautiful breezy dark together, and I started to feel so…well, you know…overly *warm*, and suddenly he just looked like the cutest most amazing man I'd ever seen and so I kissed him like crazy, and then he just…"

"Just what?"

"Just stood there." She pounded her fist in her lap. "I mean I'm so unsexy I can't even make *geeks* horny."

"No. No. that's totally untrue. I'm sure you've made *plenty* of geeks—that is, all *kinds* of—I mean you are totally sexy." Cynthia bit her lip. Not helpful. "How do you *know* he wasn't horny?"

"I looked. In that…place men get horny. He wasn't."

"Oh." Cynthia clenched her fists to keep from running out to track Ken down and make sure he entirely lost the ability to get horny again.

"Oh, Cynthia. I wanted him so badly. Now I'm probably never going to have him."

"Nonsense." Cynthia got up and started pacing the office, urging her tired mixed-up brain to go one more round and help her friend out of this one. "You probably just shocked him. Some guys are turned off by aggressive women, you know? Maybe you need to send more subtle signals."

"I guess jumping on him wasn't very subtle." Missy sniffed and wiped her eyes. "Except…at one point he said he wanted *you*. And you're not at all subtle."

"Ahem." Cynthia pretended to be offended, then grinned when Missy looked contrite. "Look. Call him up and talk. Lead him into arranging a date. Wear that dress we bought. Make yourself…available. I bet you anything he comes around."

"I don't know." Missy sniffed again, but her mouth curved in a tiny smile and a spark of hope lit her eyes. "You think?"

"Yes, I think. Absolutely, I think. Definitely, I think. I'll even help you. Okay?"

"Oh, thank you, Cynthia." Missy's expression swelled into rapture, then shut down again into sudden curiosity. "So..."

Cynthia's body stiffened. "So?"

"What about you and Adam?"

"Oh, him." Cynthia made a dismissive gesture. "He's a lot of fun, but I...I..." She cleared her throat, which had suddenly closed up on her.

"You what?"

"Well he's just a lot of fun...is all..." Her voice trailed off in a choked whisper.

Missy's eyes got hugely round. "You?"

Cynthia scowled and stalked over to her big solid protective desk. "Me, what?"

"Oh!" Missy's mouth stretched into a huge grin. "You!"

"Me...*what?*" Cynthia put her hands on her hips and turned her face into a thundercloud of doom.

"You are in *love!*"

"Ohhhh, no." She waggled her finger back and forth. "Oh, no-no-no-no-no."

"Oh, yes!" Missy rose and clasped her hands together, eyes shining. "Oh, Cynthia, I'm so *happy* for you."

"What the *hell* are you talking about?" Cynthia

picked up some papers from one side of the desk and put them down on the other side. "I had sex with the guy, that's it."

"Was it good?"

"It was…amazing." She arranged her stapler so it was more perfectly parallel with the edge of a nearby pad of paper.

"Did he say he loved you?"

Cynthia picked up a pencil and put it in her pewter beer mug holder. "Well…sort of."

"Oh! This is so amazing!" Missy ran around the desk and attempted to squeeze the life out of Cynthia with a bear hug.

"Well, I guess it is *sort of* amazing." She shrugged and attempted to make it look like the fact that she was falling in love ranked a one-point-five on the importance scale. "You promise not to tell Allegra?"

"Of course." Missy patted her shoulder. "If that's what you want. But why?"

"I don't know." She sank into her chair, pulled the pencil back out of her pewter beer mug holder and tapped it on her blotter. "I just want it kept…private."

"But Cynthia, there's nothing shameful about falling in love."

"I know that." She took two pencils out this time, and let them drop so they made a fascinating H-pattern with the third one. "I'm not ashamed. I'm just…"

"Ashamed."

"Well it's just not *like* me." She gestured in exasperation and knocked the entire mug of pencils onto the beige wool carpet. "I mean I've always been so strong and so—"

"Cynthia." Missy's brow furrowed at the same time she managed to look shocked. "Why do you think falling in love is a weakness?"

Cynthia stood abruptly. She put her hands on her hips, folded them across her chest, then put them back on her hips. She glared down at her desk and the three pencils and the rest of the stuff organized to within a millimeter of perfection and a stupid, ridiculous, sappy, frightened little tear put in a brief appearance on her cheek, ran down her nose, and dripped off onto her embossed letterhead.

"I don't know."

8

MISSY STARED at the array of flowery dresses hanging in her closet. Cute. More cute. Pretty. Sweet. Shy. Soft-spoken. Darling little Missy, so obliging, so...nice!

Just once, she wanted to be the bad girl. Cynthia had said the other day that she'd help Missy get dolled up enough to get a...she giggled...*rise* out of Ken.

But she was always leaning on Cynthia to help her. Just once, she wanted to do it all on her own. She bet she could, too.

She reached in for the hanger that had that fabulous black dress on it. She *knew* she could do it. She knew. In that dress she looked every inch the red-blooded American female she knew she was. Every inch the red-blooded American female Ken saw and wanted when he looked at Cynthia.

It's just that she was old-fashioned enough to believe that talking about sex and dressing and acting as if you were inviting sex, the way Cynthia did—to Missy's constant mortification—belonged behind closed doors alone with the man you loved. Cynthia thought it was okay to discuss her sex life with telephone operators.

But Missy wasn't totally naive by any means. She'd actually been in bed with quite a few guys. Not like Cynthia of course, but at least…three. Or okay, four if you counted that…well, never mind. And none of them had complained.

She rolled her eyes. Like any guy would *complain* about getting sex. But she'd even gotten the distinct impression they thought she was good at it. Maybe because like Cynthia, she really, really enjoyed sex. She felt so powerful and beautiful when she could make a man lose his mind over her. Which didn't happen all that often. Because men never lost their minds just from looking at her or speaking to her the way they did over Cynthia. And she wouldn't really want them to. But when she found someone really special as she was pretty sure she had found this time in Ken, she got tired of being overlooked. The way he compared her to Cynthia had smarted extra hard since Missy was quite sure *she* was the woman he was destined to spend eternity with.

Missy drew the dress out of the closet and smiled at it the way you smile at a new friend you just *know* you're going to have lots and lots of good times with. So she couldn't wear it comfortably in public. She wasn't planning to be in public tonight. Ken was her knight and she would be his lady all her life. *This* time she wasn't going to be overlooked.

She threw off her sundress and put on the matching

black lace panties and bra she'd bought that afternoon from Victoria's Secret. The bra strained to hold her breasts in and that made her feel bold and excited and giddy so that she couldn't stop giggling. Wait until Ken saw that! He'd hyperventilate.

She giggled some more and tipped her head over to spray hairspray the way Cynthia taught her so her hair would emerge all fluffy and full. She wasn't sure she quite got all the makeup right, but at the end she was satisfied with how she looked. More mature. Not such a little girl. Sexy. She'd put the dress on, and without giving herself time to think, she'd call Ken and ask if she could come over tonight. She was pretty sure he'd be home. He seemed like a homebody, same as she was. They could spend most of their nights at home together watching TV, or playing board games, or making love.

At *that* thought, she flushed and started to get that wonderful warm feeling through her body and especially down *there* where it felt the best.

Time for the dress. She slipped into it, zipped up, took a deep breath and introduced herself to her reflection.

Missy, say hello to the rest of your life.

"I HAVE SOME good news for you!" Mrs. Lemmingster raised her glass of 1996 Chateau-neuf-du-Pape toward Adam's head and flashed her dentures. They were sitting at a cozy table for two at Bartalotta's Lake Park Bistro. Behind Mrs. Lemmingster's silk-clad shoulder Lake Michigan swam out to the horizon, a blue-black mat of water. "The Lemmingsters have looked over your proposal and the brochure…"

Adam leaned forward eagerly, as if he was oh, golly gee, *praying* that his instincts about what she was going to say were correct, and that she was indeed going to drop the holy bombshell of privilege onto his lowly undeserving head.

He chastised himself. He should be celebrating in earnest. The Mrs. Lemmingsters of the world made possible a lot of good. The community center would do a lot of good. Everything everywhere was bright and sunny and fabulous. Except that he was sitting here instead of lying in bed with Cynthia Parkins's body draped all over him.

He chastised himself again. He was here to accomplish something important for the city of Milwaukee. He could see Cynthia tomorrow. And the next day. And oh, man, the next.

So chill.

"…would be happy to make up the balance of funding you need to complete the project." She beamed at him, and waited.

Adam did it all. The verbal and facial version of falling to his knees, hands clasped, grateful tears streaming down his cheeks. *Oh, thank you Mrs. Lemmingster. I thank you. The City of Milwaukee thanks you. The hundreds, no, thousands of people who will benefit from the community center thank you. My left sneaker thanks you. The astronauts circling the earth thank you.*

And so on. A routine he usually enjoyed since it signified success on his part.

So what was with him today? This community center was important. It had taken the bulk of his time and talent over the past year. Now his work was finally paying off and all he could think about was Cynthia. In the space of one week, more to the point, in the space of one *night,* she had turned his life inside out, upside down, and whatever other unnatural positions his life could be in.

Since his heart attack, he'd taken up a vaguely Zen approach to life. *Be happy where you are. Make the most of the hours given to you. Enjoy the moment.*

So why wasn't he enjoying this moment with Mrs. Lemmingster and her billions? Her generosity was making possible the successful end to a crusade he'd begun years ago when city officials approached him with the idea of the center. He should be having to restrain himself from jumping up and clicking his heels all over the restaurant.

Instead, he was restraining himself from telling Mrs. Lemmingster to swallow her lamb rib chops with cumin potato crust whole so he could break speed limits getting to Cynthia's place and hold tight to the most amazing woman he'd ever come across. Attach her to him. Make her confess she loved him, too.

Enough of that. Those feelings had their place and

time, and their place wasn't here and their time wasn't now.

He fixed a smile on his face and held up his own glass. "A toast. To you, Mrs. Lemmingster. May you always be around to benefit this city you call home."

And may you finish your dinner in a major hurry so I can get the hell out of here. He gritted his teeth at the unwelcome thought and practically bit a piece out of his wineglass.

Relax. Clear your mind. Live for the moment. Take things as they come.

"Thank you, dear." Mrs. Lemmingster beamed and picked up her knife and fork to reattack her meal. "Of course Milwaukee has always been good to the Lemmingsters. Why I remember tales of my great-grandfather Theodore Lemmingster and how he prospered here within weeks of his arrival, a penniless merchant from England. He came over to this city in eighteen hundred and fifty-three…or was it earlier…or later…"

Adam concentrated on her story. Tried to take in every detail, imagine every aspect. Her great-grandfather. Arriving in Milwaukee…

He'd probably pushed Cynthia too hard to admit she loved him. But love was sure as hell where he was heading, and like a child at the entrance to a haunted house ride, he hadn't wanted to go to that scary thrilling place alone. Making love to her had been a transforming experience. He'd never felt that depth of emotion during one of his very favorite physical activities. Instinctively, he felt Cynthia had responded in kind, with every atom of her being, but instinct could be wrong. For all he knew she threw herself into sex like that with everyone she got involved with.

And man, did she throw herself into sex. She was a master. Playful, sensual, totally uninhibited, she didn't appear to harbor the slightest feeling that she was doing anything remotely improper or immoral. And she did it all.

He felt himself start to get hard remembering their night together and brought himself back to Mrs. Lemmingster with a start, hurriedly checking his features to make sure he wasn't betraying any of his true feelings. Mrs. Lemmingster would probably not appreciate thinking he was getting turned on hearing about her great-grandfather.

"Then…" Mrs. Lemmingster paused and moistened her rather large mouth with more wine. "Just when it all seemed hopeless, in walked Mary Kate with the silver!"

He smacked his hand on the table. "Imagine that!"

"Oh, I'm so glad you enjoyed that story." Mrs. Lemmingster beamed and touched her white hair self-consciously, her wrinkled cheeks rosy with pleasure. Or maybe rosy with Chateau-neuf-du-Pape. "Let me tell you another. Let's see… Oh! Here's one. This very naughty maid at my grandmother's house had a *tremendous* fondness for gingerbread. So one day…"

Adam took a bite of his salmon with black olive

tapenade and set himself to enjoy the story. About the maid. Stealing gingerbread...

The only damper on their adventure had come when Cynthia looked at the damn clock and saw it was time to go to work. In the space of an instant, she'd changed from a warm, willing sexual gymnast to the frigid work machine he itched to crosswire. He'd love to set free that drawling shy Southern belle he'd glimpsed precious few times and let her loose on Milwaukee. And on him. Oh, man, especially on him.

"Well, you know, they found gingerbread hidden away in various parts of that house for months!"

"Gingerbread!" He let out a bellow of laughter that sounded about as real as could be expected given the circumstances, ashamed that he'd tuned Mrs. Lemmingster out again. She was a perfectly nice lady, with a fascinating and vibrant family history in this city. A few days ago he would really have enjoyed her stories.

But he might as well admit it. He was a man obsessed. The minute the door closed behind Cynthia that morning, he was starving to see her again. This from the man who lived for today. Who believed life had no deeper meaning than the joy or pain found in each moment. The man who had solemnly promised to do away with the expression, "I can't wait."

Saying, "I can't wait" meant you were wasting the most precious thing you had: time. Wasting it longing for a future that you couldn't always control and which might never even arrive. Wasting it wishing your life away.

Except that in spite of all his sound reasoning, the fact stubbornly remained that he couldn't wait to see Cynthia again. Where was she tonight? Who was she with? What was she doing? Was she thinking about him? Missing him in the same inexplicably potent and doubtless adolescent way he missed her? Had he managed to make as indelible a mark on her as she had on him?

"Let me tell you about the time my grandmother absolutely *scandalized* the summer people up in Door County by appearing in what was then considered practically the nude."

Adam gave the appropriate shocked-but-curious reaction, finished his wine with a gulp and poured more for both of them. Who was he kidding? He didn't want to be here. He didn't want to hear about Mrs. Lemmingster's naked grandmother. He wanted Cynthia.

He put on his fascinated face and let himself drift off into more not-enjoying-the-moment thoughts of her. Was she chin-deep in meeting notes and corporate business plans? Or laughing in a bar with friends?

He could call her and find out.

The second the thought hit him, he pushed it away. Interrupt dinner with a fine and generous lady who deserved every second of his rapt attention to call a woman he happened to have a serious case of the hots for and could easily talk to after dinner? It would be inexcusably rude. Not to mention betray his philosophy of life.

Mrs. Lemmingster talked. He took a sip of wine. Nodded. Smiled. His cell phone was a tantalizing weight in his pocket. He ignored it. Sort of. Pretty much.

Mrs. Lemmingster kept talking. He took another sip of wine. Nodded. Smiled. Snuck his hand into his pocket to grasp smooth plastic.

One call. Just one call from his cell phone to her cell phone. To say hello. To tell her he was thinking about her. Maybe mention a few of the things he was thinking about doing to her. To keep her off balance. Make sure she wasn't having too much fun without him.

He'd be gone from the table three minutes, max. Would that really be so rude? Would he really have to ditch his belief system over one little phone call?

The answer rose into his mind in a big sexy brunette hurry.

Yes.

Tough. He half rose from the table and smiled apologetically.

"Mrs. Lemmingster, would you please excuse me?"

KEN FLICKED the channel changer at the set in his new apartment. He'd had to buy a new TV because Tina had managed to keep just about everything they bought together. She was pretty much of a witch, he realized, now that he had been able to gain some distance. He'd never let that happen to him again.

Funny how sometimes you got drawn to people for all the wrong reasons. Like you had some weird neurosis to work out. Well in his case, whatever need he apparently had to be walked all over had thankfully dissipated, because he'd be damned if he got hooked up with a female steamroller again.

He flicked the channel again and watched John Wayne tough-guy his way through a totally unrealistic scene. He never did figure out how such a bad actor could appear in so many awful movies and become a legend.

But maybe it was just that John Wayne had the balls. Balls were something he was starting to realize were extremely necessary to being a man.

He'd spent way too much of his life without them, that was for sure. He was only just starting to realize this. Even recently, when that sweet Missy had kissed him, he hadn't even had the balls to kiss her back. Worse, he'd hurt her by saying something idiotic about her friend Cynthia. Seeing the look on her face had done something to him, made him grow up or something, because he'd hurt twice as bad for doing that to her. Maybe the pain was him finally starting to grow balls.

He wrinkled his nose, aimed the channel changer and transformed John Wayne to a bear in some nature documentary.

A bear. That's what he'd been to her. A growly

spoiled brat Grizzly, pining after some ridiculous version of inappropriate womanhood embodied by that Cynthia woman.

But you know, Cynthia hadn't even been *nice* to him. What was that? Tina Two. *Sure, Ken, out of the frying pan into the fire, why don't you.*

Well he'd done a lot of thinking since that night. And he was ashamed of the fact that he hadn't recognized right off that Missy was the one for him. Even though—duh a million times—he was ten times more comfortable with her. He obviously felt their bond subconsciously the second he met her.

It's just that while he was very bright—some called him brilliant—his romantic brain obviously lagged far behind his intellectual development. It had taken some time for his adolescent fixation on Cynthia to wear off completely and be replaced by the infinitely more rich and simple and obvious and life-altering fact that Missy had answered his ad. Sweet, beautiful Missy with her stunning shy smile and breasts that could launch a thousand ships.

Who had he been kidding? He didn't want a megababe. What the hell would a man like him ever *do* with one?

He flicked the TV off with a sudden unfamiliar spurt of masculine energy, and jumped off his new white couch to stride over to his new cordless phone before he thought about what he was doing and changed his mind.

He wanted Missy, that's all there was to it.

"WOULD YOU LIKE a drink?" The waitress at Eagan's inclined her body in a questioning stance and tilted her head toward Cynthia. Cynthia nodded politely. Yes, she wanted a drink. She wanted several drinks. Anything to cushion the irritation of having to eat dinner with The Great Crotchless One.

More than irritation. Irritation and a dirty feeling that she couldn't quite rationalize away, even imagining herself accepting the award at the ceremony. Even though she wasn't going for anything more than damage control with Dicky. God knew she wasn't going to try to influence the choice; she wanted to win that award fair and square. But by being here she hoped to stop him from influencing her chances negatively. That wouldn't be fair, either. One word to his doting daddy would do it. She just wanted to make sure that one word stayed in his mouth.

Good strategy. No problem.

Except there was a problem. Named Adam. Ever since he accused her of not living life to its fullest, he'd been perched on the side of her consciousness twenty-four hours a day. Right now, he didn't like what he saw. Since when was dining with the devil high on her list of fulfilling activities?

She opened her mouth to order a bathtub-sized martini, when Dicky gave her one of his blinding perfect smiles.

"Allow me to order for you." He turned the smile on the waitress who appreciated it far more than Cynthia did. "Two ice-cold Foster's beers, please."

Cynthia entire body stiffened. *Foster's?* Their butts had barely warmed the chair and the SOB was already going for the jugular. Worse, Adam had immediately pounced on the situation and started whispering in her ear. *Was she going to allow Richard Croshallis the upper hand this soon into their meeting? Play along and go against her principles and her very personality type to kiss up to a complete jerk?*

Cynthia pulled in a breath and let it out sharply. She firmly told phantom Adam that she'd been through all this moral stuff already, and to please go back to his nicely appointed phantom apartment and wait for her in the bedroom where he belonged.

How she went about winning the Foster Award was her business. It wasn't as if she'd ever done anything unscrupulous in her professional life. Nothing that could harm a colleague or a friend. If she felt having dinner with Dicky could prevent her from losing the award unfairly, so be it. That was her decision, based on the evidence and the reality of the situation.

So Adam could just butt the hell out of her thoughts. He didn't have a clue about the kind of battles she'd faced in her life. He'd had everything handed to him since he was born into silk, hand-embroidered diapers. What did he know about the dirty tricks ordinary mortals had to use to get what they wanted? A snap of his fingers always worked for him. Pretty damn easy to be judgmental sitting on a trust fund the size of Jupiter.

She closed the argument with herself and pronounced her side victorious. From now on she would concentrate on the business at hand and on her dinner companion. Who was looking particularly vile this evening in a black rayon shirt and black pants, his dense hair parted in a ruler-straight line and cemented over to one side with greasy-looking goop. His teeth were startlingly white, as if he'd sent away for one of those miracle whitening kits advertised on TV and overdone it. Startlingly white and perfectly straight.

He was actually quite good-looking, which, considering his personality, only made him all the more repulsive. When the Foster Award was hers, she could put her new power to good use, like getting Dicky's company run out of town.

"Foster's sounds good, thanks, Richard." Betraying no emotion, she patted her hair back though it was already firmly secured in its French twist.

"Splendid." He gave her a meaningful stare, which on his end was probably meant to be ah-so-we-have-an-understanding, but which came across more like, boy-do-I-think-I'm-hot. "And please call me Dick."

"Rich—Dick." She tightened her lips before the phrase "rich dick" could make it to her humor center. "I want to talk to you seriously about some of the concerns we have regarding IT Consulting."

He took a long sip of ice water, then put the glass down, still maintaining the icky eye contact. Cynthia held herself still and returned his stare calmly. She could stare down the best of them.

Except Adam, damn him.

"And *I* want to talk to *you* seriously as well." He curved one side of his mouth up into a sleazy grin he probably thought was devastating. "About ending this evening somewhere romantic."

She didn't move, didn't react, not a twitch. For all he knew she was thinking anything from, *oh, joy, my dream has come true,* to *run for the hills the alien has landed.* Power games. Cynthia Parkins loved them.

She waited for the tingling excitement she always felt in situations like these. Situations where she had to walk a tightrope between domination and submission. If she wavered now, showed too much weakness or too much strength, the game was up.

Unfortunately, the tingle of excitement was noticeably absent. Instead, she was suddenly and unexpectedly tired. Sick of games. Wanting to be…real with someone. Natural. The way she was in bed with Adam the other night.

He saw his chance and came back out of his phantom abode, whispering "good for you" in her ear. A thrill of pride ran through her body and made her extremely cranky. *Leave me the hell alone.*

"You're beautiful, Cynthia. I am not even trying to pretend I'm not attracted to you."

She let one eyebrow climb halfway up her forehead. Keep playing. Show no emotion. Make sure the Foster stayed possible. "I noticed that."

"So why don't we call dinner off-limits to work.

Chat like friends and...get to know one another this evening.''

Because I'd like my dinner to have some hope of staying in my stomach where it belongs. Phantom Adam chuckled and told her to say it out loud next time. *Tell the bastard the truth.* Instead, she forced herself to smile politely. ''Look, Dick, you're very nice to—''

''Ah!'' Dicky clapped his hands together as the waitress arrived with their beers. He accepted his midair and lifted it toward her.

''To you, Cynthia. May this not be the only Foster's you hold in your hand this year. And think about what I said earlier about ending this evening somewhere romantic. I can always put in a good word with Dad about the award.''

Phantom Adam stepped back and waited. Cynthia could feel his expectation pulling at her. *Flatten him, right where he sits.*

Sorry, Adam. She wasn't ready to go that far.

She took a sip of beer and put her glass down, placed her elbows carefully on the table and rested her chin on her hands. ''Are you implying that if I get cozy with you, you'll see to it I get the Foster Award?''

He at least had the decency to look surprised. ''No. I'm not implying it.''

Cynthia relaxed just a tiny bit. Okay. Maybe this wasn't so bad. Maybe the situation was salvageable. ''Good, because—''

"I'm coming right out and saying it." He folded his arms on the table and leaned forward. "I think we can be very good together, Cynthia. We're so much alike."

Cynthia swallowed convulsively. "What are you talking about?"

He grinned, and she wanted to stick little pieces of spinach between those perfect teeth. "We both started from nowhere. Clawed our way up. We both go after what we want, and we don't let little things like principles get in our way."

Nausea and something like fear swept into her stomach. He dared compare them? Dared? The idea that she was anything like Dick Crotchless was too horrifying to...to...be examined closely.

"I admire that about you, Cynthia. It excites me. We're two of a kind."

Cynthia stared at him, her brain scrambled beyond all hope of producing words. Two of a kind? Was she anything like him? Anything?

He half closed his eyes and leaned closer. "We can set the sheets on fire, kid."

That did it.

No one called Cynthia Parkins "kid" and lived. And there was only one man she wanted to set the sheets on fire with. A man who had gone a long way toward giving her the strength to do the lovely satisfying thing she was about to do. She was finished with this game. Done sucking up to a Dick in name only. About time she lived life to its fullest. About time she spent her precious hours on earth doing what she was meant to do.

As soon as she emptied her glass of Foster's beer in Dick's crotchless lap, she was going to find Adam and make him work all night.

9

MISSY LAY in Ken's bed staring miserably up at the ceiling as she'd been lying and staring pretty much all night long, listening to Ken's heavy even breathing.

Misery. Humiliation. The worst night of her life. And this was going to be the worst morning, she could just *tell*.

Her intended seduction had started out so well. Ken had been glad to take her call, sounded thrilled to have her over, and his voice even held a note of sexy promise that had practically shot her through the roof.

Then she'd walked into his apartment, decked out in her sexy finery, and taken off her sweater. Immediately, his eyes had sort of bugged out and he'd seemed to have trouble with his breathing. But not in a good way.

Right then she'd wanted to go home and die. But she'd stayed, because after all, you couldn't die just by wanting to, and she had been so determined to make Ken hers that she'd had some determination left over, even after that awful beginning.

They'd sat, had some nice blush wine and talked

and talked and talked, and things had gone so much better. It was almost *freaky* how much they had in common. She'd felt herself really, really falling in love with his gentle manner and his astonishingly intelligent brain, and found herself also getting pretty worked up to what she'd already promised herself would be the fitting ending to the evening.

Things had started okay. At least this time when she kissed him, he'd responded. And how. And gosh, he turned out to be a wonderful kisser. The kind who closes his eyes and just disappears into the kissing so you feel like you've become his whole world for that wonderful special time. She'd been beside herself with love and…that crazy hot feeling. She'd even put his hand on her breast. It had felt so wonderful and he'd clearly been enjoying himself, kissing her with his eyes closed and having his hand on her breast, so she knew the really good part would be even better between them.

But then she made her first awful mistake, which had furthered her along the path into the worst night of her life of which this was going to be the worst morning after. She'd gotten up, unzipped her dress and let it fall to the floor so she stood there in the middle of his spartan apartment in her black lace bra and matching black lace panties, feeling wild and free and glorious. Ken had reacted to her wild, free glory by choking on a swallow for which he needed a glass of water and pounding on the back. Then they'd just sat there with the sexy momentum totally *ruined* for heaven's sakes. Her worst nightmare. She'd put her sweater back on over the underwear.

Then she'd made her second mistake. She'd suggested they come into his room. He'd been in agreement, she guessed, not like he'd protested or anything—what guy would? Then she'd been overcome again and tumbled him onto the bed and about three minutes into their frantic kissing, when her hand had stolen down to investigate his male equipment, she'd realized with sickening certitude that she didn't turn him on in the least.

He'd apologized, seemed really embarrassed. She'd been matter-of-fact and comforting, suggested they just lie there and talk, all the things she'd read in some magazine article a woman was supposed to do when faced with this horrifying situation.

Then when half an hour had gone by, during which they talked nicely, and they *did* have so much to say to each other, and she felt closer and closer to him with every *word* practically, she thought maybe it was time to try again.

And gosh, she'd tried just about everything…even *that,* which she didn't think any guy could resist. But after a while her jaw was tired and obviously nothing was happening, so she'd slid miserably up to lie next to him and here she still was, eight hours later, not entirely out of hope, but pretty damn—excuse the curse word—discouraged.

Missy got out of bed and took off the bra and panties, then rummaged as quietly as she could in his drawer for a T-shirt and boxers to cover herself, since there was no way in hell she'd ever wear that dress again.

After she found what she was looking for and went into the bathroom to pull them on, she washed all the leftover makeup off her face and scowled at her plain colorless features and bad case of bedhead. Who was she kidding? It would take a hell of a lot more than cosmetics and a dress to make her into Cynthia.

She used the bathroom and pulled the flush handle down as slowly as she could so as not to make too much noise that might wake him. She wasn't sure she could go out onto the street in his T-shirt and underwear, but she didn't really want to stay here and face her failure, either. Maybe she could run out to her car and call him later? They should probably talk about what happened. Later.

She let herself carefully out of the bathroom and froze when she saw Ken already out of bed.

Oh, great. If he didn't think she was sexy last night he'd probably just throw up from looking at her now.

"Hi, Ken." She hung her bedhead down to hide her plain face and pretended fascination with the relationship between her bare toes and his carpet. The worst night of her life. "I borrowed some of your clothes. I hope that was okay."

"Missy."

His voice came out in this sort of husky groan, very masculine, and kind of hot and desperate sounding, the way she'd said his name last night many, many times.

She jerked her gaze up to his and found that his eyes were blazing blue, like she'd never seen them blaze before. Her own eyes widened and then, they couldn't help it, they took a quick sneak peek down.

And then they widened farther. A lot farther. *Oh my goodness.*

She was going to have one of the very best mornings ever.

"THAT'S MY final decision. Goodbye, Ms. Parkins."

Cynthia hung up the phone and emitted a growl that would halt a charging lion. Renovating the Harbins Park playground had been her pet project. She'd done the fund-raising, attended the dinners, coaxed donated parts and labor from local contractors. And now when the rusty slide and dirty sandbox lying forlornly amid broken asphalt had been replaced by colorful plastic and sweet-smelling wood chips, the credit and publicity were going to fat old Mr. Jancus, who'd made maybe one phone call to further the project.

And why? Because fat old Mr. Jancus was a highly visible personage in Milwaukee. Having his name attached to the project gave it importance and would provide the necessary momentum to convince others to hop on board and open their wallets.

Cynthia kicked her shoes off under the kitchen table and slammed her briefcase down on top of it.

She sure as hell picked the wrong week to turn Dicky's pants into a tributary of Lake Michigan. After she'd doused him, his eyes had turned even more rodent-like and he'd delivered some bad-movie line like, "You realize this destroys any hopes you had of winning the Foster."

Yeah, no kidding.

At the time, her response had been short and to the point, accompanied by that infinitely expressive finger gesture Ken was always doing without being aware of it.

Cynthia was very aware of it. As was Richard Croshallis. She hadn't realized people's faces could turn that color. Amazing all the new things you learned every day.

Now, of course she could call it career suicide. Sure, it had been a fine and triumphant moment, but with a Foster under her belt, fat old Mr. Jancus would have welcomed her name attached to the project. Maybe she should call Croshallis and apologize. That award would give her exactly the validation she needed in this and so many other similar situations. Give her the green light toward really making a difference on her own, instead of having to ride on male suits.

Do it. Now. She darted for the phone and left Dick a message at home to call her when he got in. If she was nice enough to him when he returned the call, indulged in a little flattery, then maybe her chances were—

Cynthia closed her eyes and sank onto a chair. Had she really stooped this low? Apologizing to Bacteria Boy? Except that it was so infuriatingly unjust that she do all the work on the playground project and Jancus get the credit. If it was just this once, okay. But episodes like this had happened to her all her life. Damned if she'd sit back one more time and let the Old Boys Club walk all over her. Enough. She was woman; hear her roar.

In fact she'd start now, redouble her efforts. There were rumors that RC Industries was relocating from outside Chicago. She could join efforts to lure the company to Milwaukee. Tonight she already had analyses to write for VF Capital, but she could drink gallons of coffee and—

Her doorbell rang; she strode over to answer it, brimming with renewed energy. Probably that kid next door who said he'd be by tonight to sell her a magazine subscription.

"Hi." Adam pushed past her into her apartment, bearing a six-pack of beer and a bakery bag under one arm, a pizza under the other. "I had a feeling you were planning to work too hard tonight, so I brought dinner and distraction."

He deposited the pizza on her table, moved her briefcase to the floor, then kicked it to the kitchen's far wall.

"Adam…" She put her hands to her temples as if she had a very bad headache, which come to think of it, she did. He was relentless. For the past few weeks, since their first night together, he'd been interrupting her at every opportunity. Taking her out to lunches that stretched beyond her allotted hour. Coaxing her out of overtime get-ahead work. Calling her during client meetings under the pretense of a business emergency and whispering erotic things into her cell phone. Even persuading her once to reschedule her Friday meetings so they could drive up to Door County for a long weekend on the beach and in bed. "This was so sweet of you. Honest. But it's a really bad— *Mmph.*"

He grabbed her and kissed her, drew back, then kissed her again, a long hot kiss that, somewhat predictably, turned her brain into crème brûlée. The man had that effect on her.

"Of course it's a bad time." He kissed her again. "Every night with you is bad. But I will have my way with you. Not for nothing am I known as Super Adam."

"Who calls you that?" She sent him a look of supreme skepticism.

He pretended to ponder. "Well, there's me, and…me, and let's not forget…me."

Cynthia laughed. Somehow he could undermine even her most determined efforts to be serious and directed. The man was dangerous. Lethal. But this time she had to be strong. This time she would resist at all costs.

"Not tonight dear, I've got a headache."

"And I'm the cure." He got plates from her cabinet and plunked two slices of pizza on each. "Besides, you can't do a thing on an empty stomach. Pepperoni pizza and chocolate éclairs, a couple of beers, and you'll be raring to go."

"I'll be raring to nap." She stared at the oily shimmer on the gooey melted cheese. Heart-attack food. Lumpy-hips food. Her saliva glands kicked into action.

Maybe *one* bite…

Six or seven bites, a salad she made herself and two beers later, she pushed back her plate and pointed to Adam. "Now. You leave. I work."

"Hmm." He stretched his lean body and got up from the table, yanked her to her feet and pinned her to the wall with a don't-take-no kiss that went on for about five minutes and still wasn't remotely long enough. "Now. I stay. We play."

"Not tonight." She managed to push him away, but knew he wouldn't surrender that easily. When had he ever? "Tonight I work. I have things to accomplish, things to—"

Her phone rang. *Dicky.* Damn. She hadn't planned out what she was going to say. She glared at Adam and lunged for the receiver. "Hello?"

"Cynthia? It's Richard."

Brrrrr. No "call me Dick" today. "Richard. I'm glad you called. I wanted to—"

"Throw more beer in your lap." Adam whispered the words in her ear, enveloped her from behind in a sexy embrace and slid his hands down her thighs, then up to heaven.

She shrugged, trying to throw him off. ''—apologize for the other night.''

Adam stiffened behind her, and something very much like shame snuck into Cynthia's confidence.

''It took you this long to apologize?''

Adam moved in front of her and gave a disapproving frown, arms folded across his chest.

She turned away from him, confused and off-balance. ''Yes. I...shouldn't have thrown my drink at you.''

''You should have thrown something heavier.''

''What was that?'' Dick asked sharply.

''Oh, nothing.'' Cynthia turned and shushed Adam furiously. ''The TV is on. I wanted to see if we could meet sometime soon to discuss—''

''Soooo.'' Dick's voice oozed smug satisfaction. ''The little worm is crawling back to Papa's dirt pile. I knew you would eventually. I'm just surprised it took so long.''

Cynthia's pizza made a bid for reemergence into daylight. She clutched her stomach, and glanced up at Adam. As usual, her glance stuck to his like he had superglue on his eyeballs.

Except his playful look had gone. In fact his angry look had gone, too. He just looked sad. And sort of hurt.

She squeezed her eyes shut to block him out. This was her life. She opened one eye and shut it quickly.

He still looked that way. Like she'd disappointed him deeply. Which was probably because she had. And maybe herself, too.

But the Foster hung in the balance. The Foster. She opened the other eye. Still there. She shut it. Damn.

Adam or no Adam, she knew what she had to do.

"Richard." She took a deep breath. "I called to apologize and apologize I will. I'm sorry I threw beer at you—it was very unprofessional. I'm also sorry to tell you that VF Capital isn't going to touch your company with a sixty-foot pole let alone one-hundred million because you are a perverted pile of goat manure. Have a nice day."

She hung up the phone and grabbed Adam's collar. "*Now*. We play."

CYNTHIA WOKE UP and smiled. *Mmm*. There wasn't much in life more fabulous than waking up having been thoroughly made love to the night before. Especially by one of the world's greatest lovers. Who also happened to have made his way so far into her heart she doubted even the most skilled surgeons could extract him.

She glanced at the clock on her bedside table and yawned. Eight-thirty. No point going to work today. No point getting out of bed today.

She turned and spooned up behind Adam's broad smooth back. "Good morning?"

"*Grmph.*"

She smiled and pushed her hips closer to his extremely fabulous buns. "And how are we this morning?"

He turned, enveloped her in his powerful arms and pulled her even closer. "Suddenly wide awake."

She grinned. "Some parts apparently more than others."

"I'm an early riser."

She giggled and didn't even care that the sound spelled giddy and infatuated in letters ten-feet tall.

Adam raised his head and squinted at the clock. "Uh, Cynthia?"

"Eight-thirty, I know." She snuggled closer. "I'm not going to work today."

His jaw dropped. "Let me get this straight. *You* are calling in sick?"

"I'm calling in sexually satisfied."

"And the Foster?"

"I guess I dropped out of the running." She swallowed hard. Okay, it hurt. She couldn't be expected to let go of a years-long dream overnight.

Adam pressed his cheek against her temple and held the contact reassuringly steady. "What can I do to convince you that you are worth so much more than that empty award?"

"I bet I can think of many things." She waggled her eyebrows, hoping the dull ache in her belly would politely get up and leave.

"I bet you can." He drew his hand up her back and stroked her hair. "You know, my nephew Alex is three years old. He asks 'why' to every single state-

ment uttered by anyone within his hearing. Sometimes it's amazing the answers that come out when
you stop to ask why.''

"And your point is…"

"I want to play the 'why' game with you."

"Why?" She threw him a mischievous glance that
made him chuckle and shake his head.

"No, that's what *I* get to ask. Ready?"

"I guess."

"Why is the Foster so important?"

"Why *was* it so important?" She shrugged. "Because it's important to me to be successful."

"Why?"

"Because…being successful involves money and
power and self-esteem." Her jaw tightened and she
instructed it to remain loose. "Those things are important."

"Why?"

"Because…" She moved restlessly. "Without
them I'm…less than I want to be."

"Why?"

Her breath rushed out in a sound of frustration. "Is
your nephew this persistent?"

"Yes. Why?"

"Well…you wouldn't understand."

"Ah-ah." He wagged his finger at her. "Those
aren't the rules. Why would you be less of a person
without the Foster?"

She shook her head to try and clear it, which didn't

help in the slightest. "I didn't *say* I'd be less of a person without it."

"At the risk of sounding even more like my nephew, yes you did."

Cynthia sucked in a breath and fought to keep her emotions down. For some reason his questions were upsetting her. She felt panicked and frightened, as if he was threatening to pull the rug out from under her entire existence. "You don't know what it's like."

"So tell me."

She stirred against him and gestured into the air above her bed. "You don't know what it's like to have people assume you're not a valuable contributor to life on planet Earth because one, you're poor, two, you're from the South and strike three, you're a woman." She blinked at the ceiling, remembering the initial surprise and humiliation, and then the determination to overcome those obstacles which hadn't failed her since. Except for maybe now. "So I lost the accent, worked my ass off, and—"

"Boy you showed them."

"Yes. I did." She didn't even try to keep the pride from her voice.

"Got them back."

"Yes."

He kissed her cheek and moved his mouth to her ear. "By becoming just like them."

"No." Cynthia pushed him away. "I proved I could play with the best of them."

"Oh, I see. So you won by living your life in homage to shallow people who were cruel to you."

"What?" She tried to sit straight so she could work up a really good outraged glare, but his arm snaked around her body and kept her down on his level. "You are the most preposterous, horrendous, maddening, plague-ridden male nightmare I've ever met."

"Aw, shucks, honey, you're going to give me a swelled head." He kept her prisoner against him and slid his hand down between their bodies to do things she knew from experience that unless she stopped him, would very shortly turn her into a panting, pleading mass of hormones, current outraged fury notwithstanding. "Hmm. You know, I think you already gave me one."

She struggled to escape, but he held her tightly, kept his fingers moving slowly and gently. "I am *not* living my life in homage to those idiots."

"No. Of course not." His soothing tone had exactly the opposite effect.

"I'm not!" She heard her voice, strident and shrill and the awful possibility hammered its way into her thick head. "Am I?"

"Oh, Cynthia." He kissed her with real passion, not even caring about morning breath, which was about as accepting and wonderful as a guy could get. "It's not too late. You can still dance the funky chicken if you want to."

"This has never happened to me. All of a sudden

I don't know anything. I'm a mess." She closed her eyes and tried to figure out what the hell she was feeling, who she was, what she should do now with the rest of her life, how she could possibly be getting aroused in the middle of a life crisis. "You've made me into a mess."

"Hmm." His fingers increased their pace. "You know what this means, don't you?"

"What?" She tried to ignore her brain meltdown, tried harder to ignore his fingers and concentrate on his words, but it wasn't easy. Or successful.

"You're in love."

She rolled her eyes while her heart screamed a giant joyous affirmative. "Will you *stop* with the love stuff?"

"No." He grinned and dipped one, then two fingers inside her, to ready her for their latest unscheduled excursion to heaven. "I'm not going to stop with 'the love stuff,' as you so romantically put it. Not until you 'fess up."

He grinned again at what had to be a helpless, horny total goofball expression on her face, grabbed a condom from her nightstand where he'd tossed them the night before, and tore the package open with his teeth as if he were a beast tearing at a carcass.

Amazingly, though her entire past, present and possibly future had just been shredded, Cynthia giggled—slightly hysterically, but again unapologetically. She loved him. Of course she did. And he knew it. He loved her, too. The knowledge was awe-inspiring and terrifying, but also protecting and familiar somehow. She felt changed, lightened and at the same time heavy with something serious and somber and almost painfully beautiful.

Even more amazingly, the feeling charged her with the certainty that whatever grew out of the smoking ruins of her existence, it would be beautiful. And useful. And sexually satisfying.

Adam put on the condom and rolled her to her back. She looped her arms around his neck and welcomed him on top of her. He kissed her tenderly, then lifted his body to watch her face as he slid inside her. She held his eyes until the emotion was too much, then pulled him down again, wrapped her arms around his strong back and savored the feel of his muscles working as he moved.

Again and again, their bodies rose and fell in perfect opposition, and gradually the good-sex feelings were mixed into and enhanced by deeper emotions. Cynthia found herself trying not to cry while all these amazing and nearly overwhelming sensations buzzed around her body, making her feel disoriented and adrift.

"You're beautiful." Adam murmured the words against her skin, kissed her mouth and buried his hands under her body to pull her impossibly closer. "You are a beautiful person, Cynthia. I love you."

"I love you, too." She only managed a whisper, but by the way his body stiffened for an instant, by the way the breath rushed into his chest, she knew he'd heard her and that whatever else her currently shredded future might hold, it would most certainly hold him.

10

CYNTHIA CROSSED her legs under the cloth-covered round table she'd been assigned in the Pfister Hotel Imperial Ballroom and gave a charming smile through clenched teeth at the old geezer on her right. Apparently he had climbed Mt. Everest in a bathing suit, walked on Mars and made more money than Bill Gates within two weeks of his third birthday.

She uncrossed her legs and took a minuscule bite of the delicious thin cheesecake topped with fresh berries and chocolate sauce. Just one more nibble, before the fat monsters did any damage to her arteries or thighs. And maybe one more after that.

This dinner had been interminable. The cocktails beforehand were interminable. The ceremony about to be underway would no doubt be interminable. Of course in all probability she wouldn't get the Foster. Dicky was here, in simpering tow to his enormous, powerful father. She'd found herself irretrievably in their path and had received such an icy reception she'd been glad for her new wondrous gel-bra in case her nipples reacted to the chill.

Still…she deserved that award. She'd resurrected several businesses with sound practices and bad luck from the brink of ruin. She'd donated to charities, volunteered her time to entrepreneurs who hoped to hit the big time, networked her butt off with the old boys in high places.

As much as her time with Adam had made her reexamine her life and her goals, she hadn't found them so lacking as to ditch them entirely. Wandering through life, taking each day as it came as he did still seemed so...aimless. So lacking in purpose and power. The demons inside her wouldn't let her give up all hope. Mr. Croshallis wasn't the whole committee.

She crossed her legs and smiled again at Geezer, who now it appeared had *really* invented the Internet. The only remaining question seemed to be whether he would admit to being God before they cleared the dessert plates.

Adam's little evil face popped immediately into her brain. Was this what she was destined to be like in her old age? Bragging about her accomplishments to some thirty-something stud who smiled politely, but felt sorry for her because clearly her life had been so empty?

She uncrossed her legs. Okay, so maybe Adam was onto something. Sort of. She wasn't going to label the past ten years of her life a waste of time, but maybe she had been a little overdirected. Maybe spending all her energy on achieving publicly impressive feats wasn't going to be the road to happiness she thought.

Maybe pinning so much on winning the Foster *was* just a waste of her energy.

Or was that line of thinking just sour grapes? Who knew how much power Dicky's daddy really had? She could still be in the running. She *should* still be in the running.

Cynthia closed her eyes. She felt like the pendulum in the grandfather clock in her office. One way, then the other, with no apparent progress. An unfamiliar feeling. Not one she enjoyed.

The emcee for the evening's ceremonies stepped up to the mike. The waitstaff began clearing the dessert plates. Cynthia's stomach drew in tightly. Okay. She still wanted the award. So shoot her.

The badly toupeed announcer warbled through the usual thanks to everyone and his grandmother for everything they'd done since infancy. Cynthia crossed her legs. The announcer went on to invite a few other badly toupeed idiots to drone on forever about things no one in the entire universe gave a fig about. Cynthia clenched her fists. The emcee retook the microphone and said those dreadfully immortal words. *And now, the moment you've all been waiting for.* Cynthia gritted her teeth. *The Foster blablabla the most important blablabla given to the person who blablabla, nominated, voted on by blablabla.*

She leaned forward, and suddenly, across the room, caught the gaze of Adam, smiling at her with about six hundred gallons of love shooting out of his eyes. *Oh, man.* Didn't the Foster pale in importance when you could have someone like that to come home to? Someone who had hold of something more important than awards, who had given so much of himself trying to teach Cynthia that lesson.

She loved him. For his selflessness, for his tireless efforts to bring her something better, to bring her to a better place, to—

And the Foster goes to...

The name was announced. Cynthia whipped her head around to stare at the emcee.

Who?

She rose to her feet. No, staggered. She staggered to her feet. The man beside her put a hand to her arm. *Are you okay?* She shook him off and stumbled for the door. No. She wasn't okay. She wasn't okay in the slightest. Her entire universe had taken a nose dive and smashed itself to smithereens on the basement level of hell. At the ballroom doorway, she turned just once, just briefly, to see the victor lofting the statuette, grinning broadly to the standing ovation in front of him, holding his hands up for quiet to begin his no doubt well-rehearsed acceptance speech.

She backed through the door and sped out into the luxurious dark-panelled hallway, fighting nausea and tears.

Adam Bradson had won the Foster.

CYNTHIA TURNED the corner of her building and froze. Leaning against the front door, looking worried and exhausted and frankly gorgeous in his

tuxedo, illuminated by the front porch light, was none
other than Mr. That - award - isn't - important - so - I -
think - you - should - slow - down - and - experience -
more - of - life - so - *I* - can - win - it.

How long had he been there? She'd gone out to
Elsa's, intending a nice three-martini self-pity party,
but had ended up nursing one for two hours while the
smoky night life went on around her.

"Hello, Cynthia." He turned tired and cautious
eyes on her that made her swallow unexpected tenderness.

Tenderness? Ha! Not until she got a damn good
explanation.

She walked slowly up onto the front stoop until she
stood about a foot away from him. "Well, if it isn't
Mr. Foster."

"No." He didn't move, just watched her. "Mr.
Bradson."

"Congratulations." She jammed her hands onto
her hips. "Had I known you were in the running I
might have wished you good luck."

"Cynthia, even *I* didn't know I was in the running."

"Oh? You put your name in while you were
asleep?"

"I didn't put my name in."

"Ah! Of course. Aliens came down from planet
Scumbag and entered you. Bet they made you Scumbag king in your absence, too, didn't they?"

"If I had known, I would have told you." He spoke

wearily, heavy words that went straight to her heart. "Someone else nominated me."

"And didn't happen to mention it. And when the committee called to confirm your entry, you said yes automatically without having a clue what they were talking about and were never curious."

"I never got a call."

"Right." A hard weight pressed in her stomach, an angry burning lump of coal left by Santa for a bad girl. At the same time her throat was closing with a stupid, desperate, naive need to believe him. She felt pulled apart by warring factions. Like a human version of the former Yugoslavia. "But you happened to show up tonight and happened to have a speech planned out and happened to look wildly overjoyed waving the trophy around."

"It would have been rude to do otherwise. I was invited to come tonight by Mrs. Lemmingster. I went to watch you win, or console you if you didn't. The speech was standard I'm-so-humbly-grateful crap, and if you'd stayed to see you would have known it wasn't planned."

"You saw me leave?"

"Yes." He said the word sharply, as if it had been a painful moment. "I wanted you to get that award, Cynthia."

"Oh, you *did!*" She clenched her fists. Did he? Didn't he? Was *anyone* that generous? Not in her experience. In her experience people went after what they wanted in whatever way possible. Like her being nice to Dicky for so long, until Adam's influence had her flinging beer at him and calling him goat manure. "So that's why you sabotaged me at every turn over the past few weeks, kept telling me it didn't matter, my clients didn't matter, that—"

"Sabotage?" His eyes narrowed. "Is that what you think?"

She took a deep breath and let it out on a rush of unshed tears. "It looks that way, you have to admit."

He tightened his lips. "Yes. It does *look* that way."

"And you're telling me it's not that way."

"That's right."

She brushed impatiently at a curious moth. "And I should say sure, fine, honey, and believe you."

He nodded, still watching her intently. "It's called trust. People in love should have it."

She lifted her head to stare at the black night sky and took another deep breath. Little episodes kept intruding into her attempts to believe him. Times he'd pulled her out of work. Times he'd convinced her she'd studied a case enough, prepared plenty, researched adequately when her instincts were telling her otherwise. "I don't know if I have that much trust right now."

"Really." His voice came out flat and devastatingly chilly.

"I haven't been in many positions where I could afford to trust someone."

"Oh, come on." He laughed bitterly. "You've just been afraid to let yourself."

"I've always had to be strong."

"You think trusting someone is a weakness? You think to be strong you have to be alone?"

Tears made a more serious threat to her control. "I always have been."

"Well, I think you're just plain terrified. Terrified of your own thoughts and feelings, terrified of everyone else's. For God's sake, you're so scared you can't even eat a chicken fat bomb." He gestured into the darkness and let his hand slap onto his thigh. "If you're so strong how come you let Crotch Boy walk all over you for so long? If you're so strong, why don't you say to hell with who won the Foster award, I love this man and he's worth taking the risk to believe in?"

Cynthia's brain melted down into a white-noise irrational puddle. She took a step away from him and clapped her hands. "Bravo, bravo, give the ten-cent psychiatrist an Oscar. What the hell do you know about strength? When have you had to do anything that required more than ringing for the parlor maid? For crying out loud, you jump at a heart attack like it gives you permission to give up on life."

"I finally figured out who I am, Cynthia. It takes strength to be able to define yourself on your own terms, not other people's. When have you had the strength to be yourself without four beers in you?"

Her jaw dropped open. "God that was low. You think I drink too much?"

He shrugged. "You think I'm a scumbag."

"You know what this makes us?"

"Incompatible?"

"Incom—" She gaped at him, unable to believe he'd stolen the word. And even more unable to believe the implication. Was this really it? "Yes. Incompatible."

He pushed himself away from the door and went down the front walk. Cynthia turned as he passed and watched him go, still fuming, but sick with pain and misery as well.

At the curb, he yanked open his car door and turned his handsome weary face back to her. "I'm glad you got home safely."

She lifted her chin. "Afraid for innocent pedestrians during my drunk-driving rampage?"

He set his jaw. "I was worried about you."

"Oh." She wrapped her arms across her chest. "Well you don't have to be. I'm fine."

"So I've been told." He got in his BMW convertible and drove off, leaving Cynthia pretty sure she'd just screwed up the best thing that had ever happened to her.

ADAM READJUSTED his position on his couch, took another peanut out of the can he clutched in his lap and aimed it carefully at the empty plastic cup on his coffee table.

Missed. The peanut bounced off the rim of the cup and joined the other failed attempts in a salty scattered mess.

Well, this was jolly. After a nice night of practically no sleep, how useful and fascinating to attempt to throw peanuts into a plastic cup.

He let loose another attempt, bending back his hand and releasing his wrist forward with a carefully calculated snap.

Missed.

Of course he couldn't quite claim to be living his life to its fullest right about now. The harsh words he'd exchanged with Cynthia had left their mark. Had he gotten lax? Traded in overachievement for apathy? Last night when the award had been handed to him, amid his confusion and horror on Cynthia's behalf, there had been that tiny traitorous part of him that said, *Oh, yeah. The winner. The champ. No one can touch me.* That part of him he thought he'd left behind three years ago. At the time he'd reacted harshly. Given himself a severe scolding as if he was an alcoholic who'd fallen off the wagon. Then he'd given Cynthia an equally severe scolding.

He aimed another peanut. Let it fly.

Missed.

But somehow today in the hazy light of a sticky August day, he was starting to see things differently. Maybe not in such black and white. Maybe he was being too hard on Cynthia. Maybe she really was happy the way she was. Maybe he was arrogant wanting to make her over into his little protégé, a replica of who he was, essentially saving her not from herself, but from who *he* used to be.

But then again…

His doorbell rang, rescuing him from his unaccustomed state of confusion and indecision and truly lousy peanut-throwing.

He opened the door and his eyebrows shot up. "Ken."

But not Ken. This Ken was dressed in a short-sleeved linen shirt in a muted stripe, and pants that actually matched. His hair was trimmed short and he sported a new pair of thin wire glasses. He looked…*good.*

"Hey, Adam. Can I come in?"

Adam nodded stupidly and backed away from the door to let him in. What the hell had happened to Ken? He even moved differently. Straight to Adam's sofa where he sat and leaned back, instead of his usual collapse. Then he caught sight of the peanut display and looked questioningly at Adam.

"So." Adam put his hands into his pockets and rocked back on his heels, for once feeling like the doofus between them. "What's up?"

"Congratulations on the Foster. I imagine winning it was something of a surprise." Ken folded his hands and rested his forearms on his thighs.

"That's for—" Adam's brain gave him a little nudge. "How did you know it was a surprise?"

Ken clasped his hands behind his head and grinned. "I put your name in."

"You." Adam stared at him, not sure whether to

clap him on the back or strangle him. "What did you do that for?"

Ken's smug expression fell. "I wanted to do you the same favor you did for me with my ad. The one that found me Missy."

Adam bit his tongue. Not Ken's fault that winning the Foster turned out to be close to a disaster. Adam should be flattered and touched.

"Thanks, Ken. That means a lot to me." He collapsed onto the sofa beside Ken, concentrating on looking flattered and touched. "So things are going okay with Missy?"

Ken's face turned radiant—or whatever the masculine equivalent was. "She's everything I've ever wanted. It took me a while to figure it out, though."

"Yeah, well, the whole newspaper ad thing was a mess from the beginning."

"No." Ken pushed his glasses up onto his nose—with his index finger. "It's more than that. I thought I wanted someone like Cynthia. Even once I knew Missy had answered my ad, I wanted her to be different than she was. Like some strange combination of two people. That was wrong."

Adam picked up his can of peanuts and missed another shot. He had a feeling he knew what Ken was going to say, and that he'd been sent by a certain blonde to lecture Adam on the ways of love for her brunette friend's sake. "That was wrong?"

"Yes." Ken cleared his throat and flashed Adam a thumbs-up. "Because once I allowed myself to love

Missy for who she is, I found out she's Cynthia inside."

"She is?" Another peanut bounced onto the dark cherry finish of Adam's coffee table. Yup. The big love-her-for-who-she-is lecture. Which was unfortunately making a lot of sense, and about where Adam had gotten to in his own brain. "Okay. I'll bite. *How* is she Cynthia inside?"

"*You* know…" Ken winked and nudged Adam with his elbow. "She's…amazing. In bed. Totally hot. I feel like…Superman."

"Uh, Ken?" Adam inched away from his friend. "Do I really need to hear this?"

"Yes, you do." Ken reached over, grabbed a peanut and sent it zinging into the cup.

Adam's jaw dropped. "How'd you do that?"

"Missy called me this morning." Ken took another nut and sailed it unerringly to join its peanutty little friend in the bottom of the cup. "Cynthia is a wreck."

"What did she say? Does she want to see me?" Adam gritted his teeth. *Jeez.* He sounded like a…*geek.*

"Missy didn't say. Just that I might want to come talk to you."

"So you're here to give me advice." Adam put his peanut can down out of Ken's reach. How sad, when Ken had to give Adam advice on his love life. Though considering how Ken looked wildly happy and Adam was chucking nuts, maybe it was appropriate.

"I said I'd come talk to you." Ken put his hand

out for another peanut. "But I'm pretty sure I can't tell you anything you don't already know."

"Maybe, maybe not." Adam moved the can farther away, took a shot of his own, and missed again. He glared at the cup. So his aim was off. His whole *life* was off today. "But thanks for coming by."

Ken took the hint and stood, grabbed a peanut from the coffee table, moved to the door, took casual aim and landed that one in the cup as well, damn him. "See you around, man."

"Yeah, see you." Adam gave a half-hearted salute to Ken's departure. Nice of the guy to come over, even if Missy made him. Even if he'd just confirmed the train of thought Adam had been on anyway. Ken loved Missy for who she was and she turned out to be everything he wanted.

He lifted another peanut and let it fly to land about three inches from its target. As long as he was allowing himself to be wrong on a few things, he might as well admit that Cynthia might be partly right, too. Maybe he was allowing too much of life to wash over him. He missed that feeling of being totally focused, of not letting anything or anyone get between him and what he wanted.

What he really, really wanted was Cynthia. Right now.

He jumped to his feet, grabbed his keys off the table by the sofa, and lunged for the door. A nut tumbled from his lap and spun out onto the floor. He grabbed it and lofted it toward the cup with a hook shot over his head.

The peanut arced gracefully through the air of his living room and rattled directly into the cup.

CYNTHIA PICKED UP a donut and stared at it, startled. What was she doing? She didn't eat donuts. Tracy, back from her mushy honeymoon, and Allegra, smugly engaged, and Missy, newly and therefore even *more* smugly engaged, had come over that morning for a round of donut therapy and she'd been fooled for a second into thinking she, who always ate whole-grain toast, wanted one. What was with her?

She put the donut down. "See, the thing is, ladies, even though I know you guys are all wildly happy, I'm just not the pairing-off-permanently type."

The words sounded loud and unnatural. Tracy rolled her eyes; Allegra giggled.

Missy shushed the two women. "Cynthia, don't you think if you tried again to talk to—"

"No." She picked up the donut. "You should have heard the things he said to me."

"We did hear them. About six hundred times." Allegra took a big bite of a chocolate glazed donut and for some reason Cynthia's mouth watered where it usually dried out and wanted salad. What was with her?

She put the donut back down. "Women like me, strong women, have so much going on, and men just can't understand our needs. They're threatened by us. We—''

"Cynthia." Missy threw her donut down onto her plate so powdered sugar splashed up onto her scoop-necked red knit blouse and looked like snow. "I'm sick of this. You are full of it."

Tracy froze with a fingerful of jelly halfway to her mouth. Allegra froze midchew. Cynthia's mouth dropped open first, *then* she froze. "What?"

"I said you're full of it. All this stuff about sex and your career and how none of us understands, I think Adam was right. I think you're just a coward."

"*You* think I'm a coward?" Her voice rose into an outraged very cowardly sounding squeak. Oh no. She had this terrible edge-of-a-precipice feeling going on. That same feeling she had when Adam got closest to invading her protected inner self.

"All this talk about going after what you want, and then when what you want lands in your *lap,* you run away to eat donuts, except you can't even *eat* them because you're afraid of donuts, *too.*"

Cynthia tried to roll her eyes, but they seemed more inclined to fill with tears. "Oh, now I'm afraid of donuts."

"The ones with fake creme filling are pretty scary," Tracy said.

Missy ignored her. "Yes, and you're afraid of chicken fat bombs."

Cynthia gestured into her donut's airspace, dimly aware she was going to lose this battle and that deep down, totally uncharacteristically, she wanted to. "For God's sake, the way people go on about them, you'd think chicken fat bombs were the ultimate test of humanity."

"And mostly." Missy took a deep breath and lowered her voice. "Mostly, you're afraid of love."

"Hear hear." Tracy nodded and lifted her jellied index finger in a toast to Cynthia before she licked it clean.

"Now guys..." Allegra reached over to squeeze Cynthia's arm. "Don't be too hard on her."

"Well, you agree, don't you?" Missy asked.

Allegra nodded cheerfully, setting her three-inch beaded earrings swinging. "Oh, sure. She's chicken as they come. But we *could* phrase it a little more gently."

Cynthia let out a bellow of frustration. "You're all driving me crazy!"

"No." Allegra loosened her grip on Cynthia's arm. "You're driving yourself crazy. We're just here for the ride and to see that you don't crash."

Cynthia picked up her donut and stared at it.

"Eat it, Cynthia." Missy spoke softly. "Open wide, and take a big sweet bite."

"Don't stop to think about it," Tracy said. "Just do it."

"Be a Manhunter." Allegra smacked her fist into her palm. "Fall for that donut and go after it."

Cynthia brought the donut slowly toward her. Why

couldn't she eat donuts? Was she really so afraid to let go? Of her appetite and her heart?

Not anymore. Not with Adam at stake. No.

She opened her mouth as wide as possible and crammed in a huge, sweet, creamy bite.

The girls cheered. She started laughing and nearly choked as she tried to maneuver the enormous wad of pastry around her mouth. Sugar dripped onto her new black linen top. The too-full bite got too close to her lips and oozed spit and cake out onto her chin. She laughed harder, then reached around and pulled the pins out of her hair. She picked up the donut and crammed more in her mouth, the cream making a wide oval mess around her lips. It felt good. Next time she saw Adam she was going to try to stuff him in her mouth, too.

Her doorbell rang. She froze with the donut poised for a third assault, then opened her mouth to say, "If it's Adam, don't let him in yet," but the words sounded more like, "Fitshadmdonledmint."

"Hi, Adam." Missy's voice rang out from the front hall.

Cynthia's eyes shot open over the huge bulge in her cheek. How the hell was she supposed to appear so enticing that he'd forgive her everything and beg her to be his forever when she had an entire bakery crammed into her mouth?

Adam appeared in the doorway to her kitchen, his eyes filled with fierce determination, as if he was going to haul her over his shoulder and drag her into the bedroom. *Oh, baby.* She'd never seen anything look that good on him.

Except once his sexy fierce eyes caught a glimpse of her chipmunk donut-storage system, they slanted down into laughter.

She managed to swallow, opened her mouth to protest her humiliation and found herself laughing, too, harder than she could remember laughing in years.

"Adam." She gasped and clutched her stomach. "What are you doing here?"

He advanced and stood, huge and masculine in her clean white kitchen. "Watching you inhale fat."

She laughed again, then snorted unattractively and didn't even care. "Oh."

"And to tell you that even though you are a female achievement system, I love you."

A three-person sigh came from just beyond the kitchen door where Tracy, Allegra and Missy, aka three-quarters of the Manhunters, rooted for their fourth happy ending.

Cynthia felt her eyes wanting to go soft and tender and she let them. Encouraged them, in fact. "And even if you are a sit-back-and-let-the-world-happen kind of guy, I love you, too."

"And the Foster—"

"Is forgotten."

He grinned. "There's always next year."

She cleared her throat and gave him a sheepish glance. "Okay, well maybe that occurred to me."

"I think we can be good for each other, Cynthia."

His eyes grew serious and he took a step toward her so that she felt enveloped by his presence. "I'll hold you back from killing yourself, and—"

"I'll goose you forward when it feels right." She stood and launched herself into his arms, lifted her face and parted her lips, aching for his kiss, the kiss that would seal their futures together.

He bent his head down, then drew back from the kiss that would seal their futures together with vanilla pastry cream smeared all over his face. "You are delicious this afternoon, Ms. Cynthia. Might I suggest we retire to your bedroom so we can use our tongues to clean up?"

She giggled, a carefree happy sound. "Only if we can go out after. I have a tremendous urge."

"Mmm." He ran his hands up and down her back. "I like the sound of that. What kind of tremendous urge?"

She brought his head down for another cream-filled kiss and smiled into his eyes, feeling free and unafraid and way, way gooey-in-love. "A tremendous urge to do the funky chicken."

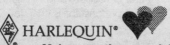

A Quiver of Longing
Trembled through Her

His head bent toward her, and she knew that he was going to kiss her. The tips of his fingers rested lightly along her jaw and the curve of her throat, holding her motionless without any pressure.

The first brush of his lips was soft and teasing, but they came back to claim her mouth with warm ease.

Her lips were clinging to his by the time he finally drew back a few inches to study the result. Slowly her lashes lifted to show the dazed uncertainty in her eyes. She glanced at his face, then lowered her gaze . . .

"Good night, Rev . . . Seth," Abbie murmured.

Books by Janet Daily

The Glory Game
The Pride of Hannah Wade
Silver Wings, Santiago Blue
Calder Born, Calder Bred
Stands a Calder Man
This Calder Range
This Calder Sky
For the Love of God
Foxfire Light
The Hostage Bride
The Lancaster Men
Mistletoe & Holly
Separate Cabins
Terms of Surrender
Night Way
Ride the Thunder
The Rogue
Touch the Wind

Published by POCKET BOOKS

For the Love of God

Janet Dailey

PUBLISHED BY POCKET BOOKS NEW YORK

POCKET BOOKS, a division of Simon & Schuster, Inc.
1230 Avenue of the Americas, New York, N.Y. 10020

Originally published by Silhouette Books.

ISBN: 0-671-55460-3

First Pocket Books printing March, 1985

10 9 8 7 6 5 4 3

POCKET and colophon are registered trademarks
of Simon & Schuster, Inc.

Printed in the U.S.A.

For the Love of God

Chapter One

The wind blowing through the opened car window held all the heat and humidity of a July day. It lifted the auburn-gold hair that lay thickly about Abbie Scott's neck, creating a cooling effect. A pair of sunglasses sat on the dashboard, looking at her with their wide, oval lenses. She had removed them earlier, not wanting the view artificially tinted.

A morning shower had brought a sharpness and clarity to the landscape of the Arkansas Ozarks. There was a vividness to the many shades of green in the trees and bushes crowding close to the highway. The air was washed clean of its dust, intensifying the lushness of the Ozark Mountain greenery.

Her hazel eyes kept stealing glances away from the winding roadway to admire the ever-changing vista of rock and tree-covered hills. The flecks of green in her eyes almost seemed like a reflection of the verdant countryside.

There was a time when Abbie hadn't appreciated the beauty around her, when she had complained about the twisting, turning double-lane roads that snaked through the Ozark hills and the lack of entertainment and shopping facilities found in cities, and the limited job opportunities in an area where the major industry was tourism.

Out of high school, Abbie had left the serenity of the rugged hills for the excitement of Kansas City. She thought she'd found it in the beginning, but the glitter had eventually faded. A year ago, Abbie had returned to her hometown of Eureka Springs after four years away.

A lot of people, her parents included, hadn't understood why she had given up a promising career with Trans World Airlines, headquartered in Kansas City, with its many travel and fringe benefits. Abbie's response, if anyone asked, and few did, was a declaration of homesickness. But that was only partially true.

She guessed that her mother suspected a man was at the root of her decision to return, but Abbie had too much pride to admit the romance she thought would lead to the altar had ended up going nowhere. Initially she had come home to lick her wounds, but a year's distance had enabled her to see it had only been the final straw and not the ultimate cause.

Now, instead of a lucrative job with a large corporation, she was her father's legal secretary, paid only a small salary compared to her previous wages. By watching her pennies, Abbie managed fairly well with some adjustments from her prior life-style. She "semilived" with her parents, which meant that she had taken her savings and fixed up the loft above the garage, once a carriage house, into a small efficiency apartment. It provided privacy, as well as low rent.

And there was Mabel—her car. She had traded in her speedy little Porsche sports car for a cheaper and older automobile. Mabel, as Abbie had dubbed the car, wasn't much to look at. Her body was showing signs of rust and dented fenders. She was accidentally two-toned blue, since the hood and the passenger door didn't match the sun-faded robin color of the rest of the car. If it was possible for vehicles to have a personality, Mabel certainly did. She was grumpy, did a lot of coughing and complaining like an old woman, but there wasn't a sick piston or plug in her body.

As the road began an uphill climb, Abbie shifted the standard-transmission car into second gear. The motor made a small grunting sound of protest but Mabel didn't hesitate. Abbie's lips curved with a faint smile.

Although July marked the height of the Ozark tourist season, there was relatively little traffic on the state highway leading into Eureka Springs. Most of the tourists used the major highways, so Abbie only had local traffic to contend with. Plus, it was the middle of a Saturday afternoon, which meant most of the tourists were at the various area attractions and few were on the road.

After experiencing city rush-hour traffic, Abbie didn't let crowded Ozark roads stop her from visiting her grandmother on the weekends. Grandmother Klein continued to live on the rocky farm she and her late husband had worked, although the acreage itself was now leased to a neighbor.

Abbie's grandmother on her mother's side still raised chickens, had a milk cow and a big garden, and canned more food than she could eat, totally ignoring the fact she was seventy years old and should slow down. No one ever visited Grandmother Klein without being loaded down with foodstuffs when they left, and no amount of protesting changed that.

On the floorboard in front of the passenger seat, Abbie had jars of pickles—sweet, dill, bread-and-butter, and cherry—as well as an assortment of homemade preserves and jellies. Plus there were two sacks on the seat. One contained tomatoes, cucumbers, and sweet corn from Grandmother Klein's garden; the other was filled with ripe peaches freshly picked from the tree, their fruity smell filling the car.

The temptation was too much to resist and Abbie reached into the sack for just one more peach as the car neared the crest of the hill. The fruit was still warm from the sun, its juice spurting with the first bite Abbie took. She had to use the side of her hand to keep it from running down her chin.

When she started to sink her teeth into the fuzzy skin for another bite, she saw the red warning light gleaming on the dashboard panel. She lowered the peach from her mouth and frowned slightly. It was rare for Mabel to overheat on these up-and-down roads.

"Don't lose your cool now, Mabel," she murmured to the car. "We're nearly to the top."

But the light stayed on even after they started the downhill run. When Abbie saw the wisps of steam rising from the hood, she knew there was trouble, and started looking for a place to pull off the road. It was another half-mile before she found a shoulder wide enough to accommodate Mabel. By then, there were more than wisps of steam coming from the hood.

Once the car was parked, Abbie made a quick glance to be sure her lane of the highway was clear of traffic before climbing out to check under Mabel's hood. She forgot she had the peach in her hand until she needed both of them to unlatch the hood. She held it in her mouth, ignoring the juice that dripped onto her blue plaid blouse.

The tails of her blouse were tied at the midriff in an attempt to beat the summer heat. When Abbie started to lift the hood, drops of scalding hot water were sprayed over the band of bare stomach between her blouse and faded Levi's. She jumped back, nearly dropping the peach, and just managing to save it while she wiped the hot water from her stomach with her other hand.

"How could you spit on me like that, Mabel?" she unconsciously scolded the car.

The upraised hood unleashed a billow of steam that quickly dissipated. Abbie moved cautiously closer to peer inside and find the cause of the spitting hot water. There was a hole in the radiator hose. Her shoulders sagged with dismay.

Abbie turned to look up the road, trying to remember how far it was to the nearest farmhouse. It was another four miles yet to the edge of town, she knew. She wasn't enthused about walking even half a mile in this heat.

A semi tractor-trailer rig zoomed by, its draft sucking at her. Abbie looked hopefully at the oncoming traffic. She knew nearly everyone in the area. Maybe someone would drive by that she knew and she could get a ride into town. Not under any circumstances would she accept a lift from a stranger.

More than a dozen vehicles passed but Abbie didn't recognize any of the drivers. A small handful slowed down when they went by her stalled car, but none stopped. And Abbie made no attempt to flag anyone down either. She took an absent bite of the peach while she debated whether to start walking until she reached the nearest house, where she could telephone her parents, or to wait a little longer.

A low-slung, dark green sports car came zipping around the curve in the road, approaching her parked car from the rear. It immediately slowed down at the sight of the upraised hood. The convertible model car had its top down, but its windshield prevented Abbie from getting a clear view of the man behind the wheel. As it edged onto the shoulder to park behind her car, she noticed the out-of-state license plates and tensed a little. Four years of living in a city had made her slightly leery of strangers.

The driver didn't bother to open the door. Instead, he lightly vaulted over the low side to walk toward Abbie's car. The man was tall, easily reaching the six-foot mark. In this land of the summer tourist, there was nothing unusual about the way he was dressed—a mottled gray T-shirt and faded cutoffs with white sneakers. It exposed an awful lot of hard, sinewy flesh, tanned to a golden brown. His hair was a toasty gold color, attractively rumpled by the wind.

Abbie couldn't see his eyes behind the mirror-like finish of his sunglasses, but she liked the strong angles and planes of his male features. She felt that instant pull of attraction to the opposite sex and experienced a twinge of regret that the man was no more than a passing stranger. There wasn't exactly a surfeit of good-looking, single men in Eureka Springs.

"Hello." His lips parted in a brief but friendly smile that showed an even row of strong white teeth. "It looks like you have some car trouble."

" 'Fraid so," Abbie admitted.

In spite of the futility of it, her interest in the man mounted as he lifted a hand to remove the sunglasses. She found herself gazing into a pair of arresting blue eyes. Their depths held a warm gleam that had a dancing charm all its own. Awareness of his sexual magnetism quivered pleasantly along her nerve ends. It had been a long time since any man had fully aroused her mating interests. The few times she had gone out on a date since her return, the desire had been mainly for companionship.

"What seems to be the problem?" As the stranger bent to look under the hood, Abbie observed the flexing muscles in his tanned arms.

Even though the busted hose had stopped spitting hot water, Abbie still advised, "Be careful. Mabel sprang a leak." The curious glance he slanted at her made Abbie realize she had referred to the car by its pet name. "That's what I call her," she explained lamely, and felt slightly foolish about it.

An interest that had not been present before entered his look as he briefly skimmed Abbie from head to foot. She was tall, nearly five foot seven, with a model's slimness—except she had curves in all the right places, although no one would ever describe her as voluptuous. Her light red hair had a gold sheen to it—strawberry blond her mother called it. Abbie would have been less than honest if she didn't acknowledge she was more than reasonably attractive. A country freshness kept her from being striking.

The stranger seemed to like what he saw without being offensive about it. Then his attention was swinging easily back to the split in the radiator hose. He tested the hose, bending it a little to discover the extent of the rupture.

"I might be able to patch 'Mabel' up." He used

her pet name for the car. The faint smile that edged the corners of his mouth seemed to share —or at least understand—her personification of the car. "Would you happen to have a rag—or an old towel?"

"Sure. I have one under the front seat," Abbie admitted. "Just a second and I'll get it for you."

Rather than use the driver's side with the road traffic to watch for, Abbie walked through the tall grass along the shoulder of the highway and opened the passenger door. It was a long stretch to reach the piece of old flannel tucked under the drivers' seat. Her elbow bumped some of the jars on the floor, rattling them together. Like a row of dominoes, they began toppling over just as her groping fingers found the rag under the seat. Abbie closed her eyes, expecting to hear one of the jars break and bracing herself for the sound, but it didn't come.

The rag was in her hand and she was half lying on the seat, preparing to push out of the car when Abbie heard the swish of footsteps in the grass. There wasn't much room on the seat for maneuvering with the two sacks of vegetables and peaches. Abbie was forced to crane her neck around in an effort to see behind her.

"Are you all right?" The man was standing on the inside of the opened car door, eyeing her with concern.

She was conscious of being in a vulnerable and ungainly position with no graceful way to alter it. "Yes. I just knocked over some jars." She pushed backward off the seat and out of the car. Her face felt red but it could have been caused by the blood rushing to her head when she had been half hanging over the seat to reach the rag.

When Abbie turned to give him the old cloth, she discovered how close she was standing to him. The cotton fabric of the mottled gray T-shirt was cleaved to his wide shoulders and lean, muscled chest. His maleness became a potent force Abbie had to reckon with, especially since she was standing nearly eye level with his mouth. Her pulse just wouldn't behave at all.

"Did you break anything?"

She watched his lips form the words but it was a full second before his question registered. Abbie pulled herself up sharply. What was the matter with her? She was reacting like a love-starved old maid who hadn't been near a man in years. A little voice argued that she hadn't—at least not with a man the caliber of this one.

Her hazel-green eyes darted a guilty look upward to meet his gaze. There seemed to be an awareness in his blue eyes of what she was thinking and feeling. It really wasn't so surprising. Experience with life—and women—was etched into the male lines in his face.

"Nothing was broken." Abbie remembered to answer his question. Her crooked smile held a measure of resignation. "Grandmother Klein loaded me down with her homemade jams and pickles before I left."

His shoulder brushed her forearm as he bent to set the jars upright. With his large hand, he was able to right them two at a time, sometimes with a thumb on the third to push it up. In next to no time, all the jars were standing again.

"Thank you. You really didn't have to do that," Abbie said when he had finished.

He raised his eyebrows in a kind of shrugging gesture. "I remember my grandmother used to make the best wild-raspberry jam. She knew it was my favorite and always made sure to have a couple of jars for me whenever I visited her. Grandmothers are like that. They either try to fatten you up or marry you off."

"That's true," Abbie agreed dryly, and resisted the impulse to look at his left hand to see if his grandmother had succeeded in the latter. "Here's the rag you wanted." She gave it to him and followed when he walked around the opened passenger door to the front of the car. "What are you going to do?" she asked. "Wrap the rag around the hose and use it as a bandage?"

"No." He appeared amused by her suggestion, but not in a ridiculing way. "I doubt if it would hold. I have some electrical tape in my car. Once I get the hose dried off, I'll wrap a few lengths of that around it. It's only a few miles to Eureka Springs, and the tape should hold until you get that far."

Abbie bit her lower lip, remembering. "Except most of the water boiled out of the radiator."

Using the rag as a protective pad, he unscrewed the radiator cap. "I always carry a gallon jug of drinking water with me. Between it and a gallon of antifreeze-coolant in my trunk,

17

we should be able to get you temporarily fixed up."

She shook her head in a gesture of bewildered amazement at how smoothly he was handling the breakdown. "I'm certainly glad you came along," Abbie declared openly. "I thought I was going to have to walk to a phone, and this isn't exactly the coolest day for walking, not to mention the tow charges you're saving me. Thank you for stopping."

"Just being a Good Samaritan," he replied, that easy smile coming again to his mouth.

With the coolant, water, and tape from his car, he patched the hose and partially filled Mabel's radiator. "The old gal ought to make it now," he said as he closed the hood and made sure it was tightly latched.

"It isn't enough to say 'thank you,'" Abbie insisted. "You not only fixed it but you used your tape and water and everything. Let me pay you for it."

He opened his mouth to refuse, then suddenly smiled. It seemed to take her breath away as her heart started thudding crazily. Love wasn't something that happened at first sight but physical attraction could. It was often equally potent, however, and Abbie knew she was suffering from a severe case of it.

"Were those fresh peaches I smelled in the sack on the car seat?" he asked instead.

"Yes." Abbie nodded while she studied the way the afternoon sun intensified the burnished gold color of his hair, antiquing it.

"If you insist on paying me, I'll take a couple of those peaches. Homegrown fruit has a taste all its own," he said.

"Okay, it's a deal." She laughed and walked to the passenger side to retrieve the sack through the opened car window. "Help yourself. You can have the whole sack. Grandmother Klein will just give me more next weekend."

"Two's plenty." He randomly picked two from the sack. "I'll follow you into Eureka Springs to make sure you don't have any more trouble with Mabel. I'll be stopping there, and I advise that you stop at the first garage and get a new hose put on."

"I will." It was a somewhat absentminded agreement, because her attention had been caught by his statement that he'd be stopping at Eureka Springs. "Eureka Springs is a quaint town. Will you be staying there awhile?"

"Yes, I plan to," he admitted, and she was conscious of his gaze running over her again.

"You'll like it," she rushed, only half-aware that he had been going to say something else. As a rule, she didn't socialize with summer tourists. A holiday romance was even more of a dead end than any other kind. But there was no doubt in her mind that she wanted to see this man again. "By the way, my name's Abbie Scott. You've already met Mabel."

"Abbie? Short for Abra?" He arched an eyebrow.

Abbie was dumbfounded. "How did you know that? Most people think my name is Abigail."

One muscled shoulder was lifted in an expressive shrug. "It just seemed appropriate. Abra was the favorite of Solomon in the Bible. A lucky guess." He extended a hand to complete the introductions. "My name's Talbot. Seth Talbot."

"That's a biblical name, too." Abbie was reluctant to admit she hadn't known anything about her namesake. Since he seemed so knowledgeable about it, she didn't want to reveal her ignorance.

"Seth was the third son of Adam," he informed her. "Not quite as well known as his older brothers, Cain and Abel."

"That's true." She smiled. Her hand tingled pleasantly in his firm clasp. He had very strong, capable hands, but they were relatively smooth, without the calluses of someone who made his living with them. It didn't really surprise her. Despite his hard physique and craggy good looks, there was the definite impression of a man who relied on his mental prowess and innate air of command for his living.

Then he was releasing her hand to gather up his empty jugs and roll of black tape. "If you start to have any trouble, just honk twice. I'll be right behind you," Seth Talbot assured her.

"Okay." She watched him walk along the grassy verge to his car and stow the things in the backseat.

Oncoming traffic permitted her to observe him as he swung over the low passenger door and into the driver's seat. Abbie waited until the road was clear to walk to the driver's side of her car and open the door. She set the sack of peaches on the seat and pushed it over to slide behind the wheel.

Mabel's motor grumbled to life at the turn of the ignition key. As Abbie turned the car onto the highway she waved to the driver of the sports car. Within seconds, she saw the reflection of the dark green sports car in her rearview mirror, following a safe distance behind her.

It was an older model car, but Abbie suspected it had been an expensive one. She tried to guess what kind of work he did, speculating that he could be a lawyer or maybe a doctor. If he was a salesman, he could sell her anything, she thought with a little laugh.

The four miles to Eureka Springs seemed to flash by. Not once did Mabel even wink her red warning light. Abbie couldn't make up her mind whether she was glad or sorry about that. Mechanical trouble would have given her an opportunity to find out more about Seth Talbot— essentials like where he was staying in Eureka Springs and some of the places he had planned to see while he was here.

Abbie couldn't believe the way she was thinking. She was actually considering chasing a man. There was nothing shy about her, but she didn't classify herself as the aggressive type either. Still, she couldn't help wondering what it would be like if he kissed her. Seth Talbot had certainly captured her fancy in a short time. Or maybe it was simply a sign that she was finally cured of her distrust for men after that disappointing romance in Kansas City. That was probably closer to the truth.

When Abbie turned her car into the service station-garage she patronized, there was a honk and a wave from the sports car before it sped on by. Abbie couldn't contain the sigh of regret that slipped out. It would be sheer chance if she ever saw him again and she knew it.

A portly, coverall clad man emerged from the service bay of the station and walked toward her car with an ambling gait. It was Kermit Applebaum, the owner of the establishment. He had serviced her parents' vehicles ever since she was a freckle-faced toddler. Thankfully, the freckles had faded with the onset of maturity, but Kermit Applebaum still called her Freckles, a nickname no one else had picked up—and Abbie was eternally grateful for that.

"Well, hello, Freckles," he greeted her as she had expected, and Abbie tried not to wince. "How's old Gladys doing?"

"Her name is Mabel," she corrected patiently, and stepped out of the car. "And Mabel has busted a radiator hose. I hope you have a spare one to fit her."

"I'll rustle up something." He wiped his greasy hands on a rag before he lifted the hood to have a look. "You didn't do a bad job of patchin' this."

"I can't take the credit for that," Abbie replied. "A tourist stopped when he saw I was broken-down and fixed it up for me, then followed me into town to be sure I made it."

"That fella that just honked at you?" the owner-mechanic asked with some surprise. When she nodded affirmatively his expression became thoughtful. "I thought it was just some guy tryin' to make time with you. I guess I did him a disservice." He closed the hood with a decisive shove and turned to Abbie. "Drive your car over to that empty bay, and I'll see what I've got for hoses to fit it."

In all, it took the better part of two hours before he had it fixed with interruptions from customers and phone calls. It was nearly suppertime when Abbie turned her trusty car onto a winding street for home.

Her hometown of Eureka Springs was filled with quaint charm. The restored and refurbished Victorian structures clinging to the steep hills gave the city an ambience of the past, a nostalgic flavor. Some visitors considered it an oddity in the middle of the Ozarks, but Abbie had always regarded it as home. It had been dubbed "The Little Switzerland of America" because of the combination of its architecture and steep terrain and had been a highly popular vacation resort since the turn of the century. Then, its appeal had been as a spa. Now, it was the town itself and its many gift, antique, and craft shops. There was even a trolley car to ease the weary feet of those unprepared for the endlessly winding streets.

And during the tourist season, people came by the thousands to see The Great Passion Play, an outdoor drama of Christ's last days, and to view the seven-story statue of Christ of the Ozarks. There were other religious attractions, too, including the Bible Museum, the Christ Only Art Gallery, and the New Holy Land with its life-size recreations of scenes from the Bible.

As much as Abbie loved her hometown and its picturesque buildings and Ozark Mountain setting, living in a town that had essentially changed little since the turn of the century had its disadvantages. Abbie became as irritated as the next motorist on city streets that were not designed to handle a lot of modern vehicle traffic. And there weren't any traffic lights, which meant relying on the courtesy of another driver in the case of making turns onto main thoroughfares or off of them.

In the summer, when the visitors came by the hundreds, she griped along with everyone else at the traffic tie-ups, but she still loved it. Maybe it was because she was like the town—a little out-of-date and out-of-step with the times—proud and old-fashioned.

All her girl friends were married, and most of them had children. She had given up a promising career and come back to—what? To fantasize about a stranger who stopped to help?

Climbing roses spilled over the fan-shaped trellises that marked the driveway of her parents' home with its gingerbread trim. The old carriage-house-turned-garage sat at the side, literally built into the hill. Her father's car was already inside the garage. Since there was only room for one and the weather couldn't hurt

Mabel's appearance, Abbie always parked out-side.

This time she stopped near the back door of the two-and-a-half story white house. Her cup-boards were already filled with jars of goods from Grandmother Klein. She knew the elderly woman wouldn't mind if her granddaughter gave some of the food and home-canned goods to the woman's daughter and son-in-law. It cer-tainly made more sense to divide it now than carry it all up a flight of stairs to her apartment, then back down to the house.

Without bothering to knock at the back door, Abbie walked into the kitchen with an armload of jars. The rush of air-conditioned coolness hit her, and she paused to savor the relief from the outside heat.

A tall, auburn-haired woman turned away from the stove where the evening meal was cooking to look at Abbie. There was a definite resemblance between mother and daughter with minor differences. Alice Scott was pencil-thin, with eyes that were more green than hazel. "You and Mother must have had quite a visit to-day," she remarked. "She isn't ill or anything?"

"No." Abbie walked to the breakfast table and carefully set the jars down. "I busted a radiator hose on the way home. I've been over at Kermit's for the last two hours getting it repaired."

"I don't see what keeps that car together at all," her mother replied with a wry shake of her head.

The unmistakable sound of her father running

down the steps and whistling a tuneless song echoed into the kitchen. In a few things, her father was very predictable. One of them was his routine after a day at the office. He immediately changed into a pair of khaki pants and either a cotton plaid shirt in the summer or a bedraggled maroon pullover sweater in the winter upon coming home from the office.

True to his pattern, he entered the kitchen in the plaid shirt and khaki pants. He sniffed at the food cooking on the stove. "Smells good, honey." He kissed his wife on the cheek and walked to the refrigerator for a beer. "When do we eat?" Then he saw Abbie standing by the table. "I thought we pushed that one out of the nest. Here she is back at mealtime with her mouth open."

"There's plenty," her mother assured her as she turned the sizzling pork chops in the skillet. "Why don't you have supper with us?"

"Not tonight, Mom. Thanks just the same." Abbie refused because it would be too easy to fall into the habit of eating her meals at home. She had become used to living on her own and liked the measure of independence the small apartment above the garage gave her.

"You're too stubborn," her father accused, but he grudgingly admired her streak of independence, too.

"I get it from you," she retorted.

"You can have Sunday dinner with us tomorrow." It wasn't an invitation from her mother; it was a statement. "It will be nice for all three of us to attend church together again."

26

Her father cleared his throat and looked uncomfortable. "Abe said something about going fishing tomorrow. I meant to mention that to you the other day."

"Drew Fitzgerald Scott, you are going to church." Her mother shook a fork at him. "It's the last time Reverend Augustus will be conducting the services. He's retiring."

"Hallelujah!" Her father raised a hand in the air in mock rejoicing.

"Drew." Her mother's voice held a warning note.

"I never did like the man," he reminded her. "I'm not going to be sorry to see him retire. If I go to church with you tomorrow, you can be sure I'll be sitting in that pew rejoicing."

"Not 'if,'" Alice Scott corrected. "You *are* going. And you're going to attend the farewell tea our ladies' club is giving him and Mrs. Augustus tomorrow afternoon."

His glance slid to Abbie, an impish light dancing in his brown eyes. "Are you going?"

"Yes, she's going." Her mother answered for her.

Abbie lifted her shoulders in a shrug that said the decision had been taken out of her hands. "You heard her, Dad." A smile widened her mouth. "I'm going."

"I guess I don't have a choice either," he replied affably, then took a deep, sighing breath. "I just hope we don't get another 'hell and damnation' minister. I like to go to church and be inspired, not threatened." He leaned a hip

27

against the butcher-block table in the middle of the sunny yellow kitchen. "What about it, Mother? What's the word on our new minister?"

Her mother switched off the burner under the skillet and paused. "I don't remember anyone discussing him in specifics, except that he's supposed to be highly qualified." She seemed surprised that her information was so scanty. "But we'll meet him and his family tomorrow. Reverend Augustus will be introducing them to the congregation, and I'm sure they'll attend the tea. You'll be able to draw your own conclusions."

With that subject apparently closed, Abbie had the chance to ask the question that had been buzzing around in her mind since this afternoon. "Mom, what made you choose the name Abra for me? Does it have any special meaning?"

"That's a strange question to ask after all these years," her mother declared with a faint laugh. "One of my girl friends had an aunt by that name and I liked it. Why?"

"I just found out Abra was the name of Solomon's favorite wife in the Bible. I guess I wondered if you had known that." Abbie shrugged.

"How interesting." Her mother looked pleasantly surprised. "Who told you this?"

"A tourist who stopped to help me when Mabel broke down—" Abbie didn't have a chance to complete the sentence in its entirety.

"What's this about Mabel breaking down?" her father interrupted.

And Abbie explained again about the busted radiator hose and her delay getting it fixed at the garage. By the time she had finished answering —or trying to answer—all his mechanical questions, her mother was dishing up their evening meal. Abbie refused a second invitation to join them and left the house to carry the bounty from her grandmother up to her apartment.

Chapter Two

The incessant pounding roused Abbie from her sleep. She rolled over with a groan and buried her head under the pillow, but she couldn't drown it out. Whoever was doing all that hammering should be put in jail for making so much noise on a Sunday morning, she thought.

Sunday morning. There wasn't anyone hammering, she realized. Someone was knocking on her door. Abbie threw aside the pillow and tossed back the covers to sit up in the single bed. The grogginess of sleep blurred her eyes as she grabbed for the robe draped over the foot of the bed.

"I'm coming!" she called while she hurriedly tried to pull on her robe, but she wasn't too coordinated.

Her alarm clock sat on the oak dresser, far enough from the bed so she would be forced to get up to turn it off. Abbie peered at it. The hour hand pointed to one. Sunshine was streaming through the bedroom window. It surely didn't mean it was one o'clock in the afternoon! With a groan she realized the clock had stopped. She must have forgotten to wind it last night.

It was obviously late, but Abbie had no idea what time it was. She hurried through the main room of her loft apartment, which included a living room, dining room, and kitchen, to the staircase door. As she opened it she lifted the weighty mass of auburn-gold hair away from her face.

Her father stood outside, dressed in a suit and tie. His gaze wandered over her while a smile deepened the corners of his mouth. "I don't think that's exactly the proper attire for church," he observed.

"My clock stopped." Abbie didn't mention that she had forgotten to wind it. "What time is it?" Her voice still contained the husky thickness of sleep.

"There's about ten minutes before the church service starts. Is that any help?" he asked with an amused slant to his mouth.

"I can't get ready in five minutes," Abbie groaned. "You and Mother will just have to go without me."

A rueful expression added lines to his face. "She isn't going to be too happy about that," he warned Abbie but not without understanding. "Too bad I didn't think of it." A boyish grin showed.

"Mom is your alarm clock," she reminded him. "She would have gotten you up in plenty of time."

A horn honked an impatient summons from the driveway. Her father glanced in the direction of the sound. "Your mother hates to be late. What shall I tell her?" he asked. "Will you be coming later on?"

"The service will be half over by the time I could make it there." Abbie shook her head to indicate she wouldn't be attending church that morning. "You'll have to convey my apologies to Reverend Augustus and assure him that I'll be at the afternoon tea."

"I think I'll let your mother have that pleasure." He began moving away from the door to the white-painted staircase. "See you after church."

With no reason for haste, Abbie took her time in the shower while coffee perked in the kitchen. The warm spray awakened her senses and eliminated the last traces of sleep and she stepped out of the shower feeling refreshed and invigorated. With a towel wrapped around her wet hair, she donned the yellow cotton robe again and ventured into the kitchen area of the apartment.

A counter bar separated the kitchen area from the rest of the room. Although there was a small wooden table and chairs, Abbie usually ate most of her meals at the counter, using the table only when she had friends over for a meal.

It was too close to dinnertime for breakfast, so Abbie settled for a glass of orange juice and a cup of freshly perked coffee, sitting on a tall, rattan-backed stool at the counter-bar. By the time she had drunk a second cup, the towel had absorbed most of the moisture from her hair. It took only a few minutes to finish drying it with the blow dryer. Its natural-bodied thickness assumed a casually loose and free style that curled softly about her neck. Choosing a dress to wear that would be both suitable for the minister's farewell party and comfortable in the July heat was relatively easy, because she had so few choices. Abbie picked out a sundress designed with classic simplicity, a white material with small, navy-blue polka dots. Its neckline was modest, while the close-fitting bodice flattered the thrusting curves of her breasts. A wide leather belt in navy-blue accented her slender waist, with the skirt flaring out to near fullness. Abbie had a pair of navy-blue sandals with stacked, wooden heels to complete the outfit. She had a three-banded bracelet and matching hooped earrings to wear with it for the finishing touch, but Reverend Augustus frowned on jewelry. After debating silently with herself for several minutes, Abbie wore them anyway.

The only clock with the right time was in the kitchen. It warned her that it was nearly time for church to be let out. She crossed the driveway to the house. Unlike Abbie, her parents had never acquired the habit of locking their doors. In this small community, there had never been any reason to worry about it.

Her mother was a terribly organized person. All the preparations for Sunday dinner were completed, from the meat and vegetables baking in the oven to the relish tray and salad sitting in the refrigerator. Abbie went ahead and put the latter on the table, already covered with their best linen tablecloth, china and silverware. There was even a bouquet of freshly cut flowers adorning the center.

When she heard her parents' car turn into the driveway, Abbie tied an apron around her waist and took the roaster from the oven. She was forking the tender roast onto the meat platter when her parents walked in the back door. Abbie sent a smile in their direction.

"How was the service?" she asked brightly, already warned by the disapproving glint in her mother's eye that she was still upset with her for missing church.

"Reverend Augustus gave an excellent farewell sermon. You should have been there, Abbie," her mother stated. Her tone held more disappointment than anger.

"She means it was brief," her father inserted in a teasing fashion. "For once he didn't rant and rave until he was drowned out by growling stomachs."

Her mother took another apron from the drawer and tied it around her middle to help Abbie dish up the food. "His sermon was quite poignant."

"Maudlin," her father declared with a wink at Abbie.

"He did wander a bit," her mother admitted. "But I thought it was just all the more touching."

Abbie turned to her father, going off the subject for an instant. "Are you going to carve the roast?" At his nod, she laid the carving knife and fork across the meat platter. "What is the new minister like?"

"Old Augustus got so choked up with sentimentality he forgot to introduce him." Her father laughed. "I guess he was sitting in one of the front pews but the church was so crowded I never got a look at him. I had the impression that the reverend didn't totally approve of his replacement though."

"Oh?" Abbie gave him a curious look. "Why?"

"I don't know." He admitted his uncertainty. "It was something in his tone of voice when he talked about the church having young blood in its ministry."

"I'm sure that he only meant to imply that the new minister and his family were young people," Alice Scott insisted. "It was merely an oversight that he forgot to introduce the new reverend to the congregation."

"Oversight or not, if Reverend Augustus disapproves of him, I think I'll like him," her father stated.

"You really should show more forbearance, Drew," her mother admonished as she passed him the platter of meat. "Take this into the dining room."

The tea was set for four o'clock in the church basement. Since it was Alice Scott's ladies' club that was giving it for the retiring minister, she had to be there early to help get everything set up. Somehow, Abbie and her father were persuaded to offer their assistance in setting up the rows of folding chairs and the long serving tables.

Abbie was busy setting out the trays of fancy-cut sandwiches when the guests of honor, Reverend Augustus and his wife, arrived in the company of a dozen or so of their closest friends in the church. With the napkins and silverware still to be laid out in a fanning display, Abbie hadn't the time to leave her work to greet them and managed only a brief glance in their direction. After their arrival, people seemed to flood into the large room. Abbie hurried to finish before someone approached the refreshment table.

She was still holding a handful of spoons when she heard footsteps behind her. There was no quick way to arrange so many, so she continued to place them one by one and hoped the person would be patient for a minute or two longer.

"Well, hello, Miss Scott," a man's voice greeted her with warm pleasure. The familiarity of it seemed to tingle through her as her lips parted in a silent breath of delight.

Abbie was so taken by surprise when she recognized the voice of the man, Seth Talbot, who had stopped to help her yesterday, that she didn't even wonder what he was doing at the tea. She swung around to face him.

"Hello, Mr. Talbot." At first her gaze went no farther than his magnetically blue eyes. They seemed sexier than she remembered, so blue against his darkly bronzed features.

Just what drew her attention to his attire, Abbie couldn't have said, because dumb shock set in immediately afterward. She couldn't seem to tear her gaze away from the narrow strip of a white collar that circled his neck, the symbolic garb of an ordained minister.

"Did you get a new hose for Mabel?" he asked.

Abbie heard him but her vocal chords were frozen. All she could do was nod, but his question did succeed in lifting her rounded gaze to his face. Looking at his ruggedly handsome face and darkly gold hair made it seem all the more incredible. There was nothing benign about his countenance, nothing to lead a person to suspect he was a man of God. There was too much virility, too much hard masculinity, too much that suggested male passions.

Something flickered over his expression. "Is something wrong?"

"Yes. No. That is . . ." She stumbled over the words, realizing how rudely she had been gaping at him. Finally, honesty won out. "I never guessed that you were a minister. You don't look like one."

"I see." The corner of his mouth deepened with amusement, attractive lines fanning out from the corners of his eyes.

"I meant . . . yesterday, on the road, you didn't

look like one." She was making a terrible mess of the explanation. "It's obvious by what you're wearing today that you are but . . ." Abbie paused to gather her scattered wits. "I'm sorry."

"For what?" he challenged lightly. "It was a natural reaction. I hadn't realized that you lived in Eureka Springs, or I would have mentioned my transfer to this church."

"But . . ." As her mind played back their previous day's meeting, Abbie discovered that she hadn't mentioned that she lived here. ". . . I guess I didn't tell you."

"I'm glad you're a member of my new congregation." That tantalizing half-smile seemed permanently affixed to his mouth. "I was beginning to think no one under forty belonged to this church."

There was so much potent male charm in that look, Abbie had to glance at his collar to remind herself of his profession. It would be so easy to forget.

"With summer and all, a lot of the members my age have other plans," she said tactfully, rather than criticizing the outgoing pastor for not doing more to encourage the attendance of younger members.

"Maybe you can help me persuade some of them to include Sunday-morning church service in their plans," Reverend Seth Talbot suggested.

All her impulses were to leap on the suggestion, but Abbie seriously questioned whether she was motivated by a desire to help the church or wanted to accept because she was physically attracted to him. She strongly suspected it was the latter. All her responses to him at the moment were purely feminine.

"I'm afraid I'm not a very active church member myself . . . Reverend." Abbie had trouble getting his professional title out. It seemed at such odds with his compelling manhood. She was conscious of the little vein pulsing in her neck.

If he noticed her hesitancy in addressing him, he tactfully ignored it. "Then I'll have to make you my first sheep to win back to the fold." His smile deepened with a heady force.

Abbie lowered her gaze to resist his undeniable appeal. Charisma, that's what it is, she told herself. He would attract anybody's attention—not just hers.

"Abbie, are you finished yet?" Her mother's voice broke into their conversation.

She turned with a guilty start, just as if she were a little girl again getting caught red-handed doing something naughty. It was an expression her mother recognized and it narrowed her gaze. There were still a half-dozen spoons in Abbie's hand. She glanced quickly at them, her task forgotten until that moment. "I'm almost done," she told her mother.

But Alice Scott's attention had already strayed to the man standing next to Abbie. Her eyes widened slightly at the black frock and white collar.

"I don't believe we've met." Seth took the initiative to correct that. "I'm Reverend Talbot, your new pastor."

"I'm sorry." Abbie realized she had forgotten her manners. "This is my mother, Alice Scott."

"I noticed the resemblance," he said, directing that warm, male smile at her mother. "It's easy to see that your daughter inherited her looks from you, Mrs. Scott."

The remark could have sounded so polite and commonplace, a meaningless response, but the way he said it seemed sincere, a glowing compliment. Abbie was a little astounded at the way her mother seemed to blossom under his spell, shedding years and acquiring a youthful beauty. Just for a minute, she was irritated with her mother.

"My father is here somewhere," Abbie informed Seth and glanced around the room in search of him. "But I don't see him this minute." The remark was offered in an unconscious attempt to remind her mother that she was married.

"My husband has been looking forward to meeting you, Reverend Talbot," her mother explained, then inquired, "Is your family here?"

Abbie was suddenly crushed by the idea that Seth already had a wife and children. Seth. She was thinking of him by his first name. That had to stop.

"My family?" An eyebrow quirked, then straightened to its normal line. "You mean my

40

wife? I'm one of the rare ones, Mrs. Scott, an unmarried minister."

"You're a bachelor?" Her mother's tone of voice made it a question, as if she needed more confirmation of his single status.

"Yes." His straightforward answer didn't leave any room for doubts, and Abbie felt a tremble of relief. It was bad enough being so strongly attracted to a minister. It would have been worse if he were married on top of it.

"I wasn't trying to pry, Reverend Talbot," her mother assured him. "But as you said, it is unusual."

"I guess I'm something of a bad boy." He included Abbie in his sweeping glance. "I should be busy choosing a proper minister's wife, but I prefer to wait until I can find the right woman for me—not my job."

"I suspect you are unorthodox in a number of different ways," Abbie murmured, remembering the way he had been dressed the previous day, and the racy sports car he'd been driving.

"So I've been told." There was a wicked light dancing in his eyes. It seemed totally inappropriate for a man of God. There was more than a trace of rebel in him, Abbie realized.

"What do you do when someone tells you that?" she asked.

"I pray on it." Then he addressed himself to her mother. "My way of doing things is sometimes regarded as unconventional, but it doesn't necessarily make it wrong." He seemed to be quietly warning her that his methods wouldn't be the same as those of their previous pastor.

"I'm sure we all have some adjustments to make," her mother conceded smoothly, but there appeared to be reluctant admiration in her look. "I guess we can start out by being thankful that you don't have long hair and a beard."

"You mean like Jesus," he murmured.

Her mother breathed in sharply, then smiled. "You have me there, Reverend Talbot."

"I prefer to have you at church on Sunday mornings," he replied with a silent laugh that slashed grooves in his lean cheeks.

"Our family will be there," her mother promised as her glance strayed beyond him. "Abbie, you'd better finish putting those spoons out. We want to start serving." She seemed to suddenly remember her initial purpose in coming to the refreshment table.

"Excuse me, ladies." He inclined his bronze head in their direction and withdrew.

As Abbie watched him walk away to mingle with the growing crowd, she tried not to notice how becoming he looked in black, and the way the cut of his suit showed off the tapering width of his chest and shoulders. It seemed wrong to be observing those things about him.

"Abbie." Her mother's prompting voice pulled her gaze from his compelling male figure. "Put the spoons out."

"I will." Then she asked, "What do you think of him?"

There was a long pause while her mother's gaze traveled across the room to where he was standing. "I haven't made up my mind," she answered finally.

People were starting to drift toward the refreshment table as Abbie laid the last few spoons out. She helped herself to two cups of coffee from the urn and went in search of her father. One of the cups was for him and the other for herself. Like a magnet, her gaze was drawn to Seth. She forced it to move onward until she spied her father in the far corner of the room, talking to one of his fishing buddies.

It wasn't easy to work her way through the throng of people, carrying two cups of hot coffee, but she made it. Engrossed in his conversation, her father looked startled when she extended the cup within range of his vision. He glanced up.

"Is that for me?" he asked.

"I thought you might have talked yourself dry with all your fish tales," Abbie said.

"There are fish *tales* and there are *fish* tails, get it?" His friend, Ben Cooper, chuckled at his own pun.

Abbie groaned in mock dismay at the poor humor. Ben Cooper had his insurance office next door to her father's law offices, so he was a frequent visitor, dropping in regularly for coffee.

"I'd offer you this cup of coffee, Ben, but it's black and I know you prefer yours drowned in milk," she explained.

"That's all right. I'll get my own." He hitched

the waistband of his suit pants higher around his middle as he stood up. "Save my chair for me, will you, Abbie?"

"Sure." She obligingly sat in it when he moved out of the way.

"That Ben is a character," her father murmured with a shake of his head.

"Mmmm." Abbie made an agreeing sound as she took a sip of coffee from her cup. Her gaze wandered idly over the crowd of people and stopped when it found Seth Talbot. She felt again that quiver of purely sexual reaction to his rough good looks.

"Penny for your thoughts?" Her father tipped his head curiously at her. "Who are you staring at?"

"Our new pastor," she admitted, and this time managed to keep her poise. "Have you met him yet?"

"No. Which one is he?" He turned to survey the crowd.

"That tall man over there, talking to Mrs. Smith." Abbie pointed him out with one finger, not wanting to be too obvious.

"Him?" There was vague surprise. "He doesn't look like a minister."

Laughter bubbled in her throat. "That's what I said, too," she admitted. "Unfortunately, I was talking to him at the time."

"That isn't like you," he said, smiling along with her. "You're usually more tactful."

"Everyone's entitled to stick their foot in their mouth once in a while." Abbie shrugged. "Besides, he's the motorist I told you about—the one who patched up Mabel so I could make it into town. He drives a sports car. And he was dressed in cutoffs and a T-shirt. Believe me, he didn't look like a minister then, either."

"No wonder you were surprised," he agreed, and turned his attention back to the more immediate subject of their conversation. "What does his wife look like?"

"He's a bachelor." Abbie pretended not to hear the soft whistle of surprise from her father as she took another sip of coffee. But it was difficult to ignore him when he turned a speculating look on her.

"Do I detect a note of interest?" he asked.

"Daddy, I just met him," she protested.

"So?" he challenged.

"So, I hardly know him. Besides, he's a minister," she reasoned.

"A minister—not a priest," he reminded her.

The conversation was taking an uncomfortable turn. Abbie was glad when she saw Ben Cooper sliding through the crowd with a cup of coffee and a napkinful of tea cakes and sandwiches. She quickly rose from the chair next to her father.

"You can have your seat back, Ben," she declared brightly, and pretended to eye the blueberry tart balanced on top of the small sandwiches. "I think I'll check out the sweets."

One blueberry tart and a cup of coffee later, Abbie found herself trapped in a conversation with the Coltrain sisters, two delightful ladies in their eighties who could ramble on for hours, reminiscing about the past. She'd heard nearly all their stories at least twice. It was inevitable that her attention wandered.

She seemed to have only one interest—Seth Talbot. Voluntarily or involuntarily, she had spent most of her time observing the way he casually mingled, getting acquainted with the members of his new congregation attending the tea. It wasn't just the women who seemed to take to him, but the men as well. The room seemed to buzz with conversations with the new minister as their main topic.

It might have been a farewell tea for Reverend Augustus, but Seth Talbot was stealing the man's thunder. Or was it only her imagination? Just because she was practically obsessed with him did not necessarily mean that everyone else was. Abbie sighed, pulling her attention back to the moment as she took a drink of coffee and discovered it had grown cold.

"Would you?" Isabel Coltrain turned an unblinking pair of blue eyes to Abbie.

"I . . ." She realized she hadn't heard a word of the recent conversation. "I'm sorry." Abbie pretended there were too many other people talking. "What did you say?"

"Would you type the manuscript Esther and I are writing when we're finished?" The older of the two sisters repeated the question. "We'll pay you . . . if it's not too much."

"Yes, I'd be happy to type it for you." Abbie relaxed a little, now that she knew exactly what she was committing herself to do. "I can do it in the evenings."

"I'm so glad that young man suggested that we should write a book, aren't you, Esther?" Isabel Coltrain practically sparkled with zest and energy.

"Young man?" Abbie murmured in vague confusion. She had been under the impression that the manuscript was already in progress.

"Yes, the new reverend." Esther showed equal excitement. "He was so fascinated by some of the stories we told him that he said we should write them down."

"My, but he's a handsome man, isn't he?" Isabel rolled her eyes and clutched a hand to her heart. "He makes me wish I was young again."

"Act your age," her younger sister scolded.

From past experience, Abbie knew the pair could become quite spiteful with sibling jealousy and quickly intervened. "It's a wonderful idea about the book. When do you plan to start on it?"

"Oh, right away," Esther assured her. "We're going to start by jotting down our ideas, then decide who's going to write what."

"That sounds practical," Abbie agreed, even though it could be the basis for a lot of arguments. Before she became embroiled in the middle of one, she thought it best to excuse herself. "I think I'll warm up my coffee."

"Don't drink too much. It isn't good for you," Isabel warned.

"I won't," Abbie promised while she backed away.

Chapter Three

The old Roman-numeraled clock on the office wall indicated the time was five minutes before twelve noon. Abbie opened the bottom drawer of her desk and removed her purse, a large shoulder-bag affair. Lifting the flap, she took a slightly oversized compact mirror out of a side compartment and a tube of bronzed pink lipstick.

The overhead light didn't provide the best conditions for the application of makeup but it was infinitely better than the bare light bulb in the rest room. Abbie turned in her swivel chair so she was facing the full play of light while she freshened the color of her lips and inspected the results in the mirror. She used her fingertips to fluff the ends of her copper hair, then snapped the compact mirror closed in satisfaction.

She was just replacing it in its zippered compartment in her purse when her father stepped out of his private office. His suit jacket was off and the sleeves of his white shirt were rolled back. He had a cup in his hand. It didn't require any clever deduction for Abbie to figure out he was heading to the coffee urn for more coffee. He'd been up to his elbows in law books for the last hour. Case research always seemed to go hand in hand with increased coffee consumption.

His absentminded glance at her desk took in her purse sitting atop it, which seemed to prompt a look at the antique wall clock. "It's that time already, is it?" He sighed his disbelief that the morning could have gone so quickly and walked on, then stopped. "Don't forget to make that bank deposit."

"I've got it right here." Abbie picked up the envelope from her desk top. "I plan to stop at the bank first. Are you going out for lunch, or would you like me to bring you something?"

Her father paused in the act of filling his cup to send her a frowning look. "Is Ed coming in at one or one-thirty?"

Abbie checked the appointment book. "One."

"Better bring me a sandwich then," he decided.

Standing up, Abbie slipped the long strap to her purse over her shoulder and kept the envelope with the bank deposit in her hand. "I'll be back in an hour or soooner," she said, and received an acknowledging nod from her father.

With a hot sun overhead, Abbie kept to the shady side of the street. There was a good breeze, which kept the summer heat from becoming stifling. It billowed the ice-blue material

50

of her loose, tentlike dress, cinched at the waist with a wide white elastic belt.

The streets and sidewalks were bustling with summer traffic as Abbie walked to the bank. There were so many strangers about that she stopped looking for familiar faces. When she reached to open the door to the bank, a man's hand was there ahead of her. She half turned to absently smile a polite thanks for the gentlemanly gesture. But the man leaning forward was Seth Talbot, not a stranger.

The air seemed to leave her lungs in a sudden rush. Abbie wasn't prepared for this exposure to his virile brand of sexuality. For the last three days, she'd made a determined attempt to block him out of her mind and stop weaving romantic fantasies about a minister of the church.

"How are you today, Miss Scott?" Seth greeted her with a natural friendly warmth.

It took a tremendous force of will to pull her gaze from his roughly hewn features and the arresting indigo of his eyes, but Abbie succeeded in doing so. "Fine, thank you, Reverend." She was irritated by how prim she sounded and made a stilted attempt to correct it. "And you?"

There was a hint of amusement in his gaze when Abbie dared to glance at him again. "Very well." But there was nothing in his voice to mock her as he held the door to the bank open, then followed her inside.

Her stomach felt like a quivering ball of nerves. The summer season had brought its usual mixture of sightseers and customers to the bank. Its reconstruction as a Victorian-era institution made it one of the town's attractions.

Believing the conversation was over, Abbie skirted the high-backed chairs that were arranged around a polished potbellied stove, a brass cuspidor near one foot, and headed for the brass teller cages. Then she realized he was walking beside her. Again he was dressed in an unorthodox fashion for a minister—a pair of Levi's that hugged his narrow hips and long, muscular legs, and a white sport shirt that was unbuttoned at the throat. His shoes looked suspiciously like cowboy boots.

It was one thing for him to travel in casual clothes, but Abbie was astounded that he was going around town minus his frock and white collar. This was the community he was to serve as minister, but how would anyone know it when he dressed like everyone else?

His gaze had finished its sweep of the bank's unusual interior and stopped on her. "It really carries out the town's theme, doesn't it?" he remarked.

"Yes. They have quite a display of original business machines, too," Abbie replied, feeling the tension return with the attention he was paying her.

"I looked at them when I was in here Monday." He nodded, his burnished gold hair reflecting the light from the overhead chandeliers. "Are you downtown shopping or is this your lunch break?"

The personal query caught her off guard. "My

lunch break," Abbie admitted, then felt she needed an excuse for being in the bank. She nervously lifted the hand with the envelope. "I have a deposit to make first, though."

"Where do you work?" His question appeared to contain only idle interest.

"I'm a legal secretary—for my father." It was hardly a secret.

"There's nothing like nepotism to keep out of the unemployment lines," he declared with the flash of a white smile.

Abbie stiffened, taking offense even though she knew none had been intended. "I happen to be very qualified for the job."

An eyebrow was arched briefly, his look gentling at her sensitivity. "I'm not throwing stones, Miss Scott. After all, I work for my Father." A teasing light sparkled in his blue eyes and Abbie smiled at the comparison of their respective employers. "That's better." Seth smiled too. "Would you excuse me? I have to talk to one of the officers."

"Of course." She hadn't meant to keep him from his errand, and her smile slid away. "I need to make this deposit, too." It was a defensive reply, an insistence that she had things to do as well.

The nearest teller also happened to be the one with the shortest waiting line. Abbie walked to it, aware of Seth Talbot approaching the desk of a bank officer. The two customers ahead of her had only minor transactions to make, so it was quickly Abbie's turn at the window.

"Hello, Roberta," Abbie greeted the plump, young woman teller, and slid the deposit across the counter.

"Is it as hot outside as it looks?" the teller asked as she checked to verify that there were signatures and deposit-only stamps on all the checks.

"Hotter, but there's a nice breeze," Abbie replied.

A bleached blonde crowded close to Roberta and leaned toward Abbie to whisper eagerly. "We're all just dying to find out who that gorgeous hunk of man is that you're with?" Fran was a former classmate of Abbie's, who was married and had two children, but she'd always been a little man-crazy.

"What man?" As soon as Abbie asked she realized Fran was talking about Seth—Reverend Talbot.

"What man she says." Fran gave Roberta a knowing look.

"I guess you're referring to Reverend Talbot," Abbie admitted. "He's the new pastor of our church now that Reverend Augustus has retired."

"*That* is the new pastor!" Fran's stage whisper seemed alarmingly loud. "Oh, Roberta, I think I've just been saved," she declared on a giggle.

"I don't blame you," Roberta murmured, and cast a longing eye across the bank—no doubt at Seth, but Abbie refused to turn around and look. "He's the sexiest-looking man to come to this town in a long time."

"I guess," Fran agreed effusively. "I'm going to have to buy myself a new Sunday dress to wear to church."

"Do you belong to our church?" Abbie questioned with a blank look. She couldn't recall ever seeing Fran and her husband attend Sunday services.

"I haven't been there in years—not since Butch and I got married," Fran admitted indifferently, then grinned coyly. "But I think I'm going to be among the faithful from now on."

"Heck, I think I'm going to convert." Roberta smiled impishly.

"Oh, God," Fran murmured excitedly. "He's coming over here. Oh, Abbie, you've just got to introduce us."

She was disgusted at the way the two of them were carrying on about him. One glance at the other female employees behind the cages informed her that Roberta and Fran weren't the only ones avidly eyeing the man walking up, and whispering among themselves. They were only echoing her own reaction to him, but that didn't make it any less distasteful.

Roberta passed Abbie the receipt for her deposit and spoke loudly, "Here you are, Abbie."

"Thank you." She was holding her neck almost rigidly still to avoid turning her head to look at Seth Talbot when he stopped beside her. But she had to move to put the receipt in her purse.

"Are you finished?" he asked.

"Yes." Her glance bounced away before it

squarely met his eyes. Too many sensations were clawing at her because of his presence.

"Hi, I'm Fran Bigsby." The blonde introduced herself when Abbie failed to do it immediately. "Abbie was just telling us that you're the new pastor. Welcome to Eureka Springs."

"Seth Talbot's the name and I'm glad to be here." Again, that warm smiling look was on his visage.

"I'm Roberta Flack, no relation to the singer." Roberta beamed, looking very pretty, despite the unflattering pounds she carried.

"I'm happy to meet you both," he said. When Abbie started to move away from the teller's window so Roberta could wait on the next customer, Seth started to leave with her. "Maybe I'll see you in church some Sunday," he added as a farewell remark.

"You can be sure of it," Fran called after them.

Abbie couldn't walk away from the window fast enough, embarrassed without being sure why. But Seth was undeterred by her haste, easily striding at her side.

"Was there anyplace special you were going to have lunch?" he asked.

His query startled a glance from her. "No. Why?" There were others leaving the bank, and Abbie was forced to slow her pace as she scanned his expression.

"I was on my way to lunch. You're on your way to lunch. So why don't we have it together?" Seth reasoned smoothly. "There's a restaurant just down the street. Shall we go there?"

Her acceptance of his plan seemed to be taken for granted. Actually, Abbie couldn't think of a single reason why she should refuse. "Sounds good," she agreed.

The combination of noon hour and the influx of summer visitors resulted in a crowded restaurant. Luckily, Abbie and Seth had to wait only a few minutes before they were seated at a small table, hardly big enough for two. Her knees kept bumping against his under the table no matter how she tried to angle them in the close quarters. There was another man seated in a chair directly behind her, so she couldn't even edge her chair away from the table.

"Sorry," she apologized when her knee rubbed against the side of his for the fourth time. She hoped he didn't think she was doing it deliberately.

"It's close quarters in here." Seth offered the excuse, but the light glinting in his blue eyes made her feel hot.

"Yes, it is." Abbie opened her menu to study it intently. Maybe if she sat perfectly still and didn't move, it wouldn't be so bad.

"What are you going to have?" he asked as he spread open his menu.

"A chef's salad, I think." Her stomach wasn't behaving too well. She didn't want to put a lot of food into it. "How about you?"

But when she looked up, his gaze was making a leisurely survey of her upper body and appearing to take particular note of the hint of maturely rounded breasts under the loose-fitting dress. It was the look of a man, and a hundred alarm bells rang in her ears.

"Are you on a diet?" Seth finally lifted his gaze to her face. "It's just one man's opinion, but I don't see how you can improve on your figure."

In the first place, she wasn't sure if he should notice such things, and she definitely felt he shouldn't comment on them if he did. But how on earth did you reprimand a minister? Abbie preferred to believe she had misinterpreted his glance. Maybe it had been more analytical and less intimate.

"I don't like to eat a lot of food on a hot day like today." She chose to explain away her lack of appetite.

"That's probably very wise," he agreed. When the waitress came, Seth ordered for both of them. At the last minute, Abbie remembered she had promised to bring her father a sandwich.

"I'll need a cold roast-beef sandwich to go, too, please," she added hastily, then explained to Seth when the waitress left, "My father was tied up and couldn't get away for lunch."

"He's an attorney here?"

"Yes. It's just a small practice. He keeps talking about retiring but he won't. He loves what he's doing too much." It seemed easier to talk about her father than the other choice of subjects open to her—like the weather. "Although he does complain that his practice interferes with his fishing," she added with a laughing smile.

"He's an avid fisherman, I take it." Seth smiled.

"Very avid," Abbie agreed, and couldn't help thinking that Seth was a "Fisher of Men."

"I didn't have a chance to meet him last Sunday at the tea. I'm looking forward to it, though," he said. "How long have you worked for him?"

"About a year now." Abbie leaned back in her chair when the waitress returned to set a glass of iced tea in front of her and milk for Seth. The action accidentally pressed more of her leg against his.

"Don't worry," he murmured on a seductively low-pitched note. "I'm not going to think you're playing footsy with me under the table." Abbie was positive she had never blushed in her life, but her cheeks were on fire at the moment. Her mind was absolutely blank of anything to say. Seth seemed to guess and asked, "What did you do before that? Attend college?"

"No, I worked for TWA in Kansas City." She was relieved to have the subject changed.

"As a stewardess?"

"No, I was in management, in the corporate offices."

His attention deepened. Abbie braced herself for the next question, fully anticipating that he was going to ask why she had left, but it never came. There was only the quiet study of his keen eyes.

"Thomas Wolfe was obviously wrong. It is

possible to go home again," was the only comment he made.

"I'm just a small-town girl at heart," she admitted.

Just as the waitress came with their luncheon order, a local judge paused by their table. Abbie had known Judge Sessions since she was a small child, so she wasn't surprised by his greeting when he noticed her.

"Hi there, little girl. How are you doing today?" He grabbed a lock of copper hair and tugged at it affectionately.

"I'm doing just fine, Judge." She smiled up at him.

His glance went to Seth, sitting opposite from her. "Who's this with you? A new man friend?" His teasing demand was accompanied by a broad wink.

"No, of course not." Abbie denied this quickly, conscious that Seth was already rising to be introduced. "This is the new minister of our church, Reverend Seth Talbot. Reverend, I'd like you to meet Judge Sessions, a family friend."

"Reverend?" The judge almost did a double take, then shook Seth's hand and laughed. "You could have fooled me!"

"I seem to fool a lot of people," Seth admitted with a brief glance at Abbie.

"You do look more like a man of the flesh than a man of the cloth," the judge stated.

"I'm the usual combination of both," Seth replied, not at all bothered by the remark.

Abbie thought the judge's description was very accurate. Seth was made of flesh and blood, all hard, male sinew and bone. Not even the cloth could conceal that.

"I'm glad to hear it." The judge nodded. "We need a change from sanctimonious old fogies, too old to sin anymore." He laid a hand on Abbie's shoulder. "Be nice to this little girl here. They don't come any better than Abbie." Then he was moving away from their table with a farewell wave of his hand.

This time it was Seth who brushed his knee against hers when he sat down. Abbie wondered if she wouldn't feel more relaxed if it weren't for this constant physical contact with him. Her skirt had inched up above her knees, but it was impossible to pull it down without touching him. He couldn't see it, not with the table in the way, so she made no attempt to adjust it downward.

"Have you known the judge long?" Seth asked as he picked up his silverware to begin eating his chicken-fried steak with gravy smothered over it and the mound of mashed potatoes.

"Practically all my life." She stabbed a piece of lettuce and sliced ham with her fork. "It's not surprising that people are taken aback when they find out you're a minister. You really should wear your collar, so they'll at least have some advance warning."

If he'd been wearing it, the judge wouldn't have assumed he was her boyfriend, and the girls at the bank wouldn't have been lusting over him—and maybe she would feel a little safer.

The last seemed silly, yet Abbie felt the collar would provide some sort of protection for her.

"Do you have any idea how those stiff collars chafe your neck on a hot day like this?" Seth appeared amused by her comment.

"I'm sorry. I didn't mean to criticize the way you're dressed." It had been a very rude thing to do—as well as presumptuous.

"It doesn't matter." His wide shoulders were lifted in a careless shrug. There was a dancing light in his eyes when he looked at her. "I promise you that I do wear it when I make my rounds at the hospital or call on a member of the congregation in their home."

"In some ways, this is a very conservative community. I guess that's what I'm trying to say," Abbie murmured. And he seemed liberal and at the age to know about sin, as the judge had suggested.

"Right in the heart of the Bible Belt area, I know." He nodded.

She glanced at him sharply to see if there was any mockery in his expression, but it was impossible to tell. Her gaze wandered downward to the white of his shirt. With the top three buttons unfastened, she had a glimpse of curly gold chest hairs, another example of his blatant masculinity. There was a chain of some sort around his neck, too.

"Something wrong?" Seth caught her staring, and amusement deepened the edges of his mouth without materializing into a smile.

Her pulse did a quick acceleration as Abbie

dived her fork into the salad again. "You just don't look like a minister." She sighed the admission. His latent sensuality was too unnerving for her.

His low chuckle vibrated over her tingling nerve ends. "Let's see . . . what would laymen expect a minister to look like?" he mused. "I imagine there are different categories. The intensely pious should be pale, ascetically slender, with deep-set eyes, hollow cheeks, and a fervid voice. There'd be the benevolent father figure— white hair, a round face, and a kindly air. And you have the thunderer, preaching about the wrath of God and pointing out the sinners with a long accusing finger. He'd have a beard, be very tall, with beetle brows." Seth paused to send a mocking glance across the table. "How am I doing so far?"

"I guess I've been guilty of type-casting," Abbie admitted with a faint smile.

"Everyone does it," he assured her. "Now, my idea of a legal secretary is a woman in her forties with her hair pulled back in a severe bun. She'd wear wire-rimmed glasses and tailored business suits." His glance skimmed her again. "Funny, you don't look like a legal secretary."

She laughed naturally for the first time. "I promise I won't say it again, Reverend." Inside, Abbie knew she'd think it each time she referred to him by his professional title.

"I've finally made you laugh." His gaze focused on the parted curve of her lips. She felt them tremble from the look that was oddly physical. "We've cleared the first hurdle," Seth murmured enigmatically.

"To what?" Her voice sounded breathless.

"To becoming friends," he replied.

"Oh." For some reason, Abbie was disappointed by his answer. She ate a few more mouthfuls of salad but found it tasteless. She couldn't stop being conscious of the warmth of his leg against hers, and the rough texture of the denim material brushing the bareness of her calf. It became imperative to keep a conversation going. "Are you all moved in to the parsonage?"

"More or less. I still have a lot of boxes of books to unpack." There was a rueful slant to his mouth as he glanced at her. "Have you ever been in it?"

"No." The slight shake of her head swayed the ends of her pale copper hair.

"It's a rambling monstrosity. There's more rooms there than I'll ever use. I'll probably close up half of the house."

"I imagine it was intended for a family to live in rather than a single man," Abbie suggested.

"It's practically an unwritten rule. A man is supposed to have his wife picked out *before* he graduates from the seminary and is assigned to his first church." Seth didn't appear troubled that he hadn't followed the rule.

"But you didn't." She stated the obvious.

"No, I didn't," he agreed, and let his gaze lock on to hers.

Her throat muscles tightened. "I guess it is the expected thing—for a minister to be married, I mean," Abbie finally managed to get the words out. "How long have you been in the ministry?" She guessed his age to be somewhere in the range of thirty-five.

"Thirteen years. I spent four of those years as an air-force chaplain." He dropped his gaze and began slicing off a piece of steak.

"Where was your first church?" She gave in to her curiosity and began delving into his background.

"This is my first church," he admitted.

"You mean, you were always an assistant pastor before?" A slight frown of confusion creased her forehead.

"No. I worked in the national offices of the church. My work was more business-oriented than anything else." There was a sardonic curve to his mouth. "For a variety of reasons, I requested to be assigned a church in some quiet little community. I guess I'm taking something like a sabbatical."

"I see," she murmured.

"I doubt it." He showed a bit of cynical skepticism, then hid it. "But it isn't important." His glance suddenly challenged her. "Why is it that *you* aren't married, Miss Scott?"

Her mouth opened and closed twice before she could think of a safe answer. She laughed shortly to conceal her hesitation. "Grandmother Klein says it's because I haven't looked hard enough."

"Or maybe you've been looking in all the wrong places," Seth suggested.

It was on the tip of her tongue to ask him where the right places were, but Abbie resisted the impulse. "Maybe," she conceded, and stirred the half-eaten salad with her fork. Absently she glanced at the slim, gold watch around her wrist. Her eyes widened when she saw the time. "It's after one. I have to get back to the office." She laid her napkin alongside the salad plate and reached for the luncheon check the waitress had left, but Seth was quicker. Her hand ended up tangling briefly with his fingers, the contact sending a tingling shock up her arm.

"I'll buy this time," he insisted.

"Please," Abbie protested. "I don't really have time to argue. She opened her purse to take out her money, intending to leave it on the table regardless of what he said.

"You said yourself that you're short on time," Seth reminded her. "If you insist on paying, just put whatever you feel you owe in the collection plate this Sunday."

"I . . . all right." She gave in to his persuasion and refastened the leather flap of her purse.

"Don't forget your father's sandwich." He handed her the paper sack when she started to get up without it.

"Thank you." She gratefully took it from him. It was bad enough being late without her father having to go hungry, too.

"See you Sunday."

The walk to her father's office seemed longer

than it was. Abbie suspected it was because she was late and trying to hurry so she wouldn't be later than she was already. Her father was a tolerant, easygoing man, but he was a stickler for punctuality.

When she walked in, the door to his private office was closed, but she could hear muffled conversation within. His one o'clock appointment had obviously arrived. Abbie hurried to her desk, returning her purse to the lower drawer and setting his sandwich atop her desk. She swiveled her chair to the typewriter and picked up the headset to the dictaphone. Before she had it comfortably adjusted so she could hear, his door opened.

Abbie saw his irritation as he approached her desk. "I left a file on your desk." He picked up a folder from the IN tray.

"Here's your sandwich." She handed him the sack.

"I'm surprised you remembered. What kept you?"

"I had lunch with Reverend Talbot." She knew the judge would mention it if she didn't. Besides, keeping it a secret would only mean there was something to hide. "The time just slipped away."

He harumphed but didn't comment. Instead he opened the sack to peer inside. "Roast beef?"

"Yes."

There was a relenting of his stern expression. "At least you brought back my favorite."

Chapter Four

There were more people at church than Abbie remembered seeing in a long time, especially since it wasn't Easter or Christmas. A lot of it, she guessed, was curiosity about the new minister. Seth made a striking figure standing at the pulpit in his robe while he conducted the services.

He was halfway through his sermon before Abbie realized he wasn't using a microphone, yet his well-modulated voice carried his words effortlessly to the back row. He talked easily, as if he was carrying on a conversation instead of giving a sermon. His gestures were natural rather than dramatic. There were even places where the congregation laughed at a bit of humor that contained a message.

It seemed that Seth had barely begun when he finished. Abbie would have liked him to go on, and it was the first time she could ever remember wishing a sermon had been longer. She stole a glance at her parents sitting in the pew beside her. Her father was looking at his watch with a stunned expression, while her mother continued to give her rapt attention to the man at the pulpit.

A few minutes later, they were following the people filing out of church. The line moved slowly as those ahead of them paused to shake hands with the minister on their way out the door.

Her father leaned sideways to murmur, "Your reverend isn't bad, Abbie."

"He's not *my* reverend, Dad," she corrected in an equally low voice, not liking the insinuation that she was somehow linked to Seth simply because she'd had lunch with him once.

"If you say so." He shrugged, letting her move ahead of him as it became a single-file line to greet Seth.

Abbie waited patiently for her turn, a ripple of anticipation warming her blood while she watched Seth chatting with the couple ahead of her. The black robe seemed to make his hair look darker, more brown than gold, but the trappings of the clergy didn't alter his male appeal.

His glance strayed to her and lingered briefly in recognition. The vivid blue of his eyes darkened with a glow that made her feel special. The look tripped her heartbeat but Abbie refused to flatter herself into believing it held any significance. She was just a familiar face, someone he knew after meeting so many strangers.

The exchange of glances lasted only a few seconds before his attention reverted to the

couple. Then they were moving down the steps
and it was Abbie's turn. Close up, Seth seemed
taller, more commanding in his black robe.
His hand reached to take hers in greeting and
continued to hold it when Abbie would have
withdrawn it.

"What's the verdict?" There was warm, mocking amusement in the downward glance that
took in his preaching robes. "Will I pass?" He
was teasing her about the way she had criticized
him about his dress at lunch that day.

"Yes." The corners of her mouth dimpled with
a responding smile. "And you *sounded* like a
minister, too, Reverend."

His head was tipped back to release a throaty
laugh. Its volume was subdued, but no less
genuine. Seth inclined his head to her in mocking acknowledgment. "That's the highest compliment I've received today. I thank you, Miss
Scott."

"You're welcome, Reverend." She would have
moved on, but his firm grip wouldn't relinquish
her hand. There was uncertain confusion in the
look she gave him, but his attention had
swerved to her parents.

"Is this your father?" Seth inquired in a tone
that prompted her to make the introduction.

"Yes. I'd like you to meet him." Only when she
spoke to indicate her compliance with his unspo-
ken request did Seth release her hand. "Dad,
this is Reverend Talbot. Reverend, my father,
Drew Scott. You've met my mother already."

"Yes, I have." He nodded, shaking her hand.

"It's good to see you again, Mrs. Scott. And it's a pleasure to meet your husband. How do you do, Mr. Scott."

"I've been looking forward to meeting you, Reverend," her father admitted. "Enjoyed your sermon."

"I understand you're a fisherman." Seth didn't mention that Abbie had been the source of that information, but her father guessed it. "Maybe you can point me to some good fishing holes around here later on."

"Be happy to," her father agreed, then added a qualification, "as long as you make sure the next time you take my secretary out to lunch, she's not late getting back."

"Daddy." It was a low, impatient protest Abbie made. He made it sound like she was likely to have lunch with Seth again.

But Seth wasn't bothered by the implication. "You have a deal, Mr. Scott."

There were still more people behind them waiting to leave the church. Abbie was relieved when her parents moved past Seth to descend the steps with her. Not all the congregation had dispersed once they left the church. Some were scattered along the wide sidewalk, socializing in small groups. Her parents were too well known to go directly to their car without being stopped by someone. Since Abbie had ridden with them, she was obliged to linger on the fringes each time her father or mother paused to speak to someone.

Her glance invariably wandered back to the

church doors. She recognized Fran Bigsby when she came out with her two small children. There was no sign of her husband as the bleached blonde stopped to talk to Seth. Flirt with him seemed a better description, Abbie thought cattily. There was no sign of Fran's husband but she noticed her younger sister, Marjorie, was with her.

Suddenly, Abbie realized there were a lot of women that had attended the morning service without their husbands, especially those families who weren't regular worshipers. She didn't like the conclusion she was reaching because she had the unkind suspicion they hadn't been drawn there today to welcome their new minister, but rather to meet the handsome bachelor-pastor the whole town was buzzing about.

It made her silent, and more than just a little thoughtful, while she studied her own motives. No matter how she tried, Abbie couldn't ignore the fact that she was strongly attracted to him on a physical level. She was living in a glass house and couldn't very well afford to throw stones at anyone else.

Abbie glanced at the clock as she rolled the finished letter out of the typewriter. It was close to noon, time enough to type an envelope and have the letter ready to mail before she left for lunch. It was Thursday, exactly a week to the day since she'd lunched with Seth.

The knowledge must have been hovering at the back of her mind, because when she heard the street door open, her heart did a little somer-sault. She turned, expecting to see Seth walking into the office. But Judge Sessions didn't look like him at all. It was difficult to keep her smile from dying.

"Hello, Judge." Abbie forced the cheerfulness into her voice. "Dad's in his office. You can go in, if you want. He doesn't have a client with him."

"Maybe I didn't come to see him," he challenged lightly. "Maybe I'm here to see you."

"It's possible, but I doubt it." Now that she had gotten over her initial disappointment, Abbie could respond more naturally to the judge's teasing remarks.

Her father stepped out of his private office. "I thought I heard you out here, Walter," he accused, and crossed to exchange a back slapping handshake. "What are you doing, you old crook?"

"I came to take my favorite father-daughter pair to lunch," the judge replied, then slid Abbie a glittering look. "That is, if your daughter doesn't have a previous luncheon date?"

"I believe I have a vacancy in my social calendar today," she replied, laughing.

"You could have been saving all your free time for that handsome new reverend," the judge suggested. "When are you going to see him again?"

Abbie was beginning to lose her humor at his probing remarks. "Probably Sunday at church just like everyone else," she retorted with a trace of coolness. "Just because I had lunch with him once, purely by accident, it doesn't mean it's going to become a regular event."

"Drew, I think the girl's sick," the judge declared. "She's trying to claim she's not interested in this fellow."

"I'm not," Abbie protested, and wanted to bite her tongue for telling such an outright lie.

"What makes you different from all the rest of the women in town?" He challenged her with a disbelieving look. "From what I've heard, they're falling all over themselves trying to get his attention."

"Is that a fact?" her father inserted, siding with the judge to gang up on Abbie. "All the gossip manages to get funneled to you, Walter. Why don't you let us in on it?"

"I understand that his cup runneth over. The older ladies are bringing him casseroles, cakes, salads, cookies, homemade bread, and just about anything else you care to mention. There isn't a bare shelf in his refrigerator or cupboard."

"I think that's nice," Abbie insisted in defense of the gifts. "It's the neighborly thing to do when a newcomer moves in."

"But those old ladies are wise." The judge winked slyly. "The way to a man's heart is through his stomach. Haven't you heard?"

"Come to think of it, Alice baked him a green-apple pie just this last Tuesday," Drew recalled. "Maybe I'd better keep a closer eye on my wife. She was at the parsonage for almost an hour."

"Dad, you can't be jealous of the reverend."

Abbie wasn't sure if he was serious or just razzing her.

"I don't mind if she looks . . . as long as that's all she does," he said, then laughed to show he wasn't worried.

"It seems there are a lot of young wives who have suddenly discovered they have marital problems, which came as quite a surprise to their contented husbands . . ." the judge inserted. ". . . and now they're going to the good reverend for his advice and understanding."

Abbie had the uneasy feeling that Fran Bigsby was probably one of them. She saw the point the judge was making. It was all a ruse to get Seth's undivided attention, to try to attract his interest.

"But it's more than his sympathy they're after," her father added, confirming Abbie's private thoughts.

"Women are volunteering right and left to help with anything from typing the church bulletins to doing his housekeeping." The judge gave an exaggerated sigh and looked at her father. "And they say a bachelor's life is a lonely one. One crook of his little finger and half the women in the county would come running. I'll bet the church will be filled to the rafters next Sunday."

"I wouldn't be surprised," her father agreed with this summation.

That's when Abbie made the decision that she wouldn't be one of them. She didn't want Seth to get the impression she was chasing him just like all the other women in town seemed to be. She didn't necessarily attend church every single

Sunday, so it wouldn't be out of the ordinary for her to skip a couple of weeks.

She was very casual about it when she talked to her mother on Saturday and mentioned that she was going to visit Grandmother Klein on Sunday and skip church. Her mother took Abbie's decision at face value. Her father gave her a strange look but said nothing.

On Monday morning, Abbie didn't have a chance to make the first pot of coffee before the street door opened and the two Coltrain sisters came bustling in. They always seemed to wear outfits that clashed with what the other one was wearing. Esther had on a brightly flowered dress, predominantly grape-colored, while Isabel wore a gaudy, fushia-pink dress.

"There you are, Abbie!" Esther declared happily. The fluorescent lights in the office seemed to reflect the grape from her dress and cast a lavender tint on her curling white hair. "We thought we might find you here at your papa's office."

"Yes, I work here during the week," Abbie explained, certain she had told them that before.

But neither of them had ever worked. They had been raised to believe women should stay in the home, married or not. Luckily the inheritance from their parents had left them with substantial annuities so they could.

Isabel opened her enormous black tapestry bag with its bold pink-rose design, and pulled out a stack of loose papers in assorted sizes and colors. A slim rubber band strained to hold them together.

"We were going to give you this yesterday at church but you didn't come," Isabel explained.

"What is it?" Abbie reached for it with a puzzled frown.

"Don't you remember?" Esther looked stricken. "You said you'd type our manuscript for us."

"Do you mean you've written it already?" Abbie looked up from the first piece of paper, filled with scrawly handwriting, to stare incredulously at the two sisters.

"Oh, goodness no!" Isabel laughed merrily at the thought. "We decided it would be easier if we gave you what we had finished as we went along."

"Haven't we gotten a lot done?" Esther asked excitedly. "We worked on it every single day, didn't we, Isabel?"

"It was so much fun, Abbie," Isabel declared, puffing up with proud satisfaction. "I'm so glad the reverend suggested it."

"I can imagine." Abbie couldn't recall when she had seen either sister so animated or so enthused. It was contagious. She felt herself catching their excitement too, and smiling right along with them.

"I do hope you won't have any trouble reading it." Isabel cupped a hand to her mouth to whisper secretively to Abbie. "Esther used to have such beautiful penmanship, but with her arthritis it's sometimes not very legible."

"I don't think I'll have any difficulty. But if I have any questions on a particular part, I'll call and ask," she promised.

"We aren't telling anyone what we're doing." Esther put a protective hand over the uncompleted manuscript Abbie was holding. "You're the only one who knows."

"I won't breathe a word." Abbie crossed her heart in a child's solemn promise. "In fact, I'll put it in the bottom drawer of my desk right now."

"You won't lose it." Isabel looked worried as Abbie walked to her desk to put the handwritten papers away.

"Call us as soon as you have it typed," Esther advised. "We'll have some more ready for you." She took her sister's arm. "Come, Isabel. Let's go home so we can start on the next part."

"Bye!" Abbie called as the two white-haired sisters bustled toward the door. "I'll phone you when I'm through with this."

That evening was the start of what became a nightly routine, with her portable typewriter sitting on the small dining-room table in her apartment and the pages of the manuscript setting out. The Coltrain sisters had used everything from yellow tablet paper to fancy stationery to write on. Abbie quickly discovered that the page numbers on the sheets were not necessarily correct. More often than not, they were out of sequence.

Before she could start typing, she had to decipher the handwriting and read and arrange the pages in their proper order. She had expected the manuscript to be a collection of loosely connected anecdotes of their early years and stories of some of the area's first citizens. Abbie was shocked to realize the sisters had fictionalized it into a story—a rather torrid, period romance set in Eureka Springs around the turn of the century.

Each night, Abbie sat down to the typewriter for three hours, correcting misspelled words, or finding the right one when a sister had fallen victim to malapropism, and inserting the right punctuation where none existed. It was a long, tedious process, made fascinating by the characters and stories she remembered the sisters telling as they became part of the plot. Just when she became used to reading Esther's handwriting and could get some typing speed, the next part would be written by Isabel and she'd have to slow down again.

The typing gave her a perfect excuse to miss church that Sunday, and the sisters had more written when Abbie finished the first installment. She missed the following Sunday's service as well.

The long days, working at the office and in her apartment on the nights and weekends, were beginning to wear on her. Abbie was dragging Monday morning when she arrived at the office. She was leaning on the table, waiting for the coffee to finish dripping. Her father walked out of his office, carrying his cup, just as she was in the middle of a large yawn.

"You can't keep this up, Abbie." He shook his head at her. "You need to get out and have some fun. I hear you hammering away at that typewriter every night."

"I'll take tonight off, Dad," Abbie promised, and tried to swallow another yawn.

"Not just tonight," he advised. "You take a couple or three nights off. Go to a movie—or ask some guy for a date. These are liberated times. You don't have to wait for a Sadie Hawkins' Day."

"Yes, Dad." She smiled wryly, because there wasn't anyone she was interested in asking—except Seth. She shook away that thought. The red light blinked on to indicate the coffee was done. "Coffee's ready."

"I've just got time for a quick cup, then I have to get over to the courthouse," he said with a quick glance at his watch.

By the time her father left, Abbie had drunk her first cup of coffee and felt that at least her eyes were open. She poured a second cup and sat down at her desk to see what dictation had been left for her to type. The more she thought about her father's suggestion, the more convinced she became that he was right. It was to the point where she was typing in her dreams.

When she heard someone enter the office, Abbie tried to summon a suitably cheerful smile to greet him. But the "him" was Seth Talbot.

Her hazel-green eyes widened in surprise, and she was suddenly very much awake.

In the past three weeks, she'd only had occasional glimpses of him behind the wheel of his dark green sports car. But here he was—in the flesh—and her pulse started fluttering crazily. As Seth approached her desk, so tall and lean and flashing her that white smile, Abbie felt weak at the knees. The whiteness of his clergyman's collar contrasted sharply with his darkly tanned neck, but her senses didn't have any respect for his attire. They were all reacting to his raw manliness, his roughly chiseled features, and deeply blue eyes.

"Hello, Reverend." Abbie was amazed that she sounded so calm.

"Good morning." His eyes crinkled at the corners, partially concealing the intensity of his scanning gaze as it swept over her. "How are you?"

"Fine." She nodded. It seemed logical to assume it was her father he came to see, so Abbie explained. "I'm sorry but my father is out of the office just now. I expect him back around noon."

"I'm not here on a legal matter." Seth corrected her thinking. "I came by to see you." He said it so casually, yet her reaction was anything but. A heady kind of excitement tingled through her nerves, while a breathlessness attacked her lungs.

"Oh?" She tipped her head to the side at an inquiring angle, her pale copper hair swinging free.

"I haven't seen you in church lately," he said. "I thought I would stop to see if there was anything wrong."

"Ah." Abbie nodded her head in bitter understanding. "The shepherd is out looking for the sheep that strayed from his flock, is that it?"

There was a slight narrowing of his gaze at the bite in her voice. "Something like that, yes," Seth admitted. "I miss having an honest critic in the congregation. If I say or do something you don't like, I know you'll tell me about it. You aren't the type to flatter my ego."

But he was flattering hers by trying to make her believe it mattered to him whether she was there or not. Except that was his job, to persuade members to attend church regularly.

"I'm sure you know how it is." Abbie shrugged. "A person goes to bed on Saturday night with the best intentions but somehow doesn't make it up in time for church the next day." The wryness in her smile was caused by many things. "I warned you I wasn't one of the truly faithful."

"And I warned you that I'd bring you back into the fold," Seth reminded her with a crooked slant to his mouth.

"So you did. Okay, I promise to be at church this Sunday. Is that good enough?" She didn't want him to do any arm twisting. If she spent too much time in his company, she was afraid he might guess that she was no different from any of the other women in town, attracted to him as a man.

"That was easy." He appeared to regard her quick capitulation with a degree of curiosity.

"'Ask and ye shall receive,'" Abbie quoted.

"That's an offer I'm not going to turn down," Seth replied as the corners of his mouth deepened in a faint smile. "Would you be willing to do some typing for me?"

"I understood you had a lot of volunteers," she countered.

"Ah, but not necessarily volunteers who can type," he explained with a mocking look. "Or maybe I should say—who can type with more than one finger."

"I'd like to help you out but I've already agreed to type a manuscript for—someone else." She kept the Coltrain sisters' authorship to herself, as they had requested. "Between doing that at nights and working here during the day, I don't have time to do any more."

"It sounds like all work and no play."

"It has been hectic," Abbie admitted, but refused to feel sorry for herself. "But I'm treating myself to a night off this evening."

"Do you have a date?"

In a small community like this, there was no point in lying. If she claimed to have a date, she'd have to produce one or be caught out. "No," she answered indifferently to show it didn't matter.

"Good. Then how about having dinner with me?" Seth invited, and leaned both hands on the front of her desk.

It was the last thing Abbie had expected. She

was so tempted to accept but—she shook her head. "Thanks but I was really planning to have a quiet evening and an early night."

"That's no problem. We'll have dinner and I'll bring you straight home so you can have a restful evening," he reasoned. "What do you like? Mexican food? Pizza? Steak?"

It was so hard to refuse. "I don't think you heard me," she said weakly.

"I'll wear my collar tonight—just for you," Seth mocked.

Abbie took a deep breath and held it a second. "You don't understand what it's like living in a small community like this, Reverend." She sighed. "If I had dinner with you tonight, by tomorrow morning, rumor would have it all over town that we're having an affair."

"So?" he challenged.

She wished he wasn't so close. Even with the desk separating them, the way he was leaning on it brought him much nearer. She could even smell the tangy fragrance of his after-shave lotion.

"So—you're a minister." Abbie wondered why she was reminding him. "And a bachelor. You can't afford to have that kind of talk going around."

"Empty talk can't hurt me." He hunched his shoulders in an indifferent shrug without changing his position. "It doesn't bother me, so you shouldn't let it bother you."

Abbie had run out of arguments. "It doesn't."

"Then you'll have dinner with me," Seth concluded.

"Pizza." The atmosphere at a pizza parlor would be more casual, invite less intimacy. Plus there wouldn't be any lingering after the meal. It seemed the safest choice all around.

"I'll pick you up at six-thirty. Is that all right?"

"Yes, that's fine." Abbie nodded, certain that she had lost her senses completely. "Do you know where I live?"

"Yes. Your address is in the membership files," he said, indicating he'd already checked. Deliberately or just as a matter of course, Abbie didn't know.

"It's probably my parents' address that's listed. I live in the apartment above the garage," she explained.

Seth straightened from her desk. "I lived in a garret when I was attending the seminary. My friends and I had some good times there."

"I like it," Abbie murmured in response.

"I won't keep you from your work any longer," he said. "I don't want to get into any more trouble with your father over that." But he was smiling in a way that belied his expression of concern. "I'll see you tonight."

"Yes." Abbie just hoped that she knew what she was doing.

Chapter Five

At ten after five that afternoon, Abbie was clearing her desk to leave. Her father stepped out of his office, a pair of reading glasses sitting low on his nose and a letter in his hand.

"I've changed my mind about the way I want this letter worded, Abbie. I'll need to have you retype it," he said, hardly paying any attention to what she was doing.

"You don't have to have it yet this afternoon, do you?" she asked hopefully. "It's already after five."

He bent his wrist to look at his watch. "I hadn't realized it was that late already. You don't mind staying a few more minutes while I reword this. There's no reason for you to rush home."

"As a matter of fact there is," Abbie admitted. "I have a date."

He took off his glasses to look at her. "Since when?" He was surprised. "Don't tell me you took my advice and asked a man out?"

"No." She wasn't quite *that* liberated. "Reverend Talbot stopped by this morning. He invited me to go out and have a pizza with him tonight."

"Reverend Talbot." He repeated the name with curious emphasis. "My, my."

Abbie knew that tone of voice. It always preceded a cross-examination to determine her degree of interest in a particular date.

"Dad, we're just going out for a pizza," Abbie cautioned him not to blow it out of all proportion. It was good advice for herself as well.

"I guess the letter can wait . . . just as long as you retype it first thing in the morning," he decided, and didn't pursue the discussion of her evening date.

"Thanks." Abbie waved him a kiss as she hurried out of the office to her car.

On the surface, it would have seemed more practical to ride back and forth to work with her father, but he was an early riser, often arriving at the office to work at four or five in the morning, when it was quiet and there were no interruptions. Abbie didn't need to be there until the office opened at nine, so she usually drove Mabel.

Mabel grunted her way through the traffic and grumbled up the winding street to Abbie's home. Abbie only had an hour before Seth arrived, and she used every minute of it. While the bathtub filled with water, she ran a dust cloth over the furniture and picked up the clutter of magazines and newspapers.

A quick bath and Abbie was faced with the

impossible decision of what to wear. Nothing seemed exactly appropriate. Her outfits were either too tight, or possibly too revealing, or too plain. Finally she settled on a pair of white jeans and a velour top in a rich kelly-green. Its V-neckline plunged a little. She'd have to remember to sit up straight.

She was just running a brush through her hair when she heard the roar of the sports car's motor coming up the drive. In her haste, she accidentally hooked the bristles in the gold hoop of her earring, giving her ear a painful tug.

"Ouch!" It was a soft, involuntary cry, interrupted by the sound of footsteps on the stairs.

Hurrying out of the bathroom, Abbie reached the door just as he knocked. She opened it, intending to leave with him immediately, but Seth walked in.

"I'm a couple of minutes early. I hope you don't mind," he said, and turned to look at Abbie still holding the door open.

"No, that's all right. I'm ready." She noticed he was wearing his collar. It just peeped over the light blue of his windbreaker.

"This is nice." His glance made an assessing sweep of her apartment. "I wish I had this and you lived in the parsonage." A frown flickered across her face as Abbie wondered whether a minister should be making such comments. Seth read her look, a smile slanting his masculine mouth. "Don't worry. I'm not breaking any commandments. I don't really covet your garret."

"I—"

"You weren't sure," he insisted.

"No."

"You might want to bring a scarf." His glance ran over the coppered blond of her hair. "I've got the top down on my car. The wind's likely to mess up your hair."

"Good idea." There was a nervous edge to her smile as she backed away toward the apartment's small bedroom. "It'll just take me a minute to get one."

"There's no rush," Seth replied.

But Abbie thought otherwise. In her bedroom, she rummaged hurriedly through the top dresser drawer until she found the sheer silk scarf with the green and gold print. The green wasn't the same shade as her velour top but it was close enough.

When she came out, Seth was standing by the table with her typewriter, looking at the stack of handwritten pages beside it. His fingertips were resting on the top paper as if marking a line. A thread of apprehension ran tightly through her edgy nerves.

"Is this the manuscript you're typing?" Seth asked, looking up as if sensing her presence in the room.

"Yes." Abbie tried to remember where she'd left off and what the next scene was that he was reading. Some parts of the book were rather racy.

"I'm glad the Coltrain sisters took my advice," he said, glancing back at the page.

"How did you know?" Abbie stared in stunned wonderment.

"I recognized the handwriting." A hint of a smile made indentations at the corners of his mouth. "Isabel sent me a note. No one else writes with all these flourishes and curlicues." A dark brown eyebrow was arched in query. "Why? Is their identity supposed to be a secret?"

"They asked me not to tell about the book," Abbie admitted.

"Their secret is safe with me," Seth assured her with easy amusement. He tapped a finger on the paper. "Judging by this passage, I think I know why they don't want it known."

"Which passage?" Abbie moved anxiously toward the table and stopped cold when Seth began reading it.

"'His hand cupped her breast and Sophia thought she would surely swoon with pleasure.'" The audible gasp from Abbie prompted him to pause at the end of the sentence, his glance going to her.

"The book really has a good plot," Abbie insisted. "You really shouldn't judge it by that little bit. The characters are interesting and they've done wonderful things with the background."

"I'm not judging it." Laughter and something else gleamed in his eyes. "Did you think I was offended by what I read? Or shocked?"

She bit at the inside of her lower lip, flustered and unnerved. "I don't know," she murmured.

"It can't be your normal reading." Her glance strayed unconsciously to his collar.

"For pleasure, I read mysteries." There was a mocking gleam in his eyes. "Travis McGee is one of my favorite characters. He's had his share of love scenes."

"Oh." Abbie didn't want to pursue this discussion of love and human passions. Sex was the word she was avoiding. She was too conscious they were alone in her apartment. How long had he been up here? Five minutes? Ten? What if her mother or one of the neighbors had noticed? "Maybe we'd better be going," Abbie suggested, clutching the scarf tightly in her hand.

"Of course," he agreed, but amusement continued to lurk in his expression as he followed her to the door. Abbie was conscious of the blue study of his eyes. "How long has it been since you've had a man in your apartment?" Seth asked, just as they reached the door to the stairwell.

She was startled into turning. "Not since—" Abbie almost said, not since she broke up with Jim, but there wasn't any reason to be so specific. "Not for quite a while," she answered instead, and took the door key from her purse.

"I thought you seemed ill at ease." Seth waited at the top of the steps while she locked the door. "Not many people do that around here," he observed, then explained, "Lock their doors when they leave."

"It's a habit left over from living in the city,"

she admitted as she returned the key to her purse and moved to the stairs to join him.

It was a wide stairwell, wide enough for both of them to descend side by side. The touch of his hand on the back of her waist almost stopped Abbie, not quite ready for such casual familiarity. Its warmth electrified her nerve ends and made her overly conscious of his masculine form, lean, muscled, and tall next to her. He didn't take his hand away when they reached the bottom, remaining to guide her to the passenger side of the car. Then Seth moved ahead to open the car door for her.

"Sometimes the latch is stubborn." He used the inside door handle to open it and waited while she climbed in, then pushed it securely shut.

It was a small car, the bucket seats set closely together and a stick shift on the floorboard between them. The close quarters were made even more so when Seth slid behind the wheel, his shoulder nearly touching hers. Abbie tried to hide her awareness of it by busily tying the scarf under her chin. Seth made no attempt to start the motor until she was finished.

"All set?" he asked. Abbie turned her head to nod affirmatively to him and received the full force of his gaze as he made a thorough study of her face. "Your eyes look more green in that color."

There was a crazy little lurching of her stomach. It was so difficult to keep this friendly outing in perspective that Abbie wished he hadn't noticed the way she looked. Compliments put it on a different level, more personal.

"Thank you . . . Reverend." Abbie needed to establish his profession in her mind and somehow keep it there.

His expression took on a thoughtful quality before he turned his profile to her and started the car. The powerful motor growled instantly to life. His hand closed on the gearshift knob and accidentally brushed her knee when he shifted into reverse.

He laid his arm along the top of her seat back as he partially turned to back the car out of the driveway. His carved features didn't seem to have any expression now. Abbie tried to relax now that all his attention was on driving.

The roar of the engine and the wind generated by the car's motion fairly well negated any attempt at conversation. Abbie kept her eyes to the front and her knees out of the way of his constant gearshifting.

The low-built sports car zipped down the winding, tree-shaded streets that *never* crossed at right angles with another. Throughout the hillside town, there were miles of gray stone walls to terrace and hold the steeply sloping earth. Seth avoided the business route through the historic downtown area and turned east on the main highway.

When they arrived at the pizza parlor, the parking lot was relatively full, but there were two empty tables inside. Seth directed her to the one secluded in a quiet corner. Abbie was undecided whether he had chosen it for the privacy it afforded or to avoid being noticed, aware that there was only a fine difference between the two reasons, but a telling one.

There were four chairs around the red-checkered cloth-topped table. After Abbie was seated, Seth pulled out the chair on her right for himself. Once they had ordered, Seth began talking. Before she knew it, there was an easy flow of conversation between them. She stopped being so self-conscious with him and began responding to his friendly manner.

"You can have the last slice of pizza, Abbie." Seth pushed the cardboard circle toward her but she leaned back from the table, shaking her head in refusal.

"I'm so stuffed I can't eat another bite, Reverend," she insisted. "It was really good, though. Thank you."

"You're welcome." He accepted with a mocking tip of his head. "Would you like anything else, Abbie? Another soft drink?"

"No." She reached for her glass, a third full yet. "I have plenty."

There was a moment of silence as he watched her take a sip of the cola through the plastic straw. His glance slid from her mouth to her eyes when she looked up.

"You don't go out much socially do you, Abbie?" It was in the way of an observation more than a question.

She nervously stirred the ice in her drink with the straw. "As much as I want." Abbie defended her lack of an active social life, quietly insisting it was by choice.

"What about close friends?" he asked.

"I was gone for four years and you sort of lose touch," she admitted. "Most of them are married now, with their own families to look after, or else they've moved away. But I'm not lonely, Reverend." She wanted that clear because she didn't want him feeling sorry for her. "I guess I like my own company." She made light of it with a quick smile.

"Or you're just not ready to commit yourself to a close relationship so soon after breaking up with that man in Kansas City," he suggested.

Abbie went a little white. "How did you know about Jim?"

"I could pretend that I was only guessing you'd been hurt recently by a man," Seth replied with a half-shrug. "I suspected it but—in a small town—you find out anyway. Were you very much in love with him?"

"No. I thought I was." She set the glass on the table, her tension growing. It was something she hadn't discussed with anyone. She wasn't sure if she wanted to tell him about it either. Actually there was very little to tell. "But I got over him too quickly, so I guess it wasn't the 'real' thing."

"What happened?"

"Nothing." Abbie discovered a twisted humor in the very appropriate answer. "I was ready to get serious and he wasn't. It was a relationship that had nowhere to go and nothing to keep it going, so it ended."

"I'm glad there aren't any lasting scars." His look was gentle yet contained a certain strength. Loud, laughing voices came from the front of the pizza parlor where there were young people standing. Seth glanced their way, then back to Abbie. "It's beginning to fill up in here. Maybe we should leave so someone can have our table."

Abbie signaled her agreement by pushing her chair back from the table to stand up. His questions concerning her abortive romance kept buzzing around in her mind as they left the restaurant. She began to suspect that was the reason he had invited her out. She had to know, so she wouldn't foolishly think there was another reason.

"Reverend . . ." Abbie slowed her steps when they neared the car. Impatience flickered in his eyes as he paused to meet her steady look. ". . . did you ask me out tonight because you thought I was suffering from a broken heart and needed some consoling?"

A startled frown crossed his forehead. "That never occurred to me, Abbie," he denied, and she doubted that he could have faked that reaction. She felt immensely better, smiling her thanks when he opened the car door for her. He walked around the back of the car and climbed into the driver's side. "I promised to take you straight home, but it looks like we're going to have a beautiful sunset tonight." Seth nodded to the western sky and the pink glow already tinting the clouds. "Would you like to drive up to the lookout and watch it?"

"Yes, I would." Abbie suddenly wasn't in any hurry to go back to her empty apartment.

They weren't far from the lookout point with its overview of Eureka Springs. Its location on the east end of town provided them with the ideal vantage point to observe the glowing colors of sundown.

Seth stopped the car at the farthest edge, facing the west. Turning the ignition off, he combed his fingers through his wind-rumpled hair to restore it to some semblance of order. The hush of twilight seemed to spill over Abbie, the warmth of a summer breeze softly stirring the air. She untied the scarf and let it slide from her hair, while a purpling pink streaked with red painted the horizon.

"It seems too beautiful to be real, doesn't it?" She half glanced at Seth.

"It can be like that," he agreed, and stretched his arm along her seat back. "If an artist tried to put it on canvas, it would look artificial."

"That's true." Abbie realized that her voice was barely above a murmur and laughed softly. "Why are we talking so quietly?"

"Probably because we're the only ones here." Seth smiled. His glance swept the lookout area. "That probably won't be true once it gets dark. This looks like the ideal place for teenagers to park and make out." He tipped his head at Abbie. "Is this where they come?"

"It . . . used to be the local lovers' lane," Abbie admitted, unsettled by the thought.

"Did you ever come here with your boyfriend?" He was mocking her hint of embarrassment.

"A few times, but that was several years ago, Reverend," she replied.

"Will you stop calling me Reverend every time you turn around?" he declared on a note of amused exasperation. "I do have a name, you know. It's Seth."

"I know, Reverend—" she began, suddenly uncertain.

Her pulse rocketed at the silencing finger he placed on her lips. "Seth," he corrected firmly.

She was so tied up in knots she couldn't breathe. He was leaning toward her, his other hand resting on the curve of her shoulder. She felt drawn into the dark aqua depths of his eyes. When his finger slid across her lips in a near caress, a quiver of longing trembled through her.

"Say it," he ordered huskily.

His gaze shifted to her lips to watch them form his name. "Seth," Abbie whispered.

His head bent toward her and she knew instinctively that he was going to kiss her. The tips of his fingers rested lightly along her jaw and the curve of her throat, holding her motionless with no pressure. Excitement danced through her senses, but Abbie willed them to stay under control.

The first brush of his lips was soft and teasing, but they came back to claim her mouth with warm ease. Abbie was hesitant to respond, unwilling to have him discover how much she wanted this, but he coaxed a response from her.

Her lips were clinging to his by the time he finally drew back a few inches to study the result. Slowly her lashes lifted to show the dazed uncertainty of her eyes. Her lips remained slightly parted, melted into softness by his persuasive mouth. She was motionless, but inside she was straining to be closer to him. Abbie was too unsure of herself—and him—to take the initiative. His heavily lidded gaze noted all this with satisfaction.

"Seth?" The rising inflection of her voice put a question mark at the end of his name.

His mouth curved in a compelling smile that seemed to take her breath away. "You've finally got it right, Abbie," Seth murmured, and started to close the distance between them again.

Her lips were moving to meet him halfway when the moment was shattered by the roar of another car approaching the lookout. Abbie abruptly pulled back to cast an anxious glance over her shoulder. His hand came away from the side of her neck and rested on the softness of her upper arm as if he expected her to bolt from the car. The other vehicle wasn't in sight yet, but the roar of its unmuffled engine was coming steadily closer.

Seth hung his head and cursed under a heavy sigh, "Devil damn." Then he was squaring around to place both hands on the wheel.

"What did you say?" Abbie looked at him, her eyes narrowing in bewilderment.

There was a wryness in the sidelong look he sent her. "Devil damn." One corner of his mouth was pulled up. "I had a grandfather who was Danish. Whenever he was upset or angry, that's the expression he used—devil damn or devil damn it. It's much better than breaking a Commandment and taking the Lord's name in vain."

A tremulous smile touched her mouth, inwardly thrilled that he was upset by the interruption. "Yes, it is," Abbie agreed softly.

He held her gaze for a long second that seemed filled with all sorts of heady promises. With another sigh, he reached to turn the key in the ignition just as a car full of teenagers drove into the lookout area.

"I guess I'd better get you home," he said.

While he backed onto the road, Abbie tied the scarf over her hair once more. She felt so good inside that she felt like singing, which of course she didn't do. More than once during the drive home through the back streets, she was conscious of Seth glancing at her. Maybe because she kept stealing looks at him.

Stopping the car in front of the garage, Seth switched off the engine. Abbie waited until he had walked around the car to open her door. He took her hand to help her climb out of the low car.

"I enjoyed myself this evening. Thanks for asking," Abbie said, letting her hand stay in his grasp a moment longer.

"It was *my* pleasure," Seth replied. "I'll walk you to the door."

"There's no need for you to walk me up that flight of steps," she assured him.

"Suit yourself." He shrugged with a mocking look. "I only suggested it because I thought it might bother you if I kissed you good night here—where your parents or the neighbors might see us." When Abbie released a laughing breath of shock at his statement, Seth chuckled and asked, "Would you like to change your mind?"

"It isn't fair to ask a girl that," Abbie protested, because if she said yes, it meant she wanted him to kiss her, and if she said no, it wouldn't be true, but at least she wouldn't sound so brazen.

"I see." The dimpling corners of his mouth were mocking her as he curved an arm along the back of her waist and guided her in the direction of the roofed stairwell. "A man is supposed to walk the girl to the door and take his chances."

"Something like that," she admitted, slipping off the scarf and absently fluffing the ends of her hair.

Her heart was tripping all over her ribs as they climbed the stairs. She didn't know what any of this meant or where these feelings would lead. It was too soon to know. But she liked this glow she felt when he walked beside her like this.

"Do you have your key?" Seth asked when they reached the top of the stairs.

"Yes." Abbie opened her purse and slipped the scarf inside before taking out her key ring.

When she had produced it, his hands settled onto the rounded bones of her shoulders, so she faced him. The width of his chest was in front of her, his head inclined at an angle toward her while his magnetically blue eyes held her rapt attention.

"What do you think my chances are?" he asked with a sensual curve to his hard, male mouth.

It was so easy to sway toward him, her head automatically tilting upward to provide him with the answer. The pressure of his hands increased to bring her nearer. A second before his mouth moved onto hers, a little voice inside warned Abbie that she was kissing a minister and not to respond too wantonly.

But it wasn't an easy warning to heed, not when the soft curves of her body came in contact with the hard contours of his male form, and she was reminded of the differences between the sexes. Her hands slid tentatively around his lean middle, while the breadth of his hands glided down her spine to hold her firmly.

His mouth did not explore this time, already having discovered the warm softness of her lips. There was more depth to his kiss, more subtle demand, less warmth and more fire. Abbie felt the stirrings of desire coming to life within her and pulled reluctantly away before she shocked him with her behavior.

It was difficult to breathe naturally, especially when his arms continued to encircle her and she could still feel the muscled solidity of his thighs brushing against her legs. The moist warmth of his breath was near her cheekbone. Abbie glanced at his face through the top of her lashes, then lowered it to the white collar showing above the black dickey.

"Thank you again, Rev . . . Seth," Abbie corrected herself.

He slowly brought his hands from around her and let a distance come between them. "Good night, Abbie."

"Good night," she returned the farewell. "I'll see you Sunday."

Seth paused on the first step to add, "If not before."

There was a hint of a promise there, even if it wasn't anything definite. She was smiling as she unlocked the door to her apartment, listening to the sound of his footsteps on the stairs.

Chapter Six

"Well?" Her father leaned against her desk and swung a leg over a corner to half sit on it. Abbie moved her cup of coffee to the side so he wouldn't accidentally knock it over.

"Well, what?" she asked with a frown. "Was there something wrong with that letter I just retyped for you?"

"Not a thing. I'm waiting for you to tell me how your date with Reverend Talbot went last night," he said.

Abbie avoided his gaze and began arranging the papers on her desk in neat stacks. "It wasn't a date exactly. But I had a good time—if that's what you're asking."

"A good time." The corners of his mouth were pulled down. "Funny, I had the man pegged as the kind capable of arousing more of a reaction than just a good time."

"Dad, he's a minister," she protested, knowing full well he was right.

"He's a man—made of flesh and blood, just

like the rest of us. Don't put him on a pedestal, Abbie." He studied her more closely. "Are you going to see him again?"

"I imagine." She nodded, then slid him a twinkling glance. "At church on Sunday."

"You know what I meant, did he ask you out again?" her father chided her for being facetious.

Abbie could answer truthfully, "No."

Her father thought about that for a minute and studied his empty coffee cup. "I guess a minister doesn't have a lot of free evenings, what with church youth groups, choir practices, and the civic functions he's expected to attend. It's bound to limit his social life."

"I hadn't thought about it." There was reassurance in it, though, because it offered a possible explanation why Seth hadn't been more definite about when he would see her again.

"Well." He slapped his leg and pushed off her desk. "Guess I'd better get some coffee and get back to my office so you can get some work done."

On Thursday, Abbie left the office early for lunch so she could stop by the post office and send out some registered mail. When she returned a few minutes before one o'clock, her father stuck his head out the door of his private office.

"Reverend Talbot stopped by to see you," he informed her. "He came shortly after you left."

Frustration clouded her expression. This was

the first indication that he had meant to see her before Sunday—and she had missed him.

"Did he say what he wanted?" she asked, feigning a mild interest.

"I guess he wanted to take you to lunch." Her father appeared to be a little vague on that point. "He did say he'd try to catch you another time."

"Oh." Another indefinite. "Thanks, Dad." Abbie sat down to her desk and stowed her purse in the drawer, trying not to be too disappointed.

Saturday morning, Abbie was up early, gathering up her dirty clothes and linen and driving to the laundromat to do her washing. Her mother had offered to let Abbie use her automatic washer and dryer to do her laundry, but it usually took the better part of a day, washing one load at a time. At the laundromat, it usually took just over an hour. Since she would have insisted on paying her mother for the use of the machines anyway, Abbie preferred the time she saved at the laundromat to the convenience of running next door, as it were.

With the laundry finished, she stopped at the grocery store on her way home and picked up the few items she needed. It was going on eleven when she turned Mabel into the driveway. Abbie stepped out of the car, juggling the sack of groceries while she searched her purse for the door key.

"Abbie!" Her mother called from the back stoop of the house. "You had some phone calls while you were gone. They called here when they didn't get any answer."

"Who called?" she frowned.

"Isabel Coltrain. She didn't say what she wanted, but she seemed very anxious to talk to you." Her mother was consumed with curiosity. "Do you have any idea what she might have wanted?"

To see if Abbie had finished the last stack of manuscript pages the sisters had given her? But Abbie had kept her word to the women. "Maybe it had something to do with typing," she said in a half-truth. "The word has spread that I'm doing typing on the side. I've gotten several calls."

"But what would they want typed?"

"Who knows?" Abbie shrugged to avoid an outright lie, and turned again toward the garage.

The acceleration of a car engine as it turned into the driveway pulled her glance over her shoulder. A dark green sports car zoomed toward her, its racy appearance making it seem to travel faster than it actually was. Excitement leaped along her veins when she recognized the car and the driver, and turned to meet them.

"I forgot to tell you," her mother called belatedly. "Reverend Talbot phoned, too." When he turned off the engine and vaulted out of the car, her mother explained to him, "I was just telling Abbie that you called for her."

"That's all right, Mrs. Scott. Thanks." Seth nodded to the woman, then walked toward Abbie with an easy, rolling stride. He was wearing Levi's again, and a blue chambray shirt opened at the throat—with no collar.

"I just got back." The gladness she was trying to contain shined in the emerald-green flecks of her hazel eyes.

"So I gathered. Here." He reached for the grocery sack. "Let me carry that for you."

Her resistance took only a token form as she relinquished the sack into his arms and walked to the stairway door. "I'm sorry I missed you Thursday, Reverend. Dad said you stopped by."

"Are we going to start that again?" Seth challenged.

"Start what?" Abbie paused on the first step.

"That Reverend business." The dark intensity of his gaze made her blood warm.

"I call 'em as I sees 'em." She mocked him with a provocative glance. Immediately she was attacked by pangs of self-consciousness that she had actually been flirting with him.

"Look, Abbie." He touched the tanned hollow of his throat with his free hand. "No collar. For the rest of the day, you're looking at Seth. So you be sure to call him the way you see him."

"All right—Seth," she agreed, her tone a little more subdued.

"Do you have anything on your day's agenda?" Seth asked as he mounted the stairs one step behind her.

"The Coltrain sisters are getting anxious. I was going to do some more typing on their manuscript," Abbie explained.

"It's a fine August day. What you need is fresh air and sunshine—not more hours in front of a typewriter," he insisted. "I'm here to unchain you from that."

"You are?" Abbie unlocked the door and pushed it open, walking in ahead of Seth. She was alive with pleasure. The realization that he wanted to spend the day with her swelled within her, but she didn't want to appear too eager, too overjoyed.

"Yes, I am." Seth walked to the counter-bar on the kitchen side of the room and set the grocery sack on it.

Abbie moved to the opposite side to begin putting the groceries away. The brilliance of his dark gaze was difficult to meet. There was something possessive about it that started a fire licking along her veins.

"You'll have to give me a few minutes to change clothes after I get these groceries put away," she said.

His eyes made a lazy inspection of the faded blue jeans softly hugging her slim hips and the thin white blouse with its capped sleeves and half-collar. Her auburn-gold hair was pulled back in a ponytail, a white silk scarf tied around it.

"What you're wearing is perfect," Seth insisted.

They were everyday clothes, clean but showing the wear and thinness of many washings. Abbie looked down at them, then back at Seth. If her present clothes were suitable for the occasion, it raised a question. "Where are we going?" She tipped her head to the side.

His strongly shaped mouth slanted in a half-smile. "Heaven."

"What?" Abbie blinked.

"I should have said, heaven on earth," he conceded, with the richness of amusement deepening his voice. "I found a quiet, little spot in the country. It's peaceful, beautiful—the perfect place for a picnic."

"A picnic." She smiled at the initial appeal of the idea, then became serious as she began to think about what food she had in the apartment that she could fix.

Seth appeared to read her thoughts. "I already have a picnic basket filled with more food than we can possibly eat. It's sitting in the back of my car. You don't have to worry about fixing a thing."

"Isn't there anything I can bring?" she asked.

"Just yourself." His gaze claimed her with a vibrancy that made Abbie feel shaky inside.

"All right." Her voice was tinged with a soft breathlessness as she let herself drift under his persuasive spell.

The telephone started ringing, its shrillness making a sharp intrusion between them. Abbie bit her lip in indecision and glanced at the ringing phone.

"That has to be one of the Coltrain sisters," she murmured and wondered what excuse she could give them for not having any more of their manuscript typed.

"I'll answer it." Seth was already moving toward the phone when he spoke.

"Oh, but—" Abbie started to protest, taking a step after him.

But Seth already had his hand on the receiver. He sent her a backward glance over his shoulder. "You get those groceries put away so we can leave," he ordered. "I'll handle the sisters for you."

Abbie gripped the sides of the cardboard milk container she had taken from the sack and watched anxiously as Seth picked up the phone. What would the sisters think when he answered her phone?

"Miss Scott's residence," he said into the mouthpiece and paused. "She's busy at the moment. This is Reverend Talbot. May I help you, Miss Coltrain?" He glanced over his shoulder and noticed Abbie just standing there.

His mouth curved into a wry line as he motioned her to get busy. Without taking her anxious gaze from him, Abbie moved sideways to the refrigerator and opened the door to set the milk inside.

"No, she hasn't finished the typing for you," he said into the phone. "Miss Scott planned to type more today, but I have decided she's been working too hard, so I'm taking her out for the balance of the day." Seth half turned from the waist up to send a smiling look at Abbie and nod in response to the voice on the other end of the line. "I knew you'd understand, Miss Coltrain."

There was another short pause. "Yes, I'll tell her. Good-bye."

Abbie quickly pushed the loaf of bread into the bread drawer as Seth replaced the receiver on its cradle and crossed to the counter. Her glance bounced off his masculine features.

"What did she say?" she murmured.

"Isabel apologized for rushing you about the manuscript and hoped you weren't too exhausted by all the typing you've done for them." Seth relayed the message. "She thought the outing was an excellent idea."

Abbie turned away to put the box of cereal in the cupboard. "But didn't she . . ." She didn't finish the question, concerned that she might be too sensitive and guilty of overreacting.

". . . didn't she think it strange that I answered the phone?" Seth completed the sentence, almost verbatim to what was in her mind. "Why should she?" he countered evenly when Abbie turned with a guilty start. "It's normal for a minister to call on members of his congregation in their homes."

"Yes, but . . ." She couldn't finish that sentence either.

". . . but you are a young and very attractive single woman." Again Seth accurately guessed the rest of it. "And I'm a bachelor."

"Something like that, yes," Abbie admitted.

"As romantically inclined as those two spinster sisters are, I'd guess they're tittering with the possibility a romance is developing between us." A suppressed smile deepened the corners of his mouth as he met her startled look.

"Oh." This small response was all she could manage, since he had confirmed exactly what she had guessed they'd be thinking.

"We lunched together, had pizza one evening, and now we're going on a picnic together," Seth reminded her. "It isn't unlikely that an outsider would jump to that conclusion."

"I know." Abbie nodded.

With calm deliberation, Seth walked around the counter-bar and took the sack of sugar out of her hands, setting it on the countertop. Her protest died when his hands moved over the bareness of her upper arms with caressing ease.

"Why bother to deny it?" Seth challenged softly while he looked deeply into her eyes. A shiver of sensations slivered through her veins. "It's true, isn't it?"

"I—suppose." The whispered admission was hesitant; she was wary of declaring too openly the feelings that were growing stronger with each meeting.

He tipped his head to one side, bronze lights darkening his hair. The expression on his roughly carved features mildly taunted her for her cautious reply, while his hands continued their slow, lazy kneading of her arms.

"You don't sound too sure," he said. "If this isn't the start of a romance, what else would you call it?"

"I don't know," Abbie admitted with an uncertain smile.

"What's the matter?" Seth asked. "Why does it bother you to admit it?"

"I guess I'm not used to being so candid," she suggested, then deliberately tried to side-track the conversation. "How did the Coltrain sisters find out that you knew about their manuscript?"

The faintly mocking glitter in his eyes informed her that Seth knew why she was changing the subject. "They invited me to dinner Tuesday night. I mentioned that we had been together the previous night and that I'd read a couple pages of the manuscript you were typing without revealing that I had recognized their handwriting," he explained. "They were so eager to find out my reaction that they confessed they had written it and asked what I thought." His smile became more pronounced. "So they don't think that you betrayed their secret."

"I wondered," she acknowledged.

"I also promised them I'd write a letter to some friends of mine in the publishing business and see what I could do to help them when it's finished." He let his hands come away from her arms and turned to look in the grocery sack. "Is there anything else in here that's perishable?"

"No, I've already put those items away." There were only some canned goods left.

"Then, let's leave the rest and go on our picnic," he stated.

"Okay." Abbie had the feeling she would agree to almost anything he suggested.

Within minutes after leaving town, Seth turned off the main highway onto a graveled county road that twisted along the ridges and hollows. Abbie was completely lost, having no idea where they were going. She'd never done that much exploring of the countryside to be familiar with all the hill roads.

The August heat had seared the grasses a golden brown to intersperse the thickly forested hills with patches of bright color. Abbie turned her face into the blowing force of the wind generated by the sports car, kicking up plumes of dust on the graveled road.

An azure sky contained a scattering of powder-puff clouds, drifting slowly while the golden sun-ball blazed above the earth with its light. Overhead, a hawk circled, floating effortlessly on the air currents. They were riding on a ridgeback, the Ozark Mountains undulating into the distance like ocean waves.

There was a change in the powerful hum of the engine as Seth eased the pressure on the accelerator slowing the car. A fairly straight stretch of road lay before them with no roads branching off it. All Abbie could see was a short lane leading to the gate of a fenced field, but it appeared to be Seth's destination as he braked the car to a slower speed to make the turn onto it. When the car was stopped, he switched off the engine, removing the sunglasses he'd been wearing.

"This is it," he said with a glance at Abbie while he pushed his door open to step out.

Abbie looked at the gate and the sign tacked on the post that very plainly read: PRIVATE PROPERTY—Trespassers Will Be Prosecuted. "We aren't going into that field, are we?" She climbed out of the passenger side, but eyed Seth with a bewildered frown.

The nearly bald knoll had only a scattering of tall oak trees to shade its yellow grasses. There didn't appear to be any animals grazing in the hill meadow, but the sign on the fence was very definite.

"Wait until you see the view," Seth replied after he had issued an affirmative nod. He reached behind the driver's seat and lifted out a wicker picnic basket. "Do you think you can carry this?"

"But there's a no-trespassing sign on the gate," Abbie pointed out as she took the basket from him and hooked her forearm under the handles. "We can't go in there."

"Yes, we can." Seth removed a Styrofoam cooler from the car's trunk and started walking to the gate. "This land belongs to my family."

"Your family," Abbie repeated with surprise. "I didn't know you had any relation living around here."

"I don't." He stopped at the gate and set the cooler on the ground. There was a padlock on the chain that circled the fence and gatepost. With a key from his pocket, Seth unlocked it and unwrapped the chain to let the gate sag open. "It's a case of absentee ownership, an investment for possible development or resale in the future."

"Oh." But Abbie didn't feel that she knew any more despite the enlightening remark.

"Careful you don't trip on the wire," Seth cautioned as she started to walk through the narrow opening. "I don't want to be responsible for causing a personal injury lawsuit."

It was said in jest but Abbie just wondered all the more. As she went through the gate she was close enough to read the small lettering at the bottom of the sign. The owner was identified as the Tal-bar Corporation. "The Tal-bar Corporation belongs to your family?" she asked when Seth followed her, leaving the gate open behind him.

"Yes. It's a combination of Talbot and Barlow. Barlow was my grandmother's maiden name, and her brother was one of the original partners with my grandfather," he explained. "I thought we'd have our picnic under that oak tree over there." Seth indicated the closest one with a nod of his head.

"Is it a big company?" Abbie suspected it was, since it had landholdings in the Ozarks.

"For a family-owned company, I'd say it's fairly large, but it's certainly not a major national corporation." There was a dry amusement in his tone.

117

"I guess your family mentioned they owned some land here when you were assigned to our church," Abbie guessed.

"Actually I was here a few years when we originally bought this property, so I was a little familiar with the area before I obtained my transfer."

"You aren't active in your family's company, are you?" Abbie frowned, automatically stopping under the tree when Seth did. She didn't see how it was possible when he was a minister. Yet his remark about looking at the property seemed to indicate otherwise.

"My father insists that I remain on the board of directors to act as their conscience," Seth admitted as he crouched down to set the cooler next to the tree. "There's a small blanket in your basket. We can spread it on the ground."

While she digested the information, Abbie opened the lid of the wicker basket and took out the square blanket lying on top of the plastic dishes. She shook it out and laid it out flat on the grass-stubbled ground. Kneeling on it, she began taking the dishes and utensils out of the basket. "I know it's none of my business . . ." But she couldn't help prying a little more into his personal affairs. ". . . but I have the feeling your father would have preferred that you had joined the company. . . ."

"Instead of becoming a minister?" Seth completed what she had left unsaid. There was a light shrug of his shoulders as he began taking out containers of assorted salads. "In the beginning, he was against the idea—until he was convinced that it was definitely what I wanted. I've had his full support and his blessing for several years now—as well as from the rest of my family."

She was glad that Seth's chosen profession had not created any friction between him and his family, but it sounded too trite to say so. The removal of the napkins and the salt and pepper shakers emptied the picnic basket. Abbie sat in the grass out of the way.

"We have here a private buffet." Seth indicated the various uncovered containers arranged in a semicircle on the blanket. "Macaroni salad, potato salad, ambrosia, tomato aspic, cold roast chicken, ham, fresh fruit, cheese. There's a couple things that I don't know what they're called."

Abbie stared at the array of food. "You don't expect us to eat all this?"

There was a wicked glint in his eye. "To tell you the truth, it was the quickest way to clean out my refrigerator. The ladies in the community have been more than generous about bringing me samples of their cooking."

"Maybe they thought it was the way to win the favor of a bachelor minister," Abbie suggested with a hint of a teasing smile.

"'The way to a man's heart . . .'" Seth followed her thinking and chuckled. "Unfortunately, they couldn't know that I had already

119

been tempted by a copper-haired girl on the road, who gave me fruit." He paused a second to hold Abbie's glance. "There are some who believe that it was the peach, not the apple, Adam and Eve ate in the Garden of Eden."

"Really," she murmured, a little unnerved by the sensuality of his look, so vibrant and alive with his male interest in her.

"Yes, really," he mocked, and turned to reach inside the cooler. "Don't you think you have what it takes to tempt me into sin?"

"Are you sure it's not the other way around?" Abbie countered, matching his sexual banter and not letting him see how much it disturbed her.

There was a heartiness to his throaty chuckle. "I deserved that. You know the right way to put a man in his place, don't you, Abbie?" Seth didn't appear to expect an answer as he took a bottle of chilled wine from the cooler. "Now, this happens to come from my own private stock. It's not a gift from anyone."

Abbie looked at him askance. "Are you allowed to drink wine?"

There was patience in his strong face as he uncorked the bottle and splashed a small portion of wine in two glasses. "In the Book of Matthew, Jesus explains in chapter fifteen that it is not what goes into the mouth that defiles man, but what comes out of his mouth. 'Whatever goes into the mouth passes into the stomach, and so passes on, but what comes out of the mouth proceeds from the heart. . . .'" he paused. "Anything in excess is not good for the body—sweets, fats, or alcohol."

"That's true," she agreed, taking the glass he handed her.

"In biblical times, they drank wine with their meals because the water wasn't potable, for the most part," he added. "It was the fruit of the vine that Jesus gave to his disciples at the Last Supper. That's hardly a justification for the consumption of alcohol. But there's a vast difference between drinking and having an occasional glass of wine with a meal."

"I agree." Abbie swirled the rose-red liquid in her glass. "I wasn't really criticizing you for bringing the wine."

"Weren't you?" It was a mild accusation.

"No, although it probably sounded like it," she admitted with a rueful laugh.

"Sometimes I get the feeling you are more pious than I am," Seth mocked. "No deviating from the straight and narrow."

"I've never been very well acquainted with a minister—on a personal basis." Abbie defended some of her preconceived notions. "So I don't always know what to expect."

"I have noticed." He nodded, a faint smile touching the corners of his mouth. "Right now, you're wondering if I'm going to say a blessing before we eat."

"I was," Abbie admitted on a note of bubbling laughter.

When Seth bowed his head, Abbie did, too. "We thank you, O Lord, for this bounty You have placed before us. And we pray that You will also feed the hunger of our hearts with the Grace of Your Love. Amen."

"Amen," she echoed softly, and lifted her head to glance at him in silent wonder, touched by the simple blessing.

"Shall we dig in?" Seth murmured, arching an eyebrow in her direction, and passed her the small bowl of potato salad.

Chapter Seven

Although Abbie had only taken a small sample of everything, there had been too many dishes. There was still some food left in her plate, but she didn't have room for another bite.

"I think it's a case of my eyes being bigger than my stomach." She sighed and set her fork on the plate.

"There's a lot of wildlife around here that will eat it, so it won't go to waste." Seth rolled to his feet. "If you're finished, I'll scrape your plate on that stump so the scraps won't be attracting the flies around us."

"I am finished." Abbie handed him the plate.

While he walked to the tree stump about twenty yards away, she started putting the lids on the containers and returning them to the cooler so they wouldn't spoil. When Seth came back, he lent a hand, stowing the dishes and silverware in the wicker basket. Once the blanket was cleared and shaken free of any crumbs, Abbie shifted to sit near the middle of it, leaning on her hands and stretching her legs out to ease the fullness of her stomach. Before she could guess his intention, Seth was lying down at right angles to her, with his head resting on her lap.

"Do you mind me using you for a pillow?" Seth looked up at her with deceptively innocent eyes, aware of asking permission after the fact.

"No." But she did find it disturbingly intimate. Her senses were operating on an uneven keel with his head nestled against her thighs. The faded material of her jeans had been worn thin, providing a scant barrier for her sensitive skin.

"Good." Seth closed his eyes and settled more comfortably in place, folding his hands across his chest in a gesture of contentment.

With his eyes shut, Abbie took the liberty of studying the irregular angles and planes of his strong face. There was power in the lift of his cheekbones and steady determination in the clean line of his jaw. His stubby lashes were dark and full, a shade darker than the brown of his eyebrows. There was a slight, crooked break in the line of his nose, and his mouth was well defined, neither too thin nor too full, and definitely masculine.

The dark, rumpled gold of his hair invited the smoothing touch of her fingers. Abbie curled them into the blanket to resist the urge to slide them through his hair. The body heat from his wide shoulders warmed the side of her hip and thigh and spread through the rest of her body. All sorts of dangerous thoughts were running through her mind when she let her glance stray to the even rise and fall of his chest. Starting a conversation seemed the wise thing to do.

"Where does your family live, Seth?" she asked.

A little frown creased his forehead. "Pillows aren't supposed to talk," he grunted.

Abbie laughed softly at that. "Well, this pillow does," she retorted. "Where does your family live?"

He sighed in mock resignation. "My parents live in Denver."

"Is that where the Tal-bar Corporation has its offices, too?"

"Yes."

"How did the company get started?" she asked.

Seth opened one eye. "My, but you are full of questions."

"How else do you learn anything?" Abbie reasoned with a small shrug.

"My grandfather and great-uncle started out as well drillers, then got into the oil and gas business, and backed into cattle ranching."

" 'Backed' into cattle ranching? How do you do that?" Abbie smiled at the phrase, finding it curious.

"My grandfather thought he was acquiring the mineral rights for federal land and found out he had actually obtained grazing rights instead. So he and my great-uncle turned a mistake into a business," Seth explained. "The company also has some mining interest."

"Do you have any brothers or sisters?" she wondered.

"A whole houseful." He sat up unexpectedly, and turned toward Abbie, bracing a hand on the opposite side of her legs. "I have five sisters and three brothers. My parents believed in a large family. Do you like large families?"

"Yes." Her answer was hesitant because she wasn't sure what he meant by the question.

Seth took it a step farther. "How many children do you want when you get married?"

"That's something . . . I'd have to discuss with my husband." She had trouble breathing when he leaned closer. Her heart started fluttering against her ribs.

"What would you say . . ." He tipped his head to kiss the side of her throat. There was a wild, little leap of her pulse. ". . . if your husband wanted . . ." He turned his head to mouth the sensitive cord on the other side of her neck. ". . . a lot of children?"

So many other things were happening in reaction to his nuzzling kisses that Abbie almost forgot the question. "I think . . . I'd like the idea." Tension knotted her throat until she couldn't swallow. A moan trembled somewhere inside her, waiting to be released.

"And if he wanted to adopt some children . . ." His mouth grazed along her cheek, feathering her skin with the warmth of his breath. ". . . in addition to your own?"

"Why not?" she murmured, turning her head to end the tantalizing nearness of his mouth.

It moved onto her lips with a sureness of purpose, claiming them as if it had long been his right to do so. There was no resistance to its commanding pressure. Her lips parted willingly to deepen the kiss as his hand curved itself to her spine. A heady tide of feeling seemed to swamp her, and she reeled at the whirling mist of glorious sensation. She felt drunk with his kiss and wondered if it was the wine.

Then there was no room for thinking, only feeling. Abbie was weightless, floating in a mindless bliss. She wasn't conscious of sinking backward onto the blanket, only that her hands no longer had to support her upright position and were now free to glide around his muscled shoulders and curl into the virile thickness of his hair.

Tiny little moans of pleasure came from her throat when he nibbled sensually at her earlobe and made an intimate study of her neck and throat. The hard contours of his body pressed their male shape onto her flesh while the stroking caress of his hands wandered over her.

Desire seemed a natural extension of all the raw emotion his embrace was disclosing to her. It was the purest form of passion she'd ever know, and the beauty of it swelled her heart until she ached for him. The need inside her strained to be released.

His hand glided smoothly across her ribs, nearing the heated fullness of her breasts. The sensation of skin against skin suddenly shocked her into an awareness of how far out of control she'd gone. Her blouse had fallen loose, the old material stretching to release the lower buttons.

With a stifled moan of panic at what he must be thinking of her, Abbie wiggled from under him and scrambled to her feet. Her breath came thickly as she quickly turned her back to avoid his stunned and frowning look.

"Abbie?" His voice was low and husky.

"I'm sorry." She quickly began stuffing her blouse inside the waistband of her jeans, a task made difficult by her shaking hands. She heard him stand up. "I don't know what got into me," she insisted. "It must have been those two glasses of wine."

His hands closed on her shoulders, the contact momentarily paralyzing. Her blouse was half in and half out, and Abbie couldn't seem to move to finish the job.

"That's not a very flattering thing to say," Seth declared and forced her to turn around. She looked everywhere but into his face, yet the sight of his manly chest, so broad and muscled, hardly hidden at all with his shirt clinging to the heated dampness of his skin, was almost equally unnerving. Abbie kept her hands rigidly tightened into fists so they wouldn't be tempted to touch him.

"I don't know what you mean," she murmured tightly.

"You indicated it was the wine that made you respond to me," he said in a voice that was warm and indulgent. "I was hoping it might have been my kisses."

"It was. I mean . . . I just got carried away because . . . of the wine," Abbie insisted.

Seth crooked a finger under her chin and lifted it to study her face at an angle. "It wasn't because of the wine. You were enjoying being kissed and caressed."

"I was, but . . ." She was close to tears, so anxious for him to think well of her. She had never felt so vulnerable in her life. ". . . I don't want you to think I'm immoral."

"Why should I think that?" Seth questioned with a smiling frown of confusion.

"Because—" Abbie couldn't finish it.

"Because I was touching you? Because I wanted to touch your breasts?" He was even more specific, and his bluntness was more than she could handle. "Or because you wanted me to?"

"Seth." She shut her eyes so he couldn't read how right he was in her look.

"I'm relieved you didn't call me Reverend," he mocked, and gave her a little shake to force her eyes open. "Abbie, I'm a man, not a saint. You are a beautiful woman with a beautiful body. Do you think I don't feel desire when I'm near you?"

"I don't know," she whispered.

"Well, I do." The corners of his mouth deepened with a smile. "Desire isn't necessarily sinful. Promiscuity, infidelity, adultery—those are sinful. Desire is a warm and wonderful thing between two people who care for one another. You don't need to be ashamed of it."

"I wasn't, not really. I just didn't—" She broke

off in midsentence when Seth suddenly began unbuttoning his shirt and pulling it loose from his Levi's. "What are you doing?"

"I'm unbuttoning my shirt. What does it look like I'm doing?" he countered. "You seemed embarrassed because your blouse came unfastened. I thought it might make you feel better if mine was loose, too."

"Seth, that's ridiculous." Abbie couldn't believe he was serious.

His low, throaty laugh vibrated over her. His hands were at her waist to pull her into his arms. That curling sensation started all over again in her stomach as his mouth came down to probe apart the softness of hers. Warmth flooded through her limbs as his molding hands roamed her back and hips to fit her intimately to his hard, male length.

Seth deepened the disruptively sensual embrace with consummate skill, dazzling Abbie with the ecstasy he evoked. Her hands were flattened against his bared chest, absorbing the heat of his body to add to the fire burning inside. She was trembling when he finally lifted his head to trail a butterfly kiss on her closed eyes.

Reluctantly, she started to shift away from him, thinking that he was signaling an end to the embrace, but his arms tightened to keep her fused to the muscled columns of his legs. "Stay here," he murmured, "where you belong."

His hand cupped the back of her head, his fingers tangling with the tendrils of rust-gold hair that had escaped from her ponytail, and firmly directed her head to rest on his shoulder. Of their own volition it seemed, her arms slid around his middle under his loosely hanging shirt. Abbie rested her cheek contentedly against his collarbone, breathing in the heady, male smell of him.

There was a very definite sensation of belonging in his arms. The hard line of his jaw was rubbing against her hair in a sensual caress. With a slight turn of her head, Abbie let her mouth lightly taste the warm flavor of his skin, tanned and tautly stretched across sinew and bone.

Her lips touched the coolness of a gold chain, reminding Abbie of her previous curiosity about it. She shifted slightly in his arms to lift a hand to follow the path of the long chain to where it ended in the center of the springy, silken gold chest hairs. They curled softly against the back of her hand as she held a plain, gold cross between her fingers.

"I wondered what you were wearing around your neck," she admitted softly. The edges were worn, a few scratches dulling the finish. "It looks very old."

"It belonged to my grandfather. He was a very religious man in many ways. And a very passionate man, too." His head tipped slightly downward for a glimpse of her face. "The two can go together."

The sheer naturalness of being held by him had been so overwhelming that it wasn't until his comment that Abbie realized his hand was curved to the underside of her breast, his thumb absently stroking its rising swell. Both her blouse and her cotton brassiere lay between his hand and her flesh, but his touch suddenly seemed to burn through both of them. Abbie stiffened in a delayed attack of modesty.

Guessing the reason, Seth let his hand slide down to the curve of her waist. "I knew what my right hand was doing, so I'm not about to cut it off," he mocked with gentle amusement. "I have the feeling, Abbie, that you are as steeped in Victorian traditions as this town."

Thinking he was ridiculing her for being prudish, Abbie started to pull away, but the bronzed band of his arm stopped her while he cupped his hand to the side of her face and forced her to look at him. There was smoldering pleasure in the darkness of his gaze.

"And I'm glad you are that way," Seth added to assure her that he approved of her keen sense of decorum. "Just remember there will come a time when there is no need to hold back your desires."

"Yes." It seemed very close, too. Abbie hoped, desperately, that she wasn't wrong.

There was a hard, brief kiss before Seth released her from the close contact with his body. "As enjoyable as it would be to idle away the rest of the afternoon kissing you, I think we'd better get our picnic things packed away in the car so we can visit your grandmother."

"Grandmother Klein?" She felt stupid saying

that. She was the only grandmother Abbie had—living that is.

"You usually visit her on the weekend, don't you?" he said. "At the moment, it seems the prudent way to spend the afternoon rather than yielding to the temptation of this blanket and you."

"I think you deliberately try to shock me," Abbie declared, still not quite used to his frankness.

He reached down to scoop up the blanket and begin folding it into a square. His side-glance ran to her, glittering with amusement.

"I have to do something to shatter that sexless image you have of a minister," Seth countered.

"You're succeeding," she admitted, without mentioning that it was something of a revelation.

"It's about time," he replied with a mocking slant to his mouth.

It didn't take long to stow the picnic items in the car. After Abbie had given him a general set of directions to her grandmother's farm, they started out. Less than thirty minutes later, Seth turned the sports car onto the lane leading to the white, clapboard house.

White leghorn chickens squawked and ran from the car with flapping wings when it rolled to a dusty halt in the farmyard. An old gray tomcat sauntered out to inspect the visitors to his territory and meowed an aloof welcome when he recognized Abbie, then eyed Seth with haughty inquiry.

"That's Godfrey." Abbie identified the cat. "He thinks he owns the farm."

"I had the same impression," Seth replied.

"Where's your mistress, Godfrey?" Abbie glanced at the house but there was no sign of life behind the gray-meshed screen door. The cat swished his tail and jumped lithely onto the rear fender of the car to begin cleaning himself, disdaining any notion that he would lower himself to act as guide. "She's probably in the garden," Abbie guessed. "It's around in back."

As Abbie started in that direction, Seth fell into step beside her, his hand fitting itself familiarly to the small of her back. There was something lightly possessive about his touch that made her feel she belonged to him, a sensation she definitely liked.

Just when they entered the fenced yard, a small woman in loose-fitting pants and a flowered blouse came around the corner of the house. The slight stoop to her shoulders was the only visible concession to advanced age. Her short hair was still carrot-red, the result of a regularly applied henna dye. Her sun-leathered complexion was liberally dotted with youthful freckles. She was carrying a five-gallon bucket, loaded full of sweet corn ears, and showing no indication that it was too heavy.

"Hello, Grandmother." Abbie called the greeting.

The woman stopped and waited for them to come to her, but she didn't bother to set the bucket down. Sharp, green eyes made a thorough inspection of Seth, not leaving out a single detail.

"I thought you were probably in the garden," Abbie said. "I wish you wouldn't work out there during the heat of the day."

"I've gotta keep moving at my age," her grandmother insisted, and turned her gaze once more to Seth. "So, you've finally brought a man for me to meet. It's about time." She didn't give either of them a chance to speak as her glance went past them to the dark green sports car. "Is that your car? I always wanted to go tearing down the road in one of those racy convertibles —with my hair flying in the wind. I used to wear it longer, when I was young."

"I'll take you for a ride in it anytime you say, Mrs. Klein," Seth offered with an engaging half-smile. "I'm Seth Talbot."

"I'm pleased to meet you, Seth Talbot," her grandmother replied and looked at Abbie. "You've picked out a strong, virile man. I'll wager he'll have you pregnant a week after you're married."

"Grandmother!" Abbie was aghast. She'd never said things like that before. There had always been the urgings to get married and start a family. Being a farmer's wife, she had always been very casual about the mating habits of animals. Despite this, her grandmother's remark probably wouldn't have struck her as being so scandalous except that—"Seth is a minister."

"So? He's a man, isn't he?" It didn't seem to

make any difference to her grandmother. "He might as well know that I'd like to have a great-grandchild before I die."

"There's plenty of time. You aren't that old," Abbie protested as she sought a tactful way to explain that her grandmother was misreading the situation.

"Considering how long it's taken you to find a suitable man, I wouldn't say there's plenty of time. I was married at seventeen, and had my first baby in my arms when I was eighteen. You're twenty-three years old already, Abbie. You've taken your own sweet time about becoming engaged, let alone married."

"Seth and I aren't engaged, Grandmother," she corrected.

"I thought that's why you brought him out here with you." Her grandmother looked taken aback, and perhaps a little bit embarrassed. "You haven't ever brought a man with you when you've visited me before."

"I was the one who suggested we come here this afternoon," Seth stated, taking the responsibility for the decision. "Abbie had mentioned that she usually visited you on the weekends. Since we had picnicked not far from here, it seemed logical to stop by." He took a step forward, apparently untroubled by the initial conclusion the older woman had reached. "Would you let me carry that sweet corn for you?"

"I can manage it." Her grandmother was a little flustered by her mistake, not liking to appear old and foolish.

"I'm sure you can," Seth agreed easily. "But my father would have my hide if I didn't carry it for you, the way a gentleman should."

Abbie was amazed to see her grandmother surrender the pail of corn to him. Any time she had offered to carry something heavy, her grandmother had impatiently waved her off, insisting she didn't like being fussed over.

"You can set it on the back porch," her grandmother instructed. "Then we'll all go in the house for some cold lemonade."

"These are good-looking roasting ears, Mrs. Klein." Seth complimented her on her garden produce.

"It isn't easy staying one step ahead of the raccoons. Between them and the deer, they play havoc with my garden." She always claimed to have an ongoing battle with the wildlife in the area. "I'll get you a sack, Abbie," she said as they started toward the back door. "So you can take a couple dozen ears of this corn home for you and your folks. You can take some home with you, too, Mr. Talbot. Or should I call you Reverend."

He slid a dryly amused glance at Abbie. "'Seth' will do fine, Mrs. Klein."

When Seth and Abbie walked out of the house more than an hour later, they were each laden with sacks of goods. In addition to the sweet corn, Grandmother Klein had sent along jars of her freshly made tomato preserves and peach butter. She followed them out to the car to bid them good-bye.

"Alice said she was coming out Tuesday to help me put up the corn," Grandmother Klein remarked as Abbie settled into the passenger seat. "Tell her to bring some jar lids."

"I will," Abbie promised.

"Don't forget, Seth, you promised to take me for a ride in this car sometime," her grandmother reminded him.

"How about next Saturday?" Seth suggested, setting a definite time. "You and I can go for a spin while Abbie fixes lunch."

"It sounds like a terrific idea," she agreed in youthful vernacular.

"It's a date." He started the engine and revved it up a few times for the old lady's benefit, then turned the car in a circle in the farmyard to head down the lane. "Your grandmother is quite a woman," he said to Abbie, raising his voice to make himself heard above the noise of the motor.

Abbie responded with an affirmative nod, not attempting to compete with the car or the whipping wind. The noise increased with the acceleration of the engine as they turned onto the state highway and headed for Eureka Springs.

It seemed an exceedingly short ride—and a short day, too, but it was already after five when Seth stopped the car in the driveway. Abbie climbed out of the car and reached for the sack stowed behind the seat.

"I'll carry that up for you," Seth volunteered.

"Thanks, but I'm going to divvy it up with my

parents first," Abbie explained and stood awkwardly, holding the sack in her arms. "And I had a wonderful time, and the picnic was delicious." She remembered the last time he'd taken her home and threatened to kiss her in full view of anyone looking. But she hadn't any excuse for going to her apartment, then coming directly down with the sack. It would be just as obvious to anyone watching.

"I'll see you in church tomorrow," he said and bent his head, lightly brushing her lips with his and drawing away before she could react.

It was only after he'd backed out of the drive that Abbie noticed her laundry still sitting in Mabel's backseat. She could have had Seth carry it upstairs for her. It would have been the perfect excuse. She sighed over the lack of foresight.

Her father came out the back door, carrying the kitchen wastebasket. "That was the reverend that just left, wasn't it?"

"Yes. We were out to Grandmother Klein's." She waited near the back door while he emptied the wastebasket into the garbage can. "There's a bunch of sweet corn here for you and Mom."

"Have you been with the reverend all day?" He took the sack out of her arms. "I thought you were in your apartment typing all this time."

"We went for a picnic, then to Grandmother's," she explained.

"Are those bells I hear?" he teased.

"Dad, you're impossible."

"Why?" he countered lightly. "Is the reverend the type that fools around? I've heard Bible salesmen are notorious philanderers. Maybe ministers are too."

"That isn't funny." She didn't want to think that Seth might just be toying with her.

Chapter Eight

The menu lay unopened on the table in front of her. Abbie took another sip from her water glass and glanced at her watch. With the advent of September and the start of school, there was a lull in the tourist trade. She hadn't taken it into account when she left the office early to stop at the post office before meeting Seth for lunch. They had agreed to meet at twelve noon, and it was still five minutes before the hour.

In the last month, she'd seen him on a fairly regular basis. They usually lunched together twice a week and went out to dinner or a local show one evening a week. Unless he was working on his sermon, they usually spent part of Saturday together, too, sometimes visiting her grandmother, who was positively mad about his car.

"George, isn't that the young Reverend Talbot talking to the judge by the door over there?"

Abbie perked up visibly when she heard the woman in the next booth mention Seth sotto voce. She looked around, but she couldn't see him from where she was sitting.

"I think it is," the man in the next booth, obviously George, responded to the woman's low question.

"He isn't wearing his collar again," the woman said in disapproval, and Abbie hid a smile, reaching for the water glass. "His behavior isn't at all proper for a minister."

"You can't very well condemn the man just because he takes his collar off once in a while," George defended him carefully. "It's probably like wearing a tie. When I'm not working, I don't want one around my neck."

"It isn't only that, George," the woman insisted. "It's the way he's carrying on with that Scott girl."

Once she had started eavesdropping, it was impossible for Abbie to stop. She knew the gossip was running rampant because of the frequency of her dates with Seth. It was to be expected.

"Both of them are single. I don't see that there's anything wrong in him dating her," the man said. And Abbie thought, Hooray for George. At least he was sticking up for them against the malicious intonations of his wife, assuming the woman was his wife.

"She doesn't live with her parents, you know, although a lot of people think she does," the woman went on. "She fixed up an apartment for herself in the loft above the garage. It's completely private from the house." The woman's voice lowered to a conspiratorial whisper that Abbie was just barely able to catch. *"They say the reverend has been in her apartment."*

"Really." George's voice was dry with disinterest.

"Don't you think it's strange the way she came back so suddenly from Kansas City? Supposedly she gave up a good job." The remarks were full of malicious innuendos that had Abbie bristling. "If you ask me, there has to be a reason why someone as attractive as the Scott girl hasn't gotten married. I'll bet she's hiding something."

"You have a remarkable talent, Maude, for seeing sin in other people," George muttered.

"I still think he should be dating a nice girl instead. . . . Don't look now, George, but he's coming this way." In a louder voice, the woman issued a sweetly bright greeting. "Hello, Reverend. How are you today?"

"Fine, thank you," Seth's voice replied.

In the next second, he entered Abbie's side vision. She glanced at him briefly, her smile a little stiff. He slid onto the opposite booth seat, a warm light gleaming in his blue eyes for her.

"Hello, Abbie. You're early," he observed. "I thought I'd have to wait for you."

"I had a couple of errands to run." She opened her menu, willing herself not to pay any attention to the idle gossip she'd overheard.

But Seth was too well acquainted with her moods, too able to read her mind. "Is something wrong?" He tipped his head to one side, the thickness of his dark bronze hair showing signs

143

of having been ruffled by the wind and then tamed with combing fingers.

Abbie started to deny that there was anything the matter, then she thought about the woman in the next booth, who must have realized she'd been sitting there all the time. When Abbie spoke, her voice was a little louder than it needed to be.

"I was just thinking about 'sticks and stones,'" she replied. Seth drew back, his gaze narrowing slightly to study her with a considering look. Abbie turned her attention on the menu, missing his glance at the booth behind her. "Meat loaf is the luncheon special today. It sounds good. I think that's what I'll have."

When the waitress came to take their order, Seth echoed her choice. "Might as well make it two luncheon specials." He waited until the waitress had left to ask, "How have you been?" As if it had been awhile since he'd seen her when it was only two days ago.

"Fine. By the way, I finished typing the manuscript," Abbie informed him. "It's safely delivered into the writers' hands already." Abbie was careful not to mention the Coltrain sisters by name, not with the possibility of a big set of ears listening.

"That's good timing," he replied.

It seemed a curious response. "Why is that?" She laughed shortly.

"Because I could use some help typing up some church notices I want to mail out next week. It shouldn't take you more than one evening."

"That sounds as if I've already volunteered," Abbie retorted in amusement.

"I knew you'd agree." Seth mockingly pretended she had. "Is there anything wrong with doing it tonight?"

"I suppose not," she replied, acknowledging that she would do it.

"Why don't you stop by the parsonage a little before seven?" he suggested. Abbie tensed, wondering what the woman in the next booth was making out of her going to the parsonage. "I have to be at the church shortly after seven for a wedding rehearsal," Seth added, and she breathed a silent sigh of relief. "You can have the office all to yourself. I wouldn't want to be accused of disturbing you while you were working."

"I should hope not. Shall I bring my typewriter or do you have one?" she asked.

"A manual."

"I'll bring my portable electric," Abbie stated.

Halfway through their lunch, a member of the church board stopped by the booth and sat down to chat a moment with Seth. Abbie heard the couple in the adjoining booth leave and relaxed a little.

Inevitably the conversation between Seth and the director turned to church matters, which fairly well left Abbie out of it. From church business, there was a natural transition to a discussion of the Bible, and a pointed, but amicable, difference of opinion about the correct interpretation of a particular passage of the Scriptures.

"You settle it, Miss Scott." The board member turned to her for a third opinion. "What do you think it means?"

She felt suddenly trapped, and embarrassed, because she wasn't familiar with the passage they were talking about at all. Seth came to her rescue.

"I think Abbie is going to insist on remaining neutral," he said. "She doesn't profess to be a student of the Bible, so it isn't fair to ask her to referee."

"The reverend is right." Abbie used his title when referring to him in the company of others. "I stay quietly neutral about such matters."

"I imagine you and the reverend have other things to discuss besides the Bible." The man winked.

It was an innocent remark, without any critical intention, yet Abbie wondered if she shouldn't become more familiar with the Bible. Just as this man had, others would expect her to be more knowledgeable about it than she was. The thought continued to prey at the back of her mind through lunch, and the rest of the day as well.

Abbie slowed the car as she neared the parsonage that evening. "I guess we might as well park right out in front, Mabel. The whole town probably knows I'm going to be here tonight anyway," she murmured aloud to the car, and maneuvered the cranky vehicle close to the curb.

With the brake set, she stepped out of the car and walked around to the passenger side where her typewriter was sitting on the seat. The screen door to the parsonage banged shut. Abbie half turned to see Seth running lightly down the steps. He looked so striking, dressed all in black, with only the narrow band of his white collar for contrast.

"Let me carry that typewriter for you," he said as he approached the car.

"It's lightweight." Abbie objected to the notion that she needed any help, but he firmly took it out of her grasp.

"How would it look to the neighbors if I let you carry this into the house when I'm empty-handed?" Seth reasoned with a mocking gleam. "They'd think I didn't have any manners at all."

"And do you?" she challenged, and moved ahead of him to open the door, letting him enter the house first.

It was an old house with typically high ceilings. The screen door opened into a wide foyer with doors leading off from it. A throw rug didn't quite cover the worn patches of the carpet and layers of dark varnish covered the woodwork. The fern-patterned wallpaper probably had once matched the carpet on the floor but it had faded.

"The office is through here." Seth pushed open the door to the right with his foot.

Abbie followed him into the office. There was

an immediate difference. The entryway had created the overall impression of something tired and worn down, but the study had a vibrant warmth to it. A pair of plushly stuffed armchairs were covered in an ocher-gold corduroy, a color carried through in the drapes at the front window. The carpet was a pale cream shade that widened the paneled walls of the room.

"This is where you spend most of your time, isn't it?" Abbie guessed.

Seth placed the typewriter on his desk and turned to lean against the front side of the old walnut desk, letting his gaze sweep around the room before settling on Abbie. "It shows, does it?"

"Yes."

"I had the chairs recovered and bought new drapes and carpeting," he admitted. "The whole house needs something done to it, but I don't know what."

"It has a lot of possibilities."

"Such as?" Seth challenged dryly, and pushed away from the desk to walk to the middle of the room where she was standing.

"As old as this house is, I wouldn't be surprised if there are hardwood floors under that carpeting in the entryway. You could paint the walls a sunny yellow and brighten it up a lot," Abbie said, throwing out ideas off the top of her head.

"Would you like to fix the place up? I'll give you a free hand to do whatever you want," he offered.

It would be a challenge, but Abbie shook her head, expressing skepticism. "I don't think the church would go along with spending that much money on the parsonage. You'd have to go to the board with plans and estimates."

"The board wouldn't care if I paid for it out of my own pocket." Seth dismissed that obstacle. "What do you say? Do you want to do it?"

Again she shook her head. "People are talking now. Can you imagine their reaction if I started redecorating the parsonage?" Abbie eyed him as if he had taken complete leave of his senses.

"'Sticks and stones.'" He used her phrase from lunch that day—deliberately.

"'May break my bones.'" She continued the children's rhyme, but changed the ending to it. "But words can end up hurting you, Seth."

"And what about the words you heard today?" he challenged quietly.

"I don't know what you're talking about," Abbie protested.

"Yes, you do," he insisted, taking her by the arms and pulling her slowly toward him. "You overheard Mrs. Jones saying something before I arrived for lunch today, didn't you?"

"It was nothing. I just considered the source and forgot it. I'm not thin-skinned," she assured him, and spread her hands across the black material covering his chest.

"You have a very sensitive skin," Seth replied, and folded her into his arms to prove it, kissing her throat and the side of her neck.

Little quivers of delight ran along her flesh to

thrill her. His clean-shaven cheeks were smooth against her skin, the tangy fragrance of a male cologne stimulating her senses. It seemed every time he held her in his arms, she experienced this heady rapture that burned deep into her very soul.

"I thought you asked me here to type." The huskiness of her voice revealed how much he was disturbing her.

"Maybe I changed my mind." He burrowed his mouth into the side of her hair.

"What about the wedding rehearsal at the church?" she reminded him, then added to get his attention, *"Reverend?"*

"Now *that* was unkind." He lifted his head while his hands continued to glide up and down her back with lazy interest.

"The bride and groom can't practice without the minister." Her gaze lingered on the strong shape of his mouth, fascinated by the feelings it could evoke.

"But the minister isn't expected for another twenty minutes," Seth informed her. "That's plenty of time for Seth Talbot to—"

"Behave yourself, Seth." Her hands pushed against his chest as she suddenly realized the screen door was unlocked. Anyone could walk in and find them.

"Why?" He allowed her to create a small space between them, but kept his hands linked together behind her back. "Do you think I'm going to lose control of my prurient desires?"

"Don't you think you'd better show me what

you want typed?" Abbie suggested, unable to handle his conversation.

"I suppose." He sighed with mock reluctance. "Come on." He took her by the hand and led her to the desk where he'd set her typewriter. "Here are the envelopes." He pointed to a stack, then to a card file. "And in there are all the addresses of the names on the list."

"Is that it?" Abbie had been under the impression it was more complicated.

"That's it. Do you think you can handle it?" A light danced in his glittering blue eyes.

"It looks simple enough," she conceded. "Any schoolgirl with one semester of typing could do it."

Seth angled his body toward her, that disturbing darkness back in his look. "So you think you're overqualified for the task?" he challenged huskily.

"I didn't say that at all," Abbie denied with a reproving smile.

"Good, because there isn't anyone else I want to do it," Seth declared, then glanced at the wall clock with its swinging pendulum and sighed in regret. "It's time I was getting over to the church. Are you sure you don't have any questions?"

"None," she assured him.

"I don't know how long I'll be." He released her hand. "If anyone calls, they can reach me at the church."

"Okay." Abbie nodded.

His fingers gripped her chin to hold it still

while he pressed a warm kiss on her lips. Then he was drawing away, winking at her as he turned and walked to the door. In just that brief contact, her pulse beat at an irregular rhythm, affected by the possessive quality in his kiss.

The screen door banged shut before Abbie finally moved from where Seth had left her standing. She walked around the desk and found the outlet to plug her typewriter cord into, but her actions were all automatic, not directed by conscious thought. There had been nothing special in this parting, nothing to set it apart from others, yet Abbie had no more doubts about the way she felt toward him. Even without Seth there to disturb her senses and affect her physically, she was in love with him. The knowledge was clear and certain within her, no longer shadowed by question marks that it might be mere infatuation or physical attraction.

A small smile touched her lips as she sat down in his chair. There weren't any bells or lightning bolts, no blinding light—just the pure, warm feeling filling her whole being with the certainty of her emotion. It was a discovery to savor for the moment. Later on, she could wonder whether it was a love that was requited.

She rolled the first envelope into the typewriter and switched on the power, then went over the list of names and addresses to quickly familiarize herself with them before she started. Once she began, more time was spent taking the envelope in and out of the typewriter than typing.

A moth fluttered into the room, drawn to the goose-necked lamp that curved over the typewriter. Abbie let her fingers pause on the keys and arched her back muscles to ease their tension. With satisfaction, she noted that the stack of typed envelopes was taller than the stack of blank ones.

As she typed out the city and zip code to complete the address on the envelope in the carriage, the telephone rang. She picked up the receiver, using her shoulder to cradle it to her ear while she rolled the envelope from the typewriter.

"Parsonage." There was a faintly preoccupied tone to her voice. Silence followed on the other end of the line, drawing her full attention. She gripped the receiver in her hand and glanced at the mouth piece. "Hello?"

"Who is this?" a woman's voice sharply demanded.

"This is Miss Scott." Abbie identified herself, a defensiveness creeping into her words.

"I want to speak to Reverend Talbot. Is he there—with you?" The light emphasis on the last monosyllable made the woman's implication very plain.

"No, he isn't." Abbie made her voice very definite on that point. "Reverend Talbot had a wedding rehearsal this evening. You can reach him at the church."

"I have already tried the church, Miss Scott, and I didn't receive any answer," was the haughty reply. "Are you sure Reverend Talbot isn't there?" The question blatantly implied that Abbie was lying.

"I am very sure," Abbie retorted, just managing to keep her temper. "Perhaps you should try phoning the church again and letting it ring. It's possible Reverend Talbot wasn't able to answer it earlier."

"And it's possible he isn't there," the woman responded. "Do you have any idea what time it is, Miss Scott?"

She had been so busy typing that she hadn't paid any attention to the hour, except to note that it had grown dark outside. She glanced at the wall clock, a little surprised to learn how much time had gone by. "It's eighteen minutes after nine."

"Would you mind telling me what you're doing at the parsonage at this hour, Miss Scott?" the woman challenged.

"The reverend had some typing that needed to be done." If it weren't for the possibility that Seth might suffer the repercussions of her rudeness, Abbie would have informed the woman that it was none of her business.

"How convenient," the woman murmured dryly.

"If the reverend comes back in the next few minutes, may I tell him who called?" Abbie sweetly demanded to know the woman's identity.

But the woman ignored the question. "I'll do as you suggested, Miss Scott, and try the church again." There was a click as the connection was broken, followed by the hum of the dial tone.

Burning with indignant anger, Abbie slammed the receiver down. Her lips were pressed tightly together as she glanced at the window. She hoped the woman had to eat all her nasty little thoughts when Seth answered the phone at the church. A flicker of curiosity ran through her mind and she wondered why he hadn't answered when the woman had supposedly rang the church earlier.

The question impelled her to leave the desk and cross the room to the front window. The outer darkness created mirrorlike reflections in the glass panes, making it difficult for Abbie to see outside. There didn't appear to be any lights burning in the church. A frown narrowed her eyes. If the wedding rehearsal was over, where was Seth? Bewildered, she turned from the window and walked blindly back to the desk. She had to force herself to concentrate on typing the balance of the envelopes.

Forty-five minutes later, she took the last one out of the typewriter. A dull pain was pounding at her temples. She rubbed at it with her fingertips, but it didn't go away. Sighing heavily, Abbie turned in the chair to arrange the typed envelopes in neat stacks. The desk lamp cast a pool of light over her work area but shadows lurked in the rest of the office-study.

"All finished?"

The voice from the shadows made Abbie

jump. She hadn't heard Seth come in. His black-clad form blended with the darkened opening of the entryway. He was leaning a shoulder against the door frame, arms crossed, when she saw him. She had the impression he'd been watching her for some time.

"I didn't hear you come in," Abbie declared after the shock of discovering she wasn't alone had passed.

"Sorry." Seth pushed away from the door, unfolding his arms to lower them to his side as he walked to the desk and into the pool of light. There was something deeply disturbing about the way he was looking at her. Her heart seemed to do crazy, little flip-flops. "I didn't mean to startle you."

"It's all right. Did you just come from the church? I thought it looked dark when I glanced outside earlier," Abbie said.

He sat sideways on the front of the desk, an amused glint in his blue eyes as he surveyed her. "Checking up on me, were you?" Seth chided dryly.

Abbie hadn't meant to give him that impression and rushed to explain. "No, it's just that a woman called here for you and said she hadn't received any answer when she rang the church. I suggested she try again and let it ring. Did you talk to her?"

"No." An absent frown crossed his rugged features. "What time was it?"

"Almost twenty minutes after nine."

"I'd already left the church by then," Seth

admitted, then noticed the questioning look that flickered uncertainly in Abbie's glance. An amused line lifted the edges of his strong mouth. "The groom's parents had a late buffet supper at their house for the wedding party, which I was expected to attend. I put in a brief appearance and left," he explained. "Did the woman leave her name or a message?"

"No. When she didn't call back, I assumed she had probably reached you at the church." Since Seth hadn't been there, Abbie could easily guess what the woman had conjectured from that. She didn't mention the snide comments the woman had made to her.

"Whatever she wanted to speak to me about couldn't have been too important, or she would have called back," Seth concluded, dismissing the matter from the conversation. "Since you're all finished with the typing, how about some coffee?"

If it hadn't been for the woman's phone call, Abbie probably would have accepted the offer. But she was conscious of being alone with him in the parsonage. "It's awfully late. I'd better not." She refused with a shake of her pale auburn hair and leaned down to unplug her typewriter. It was already after ten o'clock, and someone was bound to notice her car was still parked outside.

"In that case . . ." Seth straightened from the desktop when Abbie stood up to wind the cord around the typewriter. ". . . I'll just have to come up with some other reason to persuade you to stay." He moved leisurely around the desk to come up behind her.

"Seth," she protested self-consciously as he slid his hands around to the front of her waist to pull her back against him.

Her entire back was molded to the unmistakable maleness of his solid chest, flat muscled stomach, and thrusting hips. Abbie made a token attempt to push aside the hands circling her rib cage and stopping tantalizingly near the straining swell of her breasts. But she signaled the weakness of her opposition by tilting her head to the side to give his nuzzling mouth access to the bare curve of her neck.

A rising heat flooded through her veins to melt her into pliancy while he nibbled along the sensitive cord near the base of her shoulder. Her eyes drifted closed under the waves of excited sensation. His arms tightened around her, one hand sliding lower onto her stomach and igniting another kind of ache.

The ringing of the telephone was a decidedly unwelcome intrusion, but definitely a timely one, or Abbie might have yielded to Seth's delaying tactics. She felt him stiffen in resistance to the telephone's summons.

Drawing a shaky breath, she insisted, "You'd better answer that."

"I know," he muttered, and reluctantly let her out of his embrace to step toward the desk and pick up the phone. "Reverend Talbot speaking."

Immediately Abbie took advantage of his distraction to lift her portable typewriter into her arms. If she didn't leave now, chances were that it would be much later before she did. Seth sliced her an impatient look when he realized her intention.

"Just a minute," he said to the caller, and lowered the receiver to cover the mouthpiece with his hand. "Abbie, you don't have to leave."

"Yes, I do," she insisted, and moved out of his reach, walking toward the entryway and the front door. "It's late and I have to work tomorrow."

"Abbie—"

"Is that the woman who phoned earlier?" She paused in the shadowed doorway.

"Yes, I think it is but—" It was of no consequence to him; that much was clear in his expression.

"You'd better not keep her waiting," Abbie advised, because it would probably just fuel the woman's imagination. "Bye."

Without waiting for him to respond in kind, Abbie left the office-study and walked with quick, purposeful strides to the screen door. She pushed it open with the side of her arm, her hands carrying the typewriter. As she stepped outside she heard Seth talking on the phone again.

Chapter Nine

A steady rain beat against the panes of her apartment windows. Gray, dismal clouds cast a depressing gloom into the living area. Abbie wandered restlessly from the window and the rain that showed no signs of letting up. She was at a loss for something to do.

There was nothing interesting on television and the radio offered no less passive entertainment. She paused in front of the low shelf of books and glanced over the titles. One seemed to jump out at her, its gold lettering gleaming against its maroon background—Holy Bible. It was the Revised Standard Version of the King James Bible, a gift from the church when she had become a member.

After a brief second's consideration, Abbie slipped it from the shelf and carried it over to the sofa. She curled herself on one corner of the couch with her legs tucked under her and began leafing through the pages. There was a vague thought at the back of her mind that she might accidentally run across the passage Seth had been discussing at lunch the other day.

Since Seth was a minister, the chances were good that there would be more conversations like that one, and her ignorance of the Bible would only become more noticeable. It was something she needed to correct.

A noise made itself heard above the steady patter of rain on the roof. Abbie lifted her head to listen, but she didn't hear anything more. She flipped through a few more pages, then stopped, out of loyalty to her sex, to read the Book of Ruth in the Old Testament. Halfway down the first column, she heard footsteps on the stairs.

The knowledge ran swift and sure within her that it had to be Seth. Even though there hadn't been any definite arrangement for him to see her this Saturday, she had guessed he would come by or call if he was free. She swung her feet to the floor, leaving the Bible lying open on the cushion beside her, and hurried to the door.

There was a knock just before she reached it. Abbie opened the door to see Seth standing outside, rainwater dripping from his jacket. He was wiping the wetness from his face, then shaking it from his hand.

"It's raining," he offered wryly.

"I never would have guessed." Abbie laughed and opened the door wider to let him in. "I'll get you a towel." She walked to the kitchen area to fetch him a hand towel from a cupboard drawer. "Don't you have an umbrella, or did you forget to put the top up on your car?"

"An umbrella, that's what I forgot," Seth mocked as he shrugged out of his jacket.

The rainy autumn weather had brought a damp chill to the air. Abbie noticed Seth was wearing an ivory pullover in a wide-ribbed knit as a concession to the cooler temperatures. It emphasized the width of his shoulders and the solidness of his muscular chest, tapering as it did to his narrow waist and hips. The rain had darkened his hair to a bronze brown, gleaming in the apartment's artificial light.

"Do you have any plans for this afternoon?" he asked when she returned with the towel, giving it to him and taking his jacket.

"Nothing. As a matter of fact I was becoming bored with my own company." She hooked his jacket on an arm of the wooden clothes tree by the door. "Why? Where were you thinking of going?"

"I wasn't thinking of going anywhere, but right here," Seth replied. When Abbie turned to look uncertainly at him, he looped the towel around her neck and held both ends to pull her toward him. There was a heady excitement in the lazy way he looked at her.

"And do what?" she asked, not really meaning to sound provocative.

Bending his head, Seth kissed at her lips. Weak-limbed, Abbie clutched at his forearms for support. "What were you doing when I came?" he murmured between kisses, the heated warmth of his breath mingling with hers. "Whatever it was, that's what we can do—

among other things, like this." His mouth closed onto her lips, finally giving her a chance to respond. When he lifted his head, Abbie was contentedly lost in a glorious daze. "Aren't you going to invite me to sit down?" he chided.

"Have a seat." Her hand moved through the air to obligingly second the invitation.

He released one end of the towel and swept it from around her neck, then took her hand to bring her with him as he walked to the sofa. The opened Bible occupied the middle cushion. Seth picked it up to move it so they could sit together, then recognized the holy book. He cocked a curious look at Abbie.

"What's this?" he asked, and glanced at the book it was opened to. "You were reading the Book of Ruth?"

A smile teased her mouth as she remembered his earlier question. "That's what I was doing when you came."

"Any particular reason?" An eyebrow was lifted with speculating interest. "Or are you just trying to impress me?" He sat down on the middle cushion while Abbie bent a knee under her to sit on the end.

"Since I didn't know you were coming, I can't be guilty of trying to impress you," she denied, aware his question had been only half-serious. "I admit I was slightly prejudiced when I picked out the Book of Ruth to read, since it's about a woman. It seemed to be the fair thing to do, to stick up for my sex."

"It's a very logical choice," Seth agreed, leaning against the back rest. "I apologize if I was wrong the other day at lunch when I indicated you weren't well enough acquainted with the Scriptures to offer an opinion."

"You don't need to apologize, because you were right," Abbie admitted with a rueful shrug. "That's why I picked it up to read and learn more about what's in it than the stories they taught me in Sunday school."

"I see," he murmured, absently looking at the opened pages.

"It's a shame there isn't anyone around who could tutor me." She sighed in mock regret, a teasing sparkle in her glance.

"Is that a broad hint that you want to spend the afternoon with me—reading the Bible?" Seth countered with a glittering look that lingered on her mouth, made softer by his kisses.

"You were the one who suggested we could spend the afternoon doing whatever I was doing when you arrived," Abbie reminded him with a small, dimpling smile.

"So I did." His smile was turned down at the corners but no less filled with amusement. "And ministers don't lie, so I guess I'll have to read to you from the Bible." He began turning pages. "Do you have any requests?"

"No." Abbie shook her head. "You choose."

"Let's see." Seth paused, partially closing the book to skip ahead. "What would you like to hear?" It was a rhetorical question, absently murmured aloud. "Something for Abbie. Abra, the namesake of Solomon's favorite. The Song of Solomon." He reopened the Bible to that book of the Old Testament and arched her a glance. "Does that sound appropriate?"

"Very," she agreed, and turned to lean against the sofa's armrest, facing him more squarely.

She watched him turn a couple of pages as if selecting a particular passage, then stop when he found what he was looking for. There was something vaguely enigmatic in the glance that ran over her face.

"From the Song of Solomon," Seth repeated, and began reading in a voice that was vibrant with expression and pitched low.

"How fair and pleasant you are,
    O loved one, delectable maiden!"

The words seemed to send a caressing finger down her spine. It was not what she had expected to hear. The beat of her pulse picked up a little in anticipation, her gaze locking onto his face and watching his mouth form the words when he continued.

"You are stately as a palm tree,
    And your breasts are like its clusters.
I say I will climb the palm tree
    And lay hold of its branches."

Her breathing stopped at the passion and promise in his low voice. A fiery warmth burned through her veins, heating her skin with the things he was saying—the boldness of them, and the beauty of them.

"Oh, may your breasts be like clusters of
    the vine,
And the scent of your breath like
    apples,
And your kisses like the best wine
    that goes down smoothly,
Gliding over lips and teeth."

Seth lifted his gaze from the pages, his deeply blue eyes turning their attention to her. Abbie was helpless to conceal how much the passionate selection had affected her. She was trembling with the desire it had aroused.

Taking the book, he turned it and offered it to her. "Now, it's your turn to read to me." She took it with both hands and glanced dazedly at the page. "Start from here." His fingers pointed out where she was to begin.

Her voice had a husky sound as Abbie began reading the words, and feeling them, too.

"I am my beloved's,
    and his desire is for me
Come, my beloved,
    let us go forth into the fields,
    and lodge in the villages;
Let us go out early to the vineyards,
    and see whether the vines have
    budded,

Whether the grape blossoms have
   opened
And the pomegranates are in
   bloom.
There . . ."

Abbie paused, her voice dropping to a whisper as she lifted her gaze to Seth. "'. . . I will give you my love.'"

"Will you?" he murmured and leaned toward her.

"Yes," she whispered with an aching need to give to him, seduced by her own undeniable love for him.

She didn't know he took the Bible from her hands and laid it aside. She seemed not to be aware of anything but the pounding of her own heart and the deeply blue eyes that held her forever captivated by their fire.

"Then come here, my delectable maiden." His hands closed firmly on her waist, near her hipbones, and impelled her to slide toward him.

Like a willow, she bent under the leaning force of his body. His mouth was mere inches from hers as he gently lowered her to the sofa, the weight of his hard body pressed alongside hers. It was a moment lost in time, without a beginning or an end.

It could have been seconds or minutes before Abbie felt the warmth of his mouth on her lips. It was a kiss of raw wonder that searched and explored the boundless limits of pleasure, then deepened with the insatiable hunger that grew more intense with each taste. Her lips parted under the hungry probe of his tongue to know more of her. Abbie trembled at the fullness that came with the exchange, and the appetite it aroused for still more.

Her legs were tangled with his as her hands roamed over his sweater-covered shoulders, feeling his muscles flex and ripple beneath the ribbed knit material. His mouth rolled over her parted lips while his tongue lightly traced the sensitive inside corners, drawing a moan from her throat.

"Your kisses are like wine, Abra," Seth murmured into her mouth. "Intoxicating and smooth, 'gliding over lips and teeth.'"

And he drank of them again, but Abbie was certain she was the one who was drunk with love for him. It was a shattering experience to be helpless with longing, desperately needing what another person had to give. She strained closer to the raw heat of his body, hard and aroused against her side. His mouth was on her lips, her throat, her ear, her neck, wildly delighting her wherever it touched and tasted.

His fingers were on the buttons of her blouse, deftly slipping them free from the stitched holes, surely working their way downward. Briefly her flesh was exposed to the coolness of the air until his hand warmed it, spreading his heat and making it hers.

Then his head was turning to look at the

feminine beauty he had exposed. Abbie felt no need to conceal her body from his gaze. She loved him and his desire was for her. She wanted him to be pleased with her—with all and everything that made her unique.

"You have lovely breasts, Abra," he declared thickly. "Lovely."

His hand cupped a creamy breast in his palm; his stroking fingers evoked an intimate pleasure so intense it was like pain. His mouth came down to ease the ache and make its own tactile exploration of the hills and valleys and hardened peaks of her breasts. She was a tightly coiled spring inside, wanting to absorb him into her flesh and needing the absolute closeness of love's consummation.

"Love me, Seth," she whispered, her fingers curling into the faint dampness of his hair. It was less a request for physical possession and more a prayer for emotional commitment—that it be as beautiful and meaningful to him as it was to her.

He dragged his mouth roughly across the hollow of her throat, a groan coming from deep inside him. "Abbie, don't ask that of me," he protested.

"But—" The sharp ache of rejection choked her voice, stabbing her with remorse.

"It can't be," he insisted with a trace of hard-jawed anger. "Not for you and me."

His hands pulled her blouse closed, firmly crossing the material. Then he gathered her hard into his arms, flattening her breasts against his chest and burying his face in her hair. The tautness of his long body was pressed into hers, making its male angles intimately felt. It was almost torture to have him so close and know there would be no satisfaction. Abbie wasn't sure why. Her thoughts were too muddled with unfulfilled desires to make anything clear. She clung to him.

"Abbie." Seth released her name in the middle of a long, heavy sigh. "I want you. I'm not pretending to deny that."

"Neither am I," she murmured rawly.

A sound, something like weary laughter, came from him. "What am I going to do with you, Abbie?" The rhetorical question he muttered only confused her more.

The telephone, positioned on the table at the end of the sofa, rang shrilly, almost in her ear. Abbie stiffened with a guilty start, as if the caller could see them locked so intimately in a prone position. There was a moment of indecision while she debated whether to answer it or let it ring. Seth took the decision from her, loosening his arms to let her go.

"You'd better answer it," he advised with husky reluctance. "It could be important."

She moved away from him to sit up shakily, partially turning her back to him. On the fifth ring, she picked up the receiver while the fingers of her free hand fumbled with buttons on her blouse.

"Hello." She heard the breathlessness in her

170

voice, caused not from exertion but from the softness of love.

"Miss Scott?" a woman's voice demanded.

An icy chill ran down her spine as Abbie recognized the voice as belonging to the same woman who had called the parsonage the other night.

"Yes." She was stiff and wary. "Who is this?"

"This is Mrs. Cones. I'm trying to locate Reverend Talbot. Is he there? It's urgent that I talk to him," the woman stated.

Abbie pressed the receiver to her chest and glanced over her shoulder. Seth was sitting and raking a hand through his hair. "It's a Mrs. Cones," Abbie whispered. "She wants to talk to you."

His head lifted, as if scenting trouble, then a blandness stole over his features as he reached out a hand to take the phone. "I'll talk to her."

"Just a moment," Abbie said into the phone.

"He's there? I thought as much." The woman sniffed in a haughty way.

A scorching heat burned her cheeks at the accuracy of the woman's vile imagination. Abbie avoided looking at Seth as she rose from that end of the sofa and handed him the phone. She moved to the center of the room using both hands to button the rest of her blouse and smooth the dishevelment of her clothes.

"This is Reverend Talbot speaking," she heard Seth say into the phone.

Not wanting to hear even one side of the conversation, Abbie walked to the window to stare at the falling rain. She rested a hot cheek against the coolness of a glass pane and blanked everything from her mind.

When Seth's hand touched her shoulder, she was brought back to a world of awareness. There was a slight movement of her head to acknowledge his presence, but she didn't turn from the window.

"I'm sorry that happened, Abbie," he said.

"It's all right." But the words made her hurt inside, and it was evident in the flatness of her voice.

"Wait a minute." His fingers dug impatiently into her shoulder and forced her to turn at right angles to the window and partially face him. "I'm apologizing for the phone call—not for anything else." Although her expression changed little, the dull green flecks in her hazel eyes brightened visibly. His gaze narrowed on them in satisfaction. "Not for anything else," Seth repeated for emphasis.

"I'm sorry about that phone call, too," Abbie admitted, because it seemed the safest comment to make. There didn't seem to be any point to reiterating her feelings for him. She had already expressed them very explicitly, both by word and deed.

The hand on her shoulder eased its pressure but continued to hold her. "Do you want to know why I chose that particular section from the Bible?"

"Why?" Perhaps his answer would tell her what she wanted to hear.

"Because I wanted you to see it's a book of love and passion, suffering and caring, but mainly it's a book of love," he explained. It was a subject she was intimately familiar with, since its richness filled her. "Don't look at me like that, Abbie." A muscle leaped along his jaw, revealing an inner strain for control.

"Like what?" It seemed no different to Abbie than the way she'd always looked at him.

"Like—" His mouth came down to crush her lips in a fiercely possessive kiss. It took her breath and made a mockery of her normal heartbeat. When he pulled away, his mouth was edged with tautness and his blue eyes glittered with turbulence. His voice fell somewhere between a groan and a curse. "I'm made of flesh the same as you are, Abbie."

"I think I've always known that," Abbie admitted as she leaned back against the coolness of the window to study him. "I just kept letting the collar get in the way."

"You think I haven't known that," Seth murmured dryly, including a slight shake of his head with the reply. His hand moved over her shoulder in a restless caress. "There's a lot we need to talk about, Abbie, but I don't have time now. Mrs. Cones called because her mother is in the hospital, very ill, and her father—the woman's husband—is overwrought. I promised I'd come sit with him for a while so I have to leave."

"I understand," Abbie assured him, smothering her regret that he had to go now.

"Will you wait for me after church tomorrow?

We'll have Sunday dinner together here or at the parsonage. It doesn't matter, just as long as we can have the privacy to talk," he said.

"I don't think the parsonage is a good idea." Neither place was exactly wise but Abbie suggested, "Why don't we eat here? I can put a roast in the oven so dinner can be ready when church is over."

"That's fine." His glance flicked past her to the falling rain outside, then returned to sweep her face. There seemed to be struggle going on inside him. "I have to leave now," Seth stated with grim determination, and kissed her hard before turning away to walk swiftly to the door, as if he thought he might change his mind.

He grabbed his jacket from the hall tree and opened the door, pausing to look over his shoulder at Abbie standing by the window. His mouth twitched with a quick, hard smile, then he was walking out the door, pulling it closed behind him.

Chapter Ten

Abbie followed the line of people shaking hands with Seth as they left the church. When it was her turn, she placed her hand in his and felt his grip tighten in firm possession. There was an added vibrancy in his blue eyes, an interest meant for her alone.

"Good morning, Miss Scott." He faintly drawled the words, as if mocking the formality.

"Good morning, Reverend," she echoed his greeting, a responding smile playing with the corners of her mouth. Abbie was conscious of others listening to their exchange, some critically and some with simple curiosity.

"Your parents aren't with you?" Seth observed with a questioning inflection in his voice.

"No. They went out of town today—to Missouri to visit some friends," she explained.

"I hope you've fixed a good Sunday dinner then."

"I have," Abbie assured him, fully aware that

his comment was a subtle reminder they would be sharing it together. It was written in the way he was looking at her.

Then he was releasing her hand to greet the next ones in line and Abbie moved on. At the base of the steps, she angled to the edge of the sidewalk, removing herself from the flow of people leaving the church. She lingered there to wait for Seth.

The Coltrain sisters spied her as they came down the steps in a glaring mismatch of colors— Isabel dressed in pink and Esther in bright orange. The two sisters were inseparable, yet they seemed determined to establish their own individualities, hence their clashing clothes. Abbie smiled a greeting as the pair converged on her.

"Good morning," she said, noting the excitement in their faces.

"We saw you in church and we were hoping we'd have a chance to speak to you," Isabel rushed.

"Yes." Esther echoed her sister's words and leaned closer to Abbie to whisper conspiratorially, "We mailed the you-know-what to a company in New York."

"The reverend gave us the man's name. He'd already talked to him personally about us and the man wanted to see—what we'd done. Isn't that wonderful?" Isabel nearly giggled like a giddy young girl.

"It certainly is." Abbie didn't have to pretend to be happy for them. She was hardly a judge but she had enjoyed the novel they'd written and felt certain a publisher would like it, too.

"The reverend said it might take two months before we hear what the man thought about—it," Esther explained. "But . . ." She hesitated and glanced at her sister.

"Esther and I have another idea," Isabel spoke up. "But we aren't sure whether we should start on it until we've found out about the first. We could just be wasting our time."

"Yes, and we wanted to ask you what you thought we should do," Esther finished.

"If it were me, I'd go ahead and start working on it," Abbie replied, and their faces lit up.

"Do you hear that Esther?" Isabel declared. "I just knew she'd say that. Didn't I tell you?"

"If we didn't have you and the reverend to talk to about this, I think Isabel and I would bust," Esther insisted, ignoring the "I-told-you-so" challenge from her sister.

"You'll do the typing on this one for us, won't you?" Isabel inquired anxiously.

"Of course, I will." She could hardly refuse.

"You really are a wonderful girl," Esther said, and squeezed Abbie's hand. "And you shouldn't pay any attention to all that talk going around. Those people spreading it are just nasty busybodies who don't have anything better to do." She didn't appear to notice the sudden tension that whitened Abbie's face as she turned to her sister. "We have to get home, Isabel."

"Yes. Now that you've agreed that it's the right thing to do to start on another one, we have a lot of research we need to begin. We don't mean to rush off," Isabel explained. "But you do understand."

"Of course." But it was a somewhat absent response Abbie gave as the two women hurried away.

Abbie had known her relationship with Seth had stirred up a lot of idle gossip. It was to be expected when a local minister was involved. Some of the remarks that had gotten back to her had been unfair and unkind. She had always been more concerned about all the talk affecting Seth's standing in the community rather than her own. But Esther's comment seemed to indicate Abbie was the one being maligned, and she was absolutely helpless to do anything about it. It did little good to tell herself she shouldn't be bothered by vicious gossip, because she suddenly was.

The stream of people coming out of church had ended, although the doors remained open. There was no sign of Seth, but Abbie assumed he had gone to change out of his robes. The church grounds and parking lot were virtually emptied of people and cars. She felt rather conspicuous standing near the bottom of the church steps and decided it would be more discreet if she waited inside the door.

As she entered the church she heard voices coming from the pulpit area. She recognized Seth's among them and was drawn across the small entry area by an inner need to see him. Seth and three other men were standing by the front pew. Abbie noticed he was still wearing his black robe. She had no intention of intruding or even eavesdropping. The three men were members of the governing board, so Seth was obviously discussing some church business with them.

Before she could turn away to wait near the front doors, she heard one of the men mention her name. She was held motionless, frozen by a kind of dread. Against her will, Abbie listened to what they were saying.

"We don't mean to sound critical, Reverend." A bald-headed man was speaking in a stiffly censorious voice that belied his words. "But we have an obligation to ourselves and the church to express our feelings on this matter."

"I'm sure your intentions are above reproach." Seth's murmured response was exceedingly dry. Even from this distance, Abbie could see the coldness in his blue eyes and the attitude of challenge in his stance.

"It isn't that we have anything personal against Miss Scott." A second man hurried to assure Seth of that.

"We freely acknowledge that she comes from a good family. Her parents are respected members of the community and this church," the third man said. "Miss Scott herself is probably a very nice girl."

"However?" Seth prompted the qualification that had only been implied by their tones.

"However . . ." The bald-headed man glanced at his two colleagues. ". . . she doesn't strike us as being a suitable . . . companion"—he paused before selecting the words—"for the minister of our church."

"Since Miss Scott has returned to our town, she hasn't participated actively in church affairs. She didn't even attend church on a frequent basis until you came," the third man explained.

"These are things you couldn't have known about her," the second man inserted. "Which was why we felt we should bring it to your attention."

"I'm sure you understand now why we are advising you to break off your relationship with Miss Scott. It would be in the best interest of everyone concerned," the bald-headed man concluded, with a slightly righteous tilt of his head.

Tears burned the back of her eyes as Abbie heard the final edict. She hadn't dreamed that anything like this might happen. The whole scene took on a nightmarish unreality. Her gaze clung to Seth as the silence stretched over the span of several seconds.

"I fully understand the concern that prompted you to seek me out, so this could be discussed openly." Seth's low-pitched voice was clear and concise. "And I'm in full agreement with you that Miss Scott lacks some of the qualifications that are regarded as essential for a woman to be considered as a minister's marital partner. . . ."

An involuntary gasp of pain was ripped from her throat at this ultimate condemnation from the man she loved. Abbie cupped a hand to her mouth to smother any more sounds, but it was already too late. Seth had seen her.

"Abbie!" He called to her.

But she heard the irritation in his voice and whirled away to run out the door. Tears blurred her vision as she hurried down the steps, breathing in sobs. Her high-heeled shoes restricted her pace to a running walk.

All her illusions were torn asunder. She suddenly realized why Seth had wanted to talk privately to her today. He had intended to break it to her gently that she wouldn't be a suitable wife for him. Love had led her down another dead-end road.

Yesterday, that passionate scene on her apartment sofa had been just that—passion—at least on Seth's part. Now Abbie could see what he had been trying to tell her when he had asserted he was made of flesh. The desires of the flesh—as opposed to the desires of the heart.

She remembered the way he had held her and murmured, "What am I going to do with you, Abbie?" Tears ran hotly down her cheeks as she reached her car in the church lot. It was all very clear now why he had said that. No doubt Seth had guessed that she was in love with him, but marriage was out of the question. What a fool she'd been! What an unmitigated fool!

"Abbie!"

Her glance was jerked in the direction of Seth's voice. He was half running across the lawn toward her, his black robe billowing out behind him. The flutterings of panic went through her. She couldn't face him, not yet—maybe never.

Wiping at the tears running down her cheeks, Abbie yanked open the car door and scrambled behind the wheel. Her shaking hands dived into her purse for the key and fumbled in their first attempt to insert it into the ignition lock. She glanced frantically out the front windshield. Seth was nearly to the car, a forbidding grimness etched into his rugged features.

"Don't fail me now, Mabel," Abbie pleaded with the car as she turned the key in the switch.

The motor grumbled in protest but its slowly turning noises were encouraging. Abbie pumped on the pedal to give it more gas and the grumble became a constant complaint. The gears ground together as she shifted into reverse, but it was too late.

Seth was opening the passenger door and reaching across the seat. Abbie pressed herself against the driver's door to elude him, but he wasn't intending to grab her. He was after the key. By the time she realized it, he had already turned the motor off and extracted the key from the ignition.

Cornered, Abbie squared around to face the front and gripped the steering wheel with both hands. She held herself rigid, refusing to look at him, not wanting to see the pity in his eyes.

"Will you please give me the keys?" she requested stiffly. Her jaw was white with the effort to contain her emotional turmoil.

There was a rustle of material as Seth climbed

into the passenger side and shut the door. Tension screamed through her nerves when he leaned over and inserted the key into the ignition switch.

"There's your key," he challenged.

Her chin started to quiver. Abbie had to grit her teeth to control it. "Will you please get out of my car?" she insisted, still without looking at him.

"We're having Sunday dinner together, remember?" Seth replied evenly.

"The invitation is withdrawn," Abbie retorted wildly, and blinked quickly to keep back the tears.

"That's too bad. I guess I'll just have to sit and watch you eat," he countered. "But we're going to get this misunderstanding straightened out."

"There is nothing to straighten out." She lifted her chin a little higher. "The situation has been made perfectly clear to me, so we have nothing to discuss. I understand completely."

"Do you?" he murmured dryly.

"Yes, I do," Abbie stated. "There's nothing you have to explain."

"Whether you want me to or not, I'm going to do just that," he stated. "You obviously overheard my meeting with the representatives from the church board."

"Obviously," she admitted on a bitter note, and flashed him a brief glance that was almost her undoing. The brooding intensity of his gaze seemed to reach out for her, but she succeeded in avoiding it.

"There are a great many disadvantages to marrying a minister. Your weekends are never free. Come rain, shine, sleet, or hail, you're in church on Sunday mornings. A lot of week-nights, your husband is gone attending church meetings. Everything you do is scrutinized by the good members of the congregation, from the clothes you wear to the way you fix your hair. You're expected to join every charity, every social and church group, and attend every meeting, unless your children are sick. You—"

"Stop it!" Abbie closed her eyes, unable to take anymore. "I'm fully aware I don't qualify for the position, so you don't have to give me a bunch of reasons why I wouldn't want it anyway!"

"You may not be applying for the position, Abbie," Seth said quietly, "but I'm asking you to fill it."

She caught her breath at his words, but refused to believe he meant them. Her eyes were bright with tears when she finally opened them and turned an accusing glance at him. "I heard what you said in there, Seth," she reminded him. "I don't—"

"If you had stayed to hear what else I had to say . . ." Seth interrupted, ". . . you would know I don't care whether you'd make a suitable minister's wife or not. You're the woman I want to marry."

"I . . ." Abbie stared at him incredulously, daring to listen. "Is this a proposal?"

"Yes." A slow smile began to spread across his mouth. "I'd get down on one knee but Mabel has me in cramped quarters." He hitched up his robe to reach in his pants pocket. "I was going to offer you this after dinner."

Dazed, Abbie slowly uncurled her fingers from their death grip on the steering wheel as she caught the sparkle of a diamond ring. When he reached out for her hand, she hesitantly offered him her left. She watched him slip the ring onto her third finger. "It's beautiful," she murmured.

"Does that mean you'll marry me?" Seth mocked.

"Yes . . . if you're sure." Abbie qualified her acceptance.

"I am very sure," he insisted, and proceeded to prove it.

His kiss was ardently possessive and demanding as his arm circled her waist to pull her across the seat to achieve a more satisfactory closeness. There was a wild singing in her ears, a rush of joy that was almost unbearably sweet. When he finally dragged his mouth from hers, she buried her face in the silklike robe covering his chest.

"I never realized I could be so happy." Abbie breathed out the words. "I thought I'd lost you."

"Not a chance." His fingers tunneled into her auburn hair and lifted her head so he could study her love-softened features. "You are going to be my wife . . . Mrs. Seth Talbot."

Hearing it made her tremble with happiness. "I still can't believe that you want to marry me, but I'm glad you do."

"Don't you remember the second time we met,

I told your mother that I hadn't married because I hadn't found anyone who was suitable for me," Seth reminded her. "I was never looking for a suitable minister's wife. I wanted a woman who would be right for me. You are that woman, Abbie."

"I had forgotten you had said that," she admitted.

"Maybe if you had remembered, you wouldn't have run out of the church the way you did." His mouth twisted in a wry line. "If you only knew how frightened I was at that moment—and how angry I was, too, because their unthinking remarks had hurt you."

"It wasn't just what they said, but the remarks *you* made yesterday, too," Abbie explained.

"The remarks I made?" He quirked an eyebrow. "What did I say to give you the wrong impression?"

"It was a lot of little things. When I wanted you to love me, you refused and told me not to ask that of you," she remembered.

"That's simply because I didn't want to anticipate our wedding night," Seth explained, then shook his head in stunned disbelief. "I suppose you thought I was saying that I couldn't love you."

"Not at that moment, I didn't think it—only later when I began piecing things together," Abbie admitted ruefully, because she had gotten the picture all wrong.

"What things?"

"Like when you said you didn't know what you

were going to do with me, I thought you were trying to find a way to break it to me gently that you didn't love me."

"I love you," Seth stated, so there would be no more question of that. "As for that remark, I'm not really sure what I meant other than that I'd been waiting for so long for you to finally recognize I was a man, that I loved you as a man. Because I was a minister you kept trying to put me above such things. Yesterday you nearly made me forget I was a minister, too."

"And I'll learn to be a good minister's wife," Abbie said, tracing her fingers along his jaw and trailing them across the slashing groove to the corner of his mouth.

"That's the other thing I was trying to explain to you yesterday. I don't want you to feel that because of me, it's your duty to know the Bible, or attend church, or anything else. If you want to do it, then let it be for the same reason I have. Do it for the love of God, not because you feel obligated because you are the minister's wife."

"I will," she whispered. "I promise you that."

His arms tightened around her, gathering her against him as his mouth came down to claim her lips. It was a long and passionate kiss that rocked Abbie all the way to her toes. She felt him shudder and bury his mouth in her hair.

"How I love you, Abbie," he muttered thickly.

"Seth." When she opened her eyes, her glance strayed over his shoulder to the walls of the church. "Do you realize we are practically necking in the church parking lot?"

A low chuckle came from him after a second's stillness. He lifted his head, amusement crinkling the corners of his eyes. "Can you think of a better place? I love you. In the eyes of God and the eyes of man, I want you for my wife."

"And I want you for my husband," she whispered, because she couldn't think of a better place to love him either. Then suddenly she remembered something else and pulled back from him. "The roast!"

"What about it?" Seth frowned.

"It's still in the oven." Abbie glanced at her watch. "Dinner is going to be ruined," she groaned.

"There will be plenty of other Sunday dinners," he assured her, and pulled her back into his arms where she belonged.

143